PRAISE FOR JESSICA STRAWSER

The Last Caretaker

"You're never sure who to trust or where everyone's loyalties lie in this latest from the very talented Jessica Strawser. Deftly written with an undercurrent of unease, *The Last Caretaker* is a relevant, harrowing mystery with page-turning suspense, a powerful storyline, and relatable characters that readers will think about for a long time to come. Strawser's fans will love this!"

—Mary Kubica, *New York Times* bestselling author of *Just the Nicest Couple*

"A powerful and atmospheric tale that is equal parts emotion and suspense as a woman takes over as caretaker of a remote nature reserve, only to discover the barn is part of a dangerous underground network for victims of domestic violence. In *The Last Caretaker*, Strawser perfectly captures the perils of living in an isolated part of the world and the desperate measures some women must take in order to survive. A richly emotional page-turner with an important message."

—Kimberly Belle, internationally bestselling author of *Dear Wife* and *The Personal Assistant*

"Riveting, harrowing, timely, and important. The story of a woman fleeing a difficult past who stumbles upon a network of safe houses for domestic violence victims, *The Last Caretaker* is that rare combination of page-turning thriller and an issue-driven book with deep resonance. I couldn't put it down, I can't stop thinking about it, and I know it will stay with me for a very long time."

—Michele Campbell, internationally bestselling author of *It's Always the Husband*

"*The Last Caretaker* is the best kind of book: important, surprising, brave. You'll want all your friends to read it."

—Ann Garvin, *USA Today* bestselling author of
I Thought You Said This Would Work

"In *The Last Caretaker*, Jessica Strawser's taut and beautiful prose instantly pulls us into empathy with this twisty, suspenseful tale's heroine. All women can relate to navigating the dangers in this novel: when to offer help, when to accept it, who to trust—and even how to trust our own instincts. Richly atmospheric, with a setting that both adds to and personifies the novel's razor-sharp suspense, *The Last Caretaker* offers an unforgettable tale, believable characters you'll root for, and insights that will keep you thinking about the novel long after you've finished the final compelling page."

—Sharon Short (Jess Montgomery), author of *The Echoes*

"An important book about courage and community and the lengths we'll go to in order to protect our most vulnerable. Strawser takes on the trauma of domestic abuse and its powerful vise of shame and fear that keeps victims stuck in a destructive cycle. *The Last Caretaker* will have you rooting for this colorful cast of imperfect people who create safe places for those in need no matter the consequences."

—Melissa Payne, bestselling author of *The Night of Many Endings* and
A Light in the Forest

The Next Thing You Know

"Jessica Strawser does it again—first-rate storytelling, a fresh, unique premise, and a didn't-see-that-coming twist, resulting in a book that's unputdownable! Strawser spins a wise, thought-provoking story that crackles with tension and intrigue. Perfect for book clubs."

—Lori Nelson Spielman, bestselling author of
The Star-Crossed Sisters of Tuscany

"*The Next Thing You Know* has all the things I love about Jessica Strawser's novels—intriguing characters that I love getting to know, stellar writing, fascinating conflicts . . . An emotional, powerful, and page-turning read, with characters that are sure to stay with me for a long time."

—Megan Collins, bestselling author of *The Family Plot*

"Grab the tissues!"

—*People*

A Million Reasons Why

"[*A Million Reasons Why* is] a fascinating foray into the questions we are most afraid to ask . . . [with] two massive twists you'll never see coming."

—Jodi Picoult, #1 *New York Times* bestselling author

"[*A Million Reasons Why*] is not your typical story of discovering a long-lost family member. The intricacies of the characters' lives are fascinating, their secrets unpredictable, and the challenges they face infinitely complex. With this story, Strawser reveals just how complicated life can be. Through these dynamic characters, she shows that no one is ever truly a villain or a hero, but instead, we are all a beautiful and messy mix of both."

—The Associated Press

"A standout novel . . . seamless writing style, complex characters, and layered plot."

—*Booklist* (starred review)

"*A Million Reasons Why* is a heartbreaking, absorbing story with an irresistible premise. Strawser skillfully explores what it means to be family, to rethink the pivotal hinge points in a person's life."

—Angie Kim, bestselling author of *Miracle Creek*

"Strawser's characters are so layered and flawed and human that I came to care about them deeply. Heartbreaking yet hopeful, this astute exploration of the bonds and limitations of family is a perfect book club pick."

—Joshilyn Jackson, bestselling author of *Never Have I Ever*

"*A Million Reasons Why* has it all: betrayal, lost loves, family secrets—and a killer twist I didn't see coming. A powerful and poignant tale with characters that burrowed their way into my heart and will stay with me for a long time."

—Colleen Oakley, bestselling author of
The Invisible Husband of Frick Island

Forget You Know Me

"From the very first page of *Forget You Know Me*, I was putty in Strawser's hands. From her portrayal of the changing nature of adult friendship to the seemingly harmless secrets we keep in marriage, *FYKM* is that book you can't put down and can't stop thinking about when you are finished."

—Sally Hepworth, bestselling author of *The Younger Wife*

"[*Forget You Know Me*] expertly dials up the danger; it works equally well as an airtight thriller and a memorable depiction of an old friendship growing increasingly strained. Fans of well-written suspense are in for a treat."

—*Publishers Weekly* (starred review)

Not That I Could Tell

"Ms. Strawser has written a deeply thoughtful book in *Not That I Could Tell* . . . a nuanced portrayal of domestic violence: how it begins, how it continues, and its devastating aftereffects. It's also a very necessary look at how innumerable lives are changed by abuse—not just those of the victims but the people around them as well."

—*The Pittsburgh Post-Gazette*

"[A] page-turner à la *Big Little Lies*."

—Book of the Month

"A psychological thriller of the highest order, as well written as it is structured."

—*The Providence Journal*

"Gritty, beautiful, and urgent."

—*The Daily Beast*

Almost Missed You

"A skillful, insightful debut: a deft exploration of the mysteries of marriage, the price we pay for our secrets, and just how easy it is to make the worst choices imaginable."

—Chris Bohjalian, bestselling author of *The Flight Attendant*

"A writer's writer with talent to spare: you may not have heard of Jessica Strawser today, but by tomorrow, everyone's going to be talking about her."

—Jacquelyn Mitchard, bestselling author of
The Deep End of the Ocean

"Jessica Strawser writes from the heart."

—Lisa Scottoline, bestselling author of
What Happened to the Bennetts

THE
LAST
CARE
TAKER

THE LAST CARE TAKER

A Novel

JESSICA STRAWSER

Text copyright © 2023 by Jessica Strawser
All rights reserved.

Published by Lake Union Publishing, Seattle

www.apub.com

Amazon, the Amazon logo, and Lake Union Publishing are trademarks of Amazon.com, Inc., or its affiliates.

ISBN-13: 9781662510229 (paperback)
ISBN-13: 9781662510212 (digital)

Cover design by Faceout Studio, Molly von Borstel

Image credits: © Marianne Fisher / Shutterstock; © Stephanie Frey / Shutterstock; © Viv Vivekananda / 500px / Getty

Printed in the United States of America

Barbara Poelle, this one's for you.

1

Bess had neglected to mention the guard shack. Imagine that.

Katie had pictured this so many times: the moment she'd drive up to her new home, her new job, the whole new life she'd signed on for sight unseen. She'd pored over the few photos she could find, filling in the blanks with her best guesses. And now that she was finally here, she could see right away how much she'd gotten right: The stamped wooden sign marking Grove Farm Nature Reserve. The wide, shallow creek running parallel to the entrance, and the low concrete bridge crossing it—one car width, no guardrails. The fork on the other side, separating the parking and trail access from the turnoff that presumably led to the caretaker's residence.

That was her. The new caretaker. The lone resident on these 927 acres.

But somehow, she hadn't envisioned her new driveway—this was more or less her driveway, wasn't it?—beginning at an actual guard shack with a striped metal gate blocking entry, like some prison or secret government facility. No, she corrected herself. A gated community. A resort. Where nefarious experiments were not being done inside.

Her brain went to the heart of the problem: *How will I order pizza?*

Clearly Bess, unlike Katie, had known there was no separate entrance for the caretaker. Bess was programming director at the nature center's main campus, and peripherally, at this less-trafficked annex. Plus, she was standing next to the guard shack now, waving her arms as if Katie were approaching by airplane instead of by car.

Katie rolled down her window and waved as she turned in. The car was packed nearly to the roof without any order whatsoever, as if she'd grabbed anything she could rescue from her burning house in a panic. Which she sort of had. The hodgepodge came to life behind her, cords flapping and jackets rustling in the rush of air.

Bess didn't wave back. Instead, she tossed her phone into the grass with a giddy whoop and began doing an elaborate touchdown dance across the road. Not that there was anyone around to see. Katie hadn't passed another car for miles.

Katie was already laughing, jumping out of the car before it fully jerked into Park.

Bess ran in for a hug. "I'm so glad you're here!" she squealed. "It's really happening!"

"It's really happening," Katie echoed, squeezing her tight. It was so good to see Bess. They hadn't lived in the same town since college.

They pulled back to take a good look at each other. Twice a year they had a standing date, every Fourth of July and New Year's, without fail. Except for this past New Year's, which—for Katie—had been very much with fail, and *only* with fail. Now, in the early-spring chill, Bess gushed on about how they hadn't seen each other for nine insanely long months. How they could have birthed a whole baby in that time.

Instead, Katie had birthed a humiliating divorce. And Bess had birthed a plan to save her.

"You didn't mention the guard shack," Katie said as soon as she could get a word in.

Bess glanced over her shoulder at the tiny windowed hut. It looked old and worn, but the metal stand in front was clearly new—an intercom and membership card scanner. Guests could pay to visit the main nature center, which Bess had helped grow to be one of Cincinnati's most popular attractions on the outskirts. But access to this remote annex was a members-only perk.

"It's not a guard shack," Bess insisted. "Unless you feel like coming down here and standing guard. Everything's automated."

Katie stood, hands on hips, reevaluating the life choices that had led her to this particular *Yes, sure, why not. Great idea.* Who wouldn't want to live alone in the middle of nowhere, behind a barrier? To this point, she'd focused on the positives: how badly she needed a fresh start, and how nice it would be to have Bess nearby. Now, dozens of questions flooded her mind, but she pushed them aside. She didn't want to sound ungrateful for all the strings Bess had pulled on her behalf. Her questions were mostly hypothetical anyway. Why worry how she'd have friends over after hours if Bess was her only friend here?

"But who's going to guard me?" she joked.

"The coyotes," Bess deadpanned. "Also a barn cat, who's quite friendly. A family of foxes. Rumor has it, an occasional bobcat."

Katie held up a hand. "Forget I asked. Permanently, please. I never want to hear about any of those things again. Except the barn cat."

Bess's smile turned sheepish. "Okay," she admitted. "Maybe I was a little worried you wouldn't be able to get past the guard shack." She brightened. "Get it? *Past* the guard shack?"

Katie rolled her eyes.

"Maybe too soon for that joke. But! Obviously, you *can* literally get past it. Anytime."

Katie genuinely couldn't decide if she was meant to express relief at being able to come and go freely from her own home. So she just stood there, nodding. Nodding and . . . visualizing.

"Plus, no solicitors!" Bess went on. "The kids in my neighborhood don't even bother fundraising with chocolate bars anymore. They just straight up ask for money."

"What if this gate malfunctions?" Katie asked. "Or the power goes out?"

"Oh, no," Bess said quickly. "It can't malfunction. I mean, I guess anything *can* malfunction, but . . ." She cleared her throat. "Even without power, you can override anything manually. You'll have all the master keys. I hereby crown you mistress."

"What a refreshing change," Katie said dryly, and Bess winced. *It's okay,* Katie wanted to tell her. *You can laugh at that. I think I need to laugh at it. I think that's what I've been missing.*

Back home, everyone and everything in Katie's day-to-day had been tied to Clark. They'd founded their company together, built their network of small businesses together—designing websites for so much of their old steel town on the outskirts of Pittsburgh that there was barely a locally owned restaurant or storefront where they weren't known by name—compiled their friend group together. Every bit of it had been a mistake. Clark's word, not hers. *It made no sense,* he'd said, *when we never should have been together in the first place.*

Of course, he hadn't said any of that until he'd gone out and gotten something else. Something just for him.

"How was it?" Bess asked now. "Leaving, I mean."

Katie had been trying, the whole, long drive here across two state lines, not to think about how it was. *I'm not a mistake,* she'd told Clark. *I'm a person.* What *was* leaving like when everything important had already left? It was quiet. It was sad. It was . . . anticlimactic.

"It was time," Katie said. Bess nodded. It was true.

When she announced her plans, Katie's friends had looked at her as if she'd decided to enroll in an IRONMAN. One that started tomorrow. No time for training.

"What?" she'd demanded defensively. "I love nature."

"There's nature," they'd said, "and then there's *nature.*"

It was a bit offensive, to tell the truth. And if they had a point, well, that was *beside* the point. So what if a running joke with Clark had been that having someone on hand to deal with spiders in the house was "thirty percent of the reason I got married at all"?

Anyway, the naysayers had done Katie a favor. Until then, maybe she hadn't been 100 percent certain about the *Yes, sure, why not* she'd given Bess. Maybe she hadn't been totally sold on the *great idea*. But Bess hadn't just called it great, she'd called it *perfect*. Their resident caretaker had resigned without notice. Without any other staff dedicated to the annex, they needed someone now. No time for lengthy interviews. Plus, what other job came with a furnished house?

"Anyone have any better ideas?" Katie had challenged those skeptical friends. Who were also, relevantly, Clark's friends. "Anyone think I can actually stay here? With dignity?"

They'd gotten quiet after that.

She did love nature. She loved gazing at it from mountain overlooks, soaking it up on beaches, walking through it in the park. The idea of going all in just felt a little like stamping "all natural" on a bag of cheese puffs. SIMPLY PUFFS! they proudly proclaimed, as if they'd been plucked straight from the farmers' fields, and no one objected, really. You'd kind of snort, then buy them. Because you knew it was a stretch, but you also knew there were worse things for you—and better things for you that tasted worse. That was the compromise.

That's what kind of hire Katie was. It might seem, at first glance, like her application had been sugarcoated by Bess's referral. Glazing over all the stuff on the ingredients list that didn't belong there. But Katie, though unqualified, had some things going for her. Sincerity, for one.

It was time to buck up. Her old friends might not be ready to face facts, but she was.

Besides, they weren't really her friends anymore. How relieved they must be that she hadn't made them choose. She'd given them over to Clark and her replacement. The woman she'd heard coworkers calling "the new Katie" on her last day of work.

That was the last straw. She'd marched right back, shifting her stack of boxes to her knee so she could see over them. "Trust me," she'd said, interrupting. "The last thing Clark wants is a new Katie. He didn't even want the old one."

Fortunately, one person did want a new Katie. And that was Katie herself. Introducing the new, All-Natural Katie.

Simply Katie!

No more artificial marriage, no more processed job. No more excuses.

Now, as if in agreement, Bess pulled a glossy membership card from her pocket and waved it with a flourish toward the gate. Katie's name jumped out at her in block letters. "Shall we?" Bess asked.

"After you."

The gate was easy enough to work—a swipe of the card, no need to fuss with the intercom. Katie made note of the seasonal hours posted so she wouldn't have to bug Bess about too many details. This spring, she'd ease in with a nine-to-six routine, seven days a week, but by summer the property would be humming in twelve-hour shifts, accessible from 8:00 a.m. to 8:00 p.m.

No one appeared to be here now, late afternoon on a chilly, overcast Tuesday, as Katie steered her crossover slowly behind Bess's minivan. The creek crossing was even more harrowing up close; it was easy to imagine high waters submerging the road. Katie should make sure her essentials never ran low. Groceries. Wine. Sanity. Hey, if no one could get in or out, she'd get a day off, right? Once she got used to the idea, it could be a good thing.

The turnoff was marked in large letters: **PRIVATE: CARETAKER'S RESIDENCE. KEEP OUT.** As they made the sharp-right turn, she craned her neck for a look at the main access area but couldn't see much—the hill was steep, the trees thick. They rumbled up the long driveway sloping away from the creek, and seconds turned to minutes before the old farmhouse appeared through the trees.

In Katie's view, there existed two kinds of farmhouses in the Midwest. One, where it was too easy to picture an axe murder happening any day, encompassed roughly 90 percent of Ohio's rural homes, through no fault of their own: there was just something a little too *In*

Cold Blood about an overturned bucket in the yard or an off-key wind chime. But the second kind—the other 10 percent?—was so picturesque you couldn't envision anything bad happening there. Like the set of those rom-coms where someone goes home again, reclaims their hunky first love, and maybe saves a bookstore. That was the caretaker's house. She'd devoured the photos Bess had sent, cataloging her favorite details—*Focus, Katie, on things you'll make up your mind to like*—and now, her eyes checked them off one by one as she approached, verifying with relief that they were as advertised.

She liked that the century-old home was painted a dusty blue gray, a color that didn't quite fit but that she might have chosen herself. She liked the huge corner window and the rooftop weather vane with the silhouette of a galloping horse. She liked the screened side porch, the kind her grandma reminisced about sleeping on as a girl. She liked the green canoes stacked out back, conjuring images of those sleepaway summer camps Katie's parents had never let her go to. All the nostalgic touches made the house feel relatable, like her kind of people. And she could tell it would be beautiful in all four seasons, already picturing a postcard for each one: the way the stark landscape would soon turn floral, then dense and green in summer until the vibrant autumns gave way to snow-dusted winters.

She slowed behind Bess on the wide gravel patch dividing the house from the barn and a trio of smaller outbuildings. Katie matched Bess's smile at they climbed out of their cars. "Hard to believe this used to be a real farm," she called out. "I didn't expect it to be so wooded."

"Isn't it great?" Bess beamed. "A little bit of everything, really. You'll see. There are massive fields at the top of the hill, though they're wild and overgrown now. On the perimeter trail, you can get a better picture of how it used to be. You'll find fragments of fences and troughs—they let animals roam more freely back then."

"How long, do you think, until I can walk around here without getting lost?"

"Not long. The creek is a good benchmark. Once you orient your-self to that, there's no such thing as lost. I'm telling you, Katie, this place is underrated. You're in for a treat."

Bess had such unfounded faith in her, it made Katie want to cry sometimes. Bess wasn't known for making safe, easy choices. She didn't get hung up on details. She'd changed her major so often in college, it took her six years to graduate—not including her semesters in the Peace Corps. She'd set long-term goals that would start out sounding random and crazy—like not buying any clothes for a year, or eating sweets only if she'd baked them from scratch—and by the time the experiment was up, half her friends would be doing it too. "Oh, I got sucked into Bess's thing," they'd explain, and everyone would nod, knowing Bess's enthusiasm was contagious.

Put a girls' night on the calendar, and you'd either have the time of your life or end up on some wild-goose chase. Bess was the reason Katie had missed her flight to her own Vegas bachelorette party. Bess was the friend who could lose track not just of time but of the carry-on bag with both your IDs inside. She could be a loose cannon, a flake, and a ton of fun.

The older Katie got, the more she realized how few Besses there were in the world, living life like a bumper sticker, more journey than destination. And the more Katie's own journey stalled in a construc-tion zone, the more in awe she was that none of Bess's choices ever seemed wrong. Even that day they'd been stranded in the airport for six hours, Katie churning mad, Bess had—after recovering the carry-on from security—struck up a conversation with exactly the right stranger in the bar, landing them VIP resort upgrades that were almost worth the trouble.

Katie liked the way Bess could make her believe that things were worth the time to get right. When Bess finally landed on Natural Resources as a major, Katie knew it would stick, even though Bess had had to redo half her prerequisites. She'd even married the hard choice, sticking with her boyfriend from that year abroad, surviving a long-distance relationship right up until they said *I do*. Vince had made a career of coaching youth soccer for a Christian club, though he could "take or leave" the Bible verses printed on their jerseys. Vince could take or leave almost anything but Bess, which made them a great pair. When they couldn't get pregnant, they fostered. When they ended up pregnant anyway, they adopted too. Bess's house was a mess, but it was the only actual *joyful* mess Katie had ever seen.

Deep down, this was why Katie had come.

Now, here, she was part of it again. So far, just the mess.

But she had her eye on the joy.

2

It didn't just look like someone had left stuff behind in the caretaker's house.

It looked like someone was still *living* in the caretaker's house.

Coats draped over chairs, mail on the kitchen table, dishes in the sink. A box of cereal open on the counter. Bess even called out the last caretaker's name—"Grace? You here?"—and ran up the stairs, leaving Katie to stare at the kitschy needlepoint of a Mark Twain quote framed above the banister: IT IS NEVER WRONG TO DO THE RIGHT THING. But Bess came back shaking her head.

Now, they stood surveying the living room—the kind of small but elegant front-of-house space that might have once been called a parlor. It wasn't putting on airs now. A throw blanket sat crumpled on the couch, as if someone had slipped out to refill her mug . . . only the mug was there, too, forgotten on a coaster, the dregs inside turned to crust.

A crooked stack of books teetered on the end table, and Katie reached for the title on top, a historical blockbuster she'd meant to read herself. The jacket was wrapped in the protective plastic she'd once associated with school-day afternoons, quiet corners in the young adult section, hushed chats with her favorite librarian. She flipped it over, and sure enough, there was the barcode, along with a green ADULT FICTION sticker: CLERMONT COUNTY PUBLIC LIBRARY. She ran her finger down the rest of the spines in the stack; all were wrapped the same way.

"What kind of monster moves out of town without returning her library books?" Katie meant it as a joke—what with the inspirational needlepoint and all—but she was so perplexed it didn't come out sounding like one.

Bess's frown deepened. "I can take them. The kids and I go once a week."

"You don't have to do that. I'll want a card anyway. It's just . . . Don't you find it odd?"

Bess had made it clear she hadn't really known the previous caretaker. *Kept to herself a lot,* she'd told Katie. *Maybe that's what got to her.* She'd said it like this would never be an issue for Katie. Like Katie would enjoy an entirely different role with the exact same job description.

"April Fools'?" Bess said lamely.

Katie groaned. Her sister had texted from Tennessee about this very thing: Moving on April 1st, huh? Brave. She hadn't responded. Superstition was the last thing she needed.

"Sorry," Bess hurried on. "Bad joke. I got the impression she didn't have any ties here, so . . . maybe she figured she'd never be on the hook for fees?"

The fees seemed beside the point, but Katie let it go. Maybe this Grace had been an overly trusting sort, assuming—correctly—her successor would return them on her behalf. Maybe she'd been in a rush. Or maybe she really had been that thoughtless or lazy.

Caretaking hardly seemed a job for a thoughtless, lazy person, though.

The rest of the living room was much neater than the one Katie had left behind—an aggressively open floor plan, where their sectional couch was all that distinguished their media space from the dining room from the kitchen. She'd joked that living with Clark was like living with a poltergeist. You could trace his path through the house like muddy footprints: cupboards and drawers left open, unused time blinking on the microwave, shoes on the floor, craft beer bottle caps dotting the end tables. Katie had given up nagging long ago and made peace with her daily ritual of retracing his steps, returning things to their rightful places.

If that had been the home of someone who just didn't care, this was not. This was the home of someone who could *almost* justify leaving the place as is. And apparently had.

Remote controls were tucked into a rectangular basket on the coffee table. Across the room, a flat-screen TV perched inside a wooden hutch among box speakers, a DVD player, and a turntable with a clear lid. On the bottom shelves, DVDs were stacked incongruously alongside vinyl albums. On the top, wildflowers had wilted in a vase of murky water next to a single framed photograph. Katie moved closer for a better look.

The snapshot showed a girl offering a daisy to a pretty woman who didn't look quite old enough to be her mother, though the way they were looking at each other conveyed she probably was. Both wore white eyelet sundresses and straw hats, laughing, oblivious to the camera in the way modern photographers try to stage but never quite pull off. It was tough to place how old the photo might be—it seemed timeless. Like it might have come inside the frame for show.

"Is this her?" Katie asked, pointing to the mother, and Bess came to stand beside her.

"This," she said softly, tapping the glass next to the child instead. "This is her. She's probably older now than her mom was here."

Katie scanned the walls, taken aback. There were plenty of other framed prints—landscapes of tall grasses lit by a golden sun, a series of butterflies—but nothing else so personal.

Bess met her eyes. The question seemed to go without asking, but Katie went ahead anyway. "Why would she leave *this*? Can we get it back to her?"

"Maybe she forgot it?" Bess shot an uncomfortable glance back toward the couch, as if Katie's predecessor might reappear, snatch up her blanket and mug, and ask what they were doing in *her* living room. "Sorry, Katie. They told me she'd left some stuff behind, but I thought it might be stuff you'd want. Like canned food or extra supplies. I didn't schedule the cleaning service to come until tomorrow, because I thought you'd want a chance to call dibs on anything you didn't want hauled away."

"It's okay. I do want dibs. But I don't know about hauling anything away. Maybe she'll come back?"

Katie's eyes fell on the record player. It hadn't been used lately, unless someone had had a hankering for Elvis Presley's *Classic Christmas Album* in March.

"Maybe? But there's no way you'll feel at home here with someone else's family photos. I'll help box them up. Stay with me tonight. We'll come back once the place is scrubbed."

Bess bit her lip, clearly embarrassed. Katie didn't want her to be. Even if part of her did want to laugh. Only Bess would talk her into moving out of state for a job without bothering to check the condition of the house first. It was hilariously on brand.

Still. Her friend had gone out on a limb to make this happen for her.

"Don't be silly," she said. "You've seen how Clark lives. I'm fine here. Seriously."

Bess pulled a journal off the shelf and held it between them, the light catching the gold leaf on the embossed cover. She flipped it open to a random page, and they both looked warily at the handwriting. The entries were short, dated lists, written in meticulously neat printing. *Two red foxes* jumped out at Katie. Also: *bake sale.*

"She left her *journal*," Bess protested. "I can't look. It's bad form."

"Looks like she was keeping track of stuff on property? No reason to take it, probably."

Katie was already wondering if she should read it later. To learn what she should consider keeping track of. If she tanked at this job, it was Bess who'd look bad. Bess who they'd send out here to break the news to Katie that she'd have to find something else. Bess who, in this moment, was the only true friend Katie had left. So what if this place hadn't been stripped of all signs of prior life? It had personality. A sense of whose shoes Katie was filling.

"I'm really sorry, Katie," Bess said again. "I know this is weird."

"You're sure someone talked to her? I mean, you're sure she's okay?"

"Positive. And we have a forwarding address for payroll—her sister's house in Michigan, I think. Plus a phone number. I'll call myself. Tonight. Make sure there's nothing we should, um"—Bess cleared her throat—"set aside for her."

Nothing we should know, she'd been about to say. Bess might not know much about the last caretaker, but she knew Katie. The friend who always needed a little extra convincing.

Katie knew herself too. The chicken with the overactive imagination.

You couldn't argue some of this wasn't creepy, even in daylight. It was one thing to go minimalist but another to leave the house looking like something had spooked you to run out and never look back. Like Katie might find Grace bound and gagged in the basement, the victim of some plot to . . . what? Impersonate her, resign, and hope she starved before anyone found her?

On the other hand, it was a nature center, for crying out loud. Was there anything more innocuous? And was it so surprising that after five whole years, the last caretaker had had enough, gotten bored or fed up, and walked away? Besides, Katie couldn't help but be curious. Maybe she wanted answers to all the questions *she* had been fielding for the past week.

But what would that really be like, Katie, being by yourself in the middle of nowhere?

Is a "resident caretaker" even a thing? Why am I picturing an old man in overalls?

Can you really live with giving up your fair share of everything you've worked so hard to build? Your business, your connections, your skill set?

"To be fair," Katie told Bess, "you did warn me the place came fully furnished."

"Really fully." Bess laughed. "I wonder if you two wear the same bra size?"

She was joking, of course, but it became almost comical, moving from room to room and discovering that *nothing* fit.

Katie had been a vegetarian for decades; her pantry was filled with chicken soup and beef stew. Katie was a blonde; the shower held "ravenous redhead" shampoo. Katie enjoyed unwinding with a beer or glass of wine; the fridge was all spiked seltzers and sodas. Katie had a vice-status coffee habit; the cupboards were bursting with tea. And cereal, crackers, baking staples—all half-eaten. She and Bess filled two bags for trash and one for recycling, cringing at the waste, pretending they didn't need to make sense of the elephant in the room.

"Was she butting heads with your management?" Katie asked at one point.

Bess shook her head. So not a take-this-job-and-shove-it scenario. That kind of anger didn't stick anyway. You'd storm off, then sneak back later, get your things. Even Katie had found the courage to return her library books post blowup with Clark. After hours, when the drop-off slot couldn't give her pitying looks, but still.

The Wi-Fi was surprisingly good out here. The cell phone signal serviceable. But everything else about this place seemed to have turned back time, as if it wouldn't be all that surprising to find a wagon rumbling up the road, stocked with old tonics.

Tonic sounded pretty good, actually. Katie wondered if there was any gin.

"Might she have been swept off her feet by a traveling salesman?" she suggested, and Bess laughed.

"A family emergency?" Katie tried again. "Someone sick?"

"I like your salesman idea better."

Katie didn't ask if there was any chance this was exactly what it looked like—something that might be worth worrying about. A sign. A warning.

But Bess said she would follow up, make sure. Bess, who loved her and was trying to help. Bess, whom she had to trust—*did* trust. Overall.

Bess, who, admittedly, wasn't known for asking questions or thinking things through.

There was no turning back now. Besides, for as long as she'd known her, Katie had caught herself wishing she could be more like Bess. This was her chance to try. Bess was getting by fine, wasn't she? Better than Katie, by all accounts.

If there *was* any reason this was a bad idea after all?

Katie didn't really want to know.

3

Katie wasn't sure she'd ever felt so keenly, thoroughly aware of being alone.

Alone in this unfamiliar bed, the early-morning light seeping through the curtains into the drafty room. Alone in this new life, waking to find not a single new message on her phone. Alone on these hundreds of wild acres she had yet to explore. She let the feeling wrap around her—not self-pity, but not the excitement that had carried her here yesterday either. Something in between: a *knowing* in her gut, a heightened awareness that there would be no such thing as moving through the day on autopilot anymore, not for a long time, and that was probably good, but maybe a little sad too.

She was on her own now. It was all up to her.

But first, coffee.

She pulled on a hoodie and sweats over the T-shirt she'd slept in and was padding down the stairs, silently applauding herself for having unpacked her French press the night before, when some indeterminate noise caught her attention from outside. She glanced out the window at the bottom of the stairway, expecting to see a squirrel, maybe, or some loose tree limb whipping in the wind, and froze in her tracks.

There was a man in her barn.

She wasn't sure what was more jarring: the presence of a stranger at this early hour, or the slap of realization that this new gut feeling of *aloneness* had been flat wrong. Didn't she have any instincts at all? Her body went rigid with fear, except for her heart, which began beating wildly, ready for a fight.

The intruder was tall and broad and had his back to her, half-in, half-out of the heavy sliding barn door she was positive she'd locked last night. The door had needed several awkward yanks to coax it across its track, and the padlock was no flimsy spin dial but a long push-button panel with an eight-digit code. The combination was written right next to the window she stood watching him through, inked on a strip of masking tape across the wall-mounted key rack.

Maybe he had the code too. Either that or the guts to break and enter in broad daylight. Which, come to think of it, might not require all that many guts out here after all. Anyone staking out the place might think no caretaker was present.

This time yesterday, it would have been true.

She watched with narrow eyes as he stood staring into the open space. A row of long-handled garden tools was visible in the corner within his reach, but he made no move toward them. In fact, he didn't seem to be *looking* for anything. More like he was trying to decide something, lost in thought.

Before she could stop and think, she stepped into her shoes and burst out the door. Never mind that she had no plan. She had the right—no, the duty—to confront him. Even if she didn't have the first clue what she'd do if he gave her trouble.

The storm door snapped closed behind her, and the man turned, revealing a Nature Center fleece and an employee badge like Bess's dangling from a lanyard.

Relief took her by the shoulders, and she exhaled the breath she hadn't realized she'd been holding. False alarm. Of course. Was it possible employees had access to all these buildings, even the house? Why hadn't she thought to ask?

Forcing a smile, she crossed her arms over her chest, trying to disguise her lack of a bra. He didn't smile back. He didn't look caught or surprised or apologetic either. In fact, anyone who didn't know better would think it was she who was keeping him from his morning coffee.

Before either of them could speak, a gray blur of fur darted from the open barn door and flung itself with abandon against the legs of her joggers.

"I see you've met Chevy," the man said by way of greeting, nodding at the tabby cat. He wasn't speaking loudly, but the sandpaper edge of his baritone scraped above the morning birdsong, as if even sound followed different rules on this chilly, isolated hilltop.

She bent and brushed a finger between the cat's ears. She'd found the bag of kibble and dishes after Bess left yesterday, cleaning and filling them in hopes a friendly companion might appear. Straightening, she took her first good look at the not-technically-trespasser. She supposed they were coworkers, though the word seemed out of place so far from the conference-room chatter she was used to. If Bess were here, Katie would have whispered one of their old jokes, twisting things people only said about women: *He'd be so much prettier if he smiled.*

It was true, though. She wasn't much for the brooding type, but this guy was it with a capital *B*—the rugged outdoorsman variety. His features looked hard set but maybe not on purpose, like he spent so much time doing tough, physical work with no one around, he'd need reminding to arrange the straight line of his mouth or broad box of his shoulders any other way. The kind of guy who, if he was kind beneath it all, would become increasingly attractive—a magnet of physicality—but otherwise wouldn't turn your head except maybe to give you the creeps.

He was taking her in with intense brown eyes. Not curious, exactly, but observant. A man who didn't miss much.

"Chevy, as in . . . he likes to chase things?" she asked congenially.

"Chevy as in Chevrolet," he said. "Born in the back of a pickup."

"Ah. That was my next guess."

He still didn't crack a smile, only scuffed his work boots in the dirt. He seemed about her age, but then again, once she'd passed thirty, most people seemed roughly her age. Occasionally someone would mention a number, and she'd be floored to realize a friend was only twenty-four, or already fifty-six. It made her wonder if the middle of her life would blur together, like one of those rainy weekends you waste binge-watching a show that's been on several seasons too long.

"I'm the new caretaker," she said, though it was obvious he'd already assumed as much. "Katie. Not born in a Cadillac, though." *What am I saying?* It would have been less painful to hold an actual sign that read I'M TRYING TOO HARD.

He nodded once. "Jude." If he'd been holding an equally obvious sign, it would have said CAN YOU NOT SEE I HATE PLEASANTRIES?

"Glad to meet you, Jude. Can I . . . help you with something?"

"I doubt it." She could hardly take offense. She doubted it too. "That your hatchback?" He nodded at her Honda in the driveway. Somehow the fact that it was still packed to the seams made it look even more dwarfed by the extended cab truck he'd parked beside it.

"Well," she said, feeling oddly defensive. It was the way he'd said the words, as if implying the car was some toy or imitation vehicle. "I wouldn't call it a *hatchback*. It's a crossover."

"With a hatch. In the back. Word to the wise: that thing will not get up this hill come winter. Did you ask about access to a staff vehicle? Something four-wheel drive?"

"Um," she replied with a nervous laugh. "It's only April."

"Unsure you plan to stick around that long?"

She *really* needed that coffee. "As of now, I'm just trying to get through my first day."

"Ah. Rough first night?"

That wasn't what she'd meant to imply, though last night had been weird, even by first-night-in-a-new-place standards. It had started fine:

Bess had sweet-talked Vince into bringing them takeout, and he'd arrived full of his usual sporty energy, coach's whistle around his neck and kids bouncing behind him, crowding out the stillness.

At seven and eight years old, Ethan and Emory weren't the type to shy away, even though they hadn't seen Katie in months. *We'll show you where the crawfish hide! And where the trilliums grow super thick! And the birdhouse where we saw twenty-one cardinals at once!* Dinner passed too quickly, and Katie gathered up their promises and held them to her as she stood in the driveway and watched them go, her own words to Bess echoing in her ears.

I'll be fine. Of course I'm sure. I'll call you tomorrow.

Even after she'd gone back inside, she'd been unable to shake a ridiculous feeling that the woods themselves had been waiting for her welcoming committee to leave so they could pounce. At first, she'd been relieved her bedroom was the one room her predecessor had somewhat packed up: most hangers in the closet hung empty, and the drawers held only boxy T-shirts that were no one's favorites. Carrying her toiletry bag across the hall to the bathroom—vintage rose tile that was almost in again—she found all the left-behind bottles and tubes in the trash can, Bess's doing. It was clean enough, no toothpaste on the sink or hair in the drain, but she'd washed her face and brushed her teeth touching as little as possible, as if in a questionable hotel, and made up the bed fresh with sheets she'd found folded neatly in the linen closet but washed anyway. Then she'd lain awake, lost in the sounds of her new surroundings: the rattle of the furnace, the settling in the walls, the hoot of an owl outside, all somehow both quieter and louder than what she was used to.

"Not rough," she told Jude now. "Just getting the feel for things. How well did you know Grace?" She brightened at the thought that he might know more than Bess did. After all, here he was at first light, making himself at home.

But he only shrugged. "All I know is she did a good job."

It figured. He wasn't exactly giving off a social vibe. "And . . . what do you do here?"

"Maintenance. I get the honey-do list from main campus. Got anything to add yet?"

Maintenance. A giddy laugh-cry sensation bloomed in her chest. "Oh, thank goodness. I thought *I* was on maintenance."

The corner of his mouth twitched. "Sorry to say you are. Routine stuff. Bigger stuff you'd call in a pro for—that's me."

"Right," she said quickly. "That's what I meant." If only she had some hint as to where the line between the two was supposed to be. She'd once knocked on seven doors before finding someone "pro" enough to help her open a stubborn jar of pickles. "What brings you out today?"

"Parent complained her son cut his leg playing on hay bales. Sharp wires in there."

"Ouch. You bale hay in the spring?"

He looked impressed that she'd thought to ask, though his face remained expressionless. It was in the tilt of his head, a slight recalculation. "They're winter rye, actually. Anyway—I'm here to haul the bales away. We donate to a stable, but the bosses thought they'd look photogenic rolled in the field first. Like we don't get these complaints every year."

"Couldn't we just put a sign on them that says 'No Climbing'?"

Jude blinked slowly, which she had the feeling might be as close as he came to laughing. Katie thought of the words marking her own driveway: Private: Caretaker's Residence. Keep Out.

Before he even answered her question, goose bumps rose on her arms.

"First thing you'll learn out here," he said. "Nobody ever listens to a sign."

4

Katie counted a half dozen cars in the parking lot, scattered at respectful distances from one another. It wasn't her job to account for who was here, unless one of these cars remained after hours—in which case, to be honest, she had no idea what she was supposed to do. The map showed nine hiking trails, ranging from easy and quick to moderate and miles long, each marked by corresponding colored dots on rudimentary signposts. How long would it take to walk them all in search of someone who might be turned around or hurt or, more than likely, lost track of time? She envisioned cupping her hands around her mouth, yelling, "Closing time!" Or maybe, "You don't have to go home, but you can't stay here!"

What would the farmer's wife have used, way back when? A dinner bell? Maybe there was one in the barn. She'd have to check.

Somewhere out of sight a mother called out a warning—earnest yet faint, as if to demonstrate how futile it was: "Not too far!" A giggly squeal came in response.

There was only this one partially paved lot for all the trailheads, the picnic area—the only structured feature of the place with its oversize "you are here" map and bulletin board, a shelter, a smattering of picnic tables, and two pit toilets—and the second, empty barn that groups could reserve for scout meetings or birding seminars. It had been a winding five-minute walk from Katie's back door, with glimpses of a silty pond through the trees. Now, on these parking strips surrounded by woods on one side and rolling fields on the other, she had the uncertain feeling of showing up at a party on time, only to find she was the first one there. There was no invitation to fish out of her pocket, no need to double-check the date. This was definitely the place.

But only for her, apparently.

Well, and Jude. And this handful of cars, almost comical in a lot that could hold a hundred more.

"If you were me," she'd asked Jude as an afterthought, "where would you start?"

"No one gave you a manual, huh?" He stopped short of saying he didn't care what she did, but it came through in the impatient tone of a man with a "honey-do list" waiting.

"Sure didn't." Katie had been chagrined to find herself blinking back tears. The false alarm of waking to a stranger outside her back door was sinking in: this wasn't actually her barn or her yard or her driveway. None of this belonged to her. Not even the bed she'd slept in last night.

This was going to take some getting used to.

She'd turned back toward the house, embarrassed her emotions were getting the best of her. She didn't need Jude's advice anyway.

"I'd get a map and pen and walk the property," he'd called after her. She'd stopped, her back still to him. "Get to know the trails," he'd continued. "Note where you see any sign of neglect. Limbs down across the path, deep mud that could use straw or mulch to make it passable. By the end of today, you'll have a plan for tomorrow. Only way I know to start is one step at a time."

"Thanks," she'd called softly over her shoulder. Then she'd disappeared inside. For the coffee he'd kept her from. And to restart the day on her own terms.

But she hadn't fully exhaled until she heard the crunch of gravel under Jude's tires. It hadn't escaped her that she still didn't know exactly what he'd been doing in the barn. The hay bales he'd mentioned were nowhere near, and as far as she could tell, he'd left empty-handed.

Yet his suggestion was smart, and not unkind.

The cleaning service would be here soon—the intercom at the gate was programmed so she could buzz in guests through a code on her cell phone, so best to make herself scarce. She'd eaten a granola bar at the counter, scrolling through the usual social feeds—in that disoriented zone when everyone else's life looks much more "normal" than your own—then pulled a hat over her ears, laced on her hiking boots, and headed out map and pen in hand. Bess had mentioned the perimeter trail; she'd start there.

Katie wasn't much of an off-season hiker. She wasn't used to walking without talking on her phone or popping in earbuds, but it seemed important to pay attention now, to keep her senses open. As she ventured into the tree cover, she was surprised at how far she could see with the world not yet in bloom. The forest floor was a carpet of dried leaves. Honeysuckle was budding, arching over the ground at every turn, tinting the lower third of the woods a bright lime green. Overhead, the treetops were bare but not empty. All around her, the forest was rustling with the busy work of a new season. Birds building nests, chipmunks burrowing, squirrels chasing mates in spirals up tree trunks.

She waited to feel a part of it all, but the unease of the morning followed her down the trail, echoing in the crunch of her footsteps, making her feel . . . what? Unprepared? This wasn't *that* different from what she'd expected. Why was she so out of sorts? So the previous caretaker had barely bothered to move out. So Bess hadn't called yet today. So Jude hadn't exactly been welcoming. So what? This was her fresh start. Why give anyone the power to wrong-foot her?

As she walked on, struggling to sort herself out, she considered that Grace's left-behind mess and Jude's equally unwelcoming arrival might be, by themselves, mere annoyances, but they also signaled a problem that was less easily brushed off: How could this place ever come to feel like home? She hadn't considered that caretaking was akin to living in your office: you'd always be on call because, *of course*, other people had the keys to company property.

Grace's name was all over the house. On empty prescription bottles, magazines, even business cards in the bedside drawer. *Resident Caretaker*, they actually said. (Should Katie order cards? What on earth for?) *Grace Dunbar.* It was a name that balanced its own scale, as if her parents had sought the most elegant choice to proceed a surname that sounded too close to "dumbbell" or "done" or "bar." Yet Bess said she hadn't really known Grace. Jude hadn't either. Had anyone looked at her twice? Or had she been the equivalent of the greeter you acknowledged politely on your way into Walmart? *She did a good job,* Jude had said, shrugging. Like that was all he'd ever needed to know, though the woman had been here for years.

Katie wouldn't let herself consider this had been a mistake. She would cling to the hope that Bess could get Grace on the phone today, maybe even give Katie her number. It would be reassuring to have a chance to talk to her, ask questions. True, anyone who'd left so abruptly might not be game for dispensing job advice, but you never knew. Maybe there had been other circumstances to her leaving, and once they'd been dealt with, she'd be apologetic and helpful.

Regardless, Katie certainly hadn't come all the way from Pittsburgh to run inside crying the first time a new coworker pointed out she didn't have a clue.

She had done hard jobs before.

She just hadn't done them alone.

Or hadn't she? Because if there was one thing Clark had made clear when he wondered aloud if they might have their marriage not dissolved, but annulled? Declared *void* after more than a decade and a whole business founded together? It was that he'd never really been in it.

She walked nearly thirty minutes before she saw another soul—two fifty-something women with matching ponytails, walking side by side and chatting away at full volume.

"That's exactly what I told her," the one in the purple jacket was saying. "Life is too short for that nonsense."

Katie stepped off the trail to let them pass, and they smiled at her.

"You okay out here by yourself?" the purple jacket asked. "You look a little lost."

Katie blinked, taken aback. Was she *that* obviously ill suited for this? It was one thing for Jude to be skeptical, but . . . The woman nodded at the unfolded map Katie was clutching.

"Oh, that." She offered a weak laugh. "No, I'm not lost, thanks. At least, let's hope not."

They'd stopped walking to stare at her expectantly. Like they assumed there had to be some story about why she hoped she wasn't lost. As if anyone wanted to be lost.

Then again, maybe someone did.

"I'm the caretaker," she elaborated.

The words just fell out. She certainly had no intention of announcing her role to everyone she met, like some mall cop on a power trip. In fact, she'd rather remain anonymous. The last thing she wanted was to put herself on the hook for customer service she didn't know how to do.

But the women lit up, clapping their hands, practically falling over each other in excitement.

"You're kidding!"

"Every time we catch a glimpse of that house, we say how cool it'd be to live here."

"Oh, to have this all to yourself. It's our happy place!"

"I know just what I'd do. I'd bring out a tumbler of wine and watch the sunset up around this bend right here. You know, where you can see the river?"

They sighed dreamily. Happily.

Katie tried not to look surprised by their enthusiasm. She had to admit, Bess's family had been bursting with it in the same genuine way yesterday. Not that Bess hadn't, too, but—well, Katie assumed she'd been putting her on a bit. It wasn't as if she was becoming caretaker for some quaint beach cottage in the Scottish Highlands—attempts to make Ohio sound exotic were going to ring hollow. Yet the apple had not fallen far with Ethan and Emory. She had no doubt they'd be the best, most earnest tour guides, so easily using the proper names for trees and flowers, speaking about animals as creatures to be revered. Even Vince had gone doe-eyed, saying he wished logistics were easier to bring his teams out for trail runs.

"I'm new," she admitted to the women. She'd already said too much—why not go all the way.

"Oh, lucky you!" said the one in the puffy vest.

The purple jacket nodded along. "Congratulations. Ever done anything like this before?"

"Rookie caretaker here." She raised her hand, as if to say, *Guilty as charged*. But they kept bubbling right over each other.

"Well, I'm sure you're going to love it."

"What a fantastic opportunity. Life-changing."

"I love that there's a woman in that role."

"Yes! Fierce."

Katie was oddly moved. "Thanks for the vote of confidence. See you around?"

They nodded and waved, continuing on, and Katie did too, curious to see the view up ahead that evidently called for solitude, sunset, and wine—her kind of nature after all. These two strangers were the first people who'd reacted positively to Katie's new role—well, other than Bess. If this was their "happy place," maybe they were the ones who knew what they were talking about.

She reached the bend, and sure enough, found herself at the top ridge of a steep ravine. In the distance, the muddy curve of the river forked, marking the start of Grove's creek—the one she'd driven over yesterday. It wasn't as shallow out here closer to the mouth, but the creek bed was still photogenically rocky, with rainbow-colored lines threading the limestone on both sides. Water poured between boulders like dozens of tiny waterfalls, whooshing around stepping stones and over tree roots, the soothing sound of it all rushing up the ledge to greet her.

Beside her, a thick branch protruded from an old oak, and she slid onto it, the seat of her jeans scraping the bark. It felt sturdy, immovable; if she turned sideways, she could lean into the trunk. Nature's perfect bench. She'd almost walked right by it. Most people would.

Maybe it was okay that this place would never belong to her.

Maybe it was enough—maybe it was even better—that she was the only one with unlimited access to enjoy it. *A fantastic opportunity,* the hikers had called it. *Life-changing.*

Maybe it didn't matter where Grace Dunbar had gone, or why. Maybe, instead of griping about what to do with her stuff, Katie should be thanking her for so swiftly stepping aside. Otherwise, Katie wouldn't be here. And she might not exactly belong, but she didn't fit where she'd come from either.

The new Katie would not surround herself with people who doubted her. The new Katie would have genuine friends, or she'd have no one. But either way, at least it would be honest. She was done going through motions without real feeling behind them.

That much, she couldn't blame anyone else for. It all needed to start with her. Right here at Grove. Others would come and go, but Katie alone had been asked to stay.

The sun peeked out of the cloud cover at last, and the whole creek lit to sparkling.

By midafternoon, Katie had a respectable half-day's work to take stock of. She'd done as Jude suggested and marked where a railing had come loose from a footbridge and where a birdhouse on a tall post had fallen over. She'd made a note to find out whether the bird feeders needed to be refilled with seed—there were quite a few of them. She'd also found, in no particular order, one striped, child-size glove, one torn stocking cap, a five-dollar bill (her tip for the day), a Nature Center membership card issued to Jennifer Sheridan, one steel water bottle, two granola bar wrappers, and a single sunglass lens. With nothing along to collect them in, her pockets were bursting.

Aside from the friendly women, she'd encountered a lone retiree leaning on a walking stick, who tipped his hat at her; the young mother she'd heard in the parking lot, still calling *Be careful!* every ten seconds to her toddler; and one overdressed businessman, striding fast and nodding into his earpiece with exaggerated involvement in whatever conference call he was multitasking to.

Only five people in who knew how many miles. She'd have to install one of those fitness tracker apps she'd been resisting.

"That's a pretty representative sampling," Bess said on the phone later, when Katie was back on her front porch, sitting on the stairs, her collected treasures piled beside her. "Not bad for Day One. You're getting the whos and whats of the annex already."

The scent of Pine-Sol wafted out the front door; the cleaning crew had piled rubber bins of Grace's belongings on the walk and was now loading their supplies into their van. The house didn't really look emptier, only cleaner. More like an Airbnb. They'd left everything with an obvious, transferrable use—the furniture and library, artwork and entertainment, dishware and decor.

"Do you know if there's a lost and found here?" she asked Bess. "I picked up someone's membership card."

"Oh, thanks; the office will call them. But for anything else you find, who knows? How would we even tell the difference between a lost and found and Grace's random stuff?"

How, indeed? Katie went to the stack of storage bins, peeling the lid off the top one. The contents looked to have come from the coat closet—pilled scarves, sweat-stained baseball caps, a jacket missing a button. A bulging, oversize manila envelope had been shoved down one side. Katie pulled it out and saw a single word written across the front:

MOM. It was overflowing with children's artwork: marker drawings of stick figures holding hands, spikey suns, crooked hearts.

"Excuse me," Katie called to the cleaning crew, cradling the phone with her shoulder as she held up the folder. "Do you remember where you found this?" They shrugged—purposefully, like answers cost extra up front. "You're right," she told Bess. "Everything left behind looks random. You would've mentioned . . . Grace wasn't a mom, was she?"

"A mom?" Bess hesitated, then laughed. "You had me thinking for a second . . . but no. You know those people who don't even pretend to like kids? That's Grace. Why do you ask?"

"There's a folder of kids' artwork here, labeled 'Mom.' Maybe I'm looking at the lost and found now . . . If I found something like this at the picnic tables, I'd feel bad throwing it out."

"Does that mean I should feel bad about unloading my kids' backpacks straight into the recycling pile?"

Katie laughed and repacked the bin, adding the water bottle she'd found and making an executive decision to throw away everything else broken or torn. The lost and found could live in the barn.

"No luck tracking down Grace, I take it?" Even as she hoped for news, Katie reveled in this one comfy spot in the unfamiliar day. It had been years since she and Bess checked in with each other like this. Picking up where they left off yesterday, instead of starting a call with months of catch-up. They used to know all the minutia of each other's highs and lows. Used to bring iced coffees or cute cards to each other, just because. Katie hadn't had a friend like that since. Her heart lifted at the thought, even as her brain chided her not to be needy. Bess was busy with her own job and family, and she'd already done so much.

"Not yet." Bess paused. "I wouldn't wait to hear if I were you. She had her chance; she can hardly get upset over anything you move or toss. And don't feel bad about taking time to make the place your own, okay? No one's going to ask for a stamped timecard. Settle in. Get groceries. Sit by the creek. Your main job is just to be there, so you can't not be doing it."

Katie loved that Bess was not the sort of person who'd need to be told any of these things, but *was* the sort of person who understood that Katie did. "I met Jude," she ventured.

"Ah. Did he give you any complaints to file with my office yet?"

"Nothing major. Only that I demand a more suitable vehicle." They both laughed.

"He's particular about how things are done. But honestly, it means he does a good job."

They all kept saying that about one another. Maybe it was all they cared about.

Maybe it was all that mattered.

"He's fine," Katie said. "It's fine. It just startled me, seeing him in the barn, and I was wondering . . . Should I have a sense of how many people have access to these buildings behind my house?" Katie hadn't investigated them herself yet. A detached garage or workshop stood kitty-corner to the barn, nearly three times as wide as its one roll-up door. There were also two oversize sheds, one by the canoes and another closer to the pond. *Storage, mostly*, Bess had said yesterday. *You know the crap you never have a good home for? Stuff you use a week out of the year? That's basically what's in there.*

"No one has access to the house without knocking," Bess assured her. "As for the rest, I'm not sure. Closer to summer, we'll have staff out there training camp counselors, that sort of thing. Do you want me to ask people to give you a heads-up when they're headed your way?"

"Oh, no. I'm not trying to micromanage. Just . . . to know what to expect."

"Well, if Jude oversteps, let me know. What's the damage now that the crew has boxed up the house? I told them to let you be the one to stow everything in case you wanted one more look through. Want me to come back out and help?"

Katie did, of course. But also, she sort of didn't.

"I've got it," she told Bess. "Besides, only I can do what you said." And what do you know: she didn't have to force cheer into her voice. It was already there. "Make it feel like my own."

5

Something was ringing.

Disoriented, Katie reached through the fog of sleep to fumble for her phone. She squinted into the darkness as its display lit up at her touch: 1:18 a.m.

It sounded like a doorbell.

She did a quick mental calculation, as if she might've missed something. She couldn't have been asleep long. She'd spent the whole night unpacking her things in the bedroom, then read past midnight, sucked into one of Grace's library books, enjoying it so immensely she was glad Grace hadn't gotten around to returning it. She'd shut off the light when her eyelids began to droop, legs aching from the hike. Brain calming itself at last.

Ring, ring, ring.

Her last house—Clark's now, with the *not* new Katie—announced arrivals with a classic ding-dong, but this was a loud, shrill tone, between a buzz and a beep. It sounded three times in close succession, like a child playing at imaginary deliveries.

Fear seized her in the sudden silence. How could anyone have gotten past the gate at this hour? And why? Had some overzealous member gotten a notion to come hike by moonlight or watch a meteor shower, and the scanner malfunctioned and admitted them after hours? After a decade as a web designer, she was all too aware of how unreliable technology could be.

Unreliable and vulnerable.

Ring, ring, ring.

It came again. Katie bolted upright, clutching the blanket to her chest. One problem with her theory: Why on earth would they be ringing her doorbell?

Maybe it was Bess. Katie checked the phone again. No missed calls.

Maybe Jude? Someone with authorized access to scare the bejesus out of her? Or even Grace herself, returning for . . . something that couldn't wait until morning?

She couldn't just lie here. She had to go see.

Her legs swung reluctantly over the edge of the bed, bare feet gripping the braided throw rug. As her body caught up to her brain, she sprang into action. What if she didn't answer in time? What if no one was there? She wouldn't feel safe. Wouldn't sleep—and not just tonight. She *had* to see who.

She flicked every light switch she passed on her scramble to the door, intent on signaling she was up, on her way.

That and a ridiculous childlike urge, like nothing scary could get her if the lights were on.

At the bottom of the stairs, she saw no silhouette through the sheer-curtained window. Were there woodland creatures that could do this? Rodents running up the wall, over the button? With one finger, she moved the curtain aside and there, standing close enough to the door to press her nose to the wood, was a woman of maybe forty. Her hair was a mess of disheveled waves, and she was shifting from one foot to the other, from cold or nerves or both. Her hands clutched a pastel knit cap to her chest. It had ugly dark smears on one side.

The woman reached out to ring the bell yet again—shrill, shrill, shrill—and Katie caught sight of her forehead. The skin was broken in a thick, curved line. Blood streamed down the side of her face and onto the neck of her jacket.

"Oh, my God!" Pushing back from the window, Katie lunged at the dead bolt and flung open the door. "Oh, my God," she repeated.

Face-to-face, she could see the wound was recent but not fresh—the blood had begun to dry. "What's happened? Are you all right?"

"Thank you!" the woman cried, a sob escaping her. She pushed past Katie into the house before Katie could react. "Thank you so, so much."

Katie slammed the door behind her with the whole weight of her body, even as she realized she was locking herself inside with the only threat she could see. What if this was some elaborate scheme? What if this woman had a cohort outside waiting to see if anyone was home, and here was Katie running out half-asleep, so obviously alone and gullible? Or what if this woman herself was armed or—

"I can't believe I made it," the woman squeaked. She was full-out sobbing now. "God is good. You're an angel. I'm so sorry. I know it's late."

Relief, Katie realized. These were tears of the purest relief, the kind that could only follow sheer terror.

"Has there been a car accident?" she asked, picturing an SUV careening off the road, the woman stumbling out and past the gate on foot. Katie's house was set back far, but then again, no one was closer. *Possibly* her porch light was visible atop the hill?

The woman looked at her strangely, gasping still, trying to pull herself together. "No, I . . . I got dropped off. Like the instructions said."

"What instructions?" Katie asked.

"Oh no. Are you not the caretaker? The sign said—"

"I'm the caretaker," Katie assured her, though she still didn't understand.

So this woman wasn't here by accident, exactly, but some other wires were clearly crossed. "Let's take a breath and you can tell me what happened. Is there someone I can call for you? Or 9-1-1?"

The woman took an obedient, deep breath, then another, but looked no calmer. "I thought *you* would know who to call." She pulled something from her pocket and held it out, fingers trembling. Katie took it—a wrinkled piece of white cardstock about the size of an index card.

WHEN YOU ARE READY, someone had handwritten across the top. *NO PHONE, SMART WATCH, ETC.* Then, impossibly, they'd scrawled Katie's new address: *961 GROVE FARM ROAD.*

The rest of the card was in a typeface slightly out of alignment, as if printed on an old ink-jet.

THE FIRST STEP.
Avoid gate camera at drop-off point. Walk in alone.
Follow sign to Caretaker's House.
Ring bell 3 times. Present this card.

She had to squint to read the fine print at the bottom:

In the unlikely event of no answer, wait on screened porch. Blankets, water, and first aid kit in wicker bench. No phone calls—unless life-threatening emergency—not even to trusted sources. Do not be seen.

Katie read the card top to bottom, all the way through, then read it again. Then again.

Life-threatening emergency. Trusted sources. Do not be seen. How very Jason Bourne.

What the actual hell?

"Where did you get this card?" Katie demanded. She was no longer doing a decent job of sounding any less panicked than the woman was.

"The baker," the woman said, as if this would explain everything. As if Katie surely knew who that was. Because she had to. Because if she didn't, they were both screwed.

"What baker?" The question came out like an apology.

"You know. The trendy one. With the fancy cupcakes. And the van."

Katie fought an inappropriate urge to laugh. Nothing was remotely funny, but the implication that she'd inadvertently replaced some secret operative in this very unsecret old farmhouse . . . Actually, that *was* laughable. A bad joke on both of them.

"I'm so sorry," she managed, hating how helpless she sounded. "I feel terrible, but I don't know anything about this. There's some mistake."

The woman had stopped crying in her confusion, but she started again, crumpling inward.

"I just moved in yesterday," Katie stammered. "No one said . . ." She couldn't finish. Not the way the woman was looking at her, with abject horror.

"Yesterday?" she repeated. "And no one told you anything?"

"I'm so sorry," Katie repeated. They weren't getting anywhere. How could they? "Someone did this to you?" She gestured with concern toward the woman's bloody forehead.

"This is nothing," the woman said. "He'll kill me. He'll find me. I can't be me anymore. I'm ready—like the card says. It took me forever to get here, and now . . ." Her voice rose in desperation. "This is supposed to be Step One. To get it started."

"It'll be okay. We just have to . . ." To *what*? "Who drove you here?" Katie asked.

"I know I was supposed to go through the channels to get a ride, but I didn't have time. The baker knew I might not, which is why she gave me the card." She shook her head. "I swear, my ride was someone he doesn't even know exists. Someone he can never ask."

The *channels*. This all seemed eerily coordinated. Yet somehow, something crucial had been missed in the process. Namely, apparently, Katie.

"You're sure you can trust her?"

The woman nodded. "She's also been . . ."

Katie swallowed hard. *Shit.* "Can we call her? Ask her to come back, help sort this out?"

"No!" The woman's hands flew in front of her face, as if to catch the word and muffle it. "I can't. I promised her. I can't go back, only forward. One way or another."

"The police then. Or a women's shelter—"

"No police! No shelter. Those roads end right back where I started. You think I'd be here if this wasn't my last option?"

The woman's eyes searched the room, like some answer might be waiting in plain sight, and Katie found herself doing the same. Mark Twain's quotable adage in embroidery thread now read as a lecture from the stairwell wall. IT IS NEVER WRONG TO DO THE RIGHT THING.

Katie frowned at it. *What were you up to, Grace Dunbar? What have you gotten me into?*

Then an even grimmer question seized her. *Does this have something to do with why you left so suddenly?*

She really, really hoped not. "Can you explain exactly what you're here for?" she asked. "The first step of what?"

"Of a new life. Of leaving this one behind and never looking back."

Katie's eyes fell on the key rack mounted beside the door. Above each hook was a corresponding label written in pen on masking tape. Though for all Katie knew, they were outdated, mixed up. *Canoe gear. Front gate. Back shed. Side shed.*

She stopped short, staring.

3 Rings was scrawled in black marker above the last key.

She stared at the words, dumbstruck, then down again at the card in her hand. *Ring bell 3 times.* She looked up and saw the woman following her gaze. Drawing the same slow, strange conclusion and meeting Katie's blank stare.

"What's that key to?" The woman's voice was barely a whisper.

"I have no idea," Katie said. She slid it off the ring. The brass was cool to the touch, the ridges rough against her fingertips. *Think,* she told herself. *It's up to you to figure this out.* Who else could she call to come and help, even if she wanted to? What sense was there in yanking Bess out of bed in the middle of the night? This woman wanted answers now. And so did Katie. "Maybe this will make more sense," she ventured, "if we can find out."

Katie looked down the hallway toward the kitchen, considering. This corridor held the coat closet, powder room, and cupboard under the stairs. All doors she'd opened without a key. She'd ventured into the basement for laundry too—cracked concrete sloping to a drain in the center—where signs of water damage explained why there was nothing there but an archaic washer, dryer, and utility tub, plus some detergent and fabric softener, neither her brand. She couldn't recall any mysterious lock upstairs. The cleaners had left everything open, air-drying and fresh. The attic was through a square of plywood in the ceiling between the bathroom and the linen closet: no easy access, but no keyhole either.

She could visualize the electronic keypads on all the outbuildings. Those master keys were here, too, but they were silver, sleek, and new. Distinctly different from the one she held, which was the kind a locksmith would make while you'd wait.

Might there be locked interior doors in those buildings, though?

It was . . . a place to start. Something to try.

At least to buy time to figure out something better.

"Come look with me?" she asked. She couldn't leave a stranger in her house alone. To her relief, the woman nodded.

Katie was finding it hard to look at her. The blood at her hairline wasn't *nothing*. It had to hurt. Bad. Katie could see twin goose eggs forming beneath the broken skin.

"What's your name?" Katie asked gently.

The woman narrowed her eyes. "My real name?"

"That's up to you. What can I call you?"

She bit her lip. "Lindsay." She looked a little like a Lindsay, maybe. Maybe not.

"Lindsay." *Nice to meet you* seemed wrong, considering. "I'm Katie. How about we take care of that cut first?"

Lindsay nodded shakily, and Katie gestured toward the kitchen.

They took the first step together.

Like the card said.

6

The night was damp with cold dew. A few early-season crickets chirped, out of sync. Some nocturnal bird—or a bat, maybe—flapped overhead. Katie shivered.

Lindsay stood beside her, the clean bandage on her forehead already marred with fresh bloodstains. She swore it didn't hurt. *Adrenaline,* Katie thought.

I'm used to it, Lindsay said.

Katie had found a long, watchman-style flashlight in the pantry, and she swung it in front of them, surveying their options, even though the floodlights on the barn were bright enough to see by. Did tonight's strange turn have anything to do with why Jude was poking around out here yesterday? She didn't know whether to hope it had. Jude's involvement would at least mean someone knew what the hell was going on, but then again, what if he wasn't supposed to know?

She headed for the barn first, Lindsay close behind. At the keypad, she shielded the glowing numbers with one hand as she typed in the security code. Even if Lindsay was everything she seemed, she was obviously desperate. There was no telling what she might do, whether Katie could trust her.

They pulled open the beast of the barn door together, both of them grunting. Chevy meowed at their feet, and Lindsay crouched to pet him—reaching, Katie supposed, for any sweet, soft thing in the night.

Katie cast the beam of her light into the barn and found the string dangling from the bare light bulb inside the door. She pulled it and stood blinking in the brightness. In every direction, tools and equipment leaned in rusty tangles. The far wall held two wooden partitions that had once been animal stalls, but both had empty hinges where their doors belonged. A row of rough, unfinished cupboards stood to the right, but there was no closet, and no other door she could see. A loft stretched over the back half of the space, with a wooden ladder attached to the edge at an angle. Katie gave it a shake to verify it was sturdy, then climbed high enough to peek over. Among a lopsided mountain of cardboard boxes, bags of grass seed were stacked within easy reach, and enough birdseed for an entire pet store was sealed inside clear plastic bins. The loft was too low to stand up in without stooping, and certainly not big enough for a proper door.

She shook her head at Lindsay, and they backtracked wordlessly. Across the gravel to the garage, Lindsay held Chevy while Katie keyed in the second code written on her palm, and the garage door jolted into motion. It was the ordinary, suburban sound of remote controls clipped to sun visors, but her whole body tensed, as if something on the other side might leap out at her as soon as the panels cleared her sight line.

But nothing was on the other side. Only gaping, empty darkness— at least, compared to the cluttered barn. Even by flashlight, she could see the wide concrete floor had been swept, well maintained and clean, save for a few grease stains where a car or truck might normally park. Katie had expected the ceiling to be vaulted—she was sure she'd seen a dirt-crusted window under the pointed roof outside. But this room had the feeling of a big, empty box, low ceilinged and disproportionate to the building's exterior. Old, out-of-use signs were stacked against the far wall. Danger, High Water, the top one read. In the far-left corner was a workbench, topped with a neat row of paint cans.

And beside it, a door.

A proper, metal door, with a brass circular keyhole above the knob. Katie nodded toward it solemnly, turning to meet Lindsay's eyes. She nodded back, hugging Chevy tighter until the tabby meowed in protest and wriggled to the floor, shooting back the way they'd come. *I know how you feel,* Katie thought, and made for the door before she lost her nerve too.

"Please be it," Lindsay whispered behind her. "Please, please be it."

Katie held her breath and aligned the key with the slot in the brass.

To her amazement, it slid in. And turned with a solid click of the dead bolt releasing.

Her hand seemed not to belong to her as it twisted the knob. But here was the open doorway. Through it, a small landing, and a steep hardwood staircase to the left. Straight ahead, another piece of masking tape sprawled across a light switch. She recognized the handwriting from the key rings inside: *CAREFUL!* it said. To her right, a windowless metal door filled the stairwell's exterior wall: an emergency exit. With another dead bolt—and another strip of masking tape.

CAREFUL! it repeated.

A friendly reminder? Note to self? Or a threat?

Katie flipped the light switch, bracing for . . . what? Impact? None came. A frosted-glass ceiling fixture glowed above the stairs, revealing another closed door at the top. She turned to meet Lindsay's eyes again and something passed between them. They were thoroughly in this together now. Whatever this was.

"Careful," Lindsay whispered, trying to smile.

"I got that," Katie whispered back.

Their rubber-soled shoes echoed within the narrow walls as they scuffed up the stairs. Katie listened hard for some sign that they weren't the only ones here, but the air around them was unmistakably still, undisturbed.

Except by them.

Unlike the others, this door was no bolted metal barrier but sturdy, thick wood. Katie tried the knob, and just like that, they found themselves inside a small studio apartment with a low, sloped ceiling. Nightlights glowed from outlets on every wall—above the kitchenette sink, beside the coffee table, beneath the nightstand.

No one was here.

A roughly cut carpet remnant covered most of the floor. Katie stepped onto it: thick, plush enough to muffle footsteps. She crossed to the crooked floor lamp in the corner and switched it on. The furnishings were about what you'd expect from an over-the-garage hideaway. A blue, threadbare love seat with oversize plaid cushions. A twin mattress on a box spring but no frame. A good-size space heater, unplugged. A kitchenette consisting of a mini fridge, microwave, electric kettle, and one of those portable twin-burner stoves that campers use, plus a badly scratched circular table with two mismatched chairs. Beyond it, an open shower curtain rigged above a patch of linoleum revealed a basic toilet and shower stall.

But there were unexpected little touches too. Neatly folded on the sofa arm: a luxurious faux-fur blanket. Atop the mattress: a package of pink satin sheets tied with a ribbon. On the coatrack: a fluffy spa robe with the tag still dangling from the sleeve. On the counter, a beautiful kiln-fired bowl filled with foil-wrapped truffles—Katie recognized the signature Godiva wrapper—and beside it, a matching mug, glazed in a lovely swirl pattern, with an inviting spread of coffee pods and tea bags. Like someone had tried, under the most unideal circumstances, to show their guest that they were worth more than this. That they deserved more than this. That someone cared.

She caught Lindsay staring at the artwork—actual *artwork*—on the walls, eyes moving from one canvas to the next. A large abstract oil painting evoked a sun rising over a purple-toned mountain range. A triptych of small square watercolors added glimpses of the sea.

The effect was impressive—a room that might have otherwise seemed rock-bottom sad, turned hopeful. It took so little, Katie marveled. And yet it meant so much. She could see it all over Lindsay's face. Not just relief but astonishment. Gratitude.

"Look." Katie motioned for Lindsay to come stand with her at the dinette table. In its center, where no one could miss it, was a laminated sheet. A numbered list printed in plain font.

HOUSE RULES, it read across the top. As if they were checking into a bed-and-breakfast or joining a sorority with a watchful house mom downstairs.

1. This is *your* home for the next day or two, no more than three. You're free to use anything you'd like—don't hold back. That's what it's here for, with thanks to our generous donors.

2. A selection of clothing, toiletries, food, drinks, books, puzzles, notebooks, etc., has been provided. Any special requests, make a list and we'll do our best to accommodate.

3. Absolutely no phone calls, internet, or headphones. No exceptions. If for any reason you have not already relinquished all devices, you must do so now or be asked to leave. New devices will be provided at your final destination.

4. Do not remove the window coverings, even to peek out. You will be tempted. Resist.

5. If you have even the slightest inkling you may have been followed, notify the caretaker at once. We need this to remain a safe space. If it's not safe for you, we'll get you to a place that is.

6. Do not open the door if you hear someone downstairs. It may not be us. We will come to you, and we do promise to come, every day.

7. Please observe absolute quiet between the hours of 9:00 a.m. and 6:00 p.m., which is when the grounds are open to the public, and at any other time you hear someone in the vicinity. No running water, cooking smells, flushing the toilet, or TV/radio. This is for your protection. The caretaker will give you an all clear once the grounds are confirmed empty.

8. Our grounds are beautiful and good for the soul. You are free to enjoy the fresh air and sunshine from sunrise through 8:30 a.m., and again after closing. Use the stairwell door and lock it upon your return. Please refrain from going out after dark. Again, this is for your protection.

9. In the unlikely event that you should encounter a nature center employee before or after opening hours, say you are a guest of the caretaker if questioned and come to the house as if for breakfast or dinner. Do not reenter this building. Do not give your name.

10. IMPORTANT: anytime you must come to the house, ring three times. This alerts the caretaker to your arrival if she happens to have someone else present, so she can act accordingly.

The room fell into reverent silence as Katie and Lindsay stood reading the list together. It would have been reassuring to have such detailed instructions to follow, if only someone who knew how to implement the *other* steps of this plan was still behind them. *Your final destination,* it said. *No more than three days,* it said. Reading between the lines, it was clear the caretaker was supposed to take care of everything. It was literally right there in her job title.

Katie should be the one to state the obvious.

"They were going to hide you here," she said at last. She pulled out a chair to sit, and Lindsay did the same. It was amazing how something that loomed as large as this single laminated sheet could fit so easily between them on this table, like a plate of cookies.

"Before you ask, I did have the sense not to bring any devices." Lindsay looked down sheepishly at her bloodstained coat and muddy shoes. "I didn't bring anything at all. And I didn't know any details. I guess no one does ahead of time if they bothered to write them here."

Whoever these people were, they seemed obsessively careful about who knew what and when. Probably with good reason. "You're supposed to get a whole new identity?" Katie asked gently. It didn't escape her that she'd come here for the same thing. Just not quite as literally. "Do you know how?"

"Only that there's a system of steps, and it's supposed to feel manageable, taking one at a time. I don't know how many, or what they are. The baker called it 'smooth and speedy.'"

Katie looked around at the tiny studio and wondered how many versions of Lindsay had come here in the middle of the night. How many had cried here? Slept on satin sheets here? Played solitaire at this table? *God is good,* Lindsay had cried when she burst through Katie's door. How many broken souls had lain awake here, praying all the steps would go as planned?

How many had not slept at all, for fear they'd be found?

"Any idea how women . . . qualify?" It didn't seem the right word, yet she could think of no other.

"By being trapped, out of options. And by being ready." Lindsay bit her lip. "You don't know *anything* about this?" She was obviously trying to keep the panic from her voice, but it was in her eyes, pleading with Katie to be someone she wasn't. The caretaker she'd expected. Grace.

Was it possible Bess knew this responsibility came with the job? Or *used* to come with the job? She couldn't have. She might be flighty sometimes, but she wasn't sneaky. No way would she have knowingly brought Katie, of all people, into this role, especially without asking her first—or at the very least filling her in as soon as she arrived.

And now, this was Bess's problem too, wasn't it? Katie didn't know what to do but go straight to her with this, first thing in the morning. Maybe Bess knew something that would point them in the right direction, even if she didn't *know* she knew.

Heaven help her, Katie was thinking in mysterious double-talk already.

What they really needed was for Bess to get in touch with Grace. They had to try harder—to try everything. Surely the woman hadn't fallen off the face of the planet.

And if she had . . . Katie might have way more reasons to worry.

If you have even the slightest inkling you may have been followed, notify the caretaker, the instructions warned. *This is for your protection.*

But what about Katie's protection? A shiver ran through her.

"You can stay, of course," she heard herself promise. Because how could she turn Lindsay away? Where would she take her at two in the morning, and what would she tell her? *Sorry? Good luck?* "We'll get you settled, and I'll figure this out. You're safe here for now."

Lindsay gave her a brave smile. "I'm going to be here longer than three days, aren't I?"

"I don't know. I'll do my best." Lindsay nodded, chin trembling. She was showing an awful lot of restraint for someone in her position. Who needed help. Who needed, at minimum, for Katie not to freak out at this moment.

"Would you feel more comfortable in the house with me?" Katie asked. Would *Katie* feel more comfortable? How could she trust that this woman would really be okay out here? Or for that matter, in there?

What if she woke up and something valuable was missing or destroyed? How would she ever explain?

But Lindsay shook her head. "If this is how it worked before . . ."

Katie nodded. There *was* probably a reason they set it up this way. And in her case . . . She had no idea who might show up on her doorstep tomorrow, here for Grace's things or to switch over the cable service. As a newbie in town, she'd struggle to play off a random woman in her house. But wouldn't that be even harder if someone found Lindsay out *here*?

"I should come back and check on you, though," Katie said, realizing. "You could have a concussion."

"It looks worse than it is, honestly. Concussions are more of a concern with a blow to the top of the head, or even the back or side, but the forehead is more superficial." She smiled ruefully. "I've had reason to google that many times before."

"There's no way I'll sleep tonight anyway," Katie persisted. "I don't mind checking."

"But *I* want to sleep. You'll probably keep thinking of a million questions, and I can't thank you enough for trying to help. But it's been a day. Can we talk tomorrow? Despite all this, I'm going to sleep better than I have in years."

That's what Katie was afraid of. The only thing harder to explain than a random woman in her garage would be a random woman with a brain bleed, dead in her garage.

Katie hadn't signed up for this. If anyone had asked her, "By the way, would you be willing to shelter wounded, terrified strangers on the run in the dead of night?" she'd have said, with regret but certainty, *I am definitely not the right person for that job.*

Someone else had been, though. Someone built of stronger stuff.

Someone who'd vanished with no notice, leaving no instructions behind.

Katie had to reach Grace.

She had to keep faith that Grace was still reachable. That there wasn't some more sinister reason her post had been vacated, after all.

Grace had to be okay.

Grace would know what to do.

7

Bess gaped at Katie from the other end of her couch. "You mean to tell me this woman is out there right now?" They were each curled against an armrest, facing each other, cradling their takeout coffees. Bess had brought Katie's old order from college, a vanilla latte. Katie hadn't had one in years, and it felt decadently milky on her tongue, just on the right side of too sweet.

Katie nodded, glancing toward the front door. It remained closed, of course, the key rack beside it looking ordinary in the light of day, the "3 Rings" label too tiny to read from this distance. Even the fraying doormat seemed sprawled with a certain innocent skepticism: Could something so tired and forgettable really have staged the start of the dramatic scene she'd just recounted? "I took her breakfast first thing, but she was still asleep."

The day had dawned spitting rain, and Katie was glad. Less chance of Jude or anyone else having a reason to be out here. As early as Katie dared, she'd called Bess, knowing she sounded jittery and ridiculous as she whispered into the phone, even though she was alone in the house, *Please, can you come,* and, *This will sound dramatic, but come alone.*

"You're freaking me out," Bess had said, laughing nervously, but Katie hadn't seen any way around being vague. She'd felt more reassured after putting on her windbreaker and tramping to the loft, finding everything as she'd left it. Lindsay was true to her word, enveloped in the heavy sleep of someone who's finally, at last, found refuge. Katie had left the sliced bagel, cream cheese, and yogurt on the table in the dark, grateful for the way Lindsay briefly stirred, for signs of life.

Now, Katie trained her eyes on Bess, thinking of how vulnerable that moment with her houseguest had felt, though only one of them had been awake for it. "You honestly don't know anything about this?"

"Honest. I'd never not—I mean, this is . . . kind of a big detail to leave out."

Katie caught the subtext of annoyance with Grace, who had obviously chosen to do exactly that—deciding, for whatever reason, against entrusting Bess with this part of the job description, even on the day she turned in her resignation from all of it.

Bess was used to being underestimated, and sometimes, she even joked to Katie about the advantages of being written off as unreliable: off the hook for PTA committees and other favors she didn't want asked of her in the first place. *The other moms call me for fun stuff and leave me off everything else,* she'd crow. *Couldn't have designed this better myself!* But when someone didn't think Bess capable of rising to a challenge she wanted?

Katie knew from experience: look out.

"I don't understand," she pressed. "What did Grace expect the next time a victim showed up here in the middle of the night? That I'd magically figure this out?"

She was rethinking everything, down to the "Mom" folder of childlike drawings. What if a guest had left that behind, a sentimental keepsake they'd planned to take with them? Did that mean she should definitely keep it, just in case, or definitely get rid of it for the same reason? Everything around her suddenly seemed equally likely to mean the world to someone—or to mean absolutely nothing. How could anyone ever make sense of any of it on their own?

Bess shrugged. "That's the thing. I've already left messages she hasn't returned. What if we can't count on her to get us out of this? Or through it, or whatever? Because I have doubts."

Katie heard the truth of what Bess was saying, though she didn't want to believe it. A woman who'd outfitted that loft with soft robes and gourmet chocolates and risen from bed at all hours to welcome strangers . . . That woman *had* to care about this cause. A lot. What would it take to make her stop caring enough to leave its success to chance?

What, or who?

"Bess, level with me. Is any part of you worried that she's not okay? That she's not replying because she can't?"

"No part of me." Bess's words were surprisingly firm.

It crossed Katie's mind, fleetingly, that Bess could be withholding something about the circumstances of Grace's leaving. Something apart from this, maybe, that she wasn't allowed to share or preferred not to, even now. Office politics, a confidential issue with HR, or just bad vibes—Bess was big on avoiding those.

"If she truly can't reply," Bess went on, "it's more likely she's off celebrating her freedom somewhere, purposely offline."

Katie let it ride—for now. Bess was her only lifeline here, and Katie wasn't about to cut it by getting paranoid and giving her the third degree. But she couldn't help but feel a kinship to Grace, too, an obligation not to give up so easily. She didn't just have the woman's job title, she was sleeping in her bed.

"Okay," she conceded. "But someone must know something. I mean, other people are clearly involved in whatever these next steps are. If not you . . . Can you think of who?"

Bess shook her head. "If anyone on staff was close enough with her to be involved in something like this, they did a great job of hiding it. But you're right: we have to start somewhere. I can go now, ask around."

"No!" Katie was seized with conviction. All she could picture was Lindsay, waking to a hastily assembled committee of frowning employees. "If you ask around, you'll put this whole setup in danger."

"They're naturalists, Katie. Not vigilantes. Who will they tell? It's not like one of them will have a direct line to this woman's violent husband."

"But it's bigger than her. You'll be broadcasting this whole secret network exists."

"*Does* it exist, though, without someone to run it?" Bess wasn't being condescending; the question seemed as much for herself as for Katie. "I think we have to trust everyone to keep this in the nature center family until we figure out what's going on."

"What if someone panics and calls the cops?"

"Would that be so bad? I'm two seconds from calling the cops myself. I'm already panicking."

Only Bess could say the words *I'm already panicking,* mean them, and yet look and sound this calm.

"That's the last thing Lindsay wants," Katie insisted. "Otherwise, she wouldn't be here."

Bess bit her lip. "Let's be realistic that we might not have much choice. But we'll cross that bridge when we come to it. In the meantime, I do think we can trust the team to respect all this."

"But Grace didn't trust them. At least, as far as we know." Katie was only pointing out the obvious, but as soon as the words were out of her mouth, they sounded cruel. "I just mean . . . It's not like we're trying to keep a surprise birthday party secret here. Lives are at stake. I'll take you out to meet her, and you'll see for yourself. Can we at least try to figure this out between the three of us first?"

Bess got to her feet and began pacing. "You have to understand: I feel responsible. This is a nonprofit; it's extremely important everything be aboveboard to keep our funding. The director puts a ton of faith in my judgment. If I handle this wrong, I could get fired."

"I think I'm in the same boat."

Bess did not say, *Maybe, but you just got here.* She did not say, *Who cares? I had to talk you into even taking this job.* She did not say, *But this is my career, not something I fell into.* She was much too kind for any of that.

But she didn't have to say it. They both knew.

"Worst-case scenario," Katie ventured, "it's hard to imagine them taking issue with us keeping someone safe, isn't it?"

"I don't know the legalities of hiding someone. You're also assuming this Lindsay person is who she says she is."

"I worried about that too. But I don't see what choice we have but to believe her."

"I'm not saying I don't believe her. But staking my livelihood and the reputation of my employer on believing her is next level."

Bess had a point. Everything kept coming back to the same question. "Grace would have known we'd have to ask around as a last resort. If this is your job after hours, don't you train your replacement? Hell, don't you handpick your replacement?"

"Unless . . ." Bess stopped pacing and snapped her fingers. "This wasn't going to be anyone's job anymore?"

Katie was on her feet now too. "Like they were shutting down this whole underground system? And maybe that's why Grace left—she never wanted to be just a regular caretaker?"

"Or maybe she did want to resign, and they found a replacement somewhere else. A workaround that doesn't involve Grove anymore."

Katie finished the thought: "But Lindsay fell through the cracks somehow. A straggler."

Bess nodded slowly. "That seems more likely."

Katie's whole body tingled with the possibility. As a kid, sometimes she'd experienced a terrible rush when something went wrong. They'd had an unreliable station wagon prone to stranding them places: in a shady parking lot after a late Pirates game or on the side of the highway with eighteen-wheelers zipping by. Every time, her parents would argue and fret in the front seat while they waited for roadside assistance, while in the back seat her big sister, Gigi, bit her nails to mask her terror while Katie tried not to smile, feeling guilty at the impulse. The thing was, it was never just a disaster, it was a *story*. She could already hear them recounting the adventure: how they didn't know if the drunken fans ambling over meant to rob them or to help, how one of the semis blew a tire and sent them diving for cover.

In adulthood, as the disasters became hers to handle, she'd outgrown the thrill. When was the last time she'd felt this way and not squabbled through like her parents, or hid her face like Gigi? When was the last time she'd run toward it, eager to see how the story ended?

"You're excited about this," Bess said suddenly. Her voice sounded accusing, but she was teasing. Smiling. Eyes bright.

"Am not."

"Are too."

"Don't be ridiculous, this is serious."

"I know," Bess agreed. "Very exciting."

"Bess!" Katie elbowed her. "Truthfully? I'm terrified."

Funny enough, it was all true. Maybe it had never been bad to see a problem to solve as a kind of adventure. Maybe the impulse had never been wrong, but a gut instinct she'd had before she was old enough to follow it. Maybe she'd mistakenly thought she'd outgrown it when really, the unhappy years with Clark had just drained all sense of possibility away.

"You can be terrified and excited at the same time," Bess said now. "And I guess so can I. Listen, I got you into this. I'll help you get out of it. Okay?"

"Okay." Katie took a deep breath. *Okay.* "We'll start with Lindsay when she wakes up. If she's a straggler, we need to find out how she straggled, starting with where she got that card. I tried last night, but . . . obviously it's not exactly comforting to her that I don't know what to do here."

"Obviously." Bess was wrapping her mind around this, just as Katie had been the whole sleepless night. But the new day had brought some clarity, and less shock at the impossibility of the situation. So perhaps it would be the same for Lindsay too.

Lindsay had told her this system worked step by step. *It's supposed to feel manageable, taking one at a time.*

That's how she and Bess would take things too. They didn't need a whole plan.

Only a plan for what to do next.

8

A rainy day had never been so welcome. The soft, steady spring shower pattered on the slanted roof of the loft, enveloping the three women inside in the soothing white noise and the sense of security that no one would slosh through the maze of puddles to come knocking.

Lindsay had slept until nine but looked no less exhausted. The morning's thick, gray cloud cover seemed to have stretched even here, from the dark saucers under her eyes to the bruise blooming around the gash in her forehead. Still, she hadn't looked pained or sluggish as she'd made herself a cup of tea with honey. She moved, instead, in the slightly self-conscious way of someone determined to show *Everything is fine, this is fine, we are fine* as she joined Katie and Bess at the table, where she dug into the bagel with gusto.

Bess couldn't seem to stop looking around the room, shaking her head in amazement. Before she'd called her office to say she'd be in late—with the truthful excuse of "helping the caretaker"—she'd second-guessed whether she should come along. What if the two of them overwhelmed Lindsay, like some panel of well-meaning-but-ill-equipped do-gooders? But Katie didn't know the area, even a little bit. The bigger risk seemed that Lindsay could drop some crucial reference that would go over Katie's head but ring a bell for Bess.

Besides, Katie had never known Bess to overwhelm anyone.

"So you've worked here for years and honestly never knew this apartment was here?" Lindsay asked Bess now, mouth full of bagel, tugging at the foil seal atop the yogurt.

Bess smiled reassuringly. "We're on the private residence part of the property, and I do the public-facing stuff. I always tried not to bother the last caretaker. Most staffers do the same."

Lindsay nodded, like she hadn't really doubted it. It was Katie who needed to hear it again and again. *Bess is the best friend I've ever had,* she'd told Lindsay. *We can trust her.* Then, too, Lindsay had only shrugged, as if they'd reached some truce. Which Katie supposed they had.

"So listen," Katie said now. Might as well get right to it. "We think our best chance of helping you is to find out more about who gave you that card. You mentioned a baker."

Lindsay nodded, eyes on her yogurt as she swirled her spoon in a figure eight.

Katie cleared her throat. *Why* was she so nervous? This was just a conversation. They were just people. Outside of this, they might even be friends. Maybe they still would be. "I did a search for local cupcake shops and couldn't believe how many there are. Do you remember her name?" Katie asked gently. "What the bakery is called?"

Lindsay narrowed her eyes, trying to remember, as she mechanically swallowed one heaping spoonful of yogurt after another. "I'm drawing a blank."

That's okay, Katie told herself, refusing to let this low-grade panic rise any higher. *We'll narrow this down. We can start with how they met and—*

"I know the street it's on, though," Lindsay finished.

"Oh!" Katie's hand flew to her chest. "Excellent. Whew."

Bess leaned toward Lindsay, sprawling her hands on the tabletop in a disarming, motherly way. "Can you start at the beginning, walk us through the whole thing? Last night was all about getting you safe. But if you're up to it, the more you can tell us about how you came this far, the better our chances of making sure you can continue."

Lindsay nodded. "I woke up thinking the same thing. I just hope she'll talk to you. I mean, I think she will, but—I didn't do what she said. She might be mad."

"I don't see how she could be mad," Katie said. "She obviously wanted to help you."

"Well, she was pretty mad the last time I saw her."

Lindsay pushed her chair back from the table and pulled her knees up to sit cross-legged. She looked younger that way, and for the first time since last night, a little scared.

"So, the beginning. I was—" Lindsay stopped short. "Look, it's hard to tell this story without details of who I am. But I'm not sure if . . . I mean, my name's not even Lindsay."

"I forget all details as soon as I don't need them anymore," Bess said cheerily. "And often before I'm done needing them. Personal policy. Couldn't change it if I tried. I forget why."

Katie nodded. "I'll vouch for that. Also, she tends to rub off on me. We start talking the same, our cycles sync, and we forget the same stuff."

Lindsay—or not Lindsay—tried to smile. "I remember wishing my name was Lindsay as a kid. I thought everyone should get to pick their own names once they reached a certain age. It seemed so unfair parents got to stick you with a name your whole life." She shook her head. "I don't know when I lost that fire, you know? Not to let someone else define me?"

"Maybe you can stay Lindsay now," Katie offered. "Maybe you can pick."

"I used to wish for a different name too," Bess said. "But I forget what."

Lindsay laughed, more genuinely. "Okay." She paused to take a steadying breath. "I was walking to work one day from the bus stop. I never did that. Usually I drove and parked in the lot out back, but my right foot was in a boot, so I was stuck with the bus for six weeks."

"Crutches on a bus does not sound fun," Katie sympathized.

"It's even less fun than it sounds. But I'd had a bad fall. It was a miracle the boot was all I needed." She lowered her eyes and let the implication hang in the room. "So I'm clumping down the sidewalk, trying to get the hang of the thing, when this shop door flies open and some chick with pink hair is frantically waving me inside. I look up, see it's the cupcake place, and my first thought is, *She feels sorry for me. Free cupcakes for pathetic people.* I'm like, 'No thanks, I can't carry it anyway,' but she hissed at me. Like, *hissed* at me, 'I need to talk to you. Come in here.'"

"Weird," Bess said.

"It was. Plus, I was late for work. But she wouldn't take no. Put her arm right around me and steered me in there. The bakery was empty except for us, and she starts telling me, real matter-of-factly, that my boyfriend is stalking me."

Katie sensed Bess tensing beside her. She found herself holding very still, trying not to breathe, trying not to blink.

"It was funny," Lindsay went on, "because part of me was like, *Tell me something I don't know,* and another part was like, *Well, I think* stalking *is a strong word.* That's how you get twisted up, I guess, after years of manipulation. You feel called out and you're rationalizing, but you're not making sense."

Lindsay took her time with the story, putting them there in the empty cupcake shop: How the baker had locked the door, taken off her apron, insisted Lindsay sit down. How she'd told Lindsay her name, which Lindsay soon forgot as the horror at what was happening swelled in her brain, leaving no room for anything else. How she'd described Lindsay's longtime boyfriend, confirmed she had the right guy. Confirmed that they were on-again, off-again constantly, and when they were off, he'd come here for a vantage point of the salon where Lindsay worked kitty-corner down the block. How the baker had shown her the exact spot where he'd stood sentry at the window, recounting the orders of coffees he hadn't even pretended to drink. How the baker had hated that, how she couldn't find a polite way to make him leave, how she'd tried once and he'd gotten menacing, defensive that there was no law against a paying customer looking out the window.

The baker, Lindsay said, had a lot of questions for her then. How had she hurt her foot? What about the sling on her arm last month? What about the morning the word "Bitch" had appeared spray-painted across the salon window? What about the month she'd commuted with two busted taillights until she'd saved enough money to have them fixed? Did she have kids? Was she close to her family, and did they know? What other ties might be difficult to walk away from if it came to that? Did she understand the danger of this level of obsession? Did she have an escape plan?

An escape plan.

The baker had pulled her in to offer her one. But she'd come on much too strong, scaring Lindsay off with the sheer volume of offenses she'd been chronicling, with the length of time she'd so closely been watching. So what if she was right. So what if she *was* telling Lindsay something she didn't know—that even on days she'd thought he'd left her alone, he never had, probably never would?

It seemed to Lindsay that the baker had sort of been stalking her too. And she'd said so.

The baker had not taken this well.

When she realized she'd gone about this wrong, the baker had gotten worked up, begging Lindsay to look past all that, to focus on what mattered, on her good intentions, and to let her help. Asking if they could try again, talk later when they were both calmer. When Lindsay had more time to think. But not too much time. Because the thing about guys like this was, time could run out.

"I have to get to work," was all Lindsay could say. "You're making me late. You're making everything worse."

"I wasn't even supposed to do this," the baker had pleaded. "We're supposed to go through the proper channels." She was part of a grassroots network that helped women get away from guys like that, she'd explained. Guys who'd never be deterred by a restraining order. Guys who'd never lose interest no matter how many times you broke up. Guys who might decide that if they can't have you, no one can. But the network was careful: systematic secrecy was the only way to keep everyone involved safe. As such, the baker had rules she was supposed to follow.

"I've never done this before—obviously! Not exactly successful," she'd gone on. "But I saw you hobble off that bus, and I thought, *To hell with the rules. We might not have the luxury.*"

But Lindsay had been too taken aback to be moved. Even now, telling the story, she could only remember her embarrassment. She'd wanted to get the hell out of there, even if she was running right back toward something far more dangerous.

At least that danger was familiar. It didn't challenge her. It merely controlled her.

"You don't need my name," she'd told the baker, coldly. "If you want to help me, leave me alone." She was ashamed to think of it now, the way she'd recoiled from the offer of help, reacted with fear instead of the relief she should have felt that someone had seen the truth of her life in all the desperation it had become. The way she'd thumped on her crutches to the door and demanded to be let out, like she was being held hostage.

"I'm not supposed to do this either," the baker had said, pulling out a card, scrawling on it in pen, pressing it into her hand. "But I can't shake the feeling you're going to need it. This is only for an emergency, okay? Ideally, we'd get you in the pipeline first. When you're ready, the best thing is to come see me. But this caretaker will have my back if you have no other choice."

Lindsay—she could hardly bear to recount this last part—had thrown the card on the floor. That's when the baker stopped apologizing. She'd snatched it from the tile and met Lindsay's gaze with eyes blazing. "I'm not unlocking this door until you take the card. He stands here and tracks you, do you hear me? He is impervious to everything around him. He doesn't care about anything else. He doesn't care what anyone thinks. He stands. Right. Here."

Lindsay's eyes were glistening by the time her story was done. "I walked the long way around from the bus stop after that. I never even risked a look in the direction of the bakery. I guess that's why I can't recall the name. There's always this delivery van out front, though, with a cupcake on the side. You can't miss it. I wondered a lot about the van after that day. If it was really just delivering cupcakes. Missed my chance to find out, I guess."

Katie exchanged a look with Bess. Her instinct was to offer Lindsay words of comfort, that anyone would have been freaked out in her shoes.

But none of them would be in this mess if Lindsay had agreed right then. If she'd followed the proper channels, whatever those were.

"How long ago was that?" Bess asked finally.

Lindsay hugged her knees and pulled a face. "Before Thanksgiving." She was shivering now, shrinking before their eyes. "Please don't ask what took me so long. But you can tell her she was right. She told me so. And . . . I'm sorry. I'm so sorry."

"Hey." Bess stood and crossed to the couch, where she retrieved the throw blanket and wrapped it around Lindsay's shoulders. "She did *not* give you that card so she could say *I told you so*. It's going to be okay. We'll get you sorted."

Lindsay swallowed hard. "I just hope this network is still—I mean, it's going to save my life. That sounds so dramatic. But I get it now. I get why she was so . . ." Her voice trailed off again, and the three women sat in silence, absorbing the rhythm of the rain.

All the best new seasons started this way, didn't they? With a messy, muddy cleanse, stretches of dreariness, all that fallen dead brush to clear. And then one day the whole world was transformed, full of color and sun. New life budding even now, in the rain. *Because* of the rain.

"You said she asked about your family," Katie ventured. "Do you have people who might be worried about you right now? Looking for you?"

Lindsay shook her head. "When I told her I didn't have family, I thought she'd act like that was sad. But it seemed to be the answer she was looking for. I guess it's easier this way. I do have a sister, but . . . well, do either of you have a sister?"

"Three brothers," Bess said. "Which is every bit as insane as it sounds."

"I have a sister," Katie heard herself say. "Two years older." Even now, with this far more pressing problem right in front of her, she couldn't duck the wrecking ball of guilt that usually followed thoughts of Gigi.

"Did you go through that love-hate phase?" Lindsay asked, her expression hard to read. Expectant, yet . . . flat. "One second you're closer than best friends could ever be, the next you're clawing each other's eyes out because someone borrowed a sweater without asking?"

Funny enough, this was almost exactly how Gigi had described the relationship between her own two daughters the last time she and Katie spoke a few days ago. Katie's nieces were nine and ten. When they were babies, strangers would do double takes at Gigi's full stroller, saying, *Why, they're Irish twins in every sense, aren't they?* and Gigi never minded—until their father up and returned to Ireland. Alone. You'd think Katie and Gigi's mutual bad luck with husbands would have brought them together, but . . .

"We were never close enough for that," Katie admitted, careful not to say too much. Lindsay was prepared to walk away from anyone who'd ever known her and become someone else. And where Katie could relate on certain levels, her sister was not one of them. Gigi had needed her these past years, had needed anyone who could help her hold it together through single motherhood. And what had Katie done? Time after time, she'd ducked and dodged, wrapped up in the all-consuming task of trying to make her husband love her. And avoiding those adorable redheaded, pigtailed reminders of what she and Clark had almost had. Even then, the shame of it had burned deep within her. But not deep enough to change her singular focus. The more he'd pulled away, the more hell-bent she'd become on fixing things. Not with Gigi, her nieces, or anyone who deserved it, but with Clark. Clark. Clark.

She was determined to change all that now. The new Katie would be not just a better friend, but a better sister, a better aunt. She'd already invited her nieces to come this summer, allowing Gigi to enroll in the five-week intensive that would finally complete her MBA. It was all arranged: Gigi had secured a leave of absence from her job, with a badly needed pay raise awaiting her at the end of it. "Camp Aunt Katie," they were calling it. Gigi had cried actual tears of gratitude even as she'd seemed almost suspicious at the offer, waiting for the catch.

Katie blinked at Lindsay, realizing there might be a catch after all. She could not have children here running free if *this* was going on behind the scenes.

No. Summer was months away. Lindsay would be long gone by then. And this was surely a misunderstanding. A onetime thing.

"Well, trust me," Lindsay said, laughing ruefully. "Nothing wrong with skipping the love-hate phase. Somehow, we swung over to hate one day and stayed there. So no, she won't worry about me. No reason to start now."

Bess caught Katie's eye, looking sheepish. Her brothers lived hours away, in her hometown, but they were fiercely protective of Bess in an almost jovial I'd-like-to-see-you-try-it kind of way. The first time Katie had met them, in fact, something about Bess made more sense, like maybe she'd become who she was *because* they had her back no matter what. Bess wasn't the only one in her family who wasn't big on asking questions.

And even when Gigi had called Katie out for being distant at best, selfish at worst, hate was never in their vocabulary. Hate wasn't an option. Their parents had retired to Ft. Lauderdale, promptly divorced, and *both* remarried younger partners who still had kids in high school. Gigi and Katie didn't begrudge them their new families, but they didn't feel a part of them. And no matter what else happened between the sisters, they'd always have that in common.

They could relate to Lindsay on a lot of fronts, but only to a point. Thank goodness for that, though the thought of it felt privileged and wrong.

Katie cleared her throat. And asked, as neutrally as she could, for the address of Lindsay's salon.

9

The van was white, with the kind of hinged tailgate doors Katie associated with florists or painting companies. A peach-toned sunrise was painted on the sides, where in the place of a sun, a golden cupcake was haloed by words. WE'RE UP ALL NIGHT, they read, TO BAKE YOU A GREAT DAY. The shop's name was styled as a bold purple hashtag, #CUPCAKESFIRST.

Katie had an instant craving for a second, frosted breakfast—the name seemed to justify it. If you'd indulge in a doughnut first thing, why *not* a cupcake? She liked this woman's style.

Even if she was sort of afraid to go inside.

The storefront looked welcoming, though, painted in warm tones matching the van, with window boxes of purple flowers jutting over the sidewalk. The rain had stopped, leaving the street glistening as the midmorning sun threaded through the clouds. Bess had reluctantly gone to the office, promising to keep a lookout for anything that might be cast in a new light now that she was in the know. Meanwhile, Katie couldn't rest until she'd set into motion *some* plan for getting Lindsay out of her loft and on her way, for all their sakes.

Through the CUPCAKES FIRST logo stenciled onto the shop's picture window, she saw a line at the counter, moms in animated chitchat over their strollers, all wearing cross-trainers and a colorful array of yoga pants, as if they'd walked over from a Mommy and Me class. The first mom held a paper to-go bag, so Katie lingered outside while the rest collected their orders. She pretended to study the grab box of free monthlies, *Cincinnati Family* and *Cincinnati Parent*, one boasting a summer camp guide and the other a calendar of preschool open houses. Moments like this still gave her a pang, provoking a mental calculation: if her one and only pregnancy had stuck, she and Clark would have an eleven-year-old. A child older than even their marriage lived to be—a reminder of why it had happened at all.

Which was to say there was no reason, really, to feel this annoying nostalgia looking at photos of summer campers who were barely potty-trained. That would have been long behind her by now. It was her own Camp Aunt Katie that would have taken on new meaning, her son or daughter joining their cousins from Tennessee. Her nieces would not be the relative strangers they were now. She and Gigi would have seen each other through all the milestones, their kids so close in age they'd be thick as thieves, even across the miles. Katie would have leaned into the relationship instead of letting the pain of her miscarriage keep her away when her sister was fighting through pain of her own. It was an odd juxtaposition—how Gigi's husband had left despite their daughters; how Katie's had stayed despite their loss.

Katie supposed some degree of mutual resentment had been inevitable. Of course Gigi would see Clark as noble, even as he'd stayed for the wrong reasons, even as he'd refused to get pregnant again. Of course Katie would see Gigi as blessed by a house full of daughterly love, even when Gigi was overwhelmed and exhausted. Both sisters had been so heartbroken to begin with, the last thing they'd needed was to break each other's hearts again, but that was exactly what they'd done.

Maybe, Katie thought ruefully, Lindsay showing up at her door was life's way of throwing her privileges in her face—a wake-up call. If the distance from Clark hadn't brought immediate perspective, how about a gut check from a woman whose boyfriend made him look like a saint? A woman who'd been so threatened and wronged, she'd sooner put her faith in a clueless stranger than risk setting foot outside the loft? *What's that, Katie? You're still sad your white picket fence didn't pan out? Still wishing you could fast-forward to making things right with your sister, because deep down you both worry you're only reconciling because you finally need her as much as she needs you? Poor Katie. Poor, pathetic you.*

She tried to imagine what she'd be doing today if not for Lindsay showing up last night. The loneliness of being stuck inside on a wet day she'd hoped to spend out exploring. She might be settling in, unpacking, looking more closely through Grace's things. Or if she were honest, she might be lingering over her own boxes, paging wistfully through photo albums. Taking the Christmas record off the turntable and searching the vinyl collection for sweet, sad songs.

There was something to be said for a distraction. A good deed.

The door opened with a tingle of chimes, and the stroller-pushing moms filed past, smiles looking more forced up close. "Not wait!" one toddler was screaming. "Cu-cake now! Now!"

Inside, the young woman tidying her display case could not have been over twenty-five. She might have even passed for a teenager, except for the way she carried herself. She literally looked like she owned the place—proud posture, sure hands, nothing like the picture Lindsay had painted of the frantic girl trying to help. Her hair wasn't pink but bright purple, blunt-cut into an asymmetrical bob. Yet Katie had a strong feeling this was the baker.

The shop was even smaller than it had looked outside, no room for another person behind the counter. The door to the kitchen stood open, yet there was no clanging of pans, no chatter. Only the alternative radio station playing from a soundbar.

"May I help you?" the woman asked, tucking the long side of her bob behind her ear.

"Three cupcakes to go, please," Katie said. "Your three best flavors."

Her smile turned warmer. "Selection rotates, but today that would be . . . Lemon Raspberry, Red Velvet Buckeye, and Butterscotch Chip."

"I trust you." Katie watched closely to see if her word choice might hint this was not just about the cupcakes, but the woman only nodded and began assembling a scored sheet of pink cardboard into a box.

"First time in?" the baker asked. "A Cupcakes First first?"

"It is," Katie said. "Actually . . ." She looked over her shoulder. They were still alone. "Lots of firsts. I just moved here for a new job. As resident caretaker at Grove Reserve."

The baker turned her back to Katie to fidget with a pair of disposable gloves. "Oh, really? Never heard of it."

"I think you have," Katie said.

The baker still didn't look up. She selected a peach-frosted cupcake from the display case and placed it gingerly in the box. "What makes you say that?"

Katie slid the safe haven card onto the glass between them. The baker's eyes went wide.

"Where did you get this?" Her voice was barely a whisper. She held a red-and-white-iced cupcake suspended midair.

"She showed up," Katie whispered back. "Last night."

"She's okay?" There. There was the youthful impatience Katie had anticipated. The baker's eyes glistened, flicking past Katie to the door.

"More or less. She's . . . we're . . . awaiting instructions. For next steps?"

Abruptly, the baker returned the cupcake to the case. "You shouldn't be here."

"Hang on." The baker was unpacking the box with startling speed, tugging the folds flat. "That wasn't a ruse. I wanted those."

"You can't have them," she hissed. "None of us carry anything that can link us to the others."

"But I—"

"Her boyfriend has been in. *Today.* Didn't she tell you he comes here?"

Katie blinked, taken aback. "She did," she admitted. "But I didn't think—"

"No, you didn't think. And neither did I. I mean, I'm glad you have her, but . . . shit." The baker pursed her lips. "Can you come back at four?"

"This afternoon?"

"No. In the morning." Katie looked for some sign that she was kidding. She saw none. "Sorry, but it's safest. Come to the back door. We'll talk in the kitchen."

"Should I bring her?"

"Absolutely not." The baker closed her eyes, exhaling shakily. "Listen, the most important thing: do not say anything to anyone— either of you. Just sit tight. Shit," she repeated.

Katie shifted her weight, uncertain. She'd come determined not to leave without answers. Yet she'd given no thought to coming in broad daylight, during peak hours. Back in the relative privacy of Grove, she'd felt on high alert, paranoid they'd be caught, yet somehow in coming here she hadn't dwelled on the warnings inherent in Lindsay's story. And though Katie could not imagine how anyone could possibly link a random cupcake customer to a hairstylist who hadn't shown up for work today nearby, she hadn't tried to imagine it.

She was that out of her depth.

"Understood," she said. "Let's exchange names and numbers, just in case?"

"Nope. You've already been here too long. See you at four." She cleared her throat. "Thanks for coming in!" she announced cheerily, as if they were putting on a stage play. "Sorry I can't handle that order on such short notice. Hope your friend has an amazing birthday!"

Katie chanced another look around, confused. There definitely was no audience within earshot. But when she turned back toward the counter, the door to the kitchen was swinging closed. The baker was gone.

There was a mountain of gravel in the driveway of the caretaker's house, precisely where Katie's car had been parked an hour before. It was a ludicrously huge thing to materialize unexpectedly, like one of those Wile E. Coyote cartoons where an anvil falls from the sky.

But Katie didn't feel like laughing.

A dump truck idled noisily, blocking her path. The jumpsuited driver stood with one hand on his door, waiting while Jude walked a slow circle around the gravel as if inspecting it for quality. Both men ignored Katie's car as it rolled to a stop, though they'd left nowhere to park.

Her eyes drew a nervous triangle from the barn door to the gravel mountain to the garage where Lindsay was hidden. All appeared still, doors closed, window coverings undisturbed.

She lowered her windows, and the clattering of the truck's engine filled the car, like a thousand ping-pong balls in a spinning steel barrel. At least she didn't have to worry about anyone *hearing* Lindsay.

Still, she didn't like this.

Completing his orbit, Jude nodded his approval, and the driver handed over a clipboard for his signature.

"Hey," she called over the racket. "What's going on?"

Nobody answered, but the driver climbed back into the truck and motioned toward Katie, a gesture that meant *Get out of the way* but didn't indicate how. Irritated—no way was she backing all the way down her driveway in front of so much jeering testosterone—she did an awkward three-point turn onto the edge of her front lawn and waited while the truck ambled by, honking as it rounded the curve.

The honk was the last straw.

She whipped into the driveway, right up to the mountain, not caring if Jude had room to angle his pickup past her. He should have thought of that before showing up unannounced. Again.

"Special delivery," he greeted her.

Katie climbed out as coolly as she could. *I will not look up at the loft window again,* she told herself. *If I look, it will make him look. I will not, I will not, I will not.*

"I can see that," she replied. "And this is for . . . ?"

"High time to even out this driveway. I'm sure you saw this morning how bad the puddles get. Once they start running like creeks, they erode the surface. Not the safest, especially with your hatchback."

Katie gritted her teeth, nerves jangling. Did this mean *he* had seen the puddles this morning? And Bess's car? Had he knocked at her door and found it odd that no one answered? Or was he speaking generally of rainy spring days? "I did see," she made herself say. "But I don't see a hatchback. Only a crossover that handles puddles fine."

He raised an eyebrow. "Well, it needed done. Forecast is clear for a few days. If we tag-team it, I think we can finish before the weather turns."

A few days. A few days stuck spreading gravel with Jude, right here in the space between her house and the hidden loft. Jude, who'd been poking through her barn yesterday, grumbling about kids climbing where they didn't belong and adults ignoring warning signs. Was this all a coincidence? Or was he testing her somehow?

"You mean work through the weekend?" Katie only meant to point out that tomorrow was Friday, but she sounded like a slacker. "Not that I won't be here," she added, hoping to sound more concerned about *his* time off.

Jude shrugged. "Flexible schedules here. When a weekend makes sense, we make it up somewhere else."

She surveyed him more closely. He did seem oblivious to anything but the task at hand. Oblivious, and uninclined to take breaks or cut shifts short. This was so far from what Katie wanted to spend the rest of this day doing, let alone tomorrow or her first weekend here. She'd been talking herself down the whole drive back from the baker's, watching her rearview mirror for anyone following her home, fighting panic that 4:00 a.m. was too far away. It was too easy to picture herself arriving to find the bakery empty, locked, and dark, to imagine the baker fleeing and taking the answers with her. She'd told herself she could use the time, look for other clues Grace might have left behind, but Jude and his surprise project would derail those plans. And what about poor Lindsay? Katie envisioned her up under the eaves of the outbuilding now, crouching in fear at the commotion, wondering if she was on the verge of being discovered.

Do not even think about looking up there, Katie reminded herself. *There is no loft. There is no Lindsay. Only me, on my second full day at a new job.*

"I can get this," Katie heard herself say. "It's not a two-person job."

"It's a pretty big pile of rocks," Jude observed. "Pretty big driveway."

"I'll find a pretty big shovel."

"A big shovel," he repeated. His eyes crinkled, as if he was enjoying their banter in spite of himself. Not that he seemed to be bantering intentionally. Everything he said was so literal.

"I could use the exercise," she elaborated.

"Fine. But rocks are heavy. You might make better headway with a small shovel."

Katie appraised the gravel mountain once more. She'd spread a mulch pile this size once, having assumed Clark would help and learned the hard way that she should've asked first. *I'd have hired someone,* he'd said. It had taken almost a week, the smell permeating her hair, her nostrils, and finally, the whole house. Long soaks in the tub had done nothing to ease the bone-deep soreness, her oozing blisters, or her wounded pride.

Katie tried to smile. "Well, I'm sure the barn is full of shovels of all sizes."

"What is it with every caretaker they hire? Always trying to get rid of me."

He was looking at her in that way he had—like he didn't miss a beat—and again, her suspicions stirred. "Maybe," she said, "we're trying to prove we can do the job."

"Driveway repair isn't technically in your job description. It's in mine."

Still Katie fought the urge to check the loft window. No wonder she was such a terrible cardplayer—bluffing did not come naturally. Would she last the week out here without showing her hand? Would she ever trust that when Jude left for the day, he was gone for good?

Chevy chose that moment to come trotting toward Katie with a kittenlike exuberance. Her mouth looked strange, and it took Katie a moment to register the cat had something furry clamped in her jaws. She dropped it at Katie's feet.

It appeared to be a mole. Though it was hard to say for certain since it had no head.

"Aw," Jude said. "A welcome gift. Chevy likes you."

Katie stepped back, trying not to wretch.

"For the record?" he said. "I thought I'd do the shoveling. You can spread it with a rake. Teamwork." Then, so fast she could almost—almost—convince herself she'd imagined it, he did the thing she'd been trying not to do.

He glanced up at the eaves of the garage building.

At the covered window with the apartment on the other side.

She blanched, but by the time she registered what was happening, his eyes were back on hers. And he was offering an actual smile, like a peace offering.

Had it been nothing? A coincidence, an accident, a warning, some unspoken sign? How would she ever function with this level of paranoia?

At least here, she could keep an eye on him. If Jude was with her, he wasn't poking around somewhere else.

"Teamwork," she agreed.

Despite everything, she almost wished he were on her team after all. She didn't know yet if anyone else really was.

10

There was nighttime dark, and then there was middle-of-the-night dark.

And then? There was Grove Reserve.

Beyond the floodlights of the house stretched an encroaching, moonless black, poised to swallow any trace of color until it was one with the inky forest. Katie was not a morning person, let alone a three-thirty-in-the-morning person, yet she felt sharply alert as she steered the wide beams of her headlights down the caretaker's drive toward the creek.

She'd surprised herself by sleeping at all, though she supposed an afternoon of manual labor had helped. Lindsay had been an odd comfort, too, when Jude finally left and Katie rushed up the hidden stairs, full of apologies, only to find her calmly playing solitaire on the rug near the window, where the natural light was best. When Katie filled her in on the clumsy visit to the baker, to be continued, Lindsay said simply, "Makes sense," and excused herself for a stroll around the pond. When Katie welcomed her back with a plate of steaming pasta, Lindsay said only, "Thank you," and "I'll stay out of your hair," and "Good luck tonight."

Some of that calm must have rubbed off on Katie. She was weirdly grateful.

As Katie rolled onto the bridge across the creek—eyes on the oval of concrete lit by her headlights, like a deep-sea diver with no peripheral vision—she marveled that anyone could find their way through on foot. Maybe women like Lindsay were the only ones who could. Maybe you needed that terror to chase you, unquestionably worse than the unknown on the other side.

Yet Katie wasn't afraid.

The clouds chose that minute to slide apart, shifting the world from indistinguishable pitch to deep shadow. Katie slowed to a stop in the center of the bridge and looked up through the glass of her sunroof. There: a slice of moon, a smattering of stars. She flicked off her headlights, blinked her eyes to adjust, and yes—it was enough to illuminate the creek, a flowing ebony shimmer mere feet beneath the narrow slab where her car sat. Peering down at the rush of water, swollen from the rain, she had the surreal sensation of hovering there, suspended out of reach, safe—but only just—from the most beautiful kind of danger.

Her fingers found the panel on the door, lowering all four windows at once. She cut the engine and the car fell silent, yielding to the sound of water flowing on its endless, winding journey, beholden to nothing, to no one.

The cold wasted no time filling the car, but even as she shivered through her coat, she sensed a magical energy, as if this one spot in the world, for this one moment, belonged only to her. She closed her eyes, breathed it in through her nose, invited it in through every pore in her skin, through every small hole that had ever been ripped in her soul.

She would have missed this, if not for the baker. She wouldn't have dared venture down here at this hour alone. But this was what she'd come for, wasn't it? To be a part of something outside herself? To tap into the flow she'd always known must be there, somewhere, sustaining the world just out of sight? To go where she liked, when she liked, explaining herself to no one?

Yet she could have so easily slept through it—all the best, most unexpected parts.

Life was like that.

Katie sat that way, marveling for a few trancelike minutes, until it was time to go. But not before making herself a promise.

No matter what happened next, she would not cower at home, intimidated by her own unfounded fears. She would not be afraid of the dark.

The bakery kitchen was so bright and busy, Katie could almost forget she'd come in from the dead of night. The buttery-yellow ceiling was aglow with enough overhead lights to fill a room three times this size, like the sun itself had risen in the time it took the baker to usher her in and turn the dead bolt. The effect was amplified by so much industrial stainless steel—appliances, countertops, deep sinks—gleaming against the painted white cinder block walls, humming with its cacophony of work in progress: refrigerators sighing, ovens radiating heat, fans spinning from corners. The whole place smelled of citrus and batter rising.

"Sicilian lemon," the baker clarified. "We can talk in the office. Coffee?"

Katie hesitated, taking it all in. "Maybe? I wasn't sure if I should give up on going back to sleep."

"That's a yes." The baker grabbed two mugs and led the way to an open door in the far wall.

She stopped in the doorway, and Katie soon saw why: the so-called office was no bigger than a walk-in closet, and nearly every square foot was crammed with furniture. A standing desk filled one wall, with a chair stashed underneath, and parallel, with mere inches in between, was an Ikea daybed where two pillows and a crocheted blanket had been abandoned in a mound. The baker popped a pod into a Keurig beside her laptop.

"Do you . . . sleep here?" Katie asked.

"I try not to. Ostensibly I live at my boyfriend's. I know this room is ridiculous, but TBH, it needs to be. Otherwise, with my early-bird schedule, it would be too easy to never leave."

It took Katie a second to catch up. She'd never heard anyone say TBH out loud before. "Well. Good for power naps, right?"

"That was the original idea. Nodded off by accident once, nearly burned the place down."

She handed Katie a steaming black coffee and gestured to a bowl of creamers and sugars. "I'll take the couch and get this chair situated for you. One sec."

She turned on her heels and returned with a plate. The three cupcakes Katie had ordered yesterday. She offered it like an apology, and Katie took it, awkwardly juggling the mug and too many sweets for one person as the baker scooted by her, grabbed her own coffee, shoved the blanket aside, offered her the chair, and lowered the desk to table height between them. "There," she said, with more pride than the situation warranted. "Sort of."

Katie couldn't fathom how she could eat when her stomach was tied in this tightening knot, but she took a small bite of the butterscotch cupcake to be polite. "Wow," she said. It was by far the most decadent thing she'd ever eaten while crouched in a closet.

"Right? Sorry about earlier."

Katie smiled weakly. "I'm sorry too. Let's start over. I'm Katie."

"And I'm in trouble." The baker laughed nervously. "We try not to use names. They mostly refer to me as The Baker."

"Is there also a butcher and a candlestick maker?"

She looked at her blankly, and Katie felt old. Were nursery rhymes not a thing anymore?

"Anyhow." The baker shrugged. "Seeing as how you found me here at the shop, that's pointless. You could easily look me up, so . . . I'm Sienna."

"But I didn't hear it from you," Katie joked. Or tried to joke. Sienna squinted at her, like she wasn't sure if she was kidding.

"Okay, now spill the tea," Sienna said. "I need deets."

"I was kind of hoping you could do that for me."

"I will. But you first."

Katie briefly wondered if she should resist, keep some kind of leverage. But leverage for what? All she really wanted was to get out of this as quickly as possible. So she started at the real beginning: Bess getting her the job she wasn't qualified to do.

When she was done, Sienna shook her head. "I'd say you were the right person for the job after all. The hairdresser is really okay?"

Katie nodded. "She says you saved her life."

Sienna looked down at her fingernails. They were bitten to the quick. "Well, she's not out of the woods yet."

"She's very literally in the woods," Katie agreed.

"Who else knows about this?"

"Just Bess. In my defense, I didn't so much run and tell her as demand to know what she'd gotten me into."

"She seemed genuinely surprised?"

"To put it mildly. But the secret's safe with her. At least, provided we resolve this quickly."

"Hmm."

Katie wasn't sure she liked the tone of that sound. Like the jury was out on Bess, of all people. "Anyone else who might have even the slightest inkling? What about that Sad Keanu–type maintenance guy? Anyone else been hanging around?"

Katie laughed out loud at the description of Jude as a celebrity meme. "He's more of a Smug Keanu, but . . ." She stopped. "Did Grace mention him much? Was she worried he knew?"

"She found him generally maddening."

"Same. Anyway, no, no one else."

Only then did Sienna sink back against the couch, looking relieved. "Okay. Selfishly . . . I'm just glad she's all right."

"That is the opposite of selfish."

"Well, we usually have a jump on things we need to put in place. This is going to take some doing on short notice." Sienna cleared her throat. "I know it's a lot to ask, but can you sit tight a few more days? A week, tops. All you have to do is keep her out of sight and make sure she has what she needs."

This was only day two, and already the anxiety was doing Katie in. "I have some questions first," she said, hedging. "Starting with how big this network actually is."

"Keep in mind, the less you know, the better. For all involved. Yourself included."

"That's just it," Katie said. "You said you're all so careful to avoid anything that can link you. Not even a cupcake box. But that safe haven card seems like a pretty big exception. It's there in black and white: the caretaker's residence. My address."

"It was just that one card," Sienna assured her. "That's *not* something we typically hand out. I owe you an apology. I never should have done that. Don't leave it lying around, even at home, okay? It's been chilly; light a fire."

"It can't be just that one card. You wrote on it, but it was preprinted."

"The women we're helping get that at the drop-off point, not before. We had a huge debate about doing it, but we learned the hard way: even in the short time it takes to walk up a hill, you can forget what you're supposed to do. Panic does that. Grace was the deciding vote. She thought it was a smaller risk than having someone wandering the property in hysterics."

"Okay, that's what they were *designed* for. But how can you be a hundred percent sure no more of these are out there?"

"I'm ninety-nine. I'm the only one left who's willing to break a rule once in a while."

"The only one left," Katie repeated. "You mean without Grace?"
Sienna didn't answer.

"Can you tell me why she left? Why she stopped?"
She shook her head.

"Because you don't want to tell me," Katie asked, "or because you don't know?"

The oven timer blared, startling them both. Sienna jumped up to retrieve her cupcakes, while Katie sat processing all she'd learned. And more to the point, all she hadn't learned. She took a tentative bite of the Buckeye Red Velvet cupcake—she couldn't take it home anyway.

Hello, velvet, she thought, closing her eyes. This was not a cupcake that could be eaten with one's eyes open. Before she knew it, she was scarfing the whole thing. She had to tell Bess—these were so good they'd almost be wasted on Ethan and Emory, but worth every penny.

Then again, maybe she shouldn't. Sienna wouldn't want Bess here either.

When Sienna returned, she looked resolute. "Katie? I'm so appreciative of all you've done. I know it would've been easier to wash your hands of this. Our network is *not* that big, okay? We're a handful of people who looked at the system, saw the people it fails to help, and devised a way to pick up the slack. The key to going grassroots is keeping it simple. We each have one job, one step in the ladder, and without one of us, none of it works. So when Grace left, we thought we were done for now. And we are super grateful that with this, uh, loophole, you've figured out enough to pick up where she left off. But unless you plan to stay involved, I repeat: the less you know, the better." She flopped back onto the daybed with a sigh.

Katie almost wanted to laugh. *Unless you plan to stay involved.*

If there was one thing she didn't have right now, it was a plan. "Can you at least tell me if you've talked to Grace since she bowed out?"

"I haven't. She told me herself, though, that she was done."

"She seemed okay? Because she left in some kind of hurry. I've been worried about her. And whether I should be worried about me."

"She seemed about as okay as she ever seemed." Sienna frowned. "If it helps set your mind at ease, it wasn't a shock. She'd been burned out for probably the last year."

"I'd love to get in touch with her," Katie pressed. "Not just about this. The whole caretaker job, I mean, the real job . . . Let's say I could use some pointers."

"Even if I wanted to reach her, I don't know how. But don't get stuck on thinking you need Grace, okay? I know it's hard but try not to worry. We've helped dozens of women. We've had close calls but never a problem we can't handle. We might be paranoid, but paranoia works."

"How can I not worry? How do *you* not worry?"

"You lean into what I said about having one job. It's not my job to worry. It's my job to be the baker. It's your job to be the caretaker. That's it."

"Is it someone's job to worry?"

"Actually, yes."

It's my job to be the caretaker, Katie repeated silently, boiling it down. They'd helped dozens of women be safe again. And they couldn't do it without Grace. Which meant, reading between the lines, they couldn't do it without Katie.

But they wouldn't ask her to do it, she realized now. It was too big of a risk. That she'd say no. That she'd tell someone. As far as they were concerned, she already knew too much. They'd rather call off the whole thing than trust her.

"Why *did* you give the hairstylist that card?" she asked.

"Like she told you, because of her boyfriend. Dude picked the wrong shop for his creepy little stakeouts." She smiled, but there was no joy in it.

That smile—it was a mask. It was a wall. It was a dare.

Katie kept her voice gentle. "Why did you really give her that card?"

The silence that fell stretched out uncomfortably long, like dough rolled thin enough to fall apart.

"In college," Sienna said, finally, "I had this roommate."

She explained that she'd had five, actually. But only one who'd acquired a stalker. They'd gone on one date, and that was enough for her roommate. It was enough for him too—to become obsessed. It turns out following someone around making them uncomfortable isn't much of a crime. She'd changed her phone number. Filed police reports about incidents that could be construed as harassment, just to have a record. Finally, he crossed a line into overtly threatening her in front of a witness, and she was able to get a restraining order.

They lived in a big old house, kept busy and full by the six best friends. Four of the roommates were on the club soccer team, going out of town for a tournament the next weekend. Sienna was ashamed to admit it, but she was scared to stay back alone with a friend who'd become a target. The restraining order was only a piece of paper. What would it really do? She invited the friend to go home with her instead, spend a weekend enjoying her mom's good cooking. That, as it turned out, was a big mistake.

"She had all this pent-up anger," she told Katie, "and it exploded on me. She said I was a coward, letting this guy run my life, and I wasn't even the one being stalked. Well, *she* refused to live her life ruled by fear. She didn't *want* to leave campus for the weekend. She wanted to stay and enjoy, for once, having enough hot water for long showers and dibs on the TV. I told her forget it, I'd stay, too, but she said she didn't want me there anyway. *I'll know what you're thinking the whole time,* she said. *I don't want it to rub off on me. I want to move on.* She told me to go, just leave her alone. She'd be fine." Sienna stared into her empty coffee mug.

"She was not fine?" Katie guessed.

"She was never the same. He waited for everyone to leave, then took his opening. He kept her all weekend as his plaything. Left just in time for us to get home. Turned out he wasn't even a student—some nameless local who liked to creep on campus. They never found him, and she had no confidence they ever would. Rapists don't get that Most Wanted priority, you know?"

"So what happened then?"

"It's like she told me. She refused to live her life in fear. So when it became clear she couldn't escape that, she escaped life instead."

Katie sat with the horror of it. What it must have been like for Sienna, years later, to have another obsessed man right here in her bakery with an unsuspecting woman in his crosshairs, and not a thing she could do about it. Katie remembered how Lindsay had described Sienna pulling her into the shop, growing whiny, almost childlike when Lindsay refused help. This was a woman who still blamed herself for something that wasn't her fault. No wonder she'd decided to ask forgiveness instead of permission. Forgiveness was the thing she was up early every day trying to find.

This was a woman who'd started out as too scared to be alone with a friend who was in danger. And who'd found the courage to seek out more women like that friend ever since.

"What's your role in the network, normally?" Katie asked. Sienna had already declined to tell her, but this secret seemed insignificant compared to the one she'd just told.

"I have a van people expect to be out at all hours. I donate my unsold baked goods to the women's shelter. Sometimes when I leave, there's something in back besides cupcakes."

Katie thought of the clever marketing painted on the side panel: WE'RE UP ALL NIGHT TO BAKE YOU A GREAT MORNING. It was so brilliantly conspicuous: nothing to see here; we're just taking care of business, any odd time.

Every second since she'd taken in Lindsay, Katie had felt uneasy. Uneasy when Jude appeared, uneasy when the wind blew, uneasy at every passing stranger, and then again at seeing no one at all. Yet the way Sienna described it, maybe she wasn't such a bad fit after all. *We might be paranoid*, she'd said, *but paranoia works.*

Sienna had said very little, all things considered. But she'd told Katie enough. She'd told Katie the truth.

"What if I did plan to stay involved?" she asked.

Sienna's face lit up. "I was hoping," she said, "you might ask that."

11

For the first time in Katie's life, she was pretty sure she was less nervous than Bess.

It made no sense. Katie had every reason to be anxious. Terror would be justifiable.

And yet. It was as if the baker had fed Katie some secret recipe for a measured reaction: two cups of calm, a heaping tablespoon of trust, a teaspoon of good faith. Mix until nerves are blended, spread batter in pan, act like everything is normal, why would anything be wrong, nothing to see here, this is fine. And Katie had eaten it up and forgotten to save a slice for Bess.

Because when had Bess ever needed to cook up courage to be the cool, collected one? It was Katie who'd never been smooth at putting on brave faces. "There is no room you don't belong in," Bess used to reassure her, loyally, every time Katie was entering a room that she honestly maybe didn't belong in, like the delivery room when Gigi couldn't locate her husband, and that interview for the snobbish chamber of commerce board Clark pushed on her "for the business," and, come to think of it, the chapel itself on the day Katie told him "I do."

There was a reason Katie's brave faces tended to turn out doughy, underbaked. Because even when she wasn't being honest with anyone else about how she felt, she couldn't help being honest with herself. Katie didn't want to be anywhere she wasn't truly wanted, but didn't want to disappoint either. Which meant she'd end up trying to fix things she knew deep down weren't fixable, and Bess would end up standing by her, recognizing that Katie needed to try. Even when Gigi made a scene in the maternity ward—lashing out in misplaced anger until Katie lashed back, the pain of her own lost pregnancy too fresh—even when the chamber of commerce used Katie for a website upgrade (because *that* she could fix, thanks very much) and then publicly snubbed her from every invite Clark had been after, even when Clark gave up on the marriage, Bess was never daunted by a disastrous outcome looming before, during, or after a crisis.

Until now.

The plan had been for Katie to head straight to Bess's from the bakery, despite the ungodly hour, but something held her back. Maybe running to Bess felt too easy. Maybe, after all Sienna had told her, it felt careless. Maybe it felt unfair to unload on Bess the burden of secrets neither of them was supposed to know.

Or maybe this wasn't about the network at all. Maybe Katie needed to justify her caretaker job, the *real* job, as more than accepting a favor. When Grace left Bess in the lurch, that became Katie's chance to finally repay all those years of support by proving she belonged in this room after all. Even if this "room" was an expanse of forest that, whoops, harbored a secret safe house.

Whatever the reason, when Katie stepped out of the bakery at sunrise, all she'd wanted was to get back to Grove. So instead of heading to Bess's house as planned, Katie had texted her: Took longer than expected, need to get back—we'll talk later. No rush, nothing is urgent.

In retrospect, she should have known Bess wouldn't accept this. Bess had peeled in at lunchtime with two Greek salads as if she were beholden to a thirty-minutes-or-your-money-back pizza delivery window, tires skidding, rambling that she'd have been there sooner if not for her Wonders of the Herb Wall program. She looked horrified to find Katie covered in dirt and sweat, standing like a sentry in the space between Jude and the outbuilding that held the loft.

"Sorry . . ." Bess stammered to him. "Didn't think you were a salad guy." He muttered something about a break and pulled away in his truck extra slowly, as if to demonstrate the appropriate speed, which only provoked Bess to curse under her breath, taking it as a taunt.

Katie had had to hide her smile. Because it totally was.

But neither of them was smiling anymore.

"How do we know for sure this scumbag can't follow Lindsay here?" Bess asked for the third time. They were on a bench by the pond, neither one touching her lunch. "Stalkers gonna stalk."

"This one's stalking up the wrong tree," Katie insisted, also for the third time. "Still watching the salon. If he had any way of tracking her here, he'd have shown by now."

But Bess's questions continued, relentlessly. *What would Katie say if some staffer discovered Lindsay? What would Katie do if the baker's network never followed through? What were they supposed to think if Grace never got in touch, given that by this point, Bess had left an obnoxious quantity of urgent messages? Was it truly just happenstance Jude was so full of reasons to be at Grove? And she hated to say it, hated to even think it, but what if Katie wasn't as safe at the caretaker's house as they wanted to believe?*

It wasn't that Katie didn't have these questions too. But if she thought too much about them, she'd lose her nerve. Sienna had given her no way of checking in for updates. She'd only promised that when the time came, they'd be in touch. Right there in her office they'd created a free webmail account—harder to trace than a phone—set to forward to Katie's regular inbox. You could now reach the new caretaker via NCT123 at server-dot-com. She was to watch for instructions from a similar throwaway account: some screen name with the word "Sequence" in the mix.

With a capital *S*, Sequence was what the network called themselves, as a reminder to all involved to trust the process. To focus on their step and have faith the others would do the same. Subliminal and as power-ful as the WE'RE UP ALL NIGHT logo on the baker's van.

And effective. Katie listened patiently while Bess talked herself in circles. The calmer Katie stayed, the more worked up Bess grew. And the more worked up Bess grew, the calmer Katie felt by comparison, until there was nothing left to do but stare at each other and wonder, *Who are you and what have you done with my best friend?*

"I was wondering about cameras on the property," Katie asked finally when she could get a word in. "I know I asked before—"

"And I told you before," Bess said irritably. "It's just the obvious gate camera. It records continuously. We all have access; your log-in is in your onboarding email. But it's only there to make sure no one abuses the entry system. It barely shows anything else—it's not enough."

Katie nodded. They had indeed been over that. "I was only about to ask if there's some reason they don't have more cameras."

"Oh." Bess sighed, checking herself, and the steam went out of her. "We talked about it when we were expanding the research center at the main campus. Lots of cameras there, with university money involved. But out here, the idea never got traction. As remote as it is, our mem-bers are respectful. When people pay to get in, there's a certain security with that: anyone looking to break into parked cars or harass some unsuspecting hiker will do it at a public park, where it's free and there's no scanned record of who's been there."

"So our members are on the up and up."

"We've never had an incident. You don't shit where you eat."

"Anyone could walk in here, though," Katie pointed out.

"Yeah. But no matter which way you come, it's a long walk. It's not like you can make a quick getaway back to your car."

"Tracy!" The sharp, masculine yell startled them both as a man came into view across the pond, red-faced and huffing. "Tracy!" he boomed again, charging down the path, clearly furious, and Katie shrank back into the bench with alarm.

Her first thought was that this was Lindsay's real name. And it hadn't been brave, trying not to get as flustered as Bess. It had been stupid. They'd let Jude leave, and no one else was anywhere around. Bess clutched at her hand, clearly thinking the same, and the salad slipped off her lap with a clatter of plastic, sending lettuce and utensils flying.

That's when he saw them.

He slowed his pace, as if realizing he might look unhinged.

"Sorry!" He called across the pond. "Did a dog run through here? Beagle mix?"

Oh. Katie started to laugh it off but couldn't. What if this was a cover story? A dog with a woman's name? A *bitch*, and—

"Where's her leash?" Bess called, sounding as suspicious as Katie felt. He looked taken aback, and she pointed at her staff fleece, adding, "Rules."

"She has it," he called back. "That's the problem." Katie was still wondering if this was a ruse when she heard the faint sound of distant barking.

The man swiveled toward it. In the opposite direction. "Sorry!" he called again, then took off running. She and Bess sat in silence for an uncomfortable moment, neither wanting to acknowledge what had happened. What would keep happening if they didn't keep their heads.

Katie cleared her throat. "So Grace never pushed for more cameras?"

Bess bent and started picking up the remnants of her salad. "The opposite. She was loudest about nixing the idea. She argued people come here for solace in nature, and the last thing they want is to spot a blinking light and realize they're under surveillance. She was convincing."

"What about around the residence, though?"

"She said behind a locked gate, her house was probably safer than anyone else's."

Their eyes met, understanding at the same time. Either Grace really hadn't been afraid, at all, of anything, or . . .

"I bet cameras would have cramped her style," Katie said. She couldn't help but feel a bit of awe, picturing Grace marching into those meetings prepared to stand her ground, cleverly ensuring she remained free to serve as caretaker in every sense of the word.

Bess tossed her uneaten lunch into the carryout bag. "Yeah, well. Something cramped her style enough for her to leave."

Katie couldn't bring herself to tell Bess how she'd really left things with the baker: open-ended. Inviting the possibility that maybe, if this went well, they'd see about doing it again. When easygoing Bess had yelled "Rules!" with such ferocity, something about their role reversal started making more sense. This wasn't just Bess's area of expertise, it was the convergence of her biggest responsibilities—to her household and livelihood, the security of her children, the health of the nonprofit, even Katie. Bess had brought an old friend here to do a job she could teach her exactly how to do, only to find out that nothing at Grove had ever been as it seemed. No wonder Bess didn't know what to do but catch up, even against her better judgment.

But the Sequence wouldn't approve. None of them were supposed to act connected to the others. And breaking her link to Bess was not an option. No matter what was at stake, she'd choose Bess, every time.

Until it came to that, she was going to have to try to have it both ways.

12

That week, the daffodils bloomed. Grove Reserve shed its brown carpet seemingly overnight, the trails so perfectly lined with white and yellow it looked as if Mother Nature had sent in her own gardening team. Katie was glad of someone to share her amazement with: every morning Lindsay would wake early to walk among the blooms, and Katie would join her. Without knowing how many more days they'd have here together, they'd settled into silent agreement to enjoy what they could. Not much use in worrying when all they could do was wait.

"My boyf—I mean, my ex had a girlfriend named Daffodil," Lindsay said one morning, out of nowhere. The fields were foggy, cold condensation evaporating before their eyes in the early rays of sun, and the flowers bowed their heads as if in reverence to it all. Katie wasn't feeling especially reverent: her socks were wet inside her sneakers, and her hiking boots had rubbed painful blisters on her heels. She needed to upgrade her footwear, but when? Ordering online seemed risky with her mailbox outside the main gate, where anyone could swipe a delivery. Yet another drawback she hadn't considered.

"Daffodil, huh?" she said, treading carefully. This was the first time Lindsay had mentioned her ex unprompted. "That's a different name."

"Her sisters were Rose and Violet—it was a whole thing. I only know that because he was convinced her sisters were behind their breakup. They hated him. A whole family of vindictive bitches, luring men with their sweet flower names."

Katie laughed. "They sound great."

"Don't they? Man, it feels nice to say that out loud." Lindsay tipped her face to the sky, though she didn't break stride. "To hear him tell it, she was a total psycho, though he brought her up so often I used to worry he wasn't over her. Whenever I annoyed him, he'd say, *Don't go Daffy on me*, and launch into another story about how infuriating she was."

"Odds are," Katie said, "she was not the crazy one."

"I see that now." Lindsay shook her head. "I know it probably sounds kinda thick, but it feels symbolic, all these daffodils here. Like I made it to the other side."

Katie hesitated. This woman was on the verge of trading in her entire identity, everything she'd known and done and everyone she'd loved. Didn't Katie owe it to Lindsay to bear witness? Shouldn't someone, at least, remember her as she was?

"Can I ask what made you keep that card?" she ventured. "What made up your mind to use it?"

The trail dipped downhill, where the sun had yet to reach. Wet leaves squished beneath their shoes. Lindsay was quiet for so long Katie guessed she wasn't going to answer.

"He found out I had more male clients than he'd realized," she said finally. "I know it's just a job, but that was the one sense of purpose in my day, the one thing that still made me feel like me. I'm good at it, you know? Between my regulars and my coworkers, they were the only friends I had left after everything he'd stopped 'letting' me do. When I refused to give it up? That night was next level." She touched her forehead, where the gash was healing but clearly going to scar. They'd done their best with the bandage strips Katie had found, but she should have had stitches. Yet here she was, smiling the most genuine smile Katie had seen from her yet.

Then abruptly, she stopped.

"Do you smell a campfire?" she asked. And immediately, Katie did. It wasn't the pleasant kind of woodsmoke, but the acrid smolder of wet leaves and stubborn damp wood that refuses to light. They halted walking, listening hard, panning the hills around them, but it was impossible to distinguish any hint of smoke from the low-lying fog.

Campfires weren't allowed here, though. Plus, the gates were closed. Had been all night.

"Smoke must travel far in this damp air." Katie tried to sound surer than she felt.

Lindsay nodded uncertainly. "Someone's probably burning yard debris while it's too damp out to be a hazard."

They walked on, more harried, sharing a sudden eagerness to loop back. As if any unwanted visitors couldn't as easily find them there.

"Don't you hate that?" Lindsay huffed. Katie looked at her quizzically, keeping step. "How easy it is to be walking along, minding your own business, and have something totally innocuous make you that uncomfortable. Men don't deal with that."

"Oh, that." Katie smiled ruefully. "I do hate it. Although, these are extenuating circumstances."

"My *life* is extenuating circumstances. I'm over it. However I have to pay for it, waiting tables or cleaning hotels, I'm gonna get whatever new state license I need. I'm gonna build a bigger roster of regulars, rent my own salon booth, and never ask a man's permission again. I keep thinking of these weights I want to just let go of, just stop carrying, know what I mean? I want a daffodil to be just a plain old flower again."

Katie did know. She was clinging to a few heavy things herself. Maybe it was as simple as giving herself permission to let go. To say, *Enough, already.* The smell of smoke evaporated into the morning, and they walked on, lost in thought among the plain old flowers.

The first few days, Jude shoveled gravel while Katie raked while Lindsay hid. The upside to knowing Jude was coming was that Katie could plan. When his truck ambled up the hill, she was ready with a speaker already tuned to classic rock radio. The deejays did bits with comedians between sets, which gave her an excuse to crank the volume high enough to mask any sounds from the loft. It also gave them an excuse not to talk. To simply work and listen.

For a guy who had yet to demonstrate much sense of humor, Jude seemed surprisingly into the radio show's vibe. He had a great laugh, hearty and sincere. Whereas Katie laughed often and indiscriminately, sometimes just to put other people at ease, Jude laughed only when he really meant it. Which meant if you paid attention, you could learn, for example, that he was not big on political humor but partial to Seinfeld–style jokes "about nothing"—meandering anecdotes about misread signals and bad days. You could notice how he'd laugh when he could see himself in a joke, but not at other people's misfortune.

Sometimes Jude would get ahead of her, dotting the driveway with molehills of gravel faster than she could rake, and he'd hit the break area she'd set up on the porch. The idea was to lure him away from the outbuildings with ice water and shade, and for the most part it worked. Occasionally he'd wander down the drive on foot and might be gone a half hour. He never said where he went, but as long as he didn't go near the loft, Katie wasn't asking questions.

Bess kept coming by on her lunch break, and thankfully her initial freak-out seemed to have stabilized. She'd pull up, and Jude would take off in his truck.

"Do you think we're rude, not inviting Sad Keanu to join?" Katie asked one day.

Bess guffawed.

"Can't take credit for that one. Apparently that's what Grace called him."

"I won't ask how you know that. But that's it. A cross between a Sad Keanu meme and Christian Slater circa *Untamed Heart*? Or Ethan Hawke. A brooding Gen X dream."

"I'm only dreaming he'll find something else to do. Not that I don't love manual labor."

It wasn't so bad having a few hours of her day that were dutiful yet simple. Web design was all about troubleshooting, which meant it was all about trouble. Clients generally didn't speak the language, which added an extra challenge to explaining technical limitations and justifying costs. Her calendar had been filled with arguments disguised as meetings, made ever more argumentative because she and Clark were supposed to be on the same team. Now, there was something to be said for working side by side in companionable silence.

When the gravel was done, Katie had to admit it was a big improvement. She and Jude shook hands on it, in all their glorious mutual awkwardness.

"Cold beer?" she offered. "It's coming on five o'clock."

"Why not." He accepted the bottle she handed him. "You're not so bad, Hatchback."

She raised her drink to his. "That makes one of us."

A laugh fell out of him, and she took a long, cool sip, letting her sore muscles drink it in.

"Thanks," he said, handing her his bottle. "You done good. I should go."

She was shocked to find it empty. He was halfway gone before she could get out the word "Goodbye." But even in that hurry, he looked back at her once, twice, three times. Was he angling for a last appraising look at the gravel? For another glimpse at *her*? Or at something else? Something he had no right to see?

She pushed the thought aside. *Hold steady. Can't be much longer now.*

On the fourth day of waiting, for the first time she had a whole morning ahead of her without the handyman in her space.

But when she got home from her walk with Lindsay, something else was.

She couldn't see it, but she could hear it. Behind the ashy glass doors of the fireplace, flapping around, making a racket, sending clouds of soot seeping through the cracks into the room. She was pretty sure it was a bird, but she couldn't rule out a bat. How had it gotten in? She'd checked that the flue was closed her first day here, when the room felt drafty—before realizing *every* room felt drafty. More important, how would she get it out?

I know how I won't *get it out,* she resolved. *I will not call a man to do it for me.*

She gathered supplies: a broom, laundry basket, pillowcase, and butterfly net. Then she crouched outside the glass doors, willing herself to open them. But her *self* wouldn't listen. After spending all day, every day, feigning courage she didn't feel, critter removal was apparently one bridge too far. What if it flew at her? What if she missed the catch and lost the thing in the house, then had to sleep wondering if she'd wake up with some . . . bat disease?

So she called Bess.

It went to voice mail. She left a cheerful message asking, hypothetically, what course of action might be advised for her situation. Then she leaned her supplies against the fireplace, forming an extra wall of protection, and went to make coffee. Every now and then, the noise from the living room would stop, but just when she was hoping her winged visitor had found its own way out, it would start again. The poor creature was getting more frantic, which made her feel both more guilty about not intervening and less confident she could intervene successfully.

Lest she feel too down on herself, she tackled something else she'd been avoiding.

She called her sister. Who was, for better or worse, the only person who'd been trying to check in and see how Katie's move went.

Her younger niece, Cora, answered, lighting up Katie's phone screen with a strawberry halo of bedhead. She had wavy hair that nearly reached her waist, beautiful even when it was messy. Though at nine, she seemed not to know it. Only to want to be wild and free.

"Aunt Katie! Mom's in the shower."

"Hey, Cora. What's up?"

"I'm trying to manifest summer."

Katie laughed. When was the last time she'd given such a definite, exuberant answer to anything so simple? "You're trying to who-what?"

"Manifest summer. Like, when you release intentions or hopes and the universe gives them back to you for real? I learned about it from Willie Nelson."

Childhood manifestation lessons from Willie Nelson? Only in Nashville. And Texas probably. Although come to think of it, manifesting *was* the only technique she'd used on her chimney situation. "Better manifest harder. Here in Ohio, it's supposed to snow this weekend."

"Snow? But I already manifested spring!" Cora groaned dramatically, and Katie couldn't help but see her sister in that face. Not that she didn't in herself, too—they all shared gray-blue eyes, a heart-shaped jaw. But there was something novel about Gigi, something *extra* that was hard to put a finger on. It wasn't just the way she looked, the smoothness of her profile, or the arch of her eyebrows. Everything she did or said or touched seemed . . . bolder. Like Katie was the original and Gigi the "new and improved" version, though that was backward, because Gigi had come along first—and had no qualms about going first still. She made bolder choices, hung out with bolder friends, married a bolder man. Even her mistakes were bolder. What was Katie's meager whimper of a divorce compared to a cross-Atlantic custody battle?

"Six whole inches of snow." Katie echoed Cora's groan. "All our flowers are going to freeze."

"That's wild."

"I think so. But everyone here just rolls their eyes and says, 'Welcome to Cincinnati.'"

"Well, no snow in Tennessee. Only the boring old same."

"Is Nessa with you? Can I say hi?"

"She's not. Her sixth-grade choir thingy meets before school."

"Sixth-grade choir?" Katie frowned, doing a quick mental calculation. Was Nessa seriously in sixth grade? She'd been certain the girls were more like . . . third and fourth?

"They invite one student from each lower grade to sing at their spring concert. Nessa is the chosen fifth grader." Cora said this charitably, though she'd clearly guessed the real root of her aunt's confusion. So unlike Gigi, who never missed a chance to point out something Katie should have known or been there for. Though in Katie's more forgiving moods, it had occurred to her that if Gigi got hurt more boldly . . . maybe that was because she loved more boldly too.

"Good for Nessa," Katie said. "I didn't know she was into singing."

"You will soon." Cora rolled her eyes. "She does it all day. What she's really into is trying to be more than a year older than me. Last time it was this haircut she copied from our babysitter. Before that, it was getting her ears pierced. Now it's sixth-grade choir."

Ah. There was Gigi after all. Katie knew when to change the subject.

"So why are you trying to manifest summer?"

"Duh! Check out our countdown!" She swiveled so Katie could see, right on the fridge: Days to Camp Aunt Katie. And beneath it, on a magnetic sticky note pad, the number 67.

Sixty-seven days. Katie blinked at the digits, doing some manifesting of her own. Sixty-seven days from now, she'd be much more at home in this house. Not that she'd ever get used to wildlife flying indoors, but surely the weirdness of Grace's departure would have faded. She'd know the trails by heart; she'd be able to see her own hand at work well beyond the smooth gravel driveway. And Lindsay and the limbo they hung in here together would be long gone. Sixty-seven days should be plenty of time. Even if this open-ended arrangement in her loft continued . . . she still had more than two months to close the open end in time for company.

When Cora's eager face reappeared on screen, Katie's heart lifted and sank all at once. This wasn't just about making things right with Gigi. Her nieces wanted this too. *Needed* this too.

"What's it like there?" Cora bubbled on. "Do you love it so far?"

Did she? People didn't phrase questions that way unless they expected a resounding yes. From the living room, the fireplace doors rattled hard enough that something clattered to the floor. Cora squinted suspiciously. "It's like no place I've ever lived before," Katie answered quickly. "I wake up every day and never know what's going to happen."

"Was every day with Uncle Clark the same? And your old job and everything?"

Katie thought about this. "No," she said. "But they felt the same. *I* felt the same."

"So this is better?"

The doors rattled again: a reminder of everything else she had to have quietly in its place before she'd feel capable of honoring this promise to host Camp Aunt Katie. Before she'd feel confident saying yes. *It's a good thing. It's good for me.*

But Cora looked so hopeful. So she said, "It'll be better yet when you and your sister get here." How was that for manifesting? They both hung up smiling.

When she caught sight of Jude's truck through the window, she was only a little annoyed.

Technically, she hadn't called a man to do her dirty work.

She couldn't help it if Bess had done it for her.

"Missed me, huh?" he greeted her, pulling on thick gloves as he took the porch stairs two at a time. But he didn't tease her about not handling the situation herself. At least, not until he saw the laundry basket barricade.

She couldn't fault him for bursting out laughing then. It did look ridiculous.

"Well," he said, recovering. "Before we resort to putting the bird through the spin cycle, do you have a spare bath towel? One you don't mind getting dirty."

Another fluttering sent a fresh puff of soot out the edges of the fireplace doors, but he remained unfazed, so she hurried upstairs to the linen closet, grateful he seemed to have a plan.

When she returned a moment later, though, he hadn't moved a thing. He still stood where she'd left him, in the center of the living room, browsing the hutch's shelves of field guides.

"Those are nature center property," she said, "if you want to borrow something." It came out more curtly than she'd intended, and he glanced up guiltily.

"I know," he said. "I was thinking they hadn't left you much room to add books of your own. There's a lounge in the visitors' center if you want to transfer some of these there."

"Oh." She was oddly touched by this small consideration, even as she wondered how familiar he was with the house. He and Grace may not have been close, but he seemed to know his way around. "Thanks. I'll keep that in mind." She handed him a beach towel. "It's probably best for both our sakes if I step out and watch to see how you handle this through the window."

"Suit yourself."

As it turned out, there wasn't much to see. In a matter of seconds, it was over, and he'd swiftly bagged—or, rather, toweled—a beautiful, if dirty, blue jay.

"I'm just relieved it wasn't a bat," she told him, as they watched it fly off.

"You'd be better off with a bat. Blue jays are assholes. Territorial. I'll go up and make sure this one didn't damage your chimney cap."

Assholes? Figured. Always the best-looking ones. "But don't bats spread disease?"

"Their droppings can, but otherwise, they control bugs that *do*. You're in a sweet spot in Southwest Ohio. No wildfires, earthquakes, hurricanes, and near-zero natural predators humans need to worry about. Even venomous snakes are unusual here."

She perked up. "Really? Nothing venomous at all?"

"Only spiders."

Right. She'd add that to her list of Things Other People Find Enthusiastically Reassuring.

Sixty-seven days. Katie didn't need to put the countdown on her fridge: It was imprinted on her nerves, a constant on her mind, a guarded pocket in her heart. The next day, she woke up, confirmed that all was quiet in the fireplace, and thought, *Sixty-six.* Undeniably, the best way to make sure that was enough time to cut off involvement in the Sequence was to do it now, to throw in the towel after Lindsay. Nonnegotiable. Katie could make a whole list of reasons to say no. Bess. Cora. Nessa. Gigi. Even, and maybe especially, Grace.

But then, with sixty-five days left to go, the email came. It had been nearly a week since she'd left the warmth of the baker's kitchen, and Katie still had no idea exactly who the message was from behind SeqZero@account.com. But she didn't need to.

> Friday, ahead of the snow. Frigid day for hiking, good day for us. Forty minutes before closing I'll park in the far back of the lot. If anyone is (fool) hardy enough to be out there, wait until I'm the only one left. Have her walk out carrying no more than a backpack. We'll exit during business hours

as if we've come together. Anything goes wrong,
assume it's off. We'll try again after the snow.

As she sat with the email—the sense of duty, the thrill of victory
within reach—she was reminded of all the reasons she'd been thinking
of telling the Sequence *yes*. So she sent a reply, though they hadn't asked
for one: Would like to meet you first.

13

In the farthest corner of the parking lot stood . . . someone's grandma. Even out here, she looked like she should be wearing an apron, serving up a tray of fresh cookies. Maybe it was the brunette-dyed poodle-cut perm, the kind that hadn't been in fashion since *I Love Lucy*. Maybe it was the face, half-nurturing-matriarch, half-I-am-too-old-to-care-what-you-think. Or maybe it was the clip-on earrings: bedazzled flowers that somehow looked both cheap and yet too fancy for her sherpa jacket and comfort loafers.

Good trick, Katie thought. The baker looks like a punk rocker, and the chauffer looks like a baker. Maybe there was some other cohort who looked more like a caretaker. A bodyguard or social worker, complete with an *American Gothic* pitchfork.

The grandma cupped a hand against the cold wind and lit a cigarette, which was about the most conspicuous thing you could do out here. Then again, she'd chosen their meeting time wisely: no one was around to see. A few members had braved the barometer drop earlier in the day, but no one stuck around to see these clouds looming low with impending snow. Not even a robin, not even a squirrel.

She leaned against her car, watching Katie approach, smoking and making no move to meet her halfway. Nervous, Katie licked her lips. A bad idea. She could feel them chapping in real time.

What if this wasn't the woman she'd been waiting for?

"Hello," Katie said, maybe too softly. The wind whipped the word away, and Katie shivered, though her muscles were so tense inside her jacket she could barely feel the cold.

"NCT?" the grandma asked.

"One two three," Katie answered, spelling out the rest of the email address they'd assigned her. If this woman wouldn't even say "New Caretaker" aloud, better not to leave any doubt. Katie stopped and stood, hands in her pockets, meeting her assessing eyes.

This was it.

Whatever *it* was. The end, or maybe, the beginning.

The grandma nodded, no nonsense. "Our surprise guest: How's she holding up?"

Katie exhaled, trying to force the nervous energy out. "Remarkably calm, considering. Grateful. A good sport."

The woman didn't crack her stoic facade, only took a quick drag of her cigarette. "And how are you?" she asked, puffs of smoke escaping around the words.

It was a kind question, even if this simultaneously grandmotherly and *un*grandmotherly woman was looking at her like the question was a test, like she didn't know what to make of Katie and wasn't sure how to find out. "Happy to see you," Katie said.

Another nod. "From what I hear, you're the good sport." Again, the words were charitable, but her expression didn't quite match. "We appreciate your discretion."

"Of course. It's been . . ." What? An eye-opening adventure? A blessing in disguise? A panic attack? "An honor," she finished. It sounded cheesy, but she meant it.

"I understand you have a friend on the nature center staff who's become aware."

The end of her cigarette burned bright as she took another drag, her eyes not leaving Katie's, and Katie tried not to see the gesture as menacing. Of course she'd ask about Bess. She had to check loose ends.

"She appreciates the need for discretion as well," Katie said, borrowing her word. The grandma did not look convinced. "We've been friends a long time," Katie added. "She's one of the best people I know. We can trust her."

The woman looked at her for a long moment. "What's her name?" Something about the way she asked this gave Katie the impression she already knew exactly who Bess was.

"You still haven't told me what I should call you," she deflected.

"Call me Dottie." Katie did a double take. She'd expected some baker-esque code name, but this sounded real. At least, it fit the person standing here. Dottie must have read her expression, because she winked. "I like to dot my *i*'s and cross my *t*'s. Or so they tell me. Now look here, I respect someone who knows how to dodge a question. Not your fault we've been compromised this way. So I guess we'll have to take your word for it. But it would be best if your staffer friend forgot all about this. If you'd encourage her to do so."

Katie squirmed inside her coat. She'd come here expecting . . . what? A pat on the back? At the very least, a proposition to continue. Maybe she'd been unwise to get caught up in the baker's heartfelt story, and in Lindsay's relief to be among the daffodils "out on the other side." Maybe she was trying too hard to justify her involvement, however temporarily, creating a romanticized picture of what this really was: a mistake.

A misunderstanding.

But what if this woman, matriarch though she may seem, was just a messenger? What if none of this was actually her call? If Katie were to slink home, never to see or hear from these people again, well, that might be best. But she didn't want to do it for the wrong reasons.

"Can I ask what your role is in all this?" she heard herself ask.

Dottie dropped her cigarette to the gravel and stomped it out. Then she picked up the butt, wrapped it in a tissue, and tucked it into her pocket. As if to make a show of how meticulous she could be at cleaning up after herself. "What do you mean, my role?"

"The baker said everyone has just one job."

Dottie looked to the sky, like she was sharing an inside joke with someone up there. "How handy for her to remember that after the fact," she muttered. "Anyhoo, we should probably stay on a need-to-know basis."

"But I do need to know," Katie said. "If you want me to let Lindsay leave with you."

Dottie narrowed her eyes. "Well, well," she said. But she didn't press further. "Look here then. If the caretaker is step one, I'm step zero. I say who, I say when. At least, I'm supposed to."

Katie hadn't been on a job interview or a first date in more than a decade, but this exchange felt like an odd amalgamation of the two, and she felt woefully unprepared. She wanted to start over, make a better impression. But more than that, she wanted answers.

"How?" she asked. How could anyone be in a position to say when, who, why? Katie couldn't imagine where you'd even begin. Dottie didn't seem particularly surprised by the question, but it was clear she hadn't decided how much to divulge.

"I work at a women's shelter," she said, like this explained everything. Maybe it did.

"Wow," Katie said. "That must be . . ." She felt reluctant to finish the sentence. Rewarding? Gut wrenching? Frustrating? There must be rampant misconceptions about a job like that, given Dottie felt compelled to work around it, under the radar. Then again, she hadn't said what she did there. For all Katie knew, she was the lunch lady.

"It's both better and worse than you're imagining," Dottie said, more charitably. "Unless you've ever visited one?"

Katie shook her head. "Only the one in my loft."

The response seemed to throw Dottie off balance, like she hadn't thought of the caretaker's role that way. Or like maybe she'd already forgotten that Katie had performed the role, even though it was the reason they were here.

Dottie sighed. "Baker tells me how 'lucky' we are, to have happened into someone who's so on board with our mission. Who's so eager to learn more about what to call us, and how we operate, and all the fascinating details on how this works."

Katie felt herself blush. Hearing it put that way, she could hardly argue Dottie didn't have reason to harbor suspicions of her own. Even if they felt unfair. And even if Dottie believed in Katie's good intentions, of course she wouldn't see anything lucky about having to scramble and clean up the baker's loose ends. Katie might have gone on the defensive, pointing out the Sequence could have done way worse than her . . . but decided to level with Dottie instead.

"I get how that would rub you the wrong way," Katie said. "I came here fresh off a divorce, and through the whole mess, people keep telling me how lucky I am. Lucky we didn't have kids, they say. Lucky we didn't both want the house. Lucky he's not fighting me on the money. Lucky no one's at fault. Lucky that *at least* I still have so many things going for me, though I'm not clear on what those are. Lucky he was honest with me about developing feelings for someone else. Lucky he didn't waste any more of my time. Lucky I'm still young. Which, again, is debatable." She leveled her gaze at Dottie. "It's amazing how off-putting it is to be called lucky when it's the furthest thing from what you feel. But all I'm doing is trying to hold up the caretaker's end of the bargain here."

Dottie looked surprised by her impromptu monologue.

Katie was too.

"You one of those exceedingly polite types," Dottie asked, "when something is *off-putting*, as you call it? A people pleaser?" She said this as if a people pleaser was about the worst thing a woman could be.

"My ex-husband didn't think so."

Dottie's mouth twitched. "Then let's try this again. Here's the real reason I'm not falling at your feet with thank-yous: the last thing we want is for you to feel obligated." For the first time, she seemed sincere. "Waking up to a strange woman at your door—that alone would send most people running, and we *are* lucky you connected the dots. The baker mentioned you'd expressed a certain . . . willingness. And that was noble. But I don't want you to think anyone expects anything from you. We are not in the business of laying guilt trips on Good Samaritans. We can all call this a success if we walk away now with all parties relatively unscathed."

"I don't know if I can walk away," Katie admitted. "And given the circumstances, I don't know if I can honestly say I don't feel obligated either."

"I can absolve you of that, right here. You are not."

If this was a coy attempt at reverse psychology . . . it was working. "It's not you I feel obligated to. It's these women. If I don't help, no one does, right? You go back on hiatus?"

Dottie didn't answer, and Katie realized how much she'd been wanting to hear that she was wrong. That over the past week, they'd figured out some other safe house. She shook her head. "I can't understand why my predecessor would leave that way. After everything she'd done . . ."

"Need-to-know basis, remember? You don't need to understand her."

"I'm living in her house," Katie protested. "I'm doing her job."

A fierce gust of wind blew the bare tree branches above them into a frenzy.

"Here's what you do need to know," Dottie said. "Broadly speaking, not just Grace but everyone in the Sequence has personal reasons for getting involved—or, presumably, for getting uninvolved. And they get more personal as we go, because hard as we try to be careful, there are moments that are scary or dangerous or painfully sad. Sometimes, there are sacrifices. It's not something anyone should ever do because they feel put on the spot. It becomes a part of you."

Katie hugged herself against the cold. She'd been standing still too long. She felt it in her bones. "The baker told me a little of her history. Most of you have a story like that?"

Dottie crossed her arms. "The thing about personal reasons is, those stories aren't mine to share." The implication was clear. You couldn't possibly stumble in and belong here.

Katie felt oddly defiant. The whole time she'd been hiding Lindsay and distracting Jude and appeasing Bess and tracking down the baker, she'd fretted that she hadn't signed up for this. But she'd had no trouble grasping why someone would.

In fact, she couldn't stop thinking about why someone—anyone—*should.*

"I mean," she hedged, "I'm a woman. That's personal."

Dottie looked reluctantly amused. "Sure."

"And, you know." Katie gestured at the woods around them, as if her place in the world should be obvious. Even though she'd never been less sure of where she fit. "The patriarchy."

By now, Dottie was actively trying—and failing—not to smile. "What about it?"

Katie threw up her hands. "It's bullshit."

Dottie laughed a throaty chuckle. The argument might not have been articulate, but that didn't mean it wasn't true.

What woman, after all, couldn't relate to feeling less than? What woman didn't feel that pull of sisterhood when she least expected it, when she needed it most? It was there in breast cancer screening centers, at bridal showers, in long lines for inadequate public restrooms, in Girl Scout troops, sorority houses, and mutually dreaded PTA meetings, in women's marches and quilting bees and in courtrooms and airports and alone on dark street corners at night. It was there in *Are you getting this weird vibe* and *Did he really just say that* and *Me too.* It was there when people tried to dismiss women as catty, to pit the strongest of them against each other, to leave room only for one token female seat in a boardroom full of suits. It was there in bucking convention and smashing glass ceilings and fighting back.

The impulse to stick together.

"It is bullshit," Dottie agreed. "My husband says I see tragic stories about women everywhere I look. I tell him it's not my fault, they *are* everywhere I look. If you don't see them, either you've got blinders on or you're a man, and I hate to tell him, but it's the same damn thing." She fluffed her bangs, which impossibly reached even higher in the wind. "You cannot explain sexism to a man. Even the best ones. Trust me, sister, I've tried. It's why my hair stands up like this."

Against Katie's better judgment, she sort of liked Dottie. And she was starting to think it was mutual. Even if it was against Dottie's better judgment too.

"Sometimes I think I've seen it all," Dottie went on. "And that's why there's no shortcut to establishing trust when it comes to what we're doing here. It has to be earned. Over time."

"Sure. No offense, but I don't know if I can trust you either." Katie's distress must have started to show because Dottie softened then. The baker had been this way too—as if, different as these women were, they both had a sympathy switch. Where something would poke through the tough exterior and they'd realize, *I almost forgot you're not used to this.*

Just like that, Katie was back in her loop of second-guessing whether she wanted to be.

"Fair enough," Dottie said, carefully, like she wouldn't think less of Katie if she walked away now and didn't want Katie to think less of herself either.

If Bess were here, she'd definitely urge her to take the easy out.

But Katie was all too familiar with the easy out. And where had it gotten her?

"So we've established we'd both be crazy not to have reservations," Katie said. "None of that changes the fact that I'm here now. Or that I know now. So in case of emergency, you know how to reach me." Katie kicked at the gravel, as if she might have dropped something else she'd meant to say. "I'll send Lindsay out," she said. "Hope you weather the storm okay."

She started back toward the barn.

"Say there was one more special case," Dottie called.

Katie stopped but didn't turn. *It becomes a part of you,* Dottie had told her. Warned her. "Special how?"

"She was set to go with us a while ago, but at the last minute, wasn't eligible anymore."

Katie turned around, curious. "Like, she couldn't pay?"

An unlit cigarette had materialized in Dottie's hand, and she waved it, an irritated gesture. "Pay? We don't care about money. She took a pregnancy test."

Katie's mind raced. "Pregnant women aren't eligible?"

"No expectant mothers, no mothers. Like it or not, parental rights are the real deal, and interfering with the law in those cases isn't our place. We're out to do the right thing: we don't like murky. The last thing we need is to be accused of kidnapping or child trafficking or . . . whatever. But her circumstances have changed."

"Meaning?"

"She's not pregnant anymore."

Katie blinked at her. "Right. I could see why someone in that position would . . . take care of it."

"*She* didn't take care of anything. *He* threw her out of a moving car."

Katie gasped. "Did he not know?" She cringed at her own question. As if throwing nonpregnant women out of cars was more acceptable.

"Pregnancy brings out the real crazy in these guys. Choose your own adventure: Turn to page 19 if they refuse to believe it's theirs. Turn to page 36 if they get clingy, won't let *the mother of their child* out of sight. Turn to page 57 if they're afraid she'll love the baby more than them. People talk about women getting hormonal, but these princes don't even have an excuse. She's pretty banged up, so we'll need to wait until she's through a couple of surgeries before she's discharged from the hospital for good—maybe a week or two, depending. But we don't want to risk having her around longer than absolutely necessary."

"What's the rush? Isn't the guy who did this in jail?"

"He's posted bond. Plus, his father is a defense attorney. They're already blaming her, saying she went for the wheel, he overreacted in self-defense." Dottie looked hard into Katie's face. Katie wasn't trying to hide what she'd see there: Doubt. Uncertainty. A little skepticism, about a lot of things. "We're not doing this for kicks, you know," Dottie said. "Trust me, we'd rather the system did its job. But as it stands, sometimes it does, sometimes it sure don't."

"Isn't she safe at the shelter? Until she's fully recovered, I mean?"

Dottie twirled the unlit cigarette like a baton. "Last time she was there, we had an incident. Gave us reason to think this prince might know where it is. Which means she might not be safe at our transition houses either. We've had employees followed before. Not pretty."

Katie blinked at her. "I always thought shelters were safe."

"We have panic buttons installed, if that's what you mean."

"Do I have a panic button out here?"

"Never needed one. But for medical stuff, Dr. Clooney is always on call."

A nervous giggle bubbled up in Katie. "A McDreamy type?"

Dottie's eyes twinkled. "I'll say this: he picked his own code name. If you agree to give her a few days to rest and recover, he can check her one last time here. Like I said, she was already set to go in our system. Soon as he gives the green light, we'll have her out of your hair."

"And . . . that's it?" They both knew Katie wasn't asking about the woman anymore.

She was asking, *That's it for me?*

Dottie shrugged. "Almost everything has a free trial period, yeah? Why don't we see how it goes. You can always say stop. You can always say no. And vice versa."

It was hard to see the harm in that. "What if something goes wrong before the doctor gets here? What if she has a medical emergency in my loft?"

"We'll cover you. The doctor will. No one will ever know."

"But what if she—"

"We'll cover you no matter what happens. No matter what, you understand."

Katie was starting to think she did. They'd cover her even if the woman bled out mere yards from Katie's back door, while Katie slept obliviously in her bed.

But if that happened, she didn't know how she'd ever cover herself.

"We'll email you a heads-up as soon as we know the timing. Then, same deal. Three rings." Dottie popped her trunk and pulled out a lumpy canvas backpack stuffed with something soft. "Fresh supplies."

She held it toward Katie. Her own final question. Katie stared at the bag, tipping like a scale. She could back out, play it safe . . . but safe for whom? If this woman didn't make it out alive, that would be on Katie. Not that Katie would necessarily know . . .

But she'd always wonder.

Before she could change her mind, she grabbed the bag and slung it over her shoulder.

There was more heft to it than she'd realized at a glance.

But she wasn't about to crumple under it now.

14

Katie was finally unpacked. It should have meant the house felt more like hers, and in a way, she supposed it did. But so many of these things had belonged to Grace too.

Going through them was up next.

It started snowing not long after Dottie left Friday night, a tease at first: flurries, then nothing, off and on, off and on. She trudged out to the barn with a blanket-lined box for Chevy, but found the cat happily nestled in a pile of burlap. By Saturday morning, the snow was ready to commit. Now, late afternoon, the fluff looked as dreamlike as an old black-and-white Christmas movie: unnaturally full from lining leaves and blooms instead of bare branches. The effect was as much a time warp into the future as into the past: What would winter be like here? The first real seasonal snow was probably eight months away. Would she last that long?

Lots of layers to that question.

I'm the only one left willing to break the rules, the baker had told her.

It was time to delve deeper into what she might have meant by that.

Katie retrieved Grace's journal, or log or whatever it was, from the shelf where it had sat since she and Bess guiltily flipped through it that first day. It had seemed innocuous at a glance with its pretty embossed cover and brief notes of animal sightings and on-site events. But then again, so had the keys on the wall rack. Crossing to the desk, she pulled the messy top drawer free—the one she'd asked the cleaners to leave alone back when she thought Grace might return—and lay it on the coffee table along with the journal and a tote bag where she'd been collecting little personal things she still came across now and then: handwritten recipe cards, a braided headband, a photo booth strip showing Grace amid friends in derby-style hats. Katie had made up her mind: she would not feel bad about snooping. Nothing left behind was off-limits anymore; Grace had had ample opportunities to get in touch, follow up, return their calls. If she had personal reasons for all of this, Katie respected that. But they were personal to her now too.

She poured a glass of cabernet and was about to settle on the couch when her eyes fell on the fireplace—mercifully bird-free. Why miss this unexpected chance to use it? A roaring fire would be just the thing to make everything cozy, a true snow day. Impulsively, she donned her winter gear, grabbed the firewood sling from the hearth, and headed for the woodpile.

The snow was blowing hard, stinging her cheeks, making her eyes water, an instant reminder she'd always preferred watching winter wonderlands from inside. *Suck it up*, she thought as she trudged toward the tarp-covered mound beyond the barn. *It's worth the hassle.*

Fortunately, the wood had been split into slender, manageable pieces, and she made quick work of filling the canvas sling to the brim. She was securing the tarp back into place when the wind whipped it free, showering her with chunks of ice, and reflexively she turned her back, blinking flakes from her eyelashes, waiting for the gust to pass.

A shiver cut through her.

But not from the wind.

On the trail that crested the edge of this hilltop before veering down to the pond, she could just make out footprints being covered by the blowing snow.

Katie squinted fiercely into the trees, through them, around them, still as a whitetail deer guarding a fawn. When she was satisfied she saw no signs of life, she turned a slow circle, surveying her property more closely. The doors to the outbuildings looked secure. The windows were dark. And the footprints did not extend into her yard. Only to the edge.

She left the sling in the snow and tentatively approached the closest tracks. There was no doubt they were human, probably boots, but they were already too smoothed over to tell what kind or how large, male or female. What she could tell was that whoever had walked this way hadn't simply passed by. The footprints wandered the curve in overlapping circles before continuing down the path, stopping to tie a shoe, maybe, or angling for a photo of the pond. Katie turned to face her house. She could see it perfectly from here. But from the inside looking out, someone standing here might not *be* seen.

Katie turned another slow circle.

She had no feeling, at this moment, that anyone was watching.

But someone could be.

But someone had been.

Returning her attention to the tracks, she began to follow them, straight downhill, boots slipping, arms flinging toward the nearest branches, looking for purchase.

She'd gone maybe ten yards before she came to her senses.

What was she doing?

The tracks were fresh, but not that fresh, maybe an hour or two old and disappearing before her eyes. Even if she found the source, then what? Yes, the gate was closed for inclement weather, but there was nothing to stop an ambitious hiker from wandering in on foot, and for all she knew they were already back home, sipping cocoa.

And if it *was* a worst-case scenario? Someone tracking Lindsay, or Katie, or the Sequence in general, or even searching for Grace? Would she rather encounter a threat out here, or in her house, with heat and doors that locked? She closed her eyes and pictured exactly where she'd left her phone on the coffee table.

She'd only wanted to keep it dry. She'd thought leaving it was the safest course.

Funny how quickly things could turn on their axis.

Sure, hiding Lindsay had made her nervous. But it also meant she hadn't truly been living in solitude. This was her mind's first real chance to play tricks on her, to psych her out that she'd never know, at any given moment, if someone or something else was in these nine-hundred-plus acres of forest. Had she learned nothing from that guy calling his dog, startling Bess so badly she'd dumped her lunch? If she let paranoia take hold, it would never let go.

She had to be practical.

Could this be something to worry about? Yes.

Could there be a perfectly innocent explanation? Take your pick. In fact, couldn't these tracks be from some other staffer?

She was smarter than this. She had to put this in the same category as that campfire she could have sworn she smelled that morning with Lindsay: something curious, good to be aware of. A reason to stay vigilant. But not to panic.

She took one last, long look, three hundred sixty degrees. Then she went back for her sling of wood and returned to the house. Still on edge but trying her hardest not to be.

She'd just gotten the fire going when she heard something outside. A faint . . . buzzing? Like some distant motor. She went to the corner window and there, grinding up the hill, was a utilitarian four-wheeler. It looked like a golf cart on steroids, with tractor-like tires that could only be part of the maintenance fleet. Except it was being driven as if a crazed teenager had hotwired an ATV for a joyride: fast, swerving, and spraying snow in wide, wild arcs. The driver wore an orange snowmobile suit that could have been issued by NASA, mirrored visor included.

Above the commotion rose a high-pitched whoop. Katie watched, slack-jawed, as the vehicle cut a figure eight across her front yard and skidded to a stop at the base of her stairs, dangerously close to clipping the rickety porch boards. Katie ran to fling open the door.

"*Bess?*"

Bess pulled off the helmet, laughing, triumphant at her historic moon landing.

"Are you crazy? I can't believe that thing made it up here!" She *was* crazy. But Katie had never been so happy to see her.

"Oh, it was making it, one way or another. We have to celebrate." Bess unstrapped a pair of duffel bags from the back and stomped up the stairs. "You could freeze the teats off a cow out here! Do I smell a fire?"

"Celebrate what?" Katie held the door wide, panning the tree line for good measure. But if anyone was out there, Bess's grand entrance would have either set them straight or scared them off, surely. Besides, she was already unzipping her suit, shaking snow onto the floorboards.

"Listen to you. 'Celebrate what?' You did it! You solved the case, saved the girl, dodged Sad Keanu, and are officially done with the part of your job description you didn't sign up for."

"Oh." Katie gave a little laugh, ignoring the pang in her gut. "Only that?"

"Only!" Bess stepped out of her boots and stood in stocking feet, hands on her hips. "Look, you're doing amazing left to your own devices out here. You have literally shoveled up every load of rocks that's been dumped at your feet. But I draw the line at letting you be snowed in alone. Vince and the kids are happy to hole up with the Xbox and junk food without me."

Katie considered mentioning the footprints, unrolling the red carpet into her overactive imagination. But she thought of how rattled Bess had been, how she was finally back to herself. Bess's arrival didn't change anything Katie had decided earlier. In fact, it should make it *easier* to put it out of her mind.

Katie wasn't alone anymore. She had the best kind of company. She wouldn't ruin it.

"I haven't shoveled *every* load," Katie demurred. "Jude did have to get the blue jay."

"That's where people misunderstand feminism. Who cares if you don't want to do stuff you're skittish about? It's not a fail to hire help; he's on payroll anyway. Of all the times it's mattered for you to step up since you got here, the blue jay was not one."

Leave it to Bess to defend her over something Bess would've easily done herself. Katie's cheeks hurt from smiling so hard. She was out of practice. "Where's your car?"

"Parked by the gate. I brought provisions!" Bess rooted around in one of the duffel bags, coming up with a bottle of wine. Then another. Then another. Spotting the glass Katie had already poured, forgotten on the windowsill, she flashed Katie her "great minds" grin. "We're going to do something neither of us has had a chance to do yet: enjoy the hell out of this place. Sit by the fire, get drunk, and—"

"Snoop," Katie finished. She gestured toward the coffee table, where Exhibit A, Grace's journal, was displayed in all its guilty glory on top.

"I was going to say sleep over." Bess's grin widened. "Which everyone knows is no fun without snooping."

15

They settled around the coffee table—Bess on the couch, Katie in the circle of warm firelight on the floor—wine in hand, popcorn in a bowl, fire roaring higher.

"This is what I'm talking about," Bess said. "People pay good money for this kind of setup. What do you think? Is it going to grow on you?"

The wine was going down too easily. Katie thought about what her niece had said about manifesting the life you want, the season or stage you're longing for. Cora had the wrong idea about how to do it, but so had Katie, once. Wasn't that what she'd done with Clark? She'd thought she could want it enough for them both. She'd manifested a life that didn't love her back. Some people visualized goals, ran plays in their dreams. Others stepped right into a role and pretended they belonged. Katie had done both—nearly every day of her marriage, she'd looked her husband, friends, family, and coworkers square in the eye and smiled as if everything were fine. She'd watched Clark fake that he loved her, and she'd faked that she didn't notice he was faking. And when he finally said he was sorry, he'd tried, it had all been good on paper, she'd faked that she was surprised. And not at all soul-crushingly heartbroken.

Maybe that was Katie's secret. How this week of waiting and worrying and watching had somehow felt even less foreign and scary to her than it had to Bess.

Faking it was the only part of the job Katie had trained for.

Was the rest going to grow on her, Bess wanted to know?

"I hope so," she told her. "I want it to."

"Music!" Bess announced. "That's what we're missing. Have you looked through all this vinyl?" Bess was on her feet before Katie could stop her, lifting the turntable lid. "Oh no. Oh, sister. Bonnie Raitt? Don't tell me."

Katie scrambled over and snatched the record out of her hand. "We're supposed to be snooping on Grace. Not me."

"So you admit it wasn't Grace listening to 'I Can't Make You Love Me' on repeat?"

"I know it's pathetic, okay? You don't have to point it out."

Bess selected Carole King's *Tapestry* album. On the cover the singer posed in the half-light of a curtained window with a cat, looking cool and comfortable in her own skin.

"Then why?" Bess slid Bonnie back into her case. "You are so above pathetic."

Katie knew Bess was right. The song wasn't even the embarrassing part. Before the divorce was final, she'd related to the lyrics. But now? She'd grown envious of them. Bonnie was still turning down the lights. Bonnie was still turning down the bed. Bonnie still had at least one more night to hold on to.

Katie retreated to her spot on the floor and pulled her throw blanket around her. "I know it seems cut-and-dried. But . . . do you know I might honestly never see Clark again? It's feasible."

"A girl can dream," Bess drawled.

"You used to like him," Katie reminded her. A reflex. "Quite a lot."

In college, when they ran as a pack, Clark hadn't been the one Katie had dated. But he'd been the one she'd find herself talking to after everyone else had zonked out, huddling over late-night coffees and cigarettes. Katie usually gravitated toward opposites, like her uptight side knew it needed balancing out. While her best friend was the group's free spirit and her boyfriend aggressively easygoing, Clark was the exception, the most like Katie of them all, the one she could rely on for meandering debates, inside jokes, a study partner with the same major *and* minor. A soul match. Back then, had Bess found fault with Clark, Katie would've felt slighted too.

"He used to be quite a lot more likable," Bess pointed out.

She wasn't wrong. Obviously. Still, maybe if Katie could explain this to Bess, she'd finally understand it herself. "It's just . . . a strange thought about someone whose life was tied to yours for so long. He doesn't care what happens to you anymore, doesn't want to know. Just goes on walking the world with someone else."

"I see what you're saying. This *would* all be easier if he were dead."

"Bess! That's not what I'm saying."

"Well, it's what *I'm* saying." Bess squinted at the song list on the album cover, then dropped the needle in the middle. The opening notes of "It's Too Late" filled the room. She leaped back onto the couch, catlike.

"You have half a point," Katie conceded. "At least no one calls widows pathetic. People feel sorry for them. People are intrigued by widows. There are sexy widows, mysterious widows, scary widows . . ." Carole was singing now about the pain of something dying inside. If grieving the death of a person was sympathetic, why not the death of a relationship?

"If it's any consolation, you're definitely an intriguing, sexy, mysterious caretaker."

"But not scary?" Katie feigned offense. "What's a girl gotta do?"

Bess gave a half smile, but she didn't laugh. Instead, she narrowed her eyes. "You're not actually done, are you?"

"Done with what?"

"The Lindsay thing. That's why you're tearing your house apart instead of celebrating. You're thinking of doing it again."

Katie looked away.

"Are these step-by-step people guilting you into this? Threatening you?"

"Nothing like that," Katie said quickly. "It's hard to say no, though. Not because they're pushy, but because of what they're doing. They have this moral code . . . It's admirable."

"If you're so sure it's all on the up-and-up, what's the obsession with knowing what went down with Grace?"

Katie gestured around the room as if the answer were self-explanatory. Wouldn't it bother *anyone* that in all the puzzle pieces she'd put together—Lindsay, Sienna, Dottie—Grace remained a big, blank space smack in the middle of the picture? But Bess only blinked at her.

She tried another tack. "Clark used to do this thing where he'd start watching a movie without me. Like, without asking what I was up to or if I wanted to see it. I'd find him in the living room twenty, thirty minutes in, and he wouldn't turn it off or restart. He'd just pause and recap what I missed. You wouldn't believe how many movies I've seen only the second half of. It's a pet peeve. I mean, you pick up enough context to follow, but it's hard to fully appreciate."

"I think I get it."

"Yeah?"

"Yeah. You were married to an even bigger monster than I realized."

Katie hurled a throw pillow at her.

Bess caught it. "Look, we'd both love to know how this caretaker movie started. But from where I'm sitting maybe we don't catch the end either. Maybe it's overdue to Blockbuster."

"Maybe. As of now, I've only agreed to watch one more scene. Okay?"

Bess stared into the fireplace, and Katie knew she was picturing this all wrong. As if Dottie had been falling at her feet, begging. But she and Dottie did agree on one thing: the less Bess knew, the better. If not to protect the Sequence, then to protect Bess.

"Well," Bess said finally, "where I'm sitting doesn't matter, does it?" She downed the rest of her wine, then refilled both their glasses. "What matters is this might be the film that changes your whole life.

Who am I to stand between you and *Steel Magnolias*? You and *Thelma and Louise*? Hell, if Sad Keanu keeps hanging around, this might be your *Lake House*."

Katie rolled her eyes. "If you find letters from a time-traveling Jude, you can keep them."

Bess set to work rifling through the desk drawer—sorting and untangling one messy handful after the next. If Grace's house had been relatively neat, it was apparently only because this one wooden rectangle was magically bottomless—holding a wrinkled, torn, crunched, and ripped lifetime supply of mail, envelopes, to-do lists, coupons, and sticky notes that had lost their stick.

Katie opened the journal and settled in to read.

The brief, dated entries stretched back years. Some months had no more than one or two things logged. Other periods had multiple entries every week, sometimes every day. There were sightings of blue herons, a bald eagle nest, a six-point buck drinking from the creek. Some entries referred to group activities that had been hosted on-site: astronomy club, pollinator party, native plant sale. Also, milestones that reflected a connection to nature's cycles—harvest and strawberry moons, 2017's solar eclipse, the emergence of the Brood X cicadas in 2021.

Katie tried to read it all, but her eyes glazed over. She could find no pattern to the things Grace had and hadn't chosen to record. Nor could she read emotion into them. While Katie would have written "fourth rat snake this week" with dread, she couldn't tell whether Grace had experienced it with annoyance or awe. Had Grace simply followed things that interested her, or even things that didn't, out of some Walden-esque mission to "live deliberately"? Maybe she just wanted to be prepared if someone asked how long it had been since the last astronomy club meeting. Katie was losing interest in trying to guess.

But then the word "Clooney" jumped out at her: *Thurs, 9/7/2017: Clooney philanthropy.*

Clooney. Like the actor she'd grown up watching in scrubs on *ER.* Like the doctor Dottie had joked about choosing his own sexy Dr. Clooney alias—and who'd be here next week, checking the woman who'd miscarried.

Katie didn't want to jump to conclusions, even as the hairs on the back of her neck stood on end. She grabbed her smartphone and did a quick search. The Clooney family *was* from right across the river in Kentucky. She googled "Clooney philanthropy," "Clooney charity," then "Clooney foundation" and found a sweeping international organization to "wage for justice" for women and minorities—but no local chapter, nothing tied to a nature-based nonprofit.

She flagged the page with a sticky note and turned to the next one, running a finger down the lines as she skimmed for the word to reappear. She'd flipped dozens of pages before finding a second reference: *Clooney philanthropy.* Then a third in the very next entry. She tore off two more sticky notes, and Bess looked up from the fliers she was recycling into the bin at her feet.

"Has the nature center done any work with one of the Clooney philanthropies?" Katie asked. "Or do you have any members named Clooney?"

"I can search our database." Bess ran to get her iPad from her bag and spent a busy minute hovering over the touchscreen. "No and no. Not spelled that way. *C-l-o-o-n-e-y?*"

Katie nodded. "The Sequence has a doctor . . . She *might* have logged his visits. Though why she'd do it here with everything else and not in some separate book doesn't make sense."

"Unless she wanted it to blend in," Bess suggested. "So if anyone, oh, I don't know, decided to curl up by the fire and read the whole log, they might not notice."

"But why just that? I don't see anything else related."

"Maybe the other stuff is disguised too? If you were to keep track of anything from this network, what would it be?"

That answer seemed obvious. "Who's stayed in the loft."

"Wouldn't keeping those records be dangerous? You don't know their names anyway."

True. "It's just . . . I got to talk with Lindsay quite a bit, and it left me with this sense of wanting to remember her. Like, if not me, who?"

"Me," Bess said. "I'll remember her. The baker will too. You might feel alone in this, but you're not. Maybe that's enough—"

"Bake sale!" Katie blurted out. Bess blinked at her, startled. "Sorry, you said baker. There are multiple bake sales logged in here."

Bess frowned. "The nature center fundraises, but not with bake sales. Even if we did, we'd do it at main campus. Way more foot traffic."

Katie paged back. Sure enough, a bake sale came just before the Clooney entry.

"What if she's noting the days the baker transported the women out of the shelter with 'bake sale'? And the days she had to call the doctor with 'Clooney philanthropy'?"

"Maybe. Or maybe she let a Girl Scout troop set up a table? You could make yourself crazy with this."

Katie turned a few more pages, then tossed the journal to the floor in frustration. "You're right. I mean, the last page has stuff about 'invasive species removal' and 'blackberry bushes spreading.' Ominous warnings, or gardening tips?"

"I knew I should've brought my decoder ring," Bess quipped. "Drink your Ovaltine!"

"What we need is something in her own words. Emails or letters. There's not an old iPad or phone in there, by any chance?"

"Doubtful. Grace was low-tech. The laptop she had with her on her last day, when I had to get the router password for you, was nowhere near new."

The router. The nature center covered utilities, including Wi-Fi. Katie had changed the password right away, not knowing who might have the old one. Which meant . . .

Any backup data stored to the system should remain protected. Unchanged since the day Grace moved out.

Katie sat up straighter. "Some wireless routers have a memory. Like how your web browser stores your history. Security was never my area, but maybe I can trace her email log-in. Or at least see the last thing she searched before she left? Make sure it wasn't 'How to join the witness protection program.'"

Katie ran for her laptop. She'd barely used it since she got here. Her online activity consisted of more fleeting searches on her phone—how to check for ticks, and which venomous spiders Jude had been referring to. For someone who used to spend all day staring at a screen, the shift was drastic. And the most dramatic thing about it? That she didn't miss it.

"Seems redundant to google 'witness protection' when she was running a program of her own," Bess mused.

"Unless it was the people in the program she was trying to get away from." Bess's smile fell as she came to sit beside her on the couch. "Let's see. Router settings . . ." Muscle memory took over and Katie zipped through a series of default options. The security settings were locked tight: she had to keep reentering her admin password. But finally, she was in.

"We have a memory," she reported. "Let's see if I can filter by frequently visited URLs."

She could. There was next to no social media, confirming Katie's lackluster results when she'd tried to find Grace's accounts—hoping to friend or follow her—and found only an abandoned Tumblr of mediocre plant and insect close-ups. Grace's online habits had been more basic: shopping, local and national news, weather radar. And at the top?

Katie pointed. "Same webmail client the baker used for my account." She should've guessed. One of the tenets of web design was to remember people were creatures of habit.

Even, apparently, the secretive ones.

"Can you see her username?"

Katie shook her head, her hopes sinking as quickly as they'd risen. It was hard enough to come up with a handle that wasn't already taken, let alone guess somebody else's.

Creatures of habit. Was there any chance it could be that simple? The baker had assigned Katie as NCT123—"NCT" for "New Caretaker," and 123 presumably for the steps. On a lark, Katie keyed in "CT123" as the username, minus the *N* for "New." In the password field, she tried the same password Grace had provided Bess for the router.

She stared at the screen, hardly believing what she was seeing.

She was in.

16

Three new messages waited, unread, in Grace's unmanned inbox. Two from the week she'd left, and one from just days ago.

It was hard to believe Grace hadn't been tempted to check this account even once since her last day as caretaker. Either she really had been ready for a clean break—from everything—or something was keeping her offline. Katie didn't want to think about that possibility. After all, if Grace truly had been fed up enough to just walk out—on both the nature center *and* the Sequence—then why bother checking email?

But Dottie had been so adamant that Grace had personal reasons for doing this in the first place. *Personal* meant you looked back, at least once. *Personal* meant you couldn't help making sure everyone was okay.

Save for the three unopened emails tempting her in bold, the inbox was jarringly empty. Katie clicked through the subfolders and found not a single sent message, saved message, or random spam, not even anything in the trash. She supposed Grace wouldn't have wanted to risk leaving a record of any Sequence-related correspondence.

Assuming, of course, she'd been the one to delete them.

Bess was leaning close enough to lay her head on Katie's shoulder, practically salivating.

"Do we read these?" Katie asked, sneaking a glance sideways.

"Are you kidding? Of course we read them."

"But if she ever looks, she'll know we were in her account."

"Not if you mark them unread again."

True. But if the *senders* had that feature marking their messages "read," Katie couldn't undo that; the signal would be sent. That Grace—or someone—was out here.

Still. Assuming these messages came from inside the Sequence—and who else would know of this account?—worst-case scenario was Katie would have to own up to getting nosy. It wasn't like she could get herself into real trouble here.

Right?

Before she could second-guess herself further, Katie opened the email that had been waiting the longest—sent right after Grace's last day. It was from Seq000@account.com. Her best guess, based on the number starting with 0 instead of 123, was that this signified Dottie. It wasn't the same handle she'd used to contact Katie about Lindsay's pickup, but it stood to reason they'd change accounts as an extra safeguard when someone left the network. The actual message inside was too vague to reveal much, though. It consisted of only three clipped sentences, no greeting, no sign-off. Only the unpleasantness in between:

> For the record, we owed you nothing. You had it backward, sister. Hope you don't regret this.

"Not loving the sound of that," Bess murmured. "Considering."

Katie swallowed hard, even as she reminded herself tone was hard to read in email. Even as she remembered Dottie calling her "sister" too. Maybe this wasn't a threat. An ordinary tiff.

With an unfortunate coincidence of timing to Grace's disappearing act.

The email signature was an italicized quote attributed to Eleanor Roosevelt: "What one has to do usually can be done." Katie had seen the quote plenty of times before, and never once read those words as ominous, but in this context . . . they weren't exactly inspirational.

She scrolled down, and yes—here was the text of Grace's email that this rebuke had come in response to. Bess was hugging Katie's arm now, so tight Katie could feel her shiver—in anticipation, dread, or a cold chill, she didn't know, but Katie shivered back. Grace's original email was time-stamped earlier that same week, in what had turned out to be her final days on the job. It had taken the recipient five days to send that clipped reply.

> I won't apologize for being fed up with these excuses. Fear hasn't gotten in the way of what's important to YOU.
>
> It's not like I wanted to play this card, but . . . seriously? You owe me.
>
> We both know this would fall apart without me.

Katie scrolled up to read the response again. They must have had some offline exchange during those five days in between. The response had come after she'd quit, too late for her to see it.

"Well," Bess said weakly. "Let's not read too much into it. Quitting doesn't often go smoothly." What more was there to say? "How about the next one?"

Katie clicked forward. The second email looked to be from some later step in the Sequence, if the numbers were any indication. Seq3434@account.com.

> You really up and did it like that. Holler! I won't pretend I don't understand, but selfishly?

Damn.

Speaking of selfish: Now that you're out, Patti and I are unrestricted from begging a certain favor—at least, we think we are? No one said otherwise, and we ain't about to ask.

There's no one we'd rather officiate our long-awaited nuptials. Would you? Hell, maybe this is what we've been dragging our feet for. So it can happen this way.

It's not just how much we like and respect you, or that you helped bring us together. It's that you stand for something. For probably the only thing we both believe in except each other. Sometimes I wonder why we're even bothering to get married with the world falling apart around us. But then I remember that's exactly why we bother. You know we can't resist making a point.

We'll keep the ceremony private. We'll even come to you if you want, wherever you are. Road trips might not hold the same appeal for Patti, but I've been jonesing for a ride-along. There's only one reason why I haven't, and we're on a good long break from that, thanks to you. Don't read sarcasm into that. There isn't very much.

Let us know? The best silver lining would be to finally be allowed to call you a friend.

"Wow," Bess said. "Am I reading this right? Two women in this operation want to marry each other? So much for not being allowed to associate in public."

"Kind of brilliant, though. They can't make you testify against your spouse."

"Brilliant if you're doing something *wrong*." Bess bit her lip. "Katie, you're sure this is all aboveboard?"

"I was going to ask you the same thing. Depending on the tone of 'Hope you don't regret this,' Grace has a perceivable threat in here. You could be the last person who saw her."

Bess threw up her arms. "If anyone in the Sequence suspected she wasn't okay, they wouldn't be asking her to help them exchange vows. Right?"

Hard to argue with that logic. Though Bess was again draining her wineglass with alarming gusto.

"This last message isn't from a Sequence email," Katie said, looking more closely. "The address looks like a randomly generated password—a jumble of letters and numbers."

"What's it say?" Bess grabbed the corkscrew and got to work on another bottle.

"'Another black-eyed Susan blooming,'" Katie read. "'Thanks for the hospitality.'"

"That's it?"

"That's it."

"But it's April. Black-eyed Susans don't bloom until June."

"'Hospitality' . . . maybe she was a guest out back?" Were these women letting Grace know they'd reached the final step to safety? She couldn't imagine the Sequence being okay with any kind of digital trail. Besides, wouldn't they confirm among themselves? Katie realized with a jolt that she hadn't asked for any follow-up about Lindsay. She'd assumed she wasn't allowed.

Which was to say she'd been too tied up in showing Dottie she could be a good, compliant, rule-following player if she wanted to be.

"Bet you're right," Bess said. "'Another black-eyed Susan bloomin'' . . . I bet she's speaking in code. Sounds like she made it. That's good news, right? Whatever they're doing works."

Katie forwarded all three messages to her NCT account for safe-keeping, then deleted the forwards from the sent mail and trash and marked the inbox "unread." From now on, she'd monitor this account as obsessively as her own. If Grace ever did log on, Katie wanted to know. She wanted the peace of mind that Grace was out there, and she wanted it more than ever. If Katie had ever doubted this role was deeply meaningful to her predecessor, she didn't anymore.

This was a woman who'd asked her guests to follow up as safely as they could. A woman who'd been respected and genuinely liked by at least some of her counterparts. A woman who'd been willing to speak up when she disagreed with the others. A woman who *stood for something*.

A woman who'd sounded awfully invested for the long haul. Who'd said, in her own words, this would fall apart without her. And then what? They'd called her bluff? They'd found out she hadn't been bluffing after all?

The baker had called herself the only one left willing to break a rule. But then came this email from steps three and four, not caring if reaching out to Grace was allowed. *I ain't about to ask.* In fact, the only Sequence player she'd encountered so far who hadn't rolled her eyes at some rule? Was Dottie. *I say who, I say when.* Not necessarily the words of a team player.

Katie couldn't help but think of the way Lindsay had bristled at needing a partner's permission for anything. It was uncomfortable for any players in this network to put her in mind of the exact sort of person they'd set out to help. She sipped her wine in contemplative silence, letting her eyes roam the bookshelves where the journal had been.

That's when she saw it: A black-and-gold spine that read simply *Black-Eyed Susans*.

She got to her feet. Crossed breathlessly to the shelf. And with one swift motion, removed the fake dust jacket from the journal underneath. One vague word had been handstamped unevenly into the blue linen cover: *Stories*. She flipped it open and saw that's exactly what the volume contained. In lieu of names, a title headed each page. "Harvest Moon," read Grace's careful handwriting in one top margin. Katie recognized other line items from the log too. "Solar Eclipse." "Cicada Songs."

"I found it!" She leaped back across the room, waving the book triumphantly at Bess, laughing and teary and squealing all at once.

Bess laugh-cry squealed right back, without even knowing yet why. She was that good of a friend. Either that, or she'd had that much wine. "Found what?"

Katie hugged the book to her chest and beamed. "The secret decoder ring."

They spent the night meeting all the Black-Eyed Susans who'd found safe haven with the caretaker. They laughed with them, cried with them, raised their wineglasses to them—drunk with the knowledge that Grace had been collecting their stories after all.

She can sing Joni Mitchell a cappella, pitch-perfect. Says she hasn't let herself listen to it, much less sing it, since she was a twentysomething living alone for the first time. She forgot how much she liked it. Forgot how much she liked a lot of things—wearing baggy, soft sweatpants, and dyeing her hair back to its natural brown, and doing without gel-tip fingernails. She's thinking of picking up a guitar again too. She'd never dare step on any stage, where people might pay too much attention, but that's okay. She set that dream free long ago and doesn't need it back—but she thinks she'd like to play just for herself. She thinks she'd like that very much.

~

She had an honest-to-God fling with a movie star once. Caught his eye when she was an extra in a big-budget action flick filming in town. For one surreal month, it was champagne on private jets, room service at the Ritz. They parted on good terms. She never told anyone. She didn't want anyone else to spoil the magic for her. She still watches all his movies. She never cries until the credits roll—and even then, she's smiling, happy to have had one more night with him, and sad it's over.

~

She has marched on Washington twice for women's rights. "Keep in touch," the fast friends made there would always make each other promise. "Let us know how you're doing, okay?" She never did because she couldn't lie to those people. People who saw through bullshit and fought for justice. The next time there's a rally for a cause she believes in, she's going to go. She's going to hold hands with strangers and raise her voice to join theirs. And afterward, when groups to stay in touch are formed, she's going to be the one scheduling the first meetup.

~

She can recite the recipe for strawberry shortcake by memory—it's her favorite, but she hasn't had it in years. Too many calories. When she demonstrates how to make it, her bone-thin hands work with confident, quick movements, and she narrates as cheerfully as the host of any cooking show. She makes one after another, until the ingredients run out, and eats them three days in a row for breakfast, lunch, and dinner.

Grace managed not to use any identifying details while at the same time finding one story that could never belong to anyone else. Something memorable, brimming with spirit and light.

There was only one thing Katie didn't understand: Why go to all that trouble to honor them—to bear witness, as Katie had felt compelled to do—only to leave them behind, disguised on a shelf where they might never be found? Or, conversely, where they might be found by the wrong person? She'd walked in on Jude perusing these very shelves, even offering to take some of the books off her hands. What if that wasn't the hospitable offer it had seemed? What if he'd been looking for something—for proof, for a record, for *this*? Would Grace really have left that to chance?

Maybe she'd believed any outside threat was negligible, especially given how vague the logs were. Maybe she'd felt more strongly that they weren't her stories to take. Maybe she'd thought they belonged with the house, no matter what. Maybe the plan had been to recruit Katie all along, when the time seemed right, and the baker's slip had simply escalated things.

Or maybe Grace had, one way or another, run out of time.

When Katie couldn't read anymore, when the fire had burned down to coals and Bess had nodded off, Katie began gathering the detritus of their evening onto the coffee table tray. Judging from the empty-wine-bottles count, they'd long ago lost the ability to think clearly. It was time to call it a night. Or, more accurately, a morning.

Only with Bess could a night like this have flown by. Katie felt awash in a wave of drunken gratitude that Bess was here to stop her from spiraling. That she hadn't had to do this alone. Alone out here, without a friend . . . Of course you'd get fed up. Of course you'd get lonely.

Maybe Grace had written these stories down because without anyone to share them with, the only way to move on was to unload the weight of carrying them—to get them out of her head. Maybe that was exactly what Katie needed to do with Grace's story if she had any prayer of doing the same.

But to tell that story, she'd have to really know it. Until she did, she was going to feel like some substitute teacher out here, a placeholder where the real thing should be. That was how she'd spent her whole marriage to Clark. It couldn't be how she started over too.

Katie went to the window, surprised to find herself blinking back tears. The snow had stopped falling, and already that magical quality had gone out of the aftermath. Wind whipped at the trees, sending waves of white scattering through the dark. You could freeze to death out there. How did such things ever seem festive or fun?

She was startled by Bess, who appeared at her side and gently took the tray from her hands. "You okay?" Bess asked. "What are you thinking about?"

Katie wasn't sure she'd ever felt so vulnerable. But she was too tired to be anything but honest. "I'm thinking Grace deserves a page in this book. Writing that story is up to me. But . . . I don't know how to do it. Not yet."

Bess went silent, then nodded. "Okay," she said. "Reading that journal . . . I get it. I'll help. Whatever it takes." Katie could only nod her tearful thanks, and Bess headed for the kitchen, giving her a minute to pull herself together.

"Thank you," she whispered to the empty room.

But it wasn't really empty. Grace was still here. In the framed picture smiling up at her mom, in the handwritten *Stories* of the journal tucked beneath the *Black-Eyed Susans*. And in all the other pieces of herself that—intentionally, reluctantly, or otherwise—she'd left behind.

17

The snow melted as quickly as it came—not into slush, the way it did on warmer winter days, but straight into the soft, spongy ground, where new life beneath the surface lay greedy with thirst. There was no time to mourn those frostbitten first blooms as a thicker carpet of green emerged and hikers flocked to walk among the blue-eyed grass with its tiny lavender flowers.

Katie welcomed the company. She was easing into how it felt to be alone at Grove, the good, the bad, and the in-between. Without the routine of morning walks with Lindsay, she switched to giving things a once-over before closing instead, the way anyone might after hosting visitors for, say, a backyard barbecue. Plus, it was warmer then. But without a companion to walk with, she struggled to keep her imagination out of overdrive.

Grace was on her mind. Constantly. Grace and the Black-Eyed Susans. Where were they now? The women were strangers to her, all of them, but she so badly wanted them to be okay. Scattered to the wind like seeds, blooming where they were planted. She pictured her nieces here this summer, running wild, and thought of the roles no one ever planned to grow into. Victim, for one. And of all the things she wanted to shelter them from. Things no one really could.

She didn't see any more signs of some unidentified person on the property. But sometimes she'd be hauling birdseed or taking new trash bags to the bins, and out of nowhere, the hair would rise on the back of her neck for no reason at all.

Or maybe there was a reason. One evening, just as her stomach started rumbling about dinnertime, she rounded a bend and there, in the center of the trail, stood a mangy coyote. It cocked its head at her, and she froze in the throes of fight-or-flight, receiving the message loud and clear: she'd be shortsighted to get sidetracked by exclusively human worries. It wasn't alarmist to consider what else could befall her out here alone—a falling branch, a broken wrist, a freak animal attack. She always carried her phone now, but in that moment, she knew it wasn't enough. She needed better tools. And a better mindset.

Staring the coyote down, Katie stood her ground—broadening her stance, puffing up into the largest presence she could be. Eventually, the animal turned tail: a small victory.

She could do this. As Bess had wisely pointed out, she'd done it when it mattered.

She kept reminding herself that most of what went on at Grove had nothing to do with her. Take the bird-watchers with their binoculars, camouflaged clothes, and ability to hold so still she often didn't see them until she was upon them. They weren't trying to be creepy. Encountering another person was the last thing they wanted.

It was all just taking some getting used to.

You aren't going to go all Anne of Green Gables on me, are you? Gigi texted one day. Decide you really need a couple of strapping boys as summer farmhands?

Katie texted back: Not a chance. Unrelated question: How much can Cora bench-press?

She did have the sense not to ask how good the kids were with coyotes.

When word finally came that her next loft guest was on her way, Katie was actually glad.

She waited up, so the three rings didn't pull her from bed.

That wasn't the only way everything was quicker this time.

This new woman in the loft was no Lindsay, coming around to talk, finding meaning and beauty in the flowers, shedding the past, dreaming of the future.

She gave no name, answered no questions. She silently wrapped herself in the soft purple robe that had been stuffed in Dottie's backpack. And she cried.

Cried and slept. Slept and cried. She refused food. She looked so terrifyingly pale, it was a wonder she'd made it up the hill alone in the dark. She was a sleepwalker, a ghost, a shadow. Katie didn't worry about her making noise that might draw attention, like she had with Lindsay.

Her worries were very different. All the way at the other end of the spectrum.

Forty-eight hours. That was how long they had to wait until the doctor would arrive.

Katie checked as often as she dared.

Just to make sure the woman in her loft was alive.

Nobody had ever used the call button at the front gate except for visitors Katie knew were coming: cleaning crews, trash pickup. So when FRONT GATE INTERCOM flashed on her phone unexpectedly for the first time, she thrilled a little, feeling official. Until she remembered the button was for problems. Which she likely did not know how to solve.

"Grove Reserve caretaker," she answered, hoping someone had pushed it by accident. The property was open for the day, but she was still in her sweats, on her second cup of coffee.

"Hello?" The voice was male. Male and sheepish. "Sorry about this, but I'm a new member, and I don't think my card is working."

"Is this your first time scanning it?"

"I've used it at the main nature center. First time here, though."

"Sure you're swiping the right side? Maybe try both ways?"

"Believe me, I tried every way before pushing this button. Embarrassment is my last resort."

She laughed. "Maybe there's a malfunction. Pull aside if you can, in case anyone comes in behind you. I'll be right down."

"Thanks, I appreciate this."

Katie hid her unbrushed hair under a knit beanie, pulled on a coat and gloves, and headed out. Bess had left the monster truck golf cart in her care, and Katie had to admit, it was way more fun than her crossover. Not that she'd ever let on to Jude.

At the bridge, the melted snow had the creek running as high as Katie had seen it, and she made a mental note to ask Bess about the benchmarks that should raise concerns about crossing. Still, as she rumbled across the pavement with the water rushing beneath her, she had to admit there were worse ways to wake up. She was learning, little by little, that you couldn't pick and choose what you'd signed up for here on planet Earth—or at Grove Reserve. You took the power with the purity, the danger with the peace.

As the gate came into view, she saw a man about her age leaning against the hood of his SUV, looking very *Top Gun* in a brown leather bomber jacket and sunglasses. It wasn't an impatient pose—in fact, he wasn't watching for her at all, but looking around with admiration, up at the birdsong in the trees, around at the old wooden fences. Katie felt a swell of pride, seeing someone take in the property for the first time. Maybe it was starting to feel like hers after all.

She parked behind the guard shack and hopped out. "Hi," she called. "I'm the caretaker. Let's try this again."

He pulled off his sunglasses and flashed her a smile, and her mind went blank.

Schoolgirl-crush blank. Movie-star-in-real-life blank. First-time-meeting-Clark blank. His eyes were a piercing green, exuding an overtly friendly openness rarely seen in strangers. Especially strangers who were this mind-blankingly good looking.

"Hi, Caretaker. Sorry again about this." He met her at the gate, holding out his membership card with a gloved hand, and she took it, feeling the warmth of his fingers through the knit fabric.

They're just fingers, she told herself, embarrassed by the jolt traveling up her arm. *You've been out here what? Three weeks? Quit reacting as if you've been languishing on some man-less island.*

She sort of had, though. Jude notwithstanding.

"Don't apologize," she said, turning her attention to the scanner. Next week, operating hours would start expanding incrementally for the season. Maybe they'd made some error in preemptively reprogramming the gate. She inserted his card but met resistance before it slid in all the way. She tried again, then again, but still a half inch of plastic protruded into her palm. She lowered her eye to the reader, but it was too dark and narrow to see any obstruction inside.

"Weird." She placed her hand against the metal, which felt even colder than the air, and thought of those winter mornings in high school when there was no room for her car in her parents' garage and the old Ford's door locks would refuse her key.

"I wasn't sure how it normally worked. Your other location had a person at the gate."

"Yeah, we're self-service here. Next time, you'll want it flush with the slot, like this." She demonstrated with her index finger. "For now, I'll have to call someone. Give me a second to find the override. I'll man the gate until maintenance gets here."

She motioned for him to pull his SUV around, then fumbled with the keys at the guard shack door. She'd never been inside before and found it sparse but functional: a rickety stool at the service window, an old wired phone, a stack of trail maps. She plugged in the space heater at her feet, trying not to look too closely at the mess of cobwebs in the corner. Then, feeling déjà vu for her teenage gig working a fast-food drive-through, she slid open the window and scrolled to Jude's number in her phone. She had yet to use it, but there was no avoiding him now. She fired off a text.

Hi. Manning the front gate—scanner not accepting cards. Any chance someone can come take a look? Maybe ice stuck inside?

The SUV slowed to a stop beneath her perch, and the driver flashed that smile again. Propped in his passenger seat was a tripod and a leather bag open to reveal an arsenal of expensive-looking camera gear.

"That's a lot of equipment," Katie observed. "You're a photographer?"

"Trying to be. That's why I bought the membership. I'm revamping my portfolio for this Ohio Arts Council grant application. Thought I'd take a stab at entering your contest while I'm at it."

Katie wouldn't deflate his excitement by telling him how many other people were taking stabs of their own. Bess had invited Katie out to her office a few days ago—to see how staffers reacted to meeting the new caretaker, maybe pick up any weird vibes Bess had missed—and the visitors center had been buzzing with the overwhelming contest response. The grand-prize winner got their photo on next year's membership cards, but there were categories, too, where the best landscape or close-up or animal shot could win concert tickets, aquarium passes, and other prizes Bess had collected from top donors. *I did too good a job,* Bess had moaned. But it hadn't mattered that she'd been stressed and distracted: Katie hadn't found any new leads there anyway.

"Good for you," Katie told the photographer now. From this angle, with her open window perched above his, the rebound of spring all around them was the exact shade of his eyes. "I know how to manipulate photos digitally, but I'm too intimidated to try taking my own."

"I'll teach you if you want. I just need to figure it out quick first."

She laughed. "Still a newbie?"

"More like I got too ambitious upgrading my equipment. I'm just a hobbyist, but I'm also kind of a perfectionist, so . . . suffice to say I never get far."

"Well," Katie said, "you might be at an advantage for venturing off main campus for your shots. So many people overlook this annex."

"I hear it's the best-kept secret."

"I think so."

There was that sheepish grin again. "I'm Ryan, by the way. You might see me around a lot, but I promise to be low maintenance. At the very least I'll learn to work the card scanner."

"Katie. Nice to meet you. And no worries—that's what I'm here for."

"How long have you been caretaker?"

"Ages. I just celebrated my three-week anniversary."

He laughed. "So we're both still learning."

"We are. But I'm not entering any kind of caretaker contest."

"That's too bad. I like to root for the underdog."

Katie's stomach fluttered. Was he . . . were they . . . *flirting*? He seemed so naturally good-natured and warm, it felt presumptuous to think he was targeting these feelings toward her specifically.

Yet these feelings were unmistakably coming at her, happening in her, right now.

He draped his arm over his open window. "What all do you do out here?" he asked. "Besides rescue dolts like me?"

"I don't just rescue dolts," she assured him. "I'm an equal opportunity rescuer."

She regretted the joke immediately. Too close to home.

"Kidding, of course," she hurried on. "It's much more boring than that. Although this week I *do* get to learn to use two different types of lawnmowers. So if you're coming out to avoid yard-work noise, don't come on Thursdays."

"And if I wanted to photograph the grasses you don't mow? The fields for pollinators? The best place would be . . ."

She unfolded a trail map from the stack and handed it over, pointing. "Probably here, around this purple trail."

"Excellent. Maybe I'll see you out there sometime." He was looking at her like he could keep chatting all day—no way was she imagining this. And she was looking like . . . Yikes. She hadn't even glanced in the mirror before running down here. Her cheeks felt windburned from the ride, her nose surely red from the cold. She hoped he hadn't noticed she was basically wearing the clothes she'd slept in.

Katie's phone buzzed.

Are you aware, read Jude's response, ice does not 'stick' in temps above freezing?

She fired back: IDK, the scanner feels colder???

Her screen lit with a facepalm emoji. The nerve.

Whatever the cause, she typed furiously, it's not operational. If I could request assistance along with the science lesson, please?

She returned her attention to Ryan's expectant gaze, but before either of them could speak again, a minivan rounded the entrance. Katie could hear the kids fighting from here.

"Mommy said share!" someone screeched.

"I go first!"

"It's mine too!"

"*Moooooom!*"

Katie and Ryan exchanged a rueful look, and she gallantly pushed the button to raise the gate. "Kids are all about snack breaks," she whispered conspiratorially. "Maybe steer clear of the picnic area."

"Smart. Thanks for the hot tips." The way he said the word "hot" turned her cheeks warm.

"Sure. And thanks for . . ." She panicked. There was absolutely nothing to thank him for.

"We'll come up with something," he said with that good-natured laugh. "I owe you."

Katie couldn't stop smiling as he pulled away.

Ever since she got here, she'd been looking ahead to all her next steps with trepidation.

What a refreshing switch to have something to look forward to instead.

18

Katie had thought it might be creepy to watch security footage of her gate, but the reality was just mundane. With the photography contest rollout calming down, she and Bess had set aside this Thursday morning hour to convene for some due diligence in the wake of the scanner jam.

It turned out a tiny piece of paper had found its way into the slot, likely by accident. Plenty of members kept their membership cards in their cars' cup holders, so it wasn't hard to imagine a gum wrapper or some other scrap sticking to a card and dislodging with the swipe. In fact, it was harder to believe this sort of thing hadn't happened before.

Jude had consulted the gate's video stream and reported—with no small irritation—that the camera lens was too dirty from all the spring muck to have captured much of anything, let alone signs of tampering. Katie had never seen anyone stomp off wielding glass cleaner quite so fiercely. Meanwhile Bess, true to form, had decided the whole incident was a stroke of luck in disguise. "Now we can stop obsessing about all this covert stuff and start obsessing about your meet-cute," she teased. Not that there was much to discuss. "All I need to know," Bess had said, "is that hottie photographer's name isn't Clark. Sold!"

Still. They were overdue to check up on some other things too.

Bess's office was in a quiet rear corner of the visitors' center, private but small enough that Katie had to squeeze onto the narrow windowsill behind Bess's desk to look over her shoulder at the laptop screen. They were scrutinizing a spreadsheet of every member who'd scanned their card last month at the annex gate, working backward from the day of the jam. The names were meaningless, aside from the staffers. No surprises, no red flags.

"Here's the last visitor before the snowstorm." Bess called up the member profile. Lindy Samuelson in no way resembled the *I Love Lucy*–haired grandma Katie had met—not that they'd expected her to. Her headshot taken at the membership desk showed a woman with poker-straight hair and bright-white teeth—a forty-four-year-old single mother of three. "She's one of the most active visitors at Grove," Bess said, skimming her account history. "At least, her membership card is. It makes an appearance almost weekly, year-round, and not always at the end of the day."

That was interesting. More frequent than Katie expected. Then again, maybe Dottie was legitimately close to this legitimately active visitor—an aunt, neighbor, friend. Maybe she'd arranged to borrow her card for exactly that reason: to blend in. Bess toggled back to her browser window and pulled up the security footage of Dottie's—or Lindy's—car leaving with Lindsay ahead of the snowstorm, but Jude wasn't kidding about the dirty camera lens. They couldn't make out the driver's face or the license plate, and no passenger was visible. The best they could do would be watch for the same card to come through again, give Katie a heads-up when someone affiliated with the Sequence may be on the grounds.

"You have to admit," Katie said, "it's kind of brilliant for them to transport the women this way, hiding in plain sight." She was learning herself just how many layers of *hiding in plain sight* there could be. And maybe they were all less risky than the alternative.

Even if it didn't always feel that way.

"Great minds," Bess said. "I'm hiding in plain sight right now. Everyone knows I'm only at my desk as a last resort, so if I'm holed up in here, they don't interrupt."

Naturally, someone chose that moment to rap on the doorframe, and they both startled to see Jude walk right on in uninvited.

"Good," he said by way of greeting. "You're both here."

Bess lowered her laptop screen, clearly annoyed, as he closed the door behind him, trapping them where no one could interrupt his interruption. Was he really this oblivious to social norms? It was hard to say: he typically bypassed them entirely by being *anti*-social.

"I'll be blunt," he said, plopping down in the chair opposite Bess's desk. As if he'd ever been anything *but* blunt. "I'd like to be assigned more work out at Grove."

Katie blinked at him in confusion. Was she falling that short of expectations?

"Why Grove?" she asked, at the same time as Bess said, "What kind of work?"

"Whatever needs done."

Come to think of it, Jude had been nowhere to be seen last week when Bess brought Katie here to meet more of the main campus team. Under different circumstances, it might have been a demoralizing day, as one staffer after the next made it clear how seldom they thought of Grove, taking a little too long to connect the dots. Oh, right, *this* is Grace's replacement! It was obvious they'd forgotten to wonder whatever happened with that. As Katie had taken it in stride, it had sunk in what an outlier her outpost really was. Grove was the place they recommended to members who complained the main trails were too crowded. Grove was the place they offered to scout troops and other groups with less budget and more sense of adventure. Grove was a place where they themselves would love to spend more time . . . if they weren't getting their fill at the nature center proper. Katie asked plenty of questions, but by the end of the day, neither she nor Bess had collected any new insights about Grace—and she was starting to understand why. Not to mention feel better about how little attention anyone was paying to their goings-on.

Yet here was Jude, paying all kinds of attention. The wrong kind.

"I'll tell you the truth about why," he answered with an odd sincerity, as if lying was an option he'd decided against. Then he turned to Katie. "I know I'm rubbing you the wrong way. Anytime I set foot out there, you assume I don't think you're capable. If I've been *assigned*, maybe we can move past that. I'm not looking to ruffle feathers, only to help."

Bess bit back a smile. "Jude," she said, "I don't know how to tell you this, but you're widely regarded as a feather ruffler of the first degree. You haven't seemed to mind before."

"Haven't I?" he said coolly, and Bess's smile faded. She'd once told Katie that if the nature center had its own reality show, Jude would be the one with a montage of him saying, *I'm not here to make friends*. But if he'd never actually said that . . . how could anyone really know?

"So you . . . do think I'm capable?" Katie asked.

He blinked at her. "I think everyone new has a lot to learn, and you can learn the easy way or the hard way. The safe way or the dangerous way." He turned back to Bess. "The other day, she was cruising in that four-wheeler you gave her and—"

"How was I supposed to know there was a nest of baby rabbits?" Katie interrupted. "That could have happened to anyone."

But he went right on tattling. "She bailed," he said humorlessly, even though Bess was covering her mouth by now to stifle her laugh "Nearly flipped the thing. Imagine my surprise to find bunnies. The way she was squealing, I thought rat snakes—but those, hate to break it to her, are nesting in her barn. Along with yellow jackets."

Katie cringed, exchanging a guilty look with Bess. They'd spent so much time worrying about her nighttime duties, they *may* have neglected to make enough headway on the daytime stuff. The stuff people like Jude were bound to notice.

Another knock on the door interrupted them, and Bess waved in a delivery man holding a small package. "Sorry, need a signature on this one," he said. "Hazardous materials."

Bess took the box, puzzled. "Attn: Caretaker?" *Not now,* Katie groaned inwardly. She'd meant to give Bess a heads up—she'd only needed a reliable delivery address. But before she could stop her, Bess had torn open the seam and extracted a bubble-wrapped can. Of bear mace.

Jude shook his head at Katie. "I tried to tell you there are no bears."

Her face burned. She wasn't sure mentioning the coyote would help her case.

"Mace is never a bad idea," Bess said, shooting Katie a look as she scribbled her signature for the deliveryman. He showed himself out. "I'm sure it works on other things too."

Jude nodded, straight-faced. "Bunnies? Blue jays?"

Katie smiled tightly. "Maintenance men who show up unannounced."

"What's this really about, Jude?" Bess said. "Yes, Katie has some things to learn. But on-the-job training isn't so unusual around here. It's trial by fire."

He didn't hesitate. "This paper jam in the card reader . . . I don't like it."

Hearing him say it so matter-of-factly—*I don't like it*—Katie had a moment of doubt. But only one Sequence member she knew of ever used the card reader, and whether the woman in question was Lucille Ball or Lindy Samuelson or Carmen Sandiego, she'd been scanning that card for years without issue. Everyone else involved bypassed it, after hours. It didn't make sense anyone would tamper with the scanner to mess with *them.*

"I thought we all agreed that was a fluke," Katie said.

"Maybe it was," Jude grumbled. "But what if it wasn't? Our surveillance is inadequate. I know the budget is set for the year, but—"

"It's good enough for me," Bess cut in. "Besides, what purpose would it serve to jam the card reader? It's more annoying than concerning." Incongruously, Katie wished Dottie could see Bess now. Katie had *told* them they could count on her, and they could.

"I don't know." Jude's frustration was palpable. "I just have this feeling. I notice things, okay? Why *not* let me help out here and there? Just until we see if anything like this happens again. My other work won't slip."

It was Bess's turn to flush crimson. "Look, I know I've been more involved than usual since I'm Katie's"—she caught herself before saying *friend*—"liaison. But you know I oversee programming, not operations."

"Program something for me to do then."

Bess hesitated, shooting Katie a look, a *What do you think?* Katie's heart sank as she saw a gleam of hope in it: Bess wouldn't hate the idea of someone keeping an eye out for her. But Katie would. If there was one thing Katie didn't want right now, it was anyone having any kind of feelings about what might be going on in her loft. Especially Jude, who'd been poking around her barn, her bookshelf . . . Katie shook her head, almost imperceptibly. But Bess saw.

"I'm guessing Grace didn't like yellow jackets or snakes either," Katie pointed out, "but you never took her for a damsel in distress."

"True," Bess chimed in. "In fact, I seem to remember you resisting assignments at Grove. I've heard you refer to Grace as *difficult* more than once."

Jude looked at Katie meaningfully. A little too meaningfully. "Well, Katie isn't Grace," he said finally. "And I think we agree no one should expect her to be."

Was it possible she was reading too much into this? Possible he just had an ordinary soft spot for her, even if he did have a funny way of showing it?

"Can we stop talking about me in the third person now?" Katie asked.

"I didn't mean anything by it. Summer is coming. The high season sees way more people in and out. I just don't want you to end up feeling in over your head. That's all."

He had an awkward way with words. And with meaningful looks. With all looks, really. This was probably just . . . Jude being Jude.

Either that, or he knew something Katie and Bess didn't.

Or something they did.

Something that worried him. Something that wasn't worrying them enough. *I notice things,* he'd said. Bess must have sensed something beneath the words, too, because she didn't answer. Neither of them did.

Jude sighed, getting to his feet. "For the record," he said, "Grace made it clear she didn't want my help. Even when I—I did try." He cleared his throat. "Grace made it clear she didn't want my help," he repeated. He looked . . . well, upset, actually. "I'll leave you to it. Offer stands if you change your mind. Plenty to do that'd put me near the house if anyone needs anything."

If anyone needs anything. Katie felt a twinge of remorse as he started for the door. All this time, she and Bess had been so frustrated they couldn't get answers from anyone. Yet here they were, getting irritated at the first person who might be trying to tell them something.

Even if he wouldn't come out and say what it was.

She was about to call out when he turned. "I know you all think I'm not a people person. But I have instincts. Before I came to work here, I trained to do more than just change light bulbs. And I would have graduated fine if I hadn't decided to drop out." He opened the door and gave them a wave. "Police academy."

19

The woman in the loft had not run out of tears. Nor had she taken more than a few bites of any meal—not even the homemade noodle soup Katie made in a futile attempt at comfort through food. Katie still bristled to think of the way Dottie had assured her: *We'll cover you, no matter what happens.* As if Katie had been worried about herself. What Katie had been after was advice on how to walk this line she was now teetering on. The line between giving the woman privacy to grieve and keeping close enough watch over her well-being.

Her only consolation was that forty-eight hours was almost up.

Tonight, Dr. Clooney would make his house call.

Granted, she had new reasons to be on edge. Mainly, Jude practically flashing his police badge out of nowhere. Katie had been dumbfounded. Worse, he'd left her and Bess at odds.

Maybe we should take him up on it, Bess had whisper-shouted, once they were sure he was gone. *This can't really be about the card reader. Was it just me, or did it seem like he might be onto you?* Katie flopped into the chair he'd vacated as Bess worried on. *How do we know Grace didn't tell him everything? We shouldn't read too much into the fact that they didn't seem like friends. You said the members of this network aren't supposed to appear linked.*

If Katie had been honest, she'd have said, *Of course it's not just you.* Her knee-jerk reaction, as soon as the words were out of Jude's mouth, had been fear. She tried to reassure herself that this was unwarranted, that

Jude's background as an almost-cop need not be relevant unless she was doing something wrong. Which she wasn't. At least, she was pretty sure.

But she'd been too overwhelmed by the responsibility of it all. There was a woman in her loft right that minute. A woman who'd been thrown pregnant from a car, for crying out loud. If Katie slipped up now, misread signals, let the wrong person get too close, she wouldn't just lose the tentative trust of the Sequence. She could *ruin it*. People could suffer just because she was too chicken to go it alone.

So she'd tried to reason with Bess instead: If Grace had entrusted Jude with all this, why wouldn't he just come out and say so? Why not pull Katie aside at Grove instead of waiting for an audience in Bess's office? Besides, it was hardly unusual for a conversation with Jude to take a bizarre turn. This was complicated enough without adding him to the mix.

But Bess hadn't been reassured. Instead, she'd professed that maybe Katie didn't have any business being in the mix either. Especially if Jude was implying that he thought she needed a bodyguard. *Was* that what he'd been implying? Neither of them could be sure.

All Katie could do was take a forced, logical step back and remind Bess they'd both known this job would be out of her comfort zone. Obviously not this far out, but Katie hadn't come to be intimidated into letting someone police her personal space. Or to make Bess hold her hand through every little thing. She needed time to figure this out on her own. She'd still feel a lot better if she knew what happened with Grace. But obviously if she thought she was in real danger, she wouldn't continue down this road.

Bess had blinked back tears of frustration. *You promise? Because I brought you here. I talked you into this—I talked everyone into this. If anything happens, I'll never be able to live with myself.*

Katie hadn't wanted to fight. She hadn't wanted to have this conversation at all. But looking at Bess's obvious distress, she could see that someone else had needed to.

I promise, she'd said.

So here she was. Back to work. And hoping she didn't have some duty to tell the Sequence what had happened today. Because she had no intention of doing so.

As sunset backlit the treetops with full-spectrum pink, she switched all the outdoor lights from the motion-activated setting to the On position, thinking of those old Motel 6 commercials. "We'll leave the light on for you." She poured a glass of ice water—having read it was more effective than coffee for staying awake—and settled on the couch, determined to distract herself with a night of binge-watching. She'd moved here with a mental list of shows Clark had vetoed over the years, but nearly a month into living on her own, she'd scarcely watched a thing. Which had everything to do with being hyperaware of every moment she wasn't *on her own* at all.

Even now, she kept staring at the front door instead of absorbing the dialogue on-screen.

The hands of the wall clock crawled forward. Ten o'clock came and went, then eleven. Dottie's email had said the doctor would arrive by midnight. Katie told herself it would make no difference to stand at the window, staring into the darkness. She gave up on the TV and opened a book without seeing it. If she exuded patience she didn't feel, the doorbell would surely sound.

By 12:40, Katie was going from anxious to worried. Maybe they'd gotten their signals crossed, or he was running late. But what if something was truly wrong, and Katie was just . . . sitting here? What if something—or someone—had spooked him off or kept him away? What if—it was impossible not to think it—this had something to do with Jude's sudden interest in Grove and monitoring the gate?

She closed her eyes, forced herself to feel the ridges of the couch cushions, to focus on her breathing and slow the unwinding of endless possibilities. Why hadn't she demanded an emergency phone number to call? Why had she assumed that once the Sequence stepped in, things would run like clockwork? She'd had every indication things didn't always go as planned.

After all, that was the only reason she was here at all.

❀

Katie must have dozed off. The next thing she knew, the buzzer was cutting through the silence—once, twice, three times—and it was past 4:00 a.m.

Standing in the halo of her porch light was a man she could only describe as a caricature, stepped right off the sketch artist's easel. Everything about him was exaggerated, from his towering height to his thin, belted waist, from his bushy, white mustache and matching wild eyebrows to his soup-ladle chin and candy-cane ears. He was hunched forward, hugging a leather duffel to his chest, and she remembered how Dottie's eyes had turned teasing when Katie asked if he was "a McDreamy type." *I'll say this: he picked his own code name.*

Katie cracked open the door.

"NCT?" he asked. His eyes were kind. "I'm Dr. Clooney. Terribly sorry to arrive so late."

She swung the door open wider. "Everything okay?"

"Fine, fine. I try not to be on call on Sequence days, but as luck would have it my practice had more than one patient go into labor this evening. Must be the full moon."

She glanced up, and sure enough, it was casting such a bright glow she needn't have left the lights on at all.

"You're an ob-gyn?" He nodded, and she found herself smiling, realizing she'd been picturing some repurposed doctor, like in the movies when mobsters have veterinarians dress their bullet wounds.

"Two healthy baby girls tonight," he went on. "Beautiful and yet blissfully unaware of my after-hours schedule." He offered a weak smile. "I don't suppose I could trouble you for a cup of tea?"

"Of course." Katie was fully awake now, ushering him in, mind back to spinning. She hadn't dared hope for an audience with the doctor. This was another chance: to ask about Grace, and the next steps, and anything else that could stretch the limits of her "need-to-know" basis.

She offered him a chair at the kitchen table and filled the electric kettle. "Being an OB seems like a good cover for this gig," she ventured. "Guess it makes it easy to run out at any hour?"

"You guess correctly. My wife jokes she's counting the days until I retire because of the hours—but she's not fooling me, she's been sleeping with earplugs for forty years. She only notices me going anywhere when she's already awake." He said this with such unabashed affection toward his wife, Katie warmed to him instantly.

"You're retiring soon?"

"Soon enough that I'm the perfect person to be here. Heaven forbid someone finds out I'm making unauthorized house calls, they can hardly threaten to end my career."

Katie hadn't considered that a licensed professional like Dr. Clooney had more to lose by helping. It wasn't as if someone like Sienna was defying any state pastry chef regulations. She set a variety pack of tea bags in front of him, along with honey and a spoon.

"How often are these house calls necessary?" she asked.

"If we're doing our jobs right, they're never necessary," he said. "We get them out before they get banged up enough to need me. But realistically? Few times a year."

She wondered what he'd think if he knew that not two weeks ago, she'd had a woman here with a gash in her head and let it go unchecked. Of course, she hadn't known she had the option, and Lindsay was fine—but they'd been lucky, and Katie knew it.

"Nice of you to help," she said, weakly.

"Not sure it's nice. Only decent. When you've seen the things I've seen . . ." He accepted the steaming mug she handed him. "Thank you. I really am sorry to impose. You must be knackered." Of everyone in the

Sequence she'd met so far, he definitely had the best bedside manner. She decided to take a chance.

"You mentioned retirement. Did Gra—I mean, the last caretaker—ever mention plans to retire?"

"Not in so many words, but I can't say I was surprised." This tracked with what everyone else had been saying. The baker, the unread email in the CT123 inbox. Katie wasn't sure why she didn't find it more reassuring. "Kind of you to take up the torch."

"Not sure it's kind," Katie parroted. "Only decent."

He smiled. "Dottie warned me you'd ask a lot of questions about Grace."

So much for that tactic. Although *warned* seemed like a strong word. "I suppose she also warned you not to answer them?"

"If I were a man who heeded warnings, I wouldn't be here. My only priority is to honor the best interests of the women in my care. In a way, I always felt that included Grace—and, I suppose, now you."

It wasn't lost on Katie that in the safety of these walls, he'd said Grace's name.

"The number-one rule in caring for women—and not just in health care—is to understand nine times out of ten, they're not putting themselves first. I have women come into my office on the verge of serious medical emergencies, and all they want to know is whether the babies putting their bodies into distress will be okay. They forget the best thing they can do for the baby is take care of themselves. Dottie would never admit it's the same for her, but from where I'm sitting, the Sequence is her baby. And yours is Grove. You're both focused on the thing you're charged to take care of. I'm more concerned with looking out for the two of you."

Katie found it hard to speak. A lump was blocking her throat. Damn Jude and his vague double-talk. *Katie isn't Grace . . . and I think we agree no one should expect her to be.* She'd wanted to tell him no one did expect it. Not the Sequence—they'd made that clear. And not Bess either.

But maybe Katie did.

She slid into the seat across from the doctor, and he gave her hand a pat before taking a tentative sip of his tea.

"So you *will* tell me about Grace?" she managed.

"I'll tell you this: I wouldn't be here—or let you be—if I thought my presence would put you in any danger. As for Grace, she can take care of herself."

Katie wanted to believe him. But if he truly saw it as his priority to set her mind at ease, that didn't necessarily mean he'd follow with the truth.

"Some of the things I've found here . . ." she began carefully. "For instance, there's this folder of children's artwork labeled 'Mom.' If that was left in your waiting room, wouldn't you feel bad not asking around, trying to get that back to somebody, knowing they might be missing it?"

"Actually, if I've learned anything from my waiting room, it's that patient confidentiality is key. Asking around is a breach of that, even with good intentions." He studied her. "What did you do before you came here?"

"I helped run a web design business."

"Ah. Lots of analysis, right? Unique visitors, click rates, that sort of thing?"

"Exactly."

"Makes sense. You're programmed to analyze the Sequence. To figure out who's involved and why, and what's in it for us—the exact return on our investment. It's natural when you've been thinking along those lines for so long. But with us, not everything needs analyzed. I've had to learn to separate the two myself. My work at the hospital is complicated: Even with decades of experience, I'm required to justify my actions in mountains of paperwork, down to the last Tylenol. What's beautiful about the Sequence is that it's simple. I play a small part, do my best, and trust the others to do the same. And if the day comes when they don't want to do it anymore? I respect that too. The last thing I'd do is track them down and demand to know why."

Katie felt properly chagrined. "I—I didn't mean—" But Dr. Clooney waved his hand.

"It's neither here nor there. Of course you wish you knew Grace's whole story, and whose folder that is. Part of me still feels that way about everyone who comes through. But you can and you do move on without it. The only sane way through is to trust the process, accept the simple explanation instead of running yourself ragged and making people nervous. Nothing wrong with listening to your doctor instead of googling your symptoms until you're scared half to death."

At that, Katie couldn't help but laugh. "I appreciate the perspective."

He nodded, drinking more deeply from his tea. "Now, for your houseguest. How is she?"

"I'm worried about her. She cries constantly. Doesn't eat much. Has barely said a word."

"She's been through a lot. You're doing a good thing, providing this space for her. Maybe her kind of suffering craves privacy more than anything—and dignity. You don't get that in a hospital, and it's been a long time since she had it at home either."

She was finding it impossible not to nod in earnest agreement with everything he said. In the increasingly unlikely event that Katie ever had a baby, she'd want him as her doctor. He gave her that feeling she used to get around her mom: that at her most vulnerable, if he were to offer so much as a compassionate look or a hug, she'd lose all composure just because someone understood. Just because someone cared.

She hoped the woman in the loft would feel the same. She deserved someone she could trust. Though admittedly, it might be tough to trust anyone who woke you from your hiding place in the middle of the night for a follow-up exam.

"Was she your real patient?" Katie asked. "I mean, does she know you?"

"The patients here are the realest ones I've got," he said. "But if it'd make you feel better to walk out there with me, let's do."

"It's not that I don't trust you, it's just . . ."

"It's just that you're better suited to this than you think." He got to his feet. "Come."

20

The outbuilding was quiet, and when Katie unlocked the door to the stairwell, no glow of light shone beneath the loft door. But as she and Dr. Clooney climbed the stairs, they heard humming. They stopped, listening.

"It's a Coldplay song," Katie whispered after a minute. "'Sky Full of Stars.'"

"At least we're not waking her," he whispered back, and rapped quietly on the door. Three times, like at the caretaker's house.

The humming stopped. The face that came to the door looked puffy and sad, but the tears had dried—for now. Katie introduced the doctor, and the woman shyly extended her hand.

"I'm . . . um, I'm . . ." She froze, and Katie's heart twisted. No one's name should become that kind of crossroads. A question that, if answered honestly, could come back to haunt you.

"I love that song you were humming," Katie offered. "Maybe we could call you Sky?"

"Sky," she repeated, and there, for the first time, was the faintest shadow of a smile.

"Are you comfortable if I step out and give you and the doctor some privacy?"

She nodded. Katie was starting back down the stairs when Sky spoke again. "Wait. A bit ago . . ." Katie turned. "Did you hear a baby crying?"

Katie frowned. "A baby? Like, outside?"

"Yes. And earlier today. And last night."

Katie concentrated on not meeting Dr. Clooney's eye. Even in her peripheral vision, she could glimpse his concern. "There's a barn cat," she said. "Maybe you heard her mewing?"

Sky shook her head. "Not a cat. A baby. I hear it when you leave, when it gets quiet. I keep thinking I'm imagining it, but . . . That's why I was humming. To block it out."

Katie scrambled for some plausible explanation. She knew firsthand that grief after a miscarriage was very real. She knew a little about postpartum depression, too, and any combination of a hormone crash and severe trauma was nothing to mess with.

"I keep a radio in the barn for when I'm working outside. Maybe it got left on, and it's cutting in and out."

"Not a radio." Sky got more adamant. "A baby. I hoped you'd heard it. I need someone else to hear it, to tell me I'm not going insane." Sky blinked back tears. Katie wanted to tell her she didn't have to put on a brave face, but she wasn't sure it was true.

"You've been through the worst kind of trauma," Dr. Clooney said at last. "And layers of loss. Anyone in your shoes would be overwhelmed in every possible way."

"I know this sounds bad. I swear, I don't *feel* crazy. Just sad."

"You have every right to be sad," Dr. Clooney said. "And you have every right to be safe. That's all we want for you."

She began to cry in earnest. "He called me crazy. He doesn't mince words. He's going to be a lawyer, like his dad. The house I grew up in could fit in his family's living room. I used to feel so lucky he picked me to join his perfect life. If I was ever delusional, it was then, not now."

Katie met Dr. Clooney's eyes. Sky had spoken more in this exchange than in the last two days, and Katie hated to go. But she knew from his expression it would be best if she did.

"I can't say for sure you didn't hear something," Katie told Sky. "Only that I didn't. I'll listen for it from now on, okay?"

Futile though it might be, she intended to keep the promise. It was the least she could do.

Katie waited nearly an hour, wrapped in a blanket on the porch, before Dr. Clooney returned. The moon was dipping toward the trees, making room for the sun to rise. He had to get going. Outside the gate, his car would be hidden enough from the road in the dark. In daylight, not so much.

Katie handed him a reheated cup of tea. "How is she?"

He took a swallow and winced. From the stale tea or the question, she couldn't tell. "Physically she's healing. It's that business about hearing a baby that concerns me. I'd feel better if we could get her to the next step as quickly as possible. Here, she's alone with her thoughts so much . . ." He gazed despondently at the waning moon, and guilt washed over Katie.

"I could keep her company more," Katie said. "I was taking cues from her, but—"

"I didn't mean to imply any failing on your part. You'd put her at risk being out there during hours when someone could come looking for you. But when she reaches the next step, someone will be with her. That's safer. Though I'll need to give them a heads-up." He was thinking out loud now. "On the back end, I can see that her mental health is looked after once she gets where she's going. I just need to think of how to shepherd this. It's hard to reach Dottie early, when she's with social work and . . ." He stopped short. "I'm saying too much."

"You're not," Katie assured him. "And I appreciate you giving me the benefit of the doubt. I've been in the dark about what even happens when they leave here. Don't you think I'd be better at my role if I understood all the other pieces of this puzzle?"

His cartoonish eyebrows lifted. "That's quite the argument. Sure you're not gunning for the role of Sequence lawyer?"

"There's a lawyer?"

"Of course there's a lawyer. What kind of backwoods operation do you take this for?"

Without warning, a scuffling came from beneath the porch floorboards where they stood, followed by a series of snarls. They both startled as a furry blur bolted toward the forest, visible only for the white line down its back. Katie held her breath, waiting for the telltale stink of the skunk, and when none came, burst out laughing. Dr. Clooney joined in, his laugh hearty and warm, and soon they were both doubled over, howling at the uncanny timing.

"Not backwoods at all," Katie said, when she could finally collect herself.

Dr. Clooney's smile didn't quite fade, even as he turned serious. He looked at her for a long moment, evaluating. "The next steps happen in tandem," he began. Katie's mind flicked to Grace's unread email presumably from steps 3 and 4, two women who not only worked together but also were planning their wedding. "They get a new identity, Social Security number, the bare bones required to get a job, rent a place, start fresh. And they get a ride out of town."

"To where?"

"It varies. A trucker handles Step 4. They tag along and get off at a predetermined stop on her route."

So that was why the email had referenced road trips appealing more to one of the partners. A *ride-along*, she'd called it.

"That's all there is to it?" Katie asked.

"I'm sure there's a lot more to it. Steps three and four are the swiftest, most self-contained. This is the first time I've ever wished I knew how to reach them."

"I know how to reach them," Katie heard herself say.

He looked at her in surprise. She didn't know how the doctor would feel about her hacking Grace's inbox. Or what Dottie would think if it got back to her. "I don't want to get anyone in trouble," she hastened to add. "But I have their email address. We could reach out, see if they can take her now instead of waiting."

His fingers went to his mustache. "I wish it was as easy as them saying yes. We'd still need to make arrangements to get Sky out of here, and whatever else."

"I can take her," Katie offered. "I saw how Dottie did it. In plain sight. No one's in plainer sight than me."

She could tell he saw the sense in the suggestion, though it made him obviously uncomfortable. But their priority was Sky. How would they feel if she self-harmed or something terrible happened while they were waiting to do things by the book?

She said as much.

"You're not wrong." He shook his head. "You sure you never met Grace? Pushing the envelope was her thing. I can already hear Dottie: *What is it with these caretakers?*"

Katie tilted her head. "Why do I get the sense everyone is a little afraid of Dottie? What's so envelope-pushing about finding a creative solution? Maybe it won't work. They won't see the email, or they're not ready for her. But we can at least try."

"Okay." He hoisted his duffel over his shoulder. "Seeing as how you badgered me into it with an attack skunk." Katie laughed. "If they can fast-track this, ask them to call me—desperate times, right? Let me give you my number." Katie handed over her phone, and just like that, this was happening. "If it's a no go, just do your best to check on Sky today. If she takes a turn, well . . . you have my number now too."

"What about filling in Dottie?"

"Leave her to me."

They shook on it. He set off down the moonlit driveway, and Katie watched him go, his flashlight bobbing on, shining against the dark. Bright, true, determined.

Maybe she could be like that too.

21

Katie heard the man before she saw him. She couldn't make out the name he was calling, but the tone brought to mind a playground taunt. *Come out, come out, wherever you are . . .*

Her hands clenched the steering wheel as she slowed around the bend, shooting a nervous glance at Sky, who peered back at her, wide-eyed, from the floor of the passenger seat, where she was curled out of sight.

"Tracy! *Traaaaaaaacy!*"

The man up ahead had to be the same one she and Bess had seen across the pond, calling for the same mischievous beagle, but he wasn't facing her. He was walking down the middle of the road the same way she was headed, between her and the bridge. Between her and the gate. Between her and Sky's ticket to safety.

Why today of all days? Her heart leaped into her throat. *Stay calm.*

"I'm not Tracy," Sky whimpered before Katie could ask. Wordlessly, Katie pointed to the blanket she'd tossed on the passenger seat as an afterthought, and Sky hastened to cover herself, balling up tighter while Katie assessed the scene. She couldn't avoid him. She'd just be quick about passing. Act natural.

She slowed to a crawl, and at last he noticed the car's motor behind him. His face registered recognition as he raised an arm in an apologetic wave and moved toward the shoulder to let her pass. She saw that this time, he held a blue leash with a broken collar at one end. But the sight of it did nothing to slow the adrenaline coursing through her body.

The road was so narrow, there was no way around saying something. She lowered her window halfway. The key was to keep driving, so he wouldn't take this as an invitation to approach. Transporting Sky herself had been her idea. She couldn't botch it.

"Again?" she called out, eyebrows raised.

He threw up his arms. "Call of the wild, I guess. I'm trying not to take it personally."

Katie forced a laugh. She had a brief thought that she should ask Bess to pull up the gate footage later. Verify he really had come in with a dog. Find out his name. Anything to shake this feeling that something didn't sit right. *Plenty of things,* she assured herself, *are exactly what they seem.* It could be a coincidence that both times she'd seen him, she'd had a guest on-site.

"Well," she told him, "good luck."

The man didn't miss a beat. He waved and kept right on calling.

"We're okay," she breathed, as much to herself as to Sky, once he was behind them.

But even after they were out on the main road, even after Sky buckled in like an ordinary passenger, the cadence of the encounter echoed in Katie's mind. That taunting *Tracy, Traaaaacy.*

The fainter it played in her memory, the more it sounded like *Katie* instead.

Whoever was behind steps three and four had not asked Katie how she'd gotten their email. Nor had they balked at her request to escalate the timeline. They'd simply replied with instructions on where to bring Sky immediately: starting from not an address but an intersection of county highways twenty miles east, farther still from Cincinnati and any other sizable town. The directions were all visual: once you see a row of four tall corn silos, watch to your right for a one-lane road. After the abandoned school bus, take the gravel turnoff by the fruit stand. Katie wasn't sure if GPS got spotty out there, or if they didn't want their address on record where someone could find it.

She handed over her phone and Sky read the steps aloud as they drove past modernized farms butting up to impoverished homesteads. In one yard, a poster of a newborn has been nailed to two-by-fours. RIGHT TO LIFE, it read in block letters. Katie caught Sky's cringe.

"I had a miscarriage once." Katie just said it. She didn't think it through. But she found Sky looking back at her expectantly. "It doesn't compare to what you're going through," Katie added. "But in case it helps to know I can relate to one small aspect."

"I'm sorry," Sky said. "Were you married?" To Katie's relief, she didn't sound offended, only interested. Not that Katie really wanted to talk about this. She kept her eyes on the road.

"Not at first. He proposed after I got pregnant. It should've been obvious he was only doing it because he felt obligated. I mean, it *was* obvious. But it didn't stop me from saying yes." Over a decade later, Katie still couldn't discuss it without the humiliation flooding back. But if it would help Sky to keep chatting, take her mind off things . . . it might help Katie too. To say this aloud to someone whose very presence was a reminder that Katie's story was no great tragedy.

No comparison. No big deal.

"The father—Clark—was my college boyfriend's best friend." Katie spoke quickly, to just get through it. "My boyfriend, Steve, was one of those happy-go-lucky guys everybody likes. A human Labrador. Clark was his roommate, off studying abroad for a semester when Steve and I started dating. And it was a great semester. Fun, easy. From the moment I met Clark, though, I had this sinking feeling I'd met the wrong one of them first. I'm not proud of it."

"You two cheated?" Sky's tone wasn't judgmental.

It was still hard to explain this story wasn't like that. Reducing it to cheating felt cheap.

Though in a way, the truth was worse.

Katie had met Steve in September of their sophomore year, and he quickly became her best friend aside from Bess. Idyllically, Bess loved him just as much—which was part of the problem. Katie loved Steve pretty much the way everyone loved Steve. But her connection with Clark was something else. They could communicate across a crowded room with a single look like they were the only two in it. They could end up being the last two awake—in the duplex house their group came to split down the middle, girls on the left, boys on the right—and she'd feel overcome with pure happiness, the certainty that *this* was what they'd been waiting for all day. Even though *this* was only a nightcap on the porch, and an uninterrupted chance to talk and talk and talk.

She couldn't know if it was agony to Clark in the same way it was to her. But she knew it was unfair to Steve. By senior year, he was talking about their future, and she was in panic. Pining away on campus was one thing; this was the rest of her life. But every time she thought about breaking things off, she talked herself out of it. She couldn't bear to firebomb this once-in-a-lifetime friendship of their whole insepara-ble group. You could already picture them back on campus for home-coming as forty-year-olds with kids along, as sixty-year-olds with gray hair—ride-or-dies for life. The easier solution was to level up with Steve and get over herself about Clark. It wasn't like breaking up with Steve would give her any realistic chance with his best friend anyway. At least this way, Clark would remain in her life. She could love him like a brother.

"Except love doesn't follow logic," Sky cut in. She said this like everyone had to learn the hard way, and maybe that was true. Katie slowed for a tractor to cross the road, grateful for the distraction. The worst part was coming next.

"We were all out one night a couple months before graduation, except Steve, who had a test in the morning. It wasn't unusual for Clark and me to be the last two standing. How much we drank that night was, though. I swear to this day it wasn't me. I never would have started it, but I didn't resist. Neither of us had ever done anything like that before." Katie kept her eyes on the road, accelerating. She could still get short of breath, remembering the way Clark's hands had felt on her that night. The way his eyes had always found hers no matter where they were and finally, she had them all to herself, up close.

She was still, apparently, that stupid.

"I woke up glowing," she confessed, "even through my guilt. I lay there thinking we'd have to find a way to tell Steve, and we'd hate hurting him, but this had been unavoidable. God knows I'd tried to avoid it. In time, everyone would see it was Clark and me who were meant to be all along. Then Clark woke up—not glowing. Hyperventilating about our horrible mistake, how Steve would never forgive him. He didn't have a second thought about me, only Steve. Suffice to say my feelings were not mutual. He was adamant we tell no one."

"But you got pregnant."

"But I got pregnant. And Clark was right: it wasn't me Steve couldn't stand to look at. Later, I even wondered if a part of him always knew. He barely said anything to me, but he screamed at Clark that he was *dead to him*. In hindsight, I think Clark thought his best chance at making things right was to go along with my version. Not that he'd screwed up their friendship over some drunken lust, but that we were truly happy together. I think Clark hoped Steve would come around once he saw our little family of three."

"And you hoped Clark would come around too?"

Katie nodded. "We were both wrong. We eloped, but I lost the baby, late term. Steve never spoke to either of us again. Clark never learned to love me, no matter how big a fool I made of myself. He blamed me, for everything. I let him. And I don't think people ever stopped talking about us behind our backs. Wondering why I was still married to the guy, and vice versa."

Sky was quiet for a minute. "I think you can relate to more than one small part of what I'm going through," she said softly. "I'm sorry. No wonder you're helping with this network."

Katie opened her mouth to speak, then closed it again. Dottie had told her everyone in the Sequence had their personal reasons, and Katie had stammered about having a vagina and this being a man's world. Now she finally told the only real story she had to tell, the prolonged humiliation that defined her adult life—the story she *never* would have put on par with any real victim—and here was Sky, pointing out parallels in feeling ashamed and cornered and judged, however nonthreatening to anything but Katie's own heart. Not sneering at her but showing compassion. Katie didn't know whether to deny the connection or thank her or just cry.

Maybe this was what she'd been unable to articulate, all this time.

Why she felt this compulsion not to close the door on the Sequence, even as she faced down concern from Bess and suspicion from Jude. Even as she questioned her own sanity.

"I think that's it," Sky said, pointing to a corner storefront up ahead.

Katie's feelings about this could wait to be sorted out later. They always did.

The building was the kind of small-town-relic gas station that was usually abandoned, driven out of business by modern self-service chains. The kind with two pumps, a sun-cracked parking lot, exterior bathrooms you needed a key from the cashier to open, and an inside that doubled as the town's only convenience store.

PINKIE'S ONE-STOP SHOP, the sign read. The windows were filled with placards advertising lottery tickets, cheap tobacco, WE WIRE MONEY, homemade ice cream (TRY ALL 11 FLAVORS!), photos printed while you wait, a "cold beer cave," $9.99 Squishmallows, No CONTRACT

Cell Phones, and DIS: Discretion Investigative Solutions (We Are Licensed!).

There was only one car in the lot, an old mauve Buick Century with a broken hood ornament hanging askew. Katie pulled in a few spots away, and she and Sky sat peering at the tacky collage in silence.

"They sure take the one-stop-shop concept seriously," Katie mumbled.

"At least there's not a sign that says, 'Ask About Our Underground Transportation for Domestic Violence Victims!'" Sky joked.

Katie eyed the Discretion Investigative Solutions sign. She wasn't so sure about that. The name sounded generic and forgettable unless you took it literally. In which case it sounded an awful lot like a private investigator.

Katie hoped this was Sequence Clever and not This-Is-a-Trap Clever.

The shop door opened, and a middle-aged woman emerged.

"Stay in the car," she whispered to Sky. "I'm leaving the keys." She slipped out and closed the door behind her.

The woman smiled as she approached. She wore pink stonewashed jeans and a color-matched tee with a plunging neckline. Her layered blonde hair was flat-ironed within an inch of its life, and bright-pink lipstick gleamed on the kind of full lips celebrities ruin their faces trying to achieve. Katie did a double take. She almost didn't recognize her without the cool-weather hiking clothes and ponytail. But there was no doubt:

This was one of the two women she'd encountered her first day exploring Grove. The ones who'd encouraged her, called her fierce, and gushed that it was their "happy place."

"You?" she asked, incredulous. She couldn't decide whether to feel comforted—as if the Sequence had been looking out for her all along— or seriously creeped out.

"Good to see you again. Just hung up the phone with Dr. Clooney. Tell me, is he sexier in person?" Her voice carried a light southern accent it hadn't before: West Virginia, maybe, or Kentucky. "Not what I expected. He sounded 'bout a hundred years old."

"Closer to seventy," Katie guessed.

The woman let out a guffaw that could have been heard for miles, if anyone were around. "Just when I think I have it all figured out," she said. "Goes to show no one ever does."

"You're telling me," Katie said. "Way out here I guess I was expecting a farm."

"Well." The woman flashed her grin again. Her lipstick remained impressively perfect—not a crack, not a smudge. "If it was, then we wouldn't need you, would we?"

Katie motioned for Sky to get out of the car. If this was a trap, they were walking in. "This is Sky."

"I'm Gina. I don't do code names. At least, not on purpose. Everyone else calls me Pinkie, and I don't think it's occurred to a single one of 'em it ain't my real name."

"You do look like a Pinkie," Sky admitted.

"It's my signature color. I even painted my kitchen pink."

"You were wearing a purple coat last time I saw you," Katie observed.

"Course I was. That was incognito." She winked.

"Well, thanks again for this, Gina. My name's—"

"NCT," Gina interrupted. "You do codenames. I don't care how you figured out my email, but trust me, you're gonna be on the shit list as it is." Abruptly, she engulfed Katie in a hug. "I have a soft spot for the shit list," she whispered.

"Then I have to know," Katie whispered back. "Are you a gas station clerk *and* a PI?"

Gina pulled away to strike a pose, as if she were presenting a prize on *The Price Is Right*. "And that's not all!" she announced in a decent mimic of a game show announcer. "This place ain't the one-stop shop so much as I am, but I got tired of holding the sign." She guffawed again at her own joke and ushered them through the door.

The inside of the store was exactly as cluttered as the window display. There was remarkably little aisle space when three of the four walls were occupied by a service desk of some sort. "I've got an apron for you," Gina told Sky, pointing to the folded pink cloth on the counter. "We're making ice cream today. You'll be out of sight back by the batch freezer, real easy to use. Anyone happens to glimpse you, you're an employee. And if it sweetens the deal—see what I did there?—you can eat as much as you want."

Sky nodded shyly. "Do all the women in my shoes come and make ice cream?"

"No, ma'am. Usually your ride just pulls up to fill her tank and you hop in. But we're working around a schedule change, so you're stuck with a layover. We appreciate you rolling with it. I'm happy to pay, cash: fifteen bucks an hour fair?"

She said this smoothly, without a hint that Sky herself was the reason for the schedule change. That she was essentially here on suicide watch. Katie wondered if the woman hiking with Gina at Grove had been the "ride" but figured it would push her luck to ask.

"You don't need to pay me," Sky said quickly.

"Sure I do. A smart, capable woman like you shouldn't work for free. Look around, honey. I get paid for every single thing I know how to do."

Sky and Katie burst out laughing.

Gina unlocked the swinging door at her hip with a glittery key from a neon-pink coil around her wrist and pointed out the staff restroom at the back of the galley. Sky took the apron and closed the bathroom door behind her.

Katie looked around more closely. The merchandise displays were curated with flair—the sunglasses were affordable yet quality, the toys irresistibly cute. It was the cumulative effect of everything together, too much, that made it easy to disregard the contents as junk. Almost like Gina was doing it on purpose. Weeding out anyone who couldn't see past first impressions.

"Are you the one who secures their new IDs?" Katie kept her voice low so Sky couldn't overhear through the closed bathroom door. Gina nodded. Katie was impressed. She'd redesigned a website for a PI in Pittsburgh, and he'd struggled to fill his navigation menus. *Can't say my cases have much variety,* he'd confessed. *I spend most days sitting outside motels with my camera.*

"Seems like quite a leap from busting cheating spouses," she told Gina.

"Not such a leap when one of those spouses ends up shot in her pretty head by the guy who hired you." Goose bumps rose on Katie's arms. "Needless to say, I don't take lying spouse cases anymore—at least, not on purpose. And I only take women as clients. Not saying there ain't some bad apples with hoo-has, but that's my rule."

In spite of everything, Katie found Gina as reassuring now as she had the first time they met in passing. Or maybe Gina was just good at distraction. Because now Katie was literally picturing an apple with a hoo-ha.

"Can't help thinking Sky would have to make a lot of ice cream to fund a new start," she said.

"We fund it. Same way we get luxury goods for your loft. Through our donations manager. She's the shelter's fave Cinderella story, went on to marry an honest-to-God Prince Charming."

She said it so seriously, Katie found herself asking, "Prince of what?"

"Proctor and Gamble. And a gated suburban kingdom full of other corporate royalty."

Katie's mind spun. This meant the circle of people who might know something, anything, about where Grace had gone and why might be wider than she could ever hope to reach. "How many people are involved, altogether?"

"Tough to say. Not all our steps go in a straight line. And before you ask anything else, I do buy into the idea that the less we all know about each other, the better."

This seemed rich coming from someone who'd been staking out Katie on Day One. Not that she could blame Gina for being curious. Not that she'd seen her since. "But you got to know Grace," she pointed out. "You were obviously friends."

Gina narrowed her eyes, and Katie realized too late that Gina herself had not made this *obvious*. "And you're obviously friends with that nature center woman. Maybe you don't need more friends. Maybe you're not the only one feeling nervous about who's loyal to who." She paused. "You got into Grace's email, didn't you?"

Katie smiled guiltily. "I thought you'd want to know she hasn't logged on to see your wedding invite. I know everyone is convinced she's fine, but . . ."

Gina didn't smile back.

Instead, with one defiant question, she turned Katie's blood cold.

"Who said I'm convinced she's fine?"

22

Katie stared at Gina, every muscle in her body stopped in its tracks except her eyes, which found Gina's and held them, questioning. *Tell me I misheard you.*

"I'm not trying to toot my own horn, but if I can't find someone, either they *really* don't want to be found or someone else beat me to it." Gina shook her head. "I started looking when I didn't get a reply to that email. She was always so fast to respond. Don't know when she even slept."

Katie's spine tingled—an odd combination of validation that her instincts might have been correct all along and denial that she didn't *want* them to be. It'd been nearly a month since she'd first set foot in the caretaker's house and called this unsteady truce with all the things she didn't know. A truce she'd never stopped trying to make steadier— asking everyone she met if they truly believed Grace was okay, hearing time and again she should let it go, *almost* being convinced they were right. Even Bess and Jude, who'd fretted in their own ways over Katie, had more or less accepted Grace's resignation at face value. After all that, it was so surreal to hear someone outwardly share this concern, she'd lost sight of how a reasonable person in her shoes might feel about it.

She forced herself closer to Gina, lowering her voice even more. "Is that why you were out at Grove that day? Do you have theories? Can we compare notes?"

"I always have theories, but in this case no evidence to support any of them."

"I know some people found her to be kind of . . ."

"A pain in the ass?" Gina laughed softly. "Some people might say the same about someone brazen enough to hack her predecessor's email. Or someone who hands out safe haven cards at her bakery without permission. If you're trying to accomplish something boldly good in the world, you're probably a pain in a lot of asses." Gina's eyes narrowed. "But you never met Grace. Why are *you* obsessing? Did something happen at the house?" She waved impatiently at the air. "I mean, aside from all this?"

Where to begin? There wasn't time to get into it. But she couldn't afford not to either. A replay of her morning nagged at her subconscious. "She never said anything about someone looking for a dog, did she?"

Gina only looked at her strangely. Katie didn't want to get off track. "Level with me," she said. "If you were me, what would you be most worried about? Do you think she did something to fall out with the Sequence, and someone turned on her? Or maybe she got caught by someone on the outside? One of the husbands or . . . Maybe someone thought they'd shut the whole thing down by taking her out, not expecting anyone else to step in?"

Saying all this out loud, Katie felt real fear for the first time. *Anyone else* was her.

"Whoa," Gina said. "Whoa. Okay. I can see why you'd be spooked, but let's not go overboard. First off, I do literally trust the Sequence with my life."

"No offense, but surely you can see why I'm not there yet."

Gina gave her a hard look. "Look, I admit we all have faults. As is becoming increasingly clear. Guess that's the problem with any human network: We're only human, right? But these particular humans are doing this because we believe in our bones it's the right thing. It ain't easy, there's no reward, and there's sure as hell no reason to turn on each other." Her mouth twitched toward a smile. "Not even the pains in the ass among us."

Katie wanted to share Gina's confidence. She wanted to believe absolute trust in a network without knowing all the members wasn't a little . . . cultish. "So what *do* you think happened to Grace?"

"I don't rightly know. I only think something's wrong. When I found out she hasn't been to see her mom, that sealed it for me."

"Her mom?" Katie asked. "She did give a forwarding address at her sister's house."

Gina rolled her eyes. "Well, if that ain't a trail of bread crumbs down a dead-end street, I don't know what is. Fat chance she'll turn up there."

Given that the sister had not been receptive to Bess's calls, Katie had a feeling Gina was right. "Okay," she conceded. "Her mom then. Where is she?"

Gina's face softened. "Same place she's been for the last twenty years. Grace visits last Saturday of every month, like clockwork. Eight hours round-trip drive in one day." Before Katie could ask anything further, Gina went on. "The whole concept of the Sequence is we all bring different skills to the job, right? So leave the investigating to me. If I find something to tell, I'll tell you. Don't get yourself into a deeper mess sticking your nose where it don't belong."

"Do you want to come out and poke around? I mean, inside? I can show you what I—"

"No. I got two words for you: *Plausible deniability.* That's the only thing you should be worrying about. Besides, I've already poked around."

Katie gaped at her. "In my *house?*"

"Relax. I've got no interest in rooting around your underwear drawer. Now I'll say it again: *Plausible deniability.* Words to live by."

Katie looked at her in frustration. "I thought you never worked for free," she said. "But for the Sequence, you do. Can I ask why?"

"Besides trying to repent for the ill-begotten clients of my early investigative days?"

The bathroom door clicked open, and Sky emerged. Gina might have changed the subject, but instead she waved her over and put an arm around her.

"People always talk about wanting more," Gina said. "To eat in Paris cafes, snorkel the Great Barrier Reef. Just because I'm a midwestern homebody don't mean I don't want more too—but I find ways to get it right here. When I want a new skill, I train and hang out a shingle. When I want love, I find it in the badass trucker who's always making excuses to stop in. And when I want to make a difference, I help one person at a time. I don't care that it's not fancy or no one will ever know. I *don't* work for free. This fuzzy feeling in my cynical heart is worth everything."

She looked up at her sign and winked. "Some people might say it's too much, all in one place. But for me? It's just right."

23

Katie came armed. She loaded an axe, handsaw, and electric tree trimmer into a wheelbarrow and pushed it nearly a mile until she came to the spot where the storm had brought the trees down, blocking the yellow trail. She'd scoped it out yesterday and decided she could handle this. The trunks were thin enough; the cluster of them had fallen across the path at a diagonal, leaving the leafy tops out of the way, where they could stay. Now, she pulled on the thick gloves and safety goggles she'd found in the barn, reveling in a jolt of determined anticipation.

She couldn't think of a better way to spend this day than out here alone, where no one could critique her technique or correct her form, wielding tools she'd never dared mess with before, chopping formidable obstacles into manageable pieces.

She started with the axe, raising it high above her head and bringing it down into the trunk with a satisfying thwack. Wood shards flew, and she was glad she'd thought to bring the goggles. She swung it again, then again, finding a slow, clumsy rhythm.

Clumsy but cathartic. With each hoist of the heavy handle, each arc of the dull blade, she played back the cascade of events she was still processing. The barriers to her own path. Two weeks later, and she still wanted to go back and redo that conversation with Gina. She didn't know what, exactly, she wished she could say or do differently. Only that she couldn't shake the feeling that her strength had been tested and she hadn't quite passed.

Who said I'm convinced Grace is fine? Thwack!

Why are you *obsessing?* Thwack!

I've already poked around. Thwack!

Leave the investigating to me. Thwack!

What would it take to cut it all down to size? Two weeks of being seized with new fears about Grace. Two weeks of secret relief that Gina was on the case—and simultaneous frustration at being urged to stay out of it. Two weeks of dead-end internet searches for any rabbit trail that might lead to Grace's mom, yielding not so much as a name or a hometown. Two weeks of dodging Bess's questions about whether Katie had *done enough yet* and wishing she didn't agree she should tell Bess as little as possible. Two weeks of feeling silly about calling up footage of, as it turned out, a very real hyperactive beagle who belonged to a guy named Richard ("Get it?" Bess had crowed. "Dick and Tracy?")—and dismissing lingering worries that a dog named for a detective might be trained to track things. Two weeks of imagining Dr. Clooney at his practice, bemoaning his paperwork, believing with his gentle heart the Sequence was simpler. Two weeks of looking over her shoulder for Jude, whom she hadn't seen since the loaded exchange in Bess's office, and bracing for a third degree from Dottie that never came. Two weeks of resenting that the Sequence couldn't just trust her already, while being halfway glad they didn't, because maybe if she kept only one foot in, she could have it both ways. To have, as Gina put it, *more.*

Hadn't that been her hope for the caretaker job all along?

When her shoulders started to ache, she switched to the saw, experimenting with how fast to cut and how much pressure to apply. She was standing inches deep in mud now—mud that had clearly been a factor in the trees unrooting—and sawdust coated her pants as the freshly hewn logs fell at her feet. Then she took the electric trimmer to everything left in her way, making a spectacular racket. She had no idea if she looked foolish or fierce, if she was stretching the tool beyond its intended purpose, if she might break the blade beyond repair, but in this moment, she didn't care. Gina may have encouraged her to stop looking for answers, but what she'd really made clear was that Katie should give up hoping someone else would hand them to her.

It was time to see how resourceful she could be on her own.

When all that remained was to clear the cut pieces from the trail, she surveyed her work, hopping atop a log to free her boots from the mud. It sunk a few inches beneath her weight and held there, a stepping stone in a sea of muck. Seizing the idea, she began to arrange the logs in a neat row down the center of the path, until she'd created a sort of sideways ladder through the boggiest stretch of trail. The trees that had once blocked the path were now a part of it, as if the forest itself had this solution in mind all along and Katie was merely the conduit.

Tending to its needs as any good caretaker should.

"Hey, Hatchback," said a voice behind her. She turned and saw Jude standing a few paces away, taking in the length of her creation. "Wow. Nice work."

"Yeah?"

He nodded.

"No commentary about how I should've used a smaller shovel?"

"Doesn't look like you needed a shovel at all." He was so damn literal. One more thing she didn't know what to make of: Infuriating or endearing? "I came out because someone called this in, but you beat me to it. And did a better job than I would have."

"Well. Thanks." Katie shrugged, self-conscious. "Just wish I'd thought of it before I ruined yet another pair of shoes."

He didn't laugh. "No one is judging you by your footwear."

It was a small comment, maybe even an offhand comment, but then again, Jude didn't *do* offhand. Was it possible she'd been projecting her own insecurities onto Jude, just because he was a little abrupt, a little in her space when she happened to have something to hide?

"I might be oversensitive about being judged," she admitted.

"I get that," he said. "Believe it or not, my family doesn't exactly go around bragging that I'm a nature center maintenance man."

"No." She feigned offense on his behalf.

"Hey, I tried to do what they wanted and follow in my dad's footsteps, but it nearly broke my brain."

Katie hesitated. The last thing she wanted was to bring up their last meeting. Yet based on what he'd said then, the question was obvious. And possibly relevant, though she still didn't understand exactly how. "Is your dad a cop?"

He nodded. "He's retired now. Like I said, I did try, but . . . didn't take long to realize I didn't fit in with the rest of the guys."

"I can see that," she joked. "Not many silent brooding cop types, huh?"

But Jude didn't boomerang some snappy comeback. "Might seem like it, but . . ." He shook his head. "I think my dad knew I didn't have the right sensibility for it, but he hoped they could fix me in training. The police academy was like every personality clash we'd ever had, magnified. I respected what he did, but even as a kid couldn't help playing devil's advocate—you know, *Okay, he broke that law, but was the law fair?* To me, everything was complicated, shades of gray. I overthought everything. Anyway, eventually we both recognized no amount of training would change that. Much to his chagrin."

She'd been overthinking those shades of gray, too, ever since Jude had brought up his law enforcement tie. Just like any other layperson, she'd followed news stories where police had done everything they could to protect victims of abuse. She'd also watched viral videos of them not doing enough. And heard troubling statistics about family abuse within their own ranks. She didn't know what to think about any of it, but the point was, she understood the importance of nuance.

"Sounds like you would have made a better lawyer," she observed.

"If my grades weren't so terrible. You can guess how I did on multiple choice tests."

Katie appraised this vulnerable side of Jude, playing some devil's advocate of her own. *Possibly* he was not so much sullen but thoughtful. Not challenging ideas to be difficult but to ensure things were handled the best way. Not skeptically waiting for her to fail but trying to save her the hassle of taking the long way around. He'd acknowledged he was rubbing her the wrong way. He'd said he didn't want to. And maybe—maybe—he was treading more carefully now because he understood the importance of getting where you're going on your own terms.

Then again, he *had* made a big deal about having instincts. Some of that training must have stuck. And it wasn't exactly compatible to her line of work.

"What about you?" he asked. "What did people judge you for before you moved here?"

She tried to smile. "Oh, being trapped in a loveless marriage, I suppose." This had been her go-to divorce explanation back in Pittsburgh, just revealing and self-deprecating enough that people usually didn't pry, except occasionally to take issue with the word *loveless*. Surely it wasn't, blah blah blah, and she'd admit there had been love, but oh, how sadly one-sided.

When Jude started taking issue, it took a second to register he wasn't following the script.

"Well, that's just wrong. I've never understood the way people misuse that word. People who are free to do as they please call themselves—or each other—'trapped' all the time. Meanwhile, the few who truly are trapped are in too deep to realize."

She could only stare. Jude might not always say what was on his mind, but when he did, he sure had a way with words that seemed . . . well, intentional.

But she wasn't sure she wanted him to be.

For once, he took the hint. "Want any help getting this stuff back to the barn?"

"I'll finish up myself. But thanks."

"Sure thing. Nice day for a hike anyway. I'll take the long way back." He tackled her new sideways ladder like it was an agility course, making quick work of the logs, and turned to give her a thumbs-up. "My clean shoes salute you." She saluted back and began loading up her tools.

"By the way," he called, "did you notice those daffodils that sprouted by the pond?"

Katie froze where she stood, bent at the waist, midreach for the axe. She would not look up. She would not read into this, even as her hair stood on end. No way could he know about Lindsay and the daffodils.

Besides. This was May. Lindsay was way back in April.

Then again, the daffodils were too.

"Little late in the season, isn't it?" she answered, picking up the axe, holding it for a beat longer than necessary before dropping it into the wheelbarrow.

"Way late," he agreed. "Maybe they were smart enough to wait out the freak spring snowstorm. Or maybe they just wanted to bloom when someone would notice."

Daffodils, of all things. Why couldn't they be discussing a rose or a hydrangea? Either he was talking in metaphors, or she should have noticed too. Though in truth, she'd begun avoiding the pond. What had been an oversize murky puddle when she arrived was quickly being overtaken by algae, so thick at the edges you could barely tell water was underneath. It gave her the creeps, imagining swampy creatures slithering through, but worse, it was disappointing. Her canoes would remain stacked picturesquely by her shed all summer, uphill from the whole silty mess. No way could she let Gigi's girls use them. Hello, bacteria.

"Nope," she said. "Didn't see them."

She did look up then. Jude wasn't giving her that look he sometimes did, like he was clocking every little thing about her, trying to make up his mind about something. He looked more like he'd been pleasantly surprised to run into her. And she had to admit that maybe, if she wasn't so on edge about everything, the feeling would have been mutual.

"You should," he said, turning to go. "Something about them reminded me of you."

24

Katie was almost home when she rounded the curve into the open fields and saw a familiar figure at his tripod. His bomber jacket was unzipped, revealing a fitted gray T-shirt. His hair was windblown, his face unseasonably tanned from these days in the field. And he was still handsome enough to render her speechless, even from this distance.

Ryan.

He turned at the sound of her approach and smiled in recognition. She gave a friendly wave, and he waved back in an exaggerated, slow-motion animation. Not waving hello but waving her over—silently, like he didn't want to disturb something. She left the wheelbarrow in the path, her pulse quickening as she stepped tentatively toward his tripod. He was facing a stand of trees that had cropped up like an island in the field, his attention on the nearest trunk.

She stopped a few paces away and stared. Before them rested the largest moth she'd ever seen. Its splayed-open wings looked delicate but thick, layers of membrane folded over one another like a flat head of vibrant lime-green lettuce. The coloration would have been brilliantly camouflaged among leaves, but against the textured brown bark, it seemed to be posing for its close-up. There was something graceful about the shape of it, the way the wings entwined below the body, like slender legs crossed at the ankles. Its antennae were fuzzy, yellow-orange arms poised gracefully over its head for a pirouette.

Katie was not a bug person. Not at all. But this—this wasn't a bug. "It's a ballerina," she breathed.

"Isn't it? Otherwise known as a luna moth." Ryan's voice hovered above a whisper. "I downloaded an app to identify species. There's no mistaking this one."

"I've never seen such a thing," she whispered, not wanting to be the one to startle it away. "Are they rare?"

He leaned closer, ostensibly so they could hear each other better, and she was enveloped in the pleasant, clean smell of masculine body-wash mingling with the blooming fields. "Not as rare as people think," he whispered back, "because they're rarely seen. They fly at night." She recalled the recent full moon she'd stood under with Dr. Clooney and wondered whether the luna could possibly be in tune to the actual lunar cycle. "Also, their life spans are only about seven days."

She tore her gaze away from the moth to meet his eyes. He was even closer than she'd realized, their proximity amplified by so much open space around them, two strangers huddled against the world. "That's sad."

"They have no digestive system in moth form. They use up all the energy they stored as a caterpillar, then die." He looked disturbed by this fact, but also relieved that she was, too, like he'd been hoping for a witness right when she'd come along.

She forced herself to turn back to the moth. It hadn't moved. "What a raw deal."

"Right? They trade in a basic life necessity for beauty in another form. Like . . ."

"Ariel and the Sea Witch," she whispered.

Grinning, Ryan backed away from the trunk, and she followed. "Difference is, Ariel signed that contract herself," he pointed out. "This poor thing has no choice."

"Did you get its picture?"

"It's let me shoot for almost an hour. Take a look." He crossed to the camera atop his tripod and turned a screen on its hinge, gesturing for her to come see. Even on the tiny display, his high-powered lens had captured far more detail than her naked eye. He zoomed in, and the insect's delicate membrane became a topographical map of ridges and valleys. Then he zoomed out again, giving her the full effect of his framing.

"This is good," she said, meaning it. "Can I see more?"

They scrolled through a hundred milliseconds in the moth's short life, captured from every angle, each one drawing her nearer until she was inhaling his scent again, feeling the heat from his cheek, inches away. Here, the thickness of the body captured from the side, adding a dimension she hadn't appreciated before. Here, the markings on the wings taking center stage. Here, an optical illusion in hyperfocus, as if the moth weren't resting on the trunk but hovering above some mystical brown cloud.

"You were being modest when you called yourself an amateur," Katie said finally. "These will make a fantastic portfolio."

"I appreciate that," he said with that sincerity she remembered from the day they'd met. "You know, if you stay out here long enough, you start to wonder if you're onto something or losing your mind a little."

She knew better than he could guess. "I'm glad I got to see this," she said. "The moth and the pictures. Thanks for showing me."

"Thanks for humoring me. And the vote of confidence. I only wish I could stay till dark."

"What happens at dark?"

"Since she's nocturnal, I assume she's resting. I don't want to disturb her—I'd hoped to wait her out and catch her unfolding those wings to fly." He held out his phone, where his app showed the moth in its full glory, once-hidden markings and filigree-like curves splayed like a hang glider. "I'm not asking," he added quickly. "I know you close soon. Just wishing out loud."

"That *would* make a great shot." In fact, a less caring person could've gotten that shot already. If Clark were on commission for, say,

LunaMoths.com, he wouldn't have thought twice about using a twig to coax it from the trunk.

Ryan looked at her with surprise, then chuckled. "It would," he agreed. "Although, funny enough, I wasn't thinking about getting the shot. I just want to see it."

Oh boy. Just when the guy couldn't get more likable. Katie should not be grinning at him this way. She definitely should not be savoring the way he was grinning back, as if she, not the moth, were the rare and interesting creature he didn't want to say goodbye to.

She let herself imagine what it'd be like to simply say *Yes, why not, let's do.* After all, she was the caretaker. It was her call to invite a friend to stay after hours; it was her chance to *make* a friend. An uncomplicated friend who didn't need to know why she'd come to Grove or what she'd wrestled with since moving in. Who wouldn't pass judgment on what she should or shouldn't agree to, or anything beyond this moment, this blooming field, this pull between them. Her house wasn't far; she could run now to throw beers in a cooler, be back in minutes. The sky would grow golden as they sat talking and waiting, in no real hurry for the moth to stir. The chemistry would turn electric. All she had to do was suggest it. She could see in his eyes that he'd say yes—and how long had it been since any man had looked at her so eagerly?

And yet.

The woman in her barn was called Maria. Katie didn't know many details, only that Dr. Clooney must have convinced Dottie of Katie's worth. Because just when she started to think the Sequence had moved on without her, the email came. Can you take a pit stop from Columbus this time? ETA 2 a.m., Apologies for the late hour. Katie had stocked the fridge and set an alarm. Maria had slept, understandably, through the morning.

If Ryan stayed until dark, Maria wouldn't see the sun today.

Katie couldn't pretend to have thought this all the way through. Every day brought a new example of how the job might require sacrifices she hadn't considered. How would Katie broaden her circle beyond Bess, let alone date, if so many of her after hours were spoken for? What good was a sunset drink with a kind, interesting guy if she was going to feel selfish for doing it at Maria's expense? The gravity of it rained like stones on Katie's buoyant mood.

"I wish you could too," Katie said, averting her eyes. "Who knows, maybe Miss Luna will still be here tomorrow."

Ryan almost pulled off not looking disappointed. "Maybe," he agreed. "I've been out here all day anyway. I've been told I never know when to quit." He started detaching his equipment from the tripod. Katie turned to go.

Then she stopped short. *All day.* He said he'd been here *all day.* So had she, but she'd been sawing, chopping, and running cordless power tools. He'd been merely watching. Quietly.

I only hear it when it's quiet, Sky had said. *I swear I'm not crazy.*

"Hey," Katie said. "Odd question, but . . . I don't suppose you've heard a baby crying at any point today?"

He was in a tugging match with the zipper of his camera bag and didn't look up at first. "A baby? Why do you ask?"

"Long story. But did you?"

When Ryan did look up, his face was impassive, but it was clear he found the question strange. Strange enough that he wasn't likely to forget she'd asked, and she instantly regretted it. "Well," he said, "I can't say I have. But I should probably disclose that my ex-wife has accused me of tuning out crying babies before."

"Oh," Katie said. "You're a dad?" Why was she surprised? This was the dating pool she'd be swimming in now: divorcées like her, men who'd already started families, or singles who may have stayed that way for good reason.

"To one adorable baby girl." His face lit up when he said it, then fell a little.

"Must be hard not seeing her every day," she ventured.

"It is," he said. "I find myself in this transition phase, all the way around. Got an offer at work to opt out with a tempting severance package, so I took it. And I told myself not to panic-apply for equally miserable jobs, to use the time to try something I actually enjoy." He gestured to the camera. So *that's* why he was able to be here at all hours of the day. Katie had learned not to ask—so many visitors got touchy on the subject, mumbling they "worked remotely" and averting their eyes as if Katie were an undercover productivity tracker for human resources.

"I still don't know if that was the right call," he confessed. "Things had been rough at home for a while—we're in this sandwich genera-tion phase, so my ex moved back in with her ailing mom, and . . ." He stopped. "Does all of this make me sound like a giant loser?"

"Not at all," Katie said. "Nothing wrong with a transition phase."

"Tell that to the luna moth," he joked. "Anyway. This baby thing. What's up? Should I be paying more attention? I mean, if I do come back tomorrow?" He held her gaze, his eyes questioning. Searching.

"Foxes," she heard herself say. That had been Bess's response when Katie asked if any animal in these woods could hypothetically sound like a human baby. *I've heard fox calls likened to a woman screaming,* she'd said, suspiciously. *Maybe a young fox?* But when Katie wouldn't say why she was asking, Bess stopped volunteering possibilities.

"There's a den of pups," she told Ryan now. "That's what they sound like. Just curious if my barn cat is in their range yet."

That did the trick: His face lit up again. She wondered if he was thinking a baby fox would make a winning photo for the membership card. Less novel than the luna but cuddlier.

"I'll let you know," he promised. "I'd love to meet that cat sometime."

"I'd love to see more of your photos."

She made a point of looking him in the eye, so he could tell she meant it.

She returned home to find a burst of yellow on her welcome mat, where she couldn't miss it.

A mason jar of daffodils. Neatly cut and in water.

She looked around, but Jude was nowhere. She didn't want to mind his being here—to analyze whether this was anything more than a peace offering, a friendly overture—and if not for Maria in the loft, she wouldn't have. She *had* to get used to her roles overlapping.

She'd set out to literally cut down her frustration, and mostly she'd succeeded. What remained was all the real emotion too deep and elusive for any axe to put a dent in.

Katie carried the daffodils to the desk. Then she slid the book of Black-Eyed Susans from its shelf. If disguising these stories had been up to her, she'd have chosen a luna moth for the jacket instead: a beauty that flew by night. Not as rare as anyone assumed, only rarely seen.

She wasn't just the keeper of this book now; she was coauthor.

She opened to the first clean page, found a pen, and sat down at the desk, turning her thoughts to the first guest since Grace had left: Lindsay. Grace had taken such care to leave herself off the page. Which meant Katie couldn't write about their peaceful morning walks or how they'd laughed about her ex's disdain for the sisters named for flowers. She thought instead of what had belonged to Lindsay alone, what she'd planned to take with her. Then she wrote:

She takes pride in her work. It makes her feel capable and appreciated, and if she has to, she can take everything she needs from those few hours of the day: friendship, respect, camaraderie, gratitude, satisfaction. No one will ever stand in the way of that again.

Satisfied, she turned the page, her heart already sinking at how much more difficult Sky's story would be. And how ill equipped she was to tell it. Katie had been part of the deepest, most private loss the woman would ever live through, yet she hadn't gotten to know her beyond it. Even a cursory glance through the *Black-Eyed Susans* journal—filled with personalities, not tragedies, and sketches, not questions—made it clear this wasn't a mistake Grace had ever made.

It wasn't one Katie would make again either.

She may not have had the chance to see beyond Sky's heartbreak, but she'd felt her pain keenly. And when Katie shared something of herself in turn, even as she felt her own failed marriage and miscarriage seemed insignificant by comparison, Sky had been sensitive and gracious, relating their experiences in ways Katie wouldn't have dared.

Katie looked for a long time at the page. She didn't need more than a sentence, did she? Any words could hold power, if they were the right ones. She took a deep breath and wrote:

She's going to be a great mom someday.

She hoped it was enough. But more than that, she hoped it was true.

25

Spring thickened, filling the gaps in the forest with lush green. A few afternoons turned downright hot, movie-trailer previews of summer at Grove. Katie filled out too. Her forearms tanned, her cheeks freckled, the skin on her feet toughened until it didn't blister anymore, no matter how far she walked or how wet the ground. Mother's Day came and went, a gardener's green light for planting in the Midwest, and Katie was relieved not to spend the day in an awkward dance around Clark, neither of them acknowledging what might have been. Instead, she tilled the rectangles of soil in Grace's raised garden beds, repaired the chicken wire, and planted zucchini, cucumber, herbs, peppers, summer squash, and tomatoes.

She found pockets of peace: Adirondacks in storage that she arranged around the firepit and cushions that made the porch swing her new favorite place to read. One by one, she found new ways to preserve her sense of control too. When she buzzed in providers for service appointments, she'd load the camera feed to watch them come and go. When she ventured out on foot, she carried a belted pack with her phone, first aid kit, and bear mace, though she had yet to encounter another coyote. She heard a pack of them howling at night sometimes but no longer minded—much. And when she got that nagging feeling of being watched, she made herself big, walking tall.

Emboldened by her small successes—and by the tenuous new respect she seemed to have earned with Jude—she made another decision too: to swallow her pride and ask him to teach her more about maintaining the grounds. She still believed that for every potential upside to having him around, there was also a risk. But she rationalized that inviting him to Grove—on her own terms—remained the best way to get him to stop finding reasons to show up unannounced.

There was one other calculated reason for Katie's change of heart about Jude too. A reason in the form of a person who superseded everything else. Bess.

She'd never made a conscious decision *not* to fill Bess in about harboring poor Sky or meeting Dr. Clooney and Gina or any of the events since. It just seemed safer—especially for Bess—to be vague. Even if Katie could tell Bess not only noticed but also minded every time she dodged a question or changed the subject.

Katie minded too. On paper, they were closer than ever. They called or texted every day; Katie hosted Bess, Vince, and the kids for s'mores at the firepit; Bess invited Katie to her neighborhood book club. But there was distance between them, an undeniable tension they both tried to pretend wasn't there, which only seemed to feed it. Bess exuded a vague air of disapproval that Katie couldn't convince herself she was imagining. And Katie . . . well, she couldn't stop thinking about what Gina had said. *Maybe you're not the only one feeling nervous about who's loyal to who.*

She'd learned a long time ago that when someone's feedback made you *this* uncomfortable, it might mean they were right.

That snowed-in night, she and Bess had vowed to figure this all out together, and it wasn't Bess's fault her own attempts to help had come up empty. But what would Bess *really* do if she knew about Gina's concern for Grace, on top of their argument about Jude's implied concern for Katie? Bess might say, *Enough.* She might go whistleblower, turn them in. Or even make Katie leave, to be safe.

Katie might not know what to do, but she did know she didn't want to go. She had to give on something: the tension wouldn't defuse on its own.

"What would you say," she asked Bess one day, "if I admitted Jude was starting to grow on me?"

Bess looked surprised, then went quiet for a beat too long, until Katie was bracing for her to start catastrophizing again. She hoped Bess would see this for what it was: a signal that Katie wasn't going to let the Sequence overshadow every decision she made. It wasn't so much a lie as wishful thinking. Besides, if she wasn't going to keep Bess entirely in the loop, it wasn't fair to keep on telling her just enough to worry her either.

"I'd say that's great," Bess replied finally. She didn't need to tell Katie that it made her feel a little better . . . It was written all over her face.

Katie leaned close enough to whisper, "Don't tell anyone, okay?"

Bess burst out laughing. It wasn't an instant fix, but it was a start.

So far, Katie hadn't regretted it. Jude didn't make a fuss about her having changed her tune. He simply gave succinct tutorials and left her to the work—sensing, perhaps, that she had something to prove, if not to Bess then to herself.

He showed her how the perennials were regrowing where they'd been pruned, how to distinguish invasive plants from native ones, how to handle the most toxic invaders with care. Pokeweed and hemlock could land you in the hospital, and they weren't problems that could be cut to pieces; they had to be yanked out from the source. If they missed even one bit of pokeweed root, it'd grow back, defiant as ever.

Jude became more prone to smiling, less prone to annoying her. The second time she asked him to stay for a beer, he didn't even chug the bottle in a single gulp.

It took him at least three.

"You've been seeing him almost as much as me," Bess teased. "I hope Sad Keanu doesn't get in the way of you and the hottie photographer you rescued."

Katie ran into Ryan plenty. They never planned to, but she'd come upon him and his tripod almost every time she hoped she would, like a run of meet-cutes adding up to a natural getting-to-know-you phase.

Their divorces were equally fresh, so they kept the banter light, detached. But it was always nice to see a friendly face and feel less alone, if only for a few minutes. They'd exchange knowing smiles, he'd show her the day's photos, she'd recount her latest project and walk home savoring the sense of *possibility*. One day, Bess happened to be with her, and the three of them made an impromptu latte run, Ryan squeezing good-naturedly between the booster seats in the back of her minivan. Bess texted Katie a string of thumbs-up emojis right there in the drive-through.

"What does Jude think of him?" Bess asked later.

Katie shrugged. "As far as I know, they have yet to meet." She didn't want to think too hard about why she was happy to keep it that way.

Eventful as life was at Grove, things were equally uneventful with the Sequence. They'd made no determinations about Katie's see-how-it-goes status, nor had she. Two more women passed through without incident. One was shockingly young, though her eyes held an ageless weariness until Katie made her an ice cream sundae bar, at which point she lit up so brightly Katie had faith she'd be okay. The other requested a stack of mystery novels and spent every waking moment lost in the pages.

But time was running out. Summer was quickly approaching, and with it, Katie's nieces. Which meant this arrangement could not continue indefinitely. Could it?

No matter how she looked at pausing the Sequence again, she harbored guilt. Her covert new colleagues all seemed so much braver and surer of themselves than she'd ever been about anything. She couldn't shake the feeling that she kind of wanted to be them when she grew up. Leaving even one woman without a safe haven, let alone a whole summer's worth of women in need, felt like falling short. But she also couldn't get comfortable with the tension of keeping so many secrets, or the idea of involving her nieces in something even she should arguably not be involved in.

The closer she got to the *real* countdown to Camp Aunt Katie, the worse she felt. Katie never would've imagined she could bear this limbo for so long. Yet she did bear it, the way anyone withstood prolonged procrastination.

She didn't particularly like it, she knew it couldn't last, but she couldn't stop hoping this tangle of dilemmas might magically resolve itself.

When Gigi texted a photo of the girls posing with their countdown, Katie couldn't even laugh at the silly faces they were making with Gigi gleefully hugging her "MBA Finale" folder in the background. She could only stare in horror at the number between them: nineteen.

Only nineteen days left to go. And she felt no excitement. Only panic.

What if the only way out of this—better safe than sorry—was to call off Nessa and Cora's visit, stranding Gigi high and dry for her summer intensive? Was this like one of those ethical questions where you had to choose between saving dozens of strangers or saving only one person whom you truly love?

Katie couldn't imagine a scenario where her sister would forgive her for backing out on their plans now. Even if it was for her nieces' own good. Because she couldn't imagine how she'd explain that either. She could only imagine what a terrible ethicist she'd make.

Until the letter arrived.

The tall manila envelope, stamped from a long-term care facility in Michigan, was addressed, unusually, to "Grace Dunbar Or The New Caretaker." Katie stood at her mailbox outside the gate as a truck whooshed down the main road, and thought, *Finally.* She drove straight home and peeled it open in her driveway, unable to wait a second longer.

Inside were three childlike pieces of artwork—softer variations of the others in the folder she'd found, the bold swipes of paint replaced by finer, more blended strokes. Like the artist had not necessarily improved in skill but discovered a medium that demanded more time and care with the same subject matter: figures holding hands, lopsided hearts, a beaming sun.

A typed letter was enclosed.

Dear Grace,

I know you said you were no longer at this address, but your mom got agitated when I attempted to send this to your sister's house. She always sits with me when I address the envelopes, and I may have underestimated how well she grasps the context. She's unwilling to accept you've stopped caretaking and won't be convinced you're at your sister's either. A stubborn cookie.

I don't put words in the mouths of our non-verbal residents, but she's clearly under the impression you girls are at odds because of what happened to her. (Does it let your father off too easy to speak passively of "what happened"? Not my intention, to be sure.) Without knowing the coulda-shoulda-woulda details, for what it's worth, I've never seen her want for anything as clearly as she wishes you'd reconcile. You're both so good to her, but perhaps she understands better than anyone that the most solid tie her daughters have left is each other. You could never let her down, but she'd rather see you lift each other up. If this is overstepping, please take this motherly speech in the spirit in which it's intended.

She misses your visits. It's peak season for our garden, and on our outings with her wheelchair she never fails to point out your favorite spots—the meditation maze, the fountain, the arch of roses. I always remind her you'll be back to see them yourself as soon as you're able. I imagine being apart is equally hard for you, so I hope it brings comfort to know she's looking forward to that day, every day.

We have a new art therapist who is a marvel with watercolor pencils. Your mother is her star student, which is why we have not sent anything for so long—much of her recent work is being matted for our resident art show! You'd be proud.

I expect this letter won't reach you directly, but your successor. There was something so special in the way you spoke of that place and your role. I hope you've been able to take some sense of that with you, and your successor can find a share of it too. I also hope they can find a way to get you this envelope, wherever you are. Perhaps if you take this to heart, next time we'll find you at your sister's address after all.

Yours,

Betty

Katie read the letter twice before resting it on the steering wheel, peering through the windshield at this place that Grace had been so devoted to. Then she read it once more, cataloging the conclusions she could draw with reasonable certainty.

Each small revelation adding up to one big *personal reason*.

When Gina said Grace had uncharacteristically failed to visit her mother in the *same place she's been for the last twenty years*, that meant long-term residential care.

"What happened" appeared to be that Grace's father had, one way or another, contributed to her state where her communication skills were reduced to wordless visuals.

The folder she'd found with the Mom label indicated who the drawings were *from*, not *for*—filed away, along with Grace's rift with her sister, who'd never returned Bess's calls to apparently no one's surprise.

Katie thought back to the framed photo left in her living room, young Grace and her mother beaming at each other in matching sundresses, haloed in the golden hour. In a way, wasn't her mom still recreating that same, reassuring picture? The two of them. Love. Sunlight.

Grace had saved every version. Would she truly have left it all behind by choice?

On one hand, the letter confirmed Gina's fears: Grace still hadn't shown to visit her mom. On the other, it also implied she'd given them notice not to expect her, as she had the Sequence and the nature center. They all had something else in common, too: none of them had a clue where she really was.

Grace might never see this letter, much as Katie wished she could. But Katie had seen it. If Grace had been helping the Sequence in honor of her mom, then in a way, that's what Katie was doing, too, in filling her shoes. Grace had said herself in that scathing outbound email to Dottie: *We both know this would fall apart without me.* Katie had been trying so hard to make sure it didn't, because beneath all that frustration, she still believed it was what Grace would want. Even Grace's mom, according to her caregiver, had been *unwilling to accept you've stopped caretaking.* Which could only mean she knew what the job really entailed . . . right?

Yet it said here in black and white that what Grace's mom wanted more than anything—more than *anything*—was to see Grace make things right with her sister.

Katie wasn't about to insert herself into Grace's family drama. But she couldn't help feeling that the letter's arrival was a sign. The way it was addressed—to Grace *or* the new caretaker—the timing . . . How could she not take it to heart?

Here was a victim out on the other side, with closer ties to Grace than anyone, sending Katie a sign. Telling her exactly how to prioritize these impossibly contradictory obligations:

Family first.

Katie couldn't keep trying to be all things to all people. But she could decide right now which of her promises she was unwilling to break. The promise to Gigi. The promise to *herself* that she'd come through for her sister at last, come what may.

Now all she had to do was figure out how to keep it.

26

One blue-sky Friday at the end of May, Bess descended on the creek with a crew of polo-shirted volunteers. This was, evidently, a crucial spawning time for something called a red-spotted newt, as well as the usual suspects of toads and frogs. Across the creek's widest bends, where the water moved slowly and formed deeper pools, the volunteers stretched ropes and posted signs emblazoned with the nature center logo: This Area Reserved for Wildlife.

Bess encouraged her to stop by, maybe pick up a lesson or two for Camp Aunt Katie, and she'd quickly agreed. A training day with Bess's team seemed just the thing to help her step away from her Sequence impasse, a doable way to feel at least a little more ready for the summer ahead. Even if she was only ready to encounter a newt.

The crew was a charming mix of college students and retirees who somehow knew exactly what to do. This was clearly their jam, the thing they went home and binged more of on National Geographic. "I've never heard of the caretaker having kids out here," one of the students said with a friendly smile. "But our day camps sell out every summer. These girls will love being VIPs."

"I hope so." Katie smiled back. "Bess is kindly trying to help me look like I know what I'm doing. What's the nature-center equivalent of street cred? Creek cred?"

They all laughed, and the student held out the newt she was holding, which was mostly green with more subtle red spots than some of the others. "This is an aquatic adult," she said. "Are your nieces squeamish?"

"I have no idea." Katie peered closer at the newt's dinosaur feet and surprisingly thick tail, hoping no one could tell she was squeamish herself.

"Well, if they handle red or orange ones—the juvenile efts—make sure they don't touch their faces until they've washed their hands. Or have them wear gloves. The efts secrete toxins."

"Only the efts?"

She nodded. "As with humans, the adolescents are the touchiest. Also, discourage them from bringing these guys home. Newts do worse in captivity than other amphibians."

Katie didn't need to be told to leave the slimy things outdoors. She envisioned Nessa and Cora filling their pockets with toads to hide in her bed, like when Maria arrives at the von Trapp house in *The Sound of Music*. Maybe she could tell the kids all the animals on the property were protected—look but don't touch. Did it count as lying if it was for the best for all involved?

That was becoming the million-dollar question.

A retiree with a long white braid carried a bucket over to their huddle, introducing herself as Ruth. "How long will your nieces be staying?" When Katie told her Gigi's MBA intensive was six weeks long, she clasped her hands over her heart. "Oh, how wonderful. All children need strong women in their lives besides their mothers. And vice versa. It doesn't have to take a village, but everyone is better off when it does." For some reason, Katie had a hard time meeting her eye after that. But she forced herself to hold steady, feeling Bess watching. "Anyway, don't worry," Ruth trilled on. "You don't need to touch the newts to impress anybody. Want a look at these tadpoles? They're easy to identify once you see all the types together."

Katie nodded, grateful for her kindness, and before long found herself genuinely fascinated. Not necessarily by the newt tadpoles, which had feathered gills like baby fish, or by the fatter frog tadpoles flecked with gold, but by the crew's contagious enthusiasm and confidence. Every time they spotted larvae or eggs, they got so excited you'd think a quarterback had thrown a deep touchdown pass. Katie hovered near Ruth, asking as many questions as she dared without annoying her, until Bess finally said, "You're allowed to help, too, you know!" and tossed Katie a polo shirt. When she pulled it over her tank top, the team actually applauded.

Eventually, the volunteers moved on to collecting water samples, and Bess gave Katie a bag and rubber gloves and instructed her to walk the muddy banks, collecting anything that shouldn't be there. She found plenty: Straw wrappers from juice boxes. Lids from soda bottles. Bits of paper. Looking back, it was hard to think of anything she'd been involved with that relied so much on the goodwill of strangers to get by. *We're doing this,* Gina had assured her about the Sequence, *because we believe in our bones it's the right thing.* But Katie could see now this was modus operandi for everyone at the nature center, not just the underground night shift. The rushing creek waters from the spring rains were receding to reveal shallows prime for wading, collecting fossils, stacking rocks, skipping stones, scooping handfuls of gooey gray clay from crevasses in the limestone. All Katie had to do for Nessa and Cora to love it here was let it happen.

She rounded a bend, leaving the group's chatter behind. Here, the ridges on either side of the creek bed were higher, casting the water in deep shade. She was mentally choosing the perfect picnic spot for her and the girls, on a flat boulder overhanging a tiny waterfall, when she saw it, in a maze of fallen logs. Half floating, half beached in leafy mud.

A baby bottle.

Heart pounding, she picked her way across the rocks and bent to retrieve it, her hand shaking inside its glove. The bottle was caked with dirt—it could have been here a long time. Then again, Katie's brand-new boots didn't look any better.

Which meant the bottle could be new.

I swear, I don't feel crazy, Sky had said. When Katie promised to keep her eyes and ears open, she didn't expect to find anything. Most likely, this was nothing more than random litter she was reading too much into.

A promise was a promise, though.

Her eyes traveled up the ridge to the tree line. The bottle could have floated here from upstream—but if it hadn't, it had probably rolled from up there.

Katie slid the bottle into the pocket of her cargo pants and began to climb.

"Katie?"

In the distance, Bess was calling. She pretended not to hear. The slope was steep enough that she had to concentrate to keep hold of the ledge. She clung to each foothold, hoping there were no toxic teenage newts up here as she grabbed at ridges in the limestone and gutsy shrubs protruding at odd angles. She knew better than to look down.

"Katie?" Bess called again, closer this time. Directly below, probably. Katie kept her eyes on the ledge high above her. "What on earth are you doing?"

"Losing my mind," she called back. "Want to come?"

Bess didn't reply, or if she did, Katie was too focused to hear. The top of the slope was nearly vertical, and muddier, but above her was a cluster of three bigger trees rooted in the grassy ledge. She seized the closest trunk with both hands, then hauled her body over it in one frantic motion, feet flailing, desperate to feel solid ground on the other side. She landed in the grass, chest heaving, the forest spinning around her in her dizzy exhilaration.

She'd done it.

How about that.

She managed to sit up in time to see Bess swing herself agilely onto the grass beside her without a single sign of panting or panic.

"Show-off," she muttered.

Bess shot her a look, standing hands on hips as they oriented themselves. The forest stretched as far as they could see, nearly indistinguishable from any other Grove hilltop.

Except that not twenty feet in front of them sat a small stone building, half-reclaimed by the forest. It was scarcely bigger than a shed, with an oversize brick chimney that ran nearly the width of one wall. The roof was covered in vines, the windows boarded up with rotting wood. An overgrown stone footpath led to its wooden door, where a padlock hung from the handle.

"What is that?" Katie gasped.

"Old summer kitchen," Bess said. "There used to be a cabin up here where the foreman lived with his family. This is all that's left."

"You knew it was here?" Katie asked, incredulous. She turned in a slow half circle, searching for the nearest trail. To their far left, she caught a neon blaze marking the west perimeter detour. She'd walked it many times but never noticed the well-camouflaged structure.

"Yeah." Bess was looking at her strangely. "Why? Were you looking for a condemned building you could use to slow-roast a pig?" She stepped between Katie and the building. "Seriously. Want to tell me what we're doing up here?"

Katie did want to tell her. But then again, she didn't. Same as usual. "I don't know," she said. "Do you have the key to this padlock?"

"I can't let you go in there."

"Why not? I'm in charge of the property."

"You're *keeping an eye* on the property," Bess corrected her. "I'm in charge of it. And liable for anything that happens to an employee on my watch. As I keep trying to remind you."

Katie crossed her arms. There was absolutely no way, after all this, she was not finding out what was inside. None.

"What's this about?" Bess asked again. "One second we're talking about newts, and the next you're free-soloing the ravine." Before Katie could answer, Bess pointed at her bulging cargo pocket. "Is that a baby bottle?"

Katie looked reflexively down at the protruding nipple as if she weren't sure. "I found it in the creek." She pointed to indicate the area. "It could have been dropped from up here."

"So? Why is it in your pocket instead of your trash bag?"

"I need to rule something out."

"And what would that be?"

Katie bit her lip. Omitting details was one thing. But she didn't have it in her to lie to Bess's face. Before she could overthink it, she started talking. Fast. "A woman in my loft swore she heard a baby crying late at night. I want to make sure no one's been hanging around out here when they aren't supposed to be. Are there other abandoned buildings on the grounds?"

Bess's mouth dropped open. "Hang on. A while back, when you asked me if any animals in these woods could sound like babies crying . . . that was about this? Not foxes?"

Katie's face flushed. "I'm sorry. It's not that I didn't want to tell you. I just didn't want to . . . put you in a bad position."

Bess's eyes narrowed. "What kind of bad position?"

Katie shrugged. As if Bess had ever in her entire life accepted a shrug as an answer.

"Are you worried someone is squatting out here? Or are you worried someone is coming looking for one of these women Grace was helping?"

Katie threw up her hands. "I don't know. I'm probably being paranoid. None of the women who come through the Sequence have kids—it's against the rules. Odds are that bottle is a coincidence. But now that I know this shelter is here, I need to know it's empty. I owe it to this woman . . . She thought she was going crazy."

Bess sighed. Katie braced herself for an earful, but Bess didn't say anything at all. She just approached the summer kitchen and jammed her elbow into the rotted boards covering the nearest window. They came loose easily, and Bess switched on her cell phone flashlight with a swift nod. "I'll check," she said, leaving no room for argument. "Wait out here. And stay back. For all I know this entire thing is full of wasp nests. Or snakes. Or about to collapse."

Katie knew she should be grateful. If there was anyone she could trust to be her eyes and ears, it was Bess. If there was anyone she needed to keep on her good side right now, that was Bess too. There was no good reason to ignore her instructions and follow her in anyway.

So why did Katie feel like she should?

27

Katie inched closer to the window Bess had vanished through. The heat must be stifling in there; even from several paces away, she could feel it emanating as if from an open oven, airborne dust particles stinging her eyes. She blinked them away, straining to peer into the space where the boards had been, but saw nothing but blackness and the occasional flash of Bess's cell phone light panning the interior.

"Bess?" she called out, inching closer still. "You okay in there?"

"Hang on," Bess replied, her voice muffled. "Stay back."

Obediently, Katie stopped where she stood. The forest around her rustled and chirped, and Katie strained for any noise at all from inside the ruins of the building, any signal that something was not right. This was silly. Surely she could at least help shine a second light inside. She was about to start toward the open window again when she heard something scrape against the stone wall and Bess's face reappeared in the frame.

"Well?" Katie asked, then immediately wished she could bite back the word. She sounded juvenile, overeager, whereas Bess looked sweaty and cross.

"Suffice to say no one's been hosting Ye Olde Summer Kitchen Daycare." Bess grabbed the shoulder of her shirt and impatiently wiped a mess of cobwebs from her cheek. Even from a distance, Katie cringed. "I'll be out, but take this, would you?"

Leaning through the rotting window, Bess held out a glossy white square that appeared to be some kind of sign. "There's cord, too," she instructed. "Pull."

Katie took hold of the sign with both hands and began walking backward, trailing long strands of nylon through the opening in the wall until they tumbled to the ground. She flipped the board over in her hands. At first glance, it looked a lot like the signs Bess's team had just stretched across the creek, complete with the nature center's logo and loops to secure the cord at both sides. Except for the words, so neatly written they could almost pass for machine printing.

HAZARDOUS: KEEP OUT.

She looked up to see that Bess had hoisted herself back through the window and was twisting the boards back into place across the opening, stopping every few seconds to bat at her hair. Katie frowned down at the word "Hazardous" with a guilty pang.

"Was this supposed to be posted on the outside?" she asked.

"I don't know," Bess answered. "It's a decent mimic of our signs, but we almost never handwrite them. And it does look like someone might have tried to camp out in there, then changed their mind."

Camp out? Katie's mind whirred. "You know, I thought I smelled a campfire once, early one morning. Not far from here."

"No, I didn't know. You didn't think to tell me?"

Katie blushed. Answering that question wouldn't lead anywhere good. "What makes you think they changed their mind?"

Bess slapped the last window board into place, still swiping at her hair. "It's not habitable. Completely overtaken by wood roaches. There must be thousands of them." She moved closer, swatting her clothes now, turning in a circle. "Can you look? Are any on me?"

"Oh, gross." Katie rushed over and helped Bess shake out her shirt, checking the folds of her cargo pants. "I'm so sorry. You didn't even yell—I would have freaked."

Bess shuddered. "I respect insects, but that was a lot, even for me."

Katie wanted to hug her. Only Bess would crawl into an infested building and emerge using the words "respect" and "insects" in the same sentence.

"So what's in there? Besides the roach colony."

"This sign is pretty much it. Some ashes in the fireplace, some wrappers. My guess is someone brought in food and quickly regretted it. Could have just been kids."

"Maybe Grace caught them messing around and made a sign to deter them?"

"Maybe. But everything else in there is covered in dirt and drop-pings and I don't even want to know what else. This sign is pristine, like new. And if she bothered to make it, why take it down and put it inside? Unless someone else did, but again, why?"

Katie had never forgotten one of the first things Jude ever said to her. *First thing you'll learn out here: nobody ever listens to a sign.* Even then she'd wondered if he was being more cryptic than grouchy, trying to tell her something. She was so tired of trying to decide what was and wasn't worth worrying about. So tired in general.

"What's your actual concern here?" Bess persisted. "We're pretty far from the house. It's not like someone would be surveilling *you* out here, but . . . maybe it's time you call the cops. Get some of your suspicions on record."

Katie held up her hands. "I didn't say anything about *surveilling*."

"Well, you didn't say anything about anything. I'm just trying to figure out where this falls on the sliding scale from creepy to alarming. It's one thing to have a drunken slumber party and try to decipher Grace's journal. But now we're supposed to read threats into creek litter and track footprints in run-down buildings?"

"There were footprints?" Again, Katie thought back—this time to the footprints she'd found disappearing in the snow. Though they were probably nothing, and so was this. How much *probably nothing* could one person take? "What kind of footprints, exactly?"

Bess gave her a look. "I'm a naturalist, not an investigator, Katie. And you are neither. This is getting out of hand. You could have broken your neck climbing up here, and clearly there's more to the story. So I'm asking again: What's the real concern here?"

Katie tossed the sign to the ground at her feet, defeated. "I . . . I don't know."

"You don't know, or you won't tell me?"

The answer might have been both. Katie kicked at the dirt, sinking into the feeling that this was it. Even if she hadn't reached her own limit, she'd reached Bess's.

Bess confirmed it with a bitter laugh. "If these people are convincing you not to trust me, of all people, what else are they convincing you of? They have no concept of boundaries." Her eyes burned with anger—or was it fear? Her hands were shaking. "Look. If you honestly think someone has been stalking around where they shouldn't be, it's my job to do something about that. I don't understand how I ended up so far outside whatever is going on here at Grove, but I can't look the other way for this mystery organization at the expense of nature center operations. Or our caretaker. Maybe you shouldn't be here by yourself so much. Or maybe we do need to revisit our security measures. If the Sequence can't get around that, it's their problem."

"You mean my problem."

"No. I mean theirs. Who is paying your salary, rent, utilities? That's who you put first. Not the opportunists taking advantage, turning you into a sitting duck just to use your loft space."

Katie opened her mouth to protest. But she was stuck on the way Bess's voice had broken when she said *I don't understand*. Katie didn't either. What had Bess ever done, really, but take Katie's side, even when it went against her better judgment?

"You have a woman in your loft right now, don't you?" Bess pressed on. "Let me guess: Another special case?" Katie couldn't look at her. "Honest question: Do you really think the system can be failing this many people?"

"From what little I've seen? Unfortunately, I do."

"From what little *I've* seen," Bess spat back, "the Sequence is failing you worse."

Katie's tears didn't gently well. There was no preemptive sniffling. She just started to sob. She couldn't keep arguing when Bess wasn't wrong. Katie had been so convinced this caretaking role was the key to finding herself again. But she'd never felt more lost.

When she finally, halfway pulled herself together, she saw that Bess was crying too.

"Do you know"—Bess sniffed—"I couldn't have cared less about the newts today?"

Bess didn't look mad anymore. Only sad. Helpless.

Pretty much exactly like Katie felt.

"All I wanted was to remind you why you came here in the first place. What you have to look forward to. I didn't even know for sure if you were still doing the summer camp thing."

"Of course I'm still doing it," Katie said, but the words sounded weak, even to her own ears. As if they didn't both know exactly why Bess was asking.

"Do you also know Ethan and Emory have been bugging me to ask you if they can be Nessa and Cora's 'camp counselors'? They have this idea they could come here twice a week, share their favorite Grove hacks. And I'm big on giving them freedom to explore, so they don't understand why I'm dragging my feet about asking you. I can't tell them I don't know if I should be comfortable with *any* kid roaming out here, with everything going on. And I definitely can't tell them I've been afraid you won't say yes."

Katie wiped her face on her sleeve, chagrined. "Oh, Bess. I'm sorry. About all of it."

"Believe it or not," Bess said gently, "there are real reasons I thought this job was a fit for you. I thought you'd see that starting over doesn't have to mean starting at the bottom. The special thing about places like Grove is they're for everyone. Whether or not you know the life cycle of the newt, there's magical common ground between what people want from this space and what the reserve requires to thrive. I've always believed, with all my heart, Grove could bring you and anyone else who needs it peace. I've built my whole career around this. It's my one unshakable belief. And this has been shaking it."

She moved closer, looking at Katie so intently she almost started to cry again. "I know I'm playing devil's advocate here, but I'm so proud of you, Katie. These women you've helped—they owe you so much. I can tell it's been good for you, too, in some quiet and powerful ways, which is why I've tried not to harp on this. But at this point, it's not selfish to rethink your role. There are other ways to help, aside from becoming a full-blown activist."

Katie scrunched her nose. "I'm not an *activist*."

Bess crossed her arms, leaving Katie to sit with the word, the discomfort it conjured. Why *was* it so uncomfortable? Weren't activists merely people who were willing to take a stand for things to be better? Didn't most people, in fact, owe a debt of gratitude to earlier generations of activists, yet somehow the word carried a negative connotation of going too far, getting carried away? Katie's gaze shifted to the trees. She wanted desperately to see through them to some end, but the forest just went on and on.

Every doubt Bess was expressing, Katie had been over herself a million times before.

"I hear you," Katie said. "I do. It would be easier and probably smarter not to go further into this. But even when I'm looking over my shoulder, finding new reasons *not* to do this every day, I can't seem to let it go. Trust me, I've tried." She took a shaky breath. "Thing is, I like myself better when I'm doing this job than I have in a long time. That goes for *both* caretaker roles. If I back down from this . . ." She shrugged. "I don't want to stop liking myself again."

"Oh, Katie. I don't want that either. Obviously."

They stared at each other. Some things went without saying. That they didn't want to go on like this, surrounded by half-kept secrets and half-baked worries. That they'd been through too much together to let this break them.

Other things, though, did need to be said. Or heard.

Bess half smiled tentatively. "As your friend and coworker and the mastermind who brought you here in the first place, I have a proposition for you."

Katie half smiled back. "I'm listening."

"If this is truly what you want, tell the Sequence you'll do it—after this summer. But not until then. Not even special cases. This whole trial basis thing needs to end now, before the girls come, to let you catch your breath."

"I wish it was that simple. But that's a long time to put things on hold. If even one woman can't get help because of me, how do I get okay with that?"

"You don't. It is simple. When the air pressure drops, you put on your own oxygen mask before you assist anyone else, like the flight attendants instructed. No one would fault you for that, let alone hold you responsible for the pressure dropping in the first place."

Katie bit her lip. She had to admit, it was what she'd longed to hear. But was it true?

"Think about it: you're stretched thin as it is, and having Nessa and Cora in the mix is going to push everything to the brink. You only have what? Under two weeks left to get ready for them? Plus, this'll free you to endear yourself to more of the staff, get involved the way you did today so when the high season's over, no one is suggesting we get a more qualified caretaker."

"You think that's . . . something I have to worry about?"

"I think you won't be any good to the Sequence if you're not here long term. Plus, hello, elephant in the room. Can you honestly tell me you'd be okay with Gigi's girls, say, sleeping on the screened-in porch right now? Kids are relentless when they latch on to ideas like that. You say no, they ask, 'Why?' What reason will you give?"

Katie bowed her head. She'd been doing her best to make this up as she went, but there was no denying it was about to get harder, if not impossible.

"Put this on pause now," Bess persisted, "and you can come through for Gigi and the girls without putting them in a situation you could regret. Let me and my kids be a part of it. Invite Hottie Photographer to come take shots of the moon. Even get open to the idea of Sad Keanu being more of a Sexy Keanu." She gestured as if to say, *Stranger things have happened. I mean, look around,* and Katie managed a weak laugh. There was no stopping Bess once she hit her stride—it was why all her best ideas were so contagious. Sure enough, the speech went on.

"Have a childlike summer. Have a love triangle. Have a blast with your best friend. Have an honest go at this new gig, without constant distractions. It's okay to want those things. It's *how* you keep liking yourself without leaning on the Sequence for a sense of self-worth. Bonus, you can let the dust settle on this Grace situation and everything else that has you wound so tight random baby bottles are giving you the creeps. On the scary off chance anyone is looking for Grace or whoever else, they'll realize she's not here. Take a break, and it might sort itself out."

Bess rested a hand on Katie's shoulder. "If you're meant to be part of the Sequence, it'll be waiting for you. By then you won't be covering for Grace anymore. You'll be rising to the occasion, good and ready to be the best damn caretaker they've ever had."

For a moment, Katie could only stare back at her friend, too overcome to speak. Katie had tried so hard not to show all her inner wrestling with her conscience, the push and pull of so many decisions she'd been struggling not to make. But Bess had seen. And Bess was still here.

"Why does it sound so much more reasonable when *you* put it that way?" Katie asked at last. "In my brain, that argument felt flimsy. Like when people say they need to 'love themselves before they can love anyone else' just to end a relationship they were never into. Like a coward."

"You're not a coward," Bess said fiercely. "This isn't an emotional decision; it's practical. You can't tackle everything at once. No one could. These Sequence women, of all people, should respect that."

"You think so?"

"It'll be good for them too—they're not entirely comfortable with this yet either, right? And I'll honor whatever you decide. If you take this break now and you still want this at the end, I'll never question it again, you have my word. I'll cover you."

Katie pulled Bess into a hug. This whole time, she'd been so determined not to rely on Bess to solve all her problems.

But how wonderful would it be if Bess had gone and done it anyway?

28

Katie told Dottie in person. At the pick-up point for the woman who called herself, simply, "Z."

The last time they'd been in this corner of the parking lot, snow was blowing in. Now, it was pollen, floating so thickly through the air Dottie's car was taking on a fine yellow coating before their eyes. The contrast made it seem as if Katie had been in limbo with the Sequence far longer than she had, a stretch of uncertain seasons rather than one tumultuous spring.

Bess was right. Dottie didn't just respect Katie's decision; she seemed to respect Katie for having made it.

"Get in touch when you're ready," she said. "We all need to regroup. We didn't plan on jumping back into this either. Summer break will do everyone good."

Simple as that, the pause she'd agonized about requesting was reduced to something as ordinary as a school vacation. Dr. Clooney had told her this was all simple. Bess too. Maybe it really was Katie who'd overcomplicated things all along.

"Summer break," she agreed. Katie turned back to get Z from the barn when she heard the call from behind her.

"NCT?"

She steeled herself. This had been too easy. *Just one more favor,* Dottie would ask again, and what if she didn't have it in her to say no? She looked back. "Yeah?"

Dottie met her eyes with a sincere smile. "Turns out we really were lucky to have you. Thanks for everything."

From that point on, it became more and more clear to Katie that Bess was right. This wasn't just the best way to proceed, it was the *only* way.

Bess was right, she thought as she brightened the guest room with a coat of lavender paint, tucking pretty coverlets onto the twin beds.

Bess was right, she thought as Jude pulled up, his truck piled with wood planks, and announced he was starting a boardwalk project around the pond that would take weeks. Days ago, this news would have sent her pulse racing, her mind calculating. Now, it felt good to have nothing to hide. And to sit the manual labor out.

"Okay," she agreed. "Though why anyone would want better access to that cesspool is beyond me." Even the late-blooming daffodils had given up on the pond by now. There were lily pads, but they were heavy on the pad, light on the lily.

"Bacteria are key to pond ecosystems," he began, but stopped when he saw the look on her face. "Anyway, this won't lead to it, but around it. The far side trail is so eroded someone's bound to slip in. Also, the boardwalk will be the meeting site for the new forest bathing class."

"Forest bathing?" Should she know what this was? She could only stare blankly.

"It's what it sounds like. You go into the forest and . . ." He lifted his hands overhead as if about to lead some meditation, his face serene, inhaling deeply.

Katie lifted an eyebrow.

Jude rippled his arms slowly through the air, like a land-bound synchronized swimmer.

Her eyebrow arched higher.

"It was Bess's idea," he added, as if this explained everything. Which it sort of did.

"I see," she said. "You go into the forest and . . . do the breaststroke?"

He broke character with a loud, undignified snort, and she let loose a giggle. Soon, they were both howling with laughter.

"Seriously," Jude said, once they'd collected themselves, "they commune with nature. I don't know what it looks like. This will shock you, but I've never tried it."

"Well, as long as they don't literally bathe. Not in that pond."

"Oh no. Only in the forest. In the air, you understand."

That sent them doubling over again. Katie smiled the whole rest of the night, every time she pictured Jude, of all people, in his namaste pose. But not because of the way he'd smiled back at her when he'd done it.

Definitely not because of that.

Bess was right, she thought as she ordered matching "Happy Camper" T-shirts for her girls and Bess's little "camp counselors" too. *Bess was right,* she thought as she sailed down the frozen food aisle, filling her cart with every kid-friendly treat that caught her eye. And again when she got home to find a matted print of the luna moth in her mailbox, and her own words written across the back. "The Ballerina," Ryan had titled it. *Bess was right.*

At Pinkie's One-Stop Shop, everything all at once might be just right, but here at Grove, it was too much. And Katie wouldn't have given herself permission to say so. She might have made mistakes in this new start, but one thing she'd done right was to surround herself, at last, with people who would lift her up while she worked things out. Friends like Bess, who'd tell it like it was; colleagues like Jude, who'd give her the benefit of the doubt; artists like Ryan, who'd remind her to stop and appreciate beauty; unsung heroes like Dr. Clooney, who'd inspire her to do better. *Bess was right.*

The night before the girls were scheduled to arrive, Katie had a long phone call with her sister. Gigi had emailed ahead a manual to her daughters and wanted to talk through the highlights. Fourteen pages on how Cora got stomachaches if she ate too much dairy, Nessa had yet to be stung by a bee so they couldn't rule out an allergy, and they could read in bed as late as they wanted but should be tucked in by nine thirty or the rails would come off.

Katie sat on the porch with her printout, a gin and tonic sweating in her glass as she listened and scribbled notes in the margins.

"Don't let them talk you into everything they ask for," Gigi said. "It's okay to say no. Trust me, they're used to it."

Say yes as much as possible, Katie wrote.

"Their father might call. Let them know he's on the line, but don't force them to talk if they'd rather not. Don't be alarmed if they get emotional. He's been on about how his mum would have been happy to take them this summer. Not him, mind you, his mum. You've saved me from having to ship them all the way to Ireland. I'd have been even more of a nervous wreck."

Tell their dad to bugger off, Katie wrote.

"Don't be nervous," she assured Gigi. "I've got this. And if I get stuck with any mom-type questions, Bess is here."

"That's what I'm afraid of," Gigi joked. Then she started to cry.

"Hey. Why don't you stay over tomorrow?" Katie asked. "Do you really have to drive right back?"

"I do," Gigi cried. "It's just . . . What kind of mother am I, to be happy they're leaving?"

Finally, an answer Katie knew. "The kind who knows what it takes to do better for them. And is putting in the work, no matter what it takes. You're the best kind of mother." Katie swallowed. "I'm glad you're giving me a chance not to be the worst kind of sister for a change."

Gigi sniffled. "*I'm* the worst. I've barely even asked how you're doing without Clark."

This was the kind of thing that would have rankled Katie a few months ago. Now, she hadn't even noticed, let alone cared.

"Ever heard that expression, 'You can get bitter or you can get better'?"

"Catchy."

"Well, I've done bitter. Now I'm putting in the work too," Katie said. *No matter what it takes.* "Promise you'll come stay before you take them home? I miss you."

When Katie hung up, she flicked off the porch light and stayed in her rocking chair, finishing her drink in the dark. For the first time, she felt the true weight of the task stretching in front of her. The kind of weight you had to keep a steady hold of instead of trying to juggle.

And she thought again that Bess really had been right.

Thank goodness Katie had listened.

Katie wasn't sure what had woken her. Not three doorbell rings—she had a Pavlovian response to that by now. Something more subtle. Her windows were closed against the humid June night and its cacophony of singing insects; in the corner, the fan spun on low, helping along the weak central air. She stared at the clock on her nightstand, straining for any sound that didn't belong. It was after 3:00 a.m.

There. Faintly, coming from outside. Voices.

She slipped out of bed and to the window. The gravel between the outbuildings glowed in her floodlights. Beyond it, near the shed, she could make out two figures standing between the canoes and the tarp-covered mound of Jude's boardwalk supplies. Katie's heart began to race, her hands glued to the windowsill, her body caught in the throes of fight or flight. She watched as one of the figures took a step away from the other, arms waving through the air. There was no mistaking it: they were arguing. Facing off in hushed tones.

The other figure gestured to something between them, low to the ground. A wheelbarrow? Were they *stealing* Jude's wood, his tools? This was company property.

She should call the police, right now.

If only she'd slept through this. Reporting teenage mischief or petty theft hardly seemed worth the trouble it would cause. Police searching her outbuildings. Her sister pulling up to find officers here, taking notes. Katie squeezed her eyes shut. *Please, just go. Give up and go.*

She opened them just as one of the figures stepped into the halo of light.

Even from here, there was no mistaking the silhouette of Dottie's poodle-cut hair.

Dottie, who'd let her go without argument, so easily.

Too easily.

She hadn't wanted to believe it. But part of her must have known.

Fury flooded Katie's veins, submerging her fear. She shot through the darkness, down the stairs, clutching her phone. What could they possibly be doing, skulking around her property without so much as a heads-up? They had no right.

Bess called them "opportunists." *Taking advantage, turning you into a sitting duck just to use your loft space.* Katie had wanted to yell how wrong she was, how it wasn't like that; no one was turning her into anything she didn't want to be. How she'd left all the people who were taking advantage back in Pittsburgh, and it was condescending to imply her judgment was this consistently bad. But she knew once they started that argument, it would be hard to come back from. So she'd kept quiet.

Now, in a huff, she toed on her shoes, reaching for her hoodie—and stopped short, breathing hard, knuckles white on the doorknob, whole body trembling. It hit her like a slap:

What if.

What if Bess had been right about that too?

Should Katie be more afraid now that she knew exactly who was outside? Should she call someone—if not the police, then Bess, anyone to hear her say, "If I'm not back in fifteen minutes, send help," or, "If I'm not back in fifteen minutes, I might be finding out exactly what happened to Grace," or, "Please talk me out of doing what needs done?"

But if she hesitated, they could slip away. And she may never know why they'd come.

She had to take her chances.

29

Katie threw open the coat closet, panning the contents for anything to arm herself. She grabbed a long flashlight—heavy as a nightstick—and the bear mace, though she couldn't picture herself using it on a person, let alone someone she knew. But she couldn't go empty-handed either.

Slipping outside, she closed the door quietly behind her and set off, taking the long way around the barn to avoid the floodlights. The grass underfoot was damp, the air thick with mid-June humidity and the pulsing white noise of night insects. *Please still be here,* a voice in her brain pleaded, while another whimpered, *Please be gone.* She didn't know which was louder. She didn't know which was right. Even with only a sliver of moon, the stars lit the cloudless sky, and she hugged the shadows along the barn wall. A breeze tickled the nape of her neck, playing at the hairs pulled loose from her ponytail, carrying hints of the voices she'd heard earlier.

Still here then.

At the far end of the barn, she risked a look around the corner. The figures hadn't moved from where she'd seen them, still whispering frenetically, though she couldn't make out the words any better from here. Dottie coughed her smoker's cough, and the other figure turned away, the glow of the barn's lights illuminating her features in silhouette. Katie recognized her instantly. Sienna blew her nose into a wad of tissues. Her face was puffy from crying.

Something was definitely wrong.

Even so, Katie's body responded to the baker's presence with a slight unclenching of her shoulders, a small sigh of relief. Of everyone in the Sequence, Sienna had been the most forthcoming about why she was doing all this. She'd owned up to her mistakes with Lindsay, invited Katie in, apologized sincerely, fed her decadent sugar. She was too young and idealistic for anyone to question that her intentions were good. Pure.

Then again, she was crying. Here. In the middle of the night.

Katie stepped out of the shadows. "Can I help you with something?"

Both women startled. Sienna let out a yelp and fumbled forward. Katie had been so caught up trying to read into their exchange that she'd forgotten they had something between them on the ground, something that had made her assume they were after Jude's supplies. Sienna launched herself in front of the object now, jostling it so the handles flew out to the side.

Definitely a wheelbarrow. Some long-handled tools too. *Were* they stealing them?

Sienna righted herself, hands flying to her chest. Even in her alarm, she looked as relieved as Katie had felt to realize this was only her, not some stranger.

Dottie did not look relieved. She threw her head back. "Jesus, Mary, and Joseph," she said. "Just great."

"Sorry to sneak up on you," Katie said drily. "Then again, I live here."

"We didn't mean to wake you." Dottie's eyes darted downward, and Katie followed them. The wheelbarrow was too low to the ground for Sienna's thin frame to hide much, its contents covered in some kind of rough blanket or burlap. And maybe it was a trick of the moonlight.

But the shape of it looked distinctly human.

"What's going on?" Katie demanded.

"Nothing," Dottie said quickly.

"I thought we agreed to take a break for the summer."

"We did. We are. Go back to bed. Forget you saw us. This won't happen again."

"You say that a lot," Katie observed. "You must think I'm very forgetful." She shifted her attention back to Sienna's terrified face and pointed to the object behind her. "What is that?"

Again, Dottie answered for her. "It's nothing."

But Sienna's eyes were boring into Katie's, filling with fresh tears. "Please," she whimpered, "we don't want to involve you. We just need to borrow your pond, okay?"

"Baker!" Dottie barked. Fear shivered through Katie.

"Borrow my pond?"

"Jesus, Mary, and Joseph," Dottie muttered again. "I need a cigarette."

Katie lowered her eyes to the blanketed mound. Something dark and smooth was peeking out from one bottom corner. Something that looked an awful lot like the sole of a shoe.

The loft was one thing. She had never agreed to let anyone *borrow her pond*.

A terrible thought seized her. Before she could stop herself, it had formed into words.

"Is that *Grace*?"

Dottie's expression turned disgusted. "Of course it's not Grace!" she snapped.

"It's one of these creep abusers," Sienna clarified, and Dottie shot her a look.

"Baker, you've done quite enough."

Slowly, Katie began backing away. The first time she'd met Dottie, the woman had told her plainly: *Sometimes, there are sacrifices.* Was this—whatever *this* was—what she'd meant? If Katie broke into a run, she could get to the house, but then what? There was a *body* in this wheelbarrow. Presumably a dead one. Even if she did as Dottie asked and went back to bed, that didn't change the fact that she was a witness. A liability.

It didn't change the fact that they were, presumably, trying to *leave this body here.* Tonight. In the pond. Or that Nessa and Cora would be here tomorrow.

It didn't change the fact that Katie had come this far as a partner to these very people. That they were linked, and so were their actions—whether she condoned them or not. "If you can't get the women away safely," she asked, incredulous, "you get rid of the creeps instead?"

"No, we do *not.*" Dottie shook her head, adamant. "This one, however, hid in the baker's van." She shook her thumb toward Sienna. "He almost killed her!"

"I didn't mean to," Sienna sobbed, choking on the words. "I just wanted him off me."

Katie held up a hand. "You know what, you're right. I don't want to know. No more details. And I never saw you. But you can't 'borrow' my pond. Take him and go. Now."

"Go back inside, NCT. Tell yourself this has been a strange dream."

"Not until you leave. Don't make me call the police."

Dottie looked at her coolly. "Call them and say what? You want to tear the whole operation down because one guy came after her, and she had the balls—no, the *ovaries*—to take care of it? What the hell do you think we're doing this for?" She shook her head. "I'm still trying to get past the part where you asked if this was *Grace.*"

Somehow, she was turning this whole thing around. Like Katie was the one out of line. "I'm still trying to get past the fact that you never proved it isn't."

Dottie stomped over to the wheelbarrow and pulled back the corner of the cloth. What had looked like the sole of a shoe was in a fact a very large, very male cross-trainer. Attached to a matching leg. "More?" she asked sweetly, as if she were a server offering a coffee refill.

Katie went light-headed, dots clouding her vision.

"Go back to bed, NCT. We appreciate your concern. We've got this."

"Easy for you to say. You're not the one who will be here when he floats up!"

"He won't."

"How do you know?"

"I thought you didn't want any details?"

She didn't, of course. But she might need a few if she was going to sleep tonight. Or ever again. "Won't it smell?"

"That pond already reeks. No offense."

"Yes, but how can you—" She stopped short. "This isn't the first time, is it?"

Neither of them answered.

"Is *this* why my pond is a disgusting swamp?"

Dottie ignored the question. "Look, you're kind of downing the vibe. Good riddance to bad rubbish. You know *Thelma and Louise*? *Practical Magic*? You know that Dixie Chicks song, 'Goodbye Earl'? It's not like anyone planned this, but it's hardly a great tragedy."

Sienna nodded her shaky agreement.

"Was he looking for the hairdresser?" Katie asked, with more hope than was probably acceptable. At least she knew *that* creep's story. Maybe she could get okay with that. With the daffodils blooming late on the banks every spring to taunt what was left of him.

"No," Sienna said. "Sadly."

She had another thought, more of a long shot. More terrible. "I don't suppose he had a dog with him? Or a leash? Anyone named Tracy involved?"

Dottie looked quizzically at Sienna, then back at Katie. "Something we should know, NCT?"

She shook her head. Stupid. She was only going to make them think she was the one prone to overreacting. "Could he have been after Grace?"

"Doubtful. But if anyone did come looking for Grace, we'd have your back too."

Gina had said something similar. Everyone was claiming to have her back, but so far all they'd done was back her into a corner.

"I'm sorry," Katie said. "But I really can't let you do this."

"You're not *letting* us do anything," Sienna said softly. "You're asleep."

Katie stood her ground. "You need a different plan. The pond perimeter is under construction. Maintenance staff are on-site daily." *Maintenance staff with police training,* she almost said. But something held her back. "And classes will be forest bathing there."

Dottie made a face. "Do I want to know what on God's green Earth that is?"

Katie thought of Jude standing in this very spot, doing his nonsensical imitation, the two of them doubling over in laughter as they looked down the hillside to the water's edge. She realized with a jolt that she would never again make light of anything here, never go near the pond with a clear conscience. This was not some noble cause, this was another level, even if it had been self-defense. This, she'd never take pride in, never get used to. She would never be far enough away from it as long as she stayed on as the caretaker. Which, of course, she had to. At least for the summer. Too many people were counting on her.

For the first time in a long time, she'd even been counting on herself.

"Let us worry about that," Dottie said. "The forest bathers will never know. You have my word."

But I'll know, Katie thought. *But I live here. But there are children coming.* It did not seem wise to say any of this aloud. On the off chance that Dottie needed reminding.

"Please, Katie," Sienna said, her voice small, surprising Katie by using her real name. "There's no other plan. Only this one." Her eyes held more pleas she didn't say aloud. That she had her whole life ahead of her and was not about to let another one of these assholes ruin it. That she'd overcome so much to get here. That someone had to look out for these women, and sometimes there was a price. That playing along was the safest course for her and Katie *both*.

She was right about one thing. There was no escaping this. Not anymore.

Katie tossed the can of bear mace to Sienna.

"For heaven's sake," she said, "keep something like this in your van from now on."

Sienna stared down at the can in her hand, nodding. Like maybe it wasn't too late for a nonlethal weapon to fix this now.

But nothing could fix it, for anyone involved. Certainly not for Katie.

Even if they took their wheelbarrow and went away . . . she'd always wonder.

If it could happen again.

If it had happened before.

If one way or another, Grace had never left the property after all.

30

Katie closed the door behind her and leaned against it in the dark house, catching her breath, waiting—for what? For the bottom to drop out any second now?

One second thudded into the next, and the next, and the next.

Katie knew this feeling all too well.

If she had to think back and name the lowest time of her life, the most hopeless, the most difficult, it wouldn't have been her divorce. Nor any point in the endless string of failures that made up her marriage. Not even the miscarriage, because against all reason, there had always been hope. Hope had carried her through with a little help from its faithful cousin, self-delusion. And when it finally couldn't anymore, she'd found relief in letting go, even when the best she could manage was to coach herself through it as if it were happening to someone else. Pack up everything worth taking. Say goodbye. Let go. Accept the out-stretched hand of an old friend.

None of that was a real, rock-bottom low. For that, she had to go back further. To the night that changed everything. Or, rather, to the next morning. When Clark looked at what they'd done with abject horror and left Katie there alone, insisting this changed nothing.

As if it hadn't already changed everything. The course of her life. The makeup of her soul. The way she looked at the most precious things in her world. The way she looked at all her most formative college years, which up until now had been the best time of her life. The way she looked at herself, their friends, her memories, her wildest dreams. The way she looked at *him*.

The worst part wasn't that Clark was fooling himself, fooling them both.

The worst part was that, for a little while, Clark was right.

It was amazing she could feel so different, so inside-out wrong, and yet walk the world as the same old Katie, no one the wiser. Not even her boyfriend, who was busy planning what they'd go on to do next—together—without the slightest inkling she'd already squandered it all in one night.

How could Steve not look at her and see all her shame and guilt flaming right in front of him—behind her eyes, beneath her skin, inside her soul, burning too hot to bear, except she had to bear it, there was no way not to, this was her punishment, the only way out was through?

Worse, how could he not look at her and see all the ways she was not sorry enough? All the ways her heart was still being shredded, every time she thought of it, right now in front of him? How did he not sense her embarrassment and heartbreak over all the wrong things?

When she would not let Steve touch her, when she'd throw him just enough affection to get by, how could he accept her lame excuses, chalking it up to the emotional cocktail of graduation, affording her patience she'd done nothing to deserve, making her burn even hotter? Katie of all people should have known the depths of the human capacity to look at your relationships and see only what you want to see. But she was out on the other side now, and she'd learned nothing. She'd stretched her own yearning so far it had finally snapped in two, and now she was flat on her bottom, holding the loose ends, smarting from the fall, and *still* no one noticed. No one had to know. Clark breezed in and out like always, so chummy with Steve she might have imagined everything.

She'd gone on like that for six bottomless weeks. Every day, she'd look in the mirror and think, *I cheated on my boyfriend, who loves me.*

Me, the rule follower, the loyal friend. Me, who's spent years not feeling my feelings because I was determined not to hurt anyone—including myself. It's all undone, and on top of that, Clark rejected me. How do I live like this? How is no one calling me out? Maybe today will be the day. She'd never been a good liar, never set out to betray anyone. Apparently, just because you don't want to keep a terrible secret doesn't mean you can't.

Especially if you're the last person anyone would suspect of having one.

When she found out she was pregnant, when she knew there was no way it could be Steve's, she was overcome with a backward kind of relief. Not because she thought this would change anything with Clark—at least, not at first—but because they had no choice but to be honest now. Not just with Steve but with each other. Finally, she had an indisputable reason to confess to Clark that it had always been him. To acknowledge that *This changes nothing* had been a pipe dream.

But the truth was, if not for that pale line on the pregnancy test, it wouldn't have been.

This was the image, the feeling, the memory, that always came flooding back to her when people talked so aspirationally about being stripped of your defenses, of digging deep within.

Not everyone who finds out what they're made of likes what they see.

Of course, once you've gone there, it's too late. You can't ever forget it.

Eleven years later, you might find yourself turning on your heels. Giving up, cursing your bad judgment, unsure you can save yourself, but knowing you have to try. Knowing you have it *in you* to try. Fleeing back to bed, heart pounding, imagination running wild, piling pillows over your head, hoping it's enough to pad your hearing.

And reacquainting yourself with hope against hope—that it will pad your conscience too.

31

"Aunt Katie!" Nessa and Cora came running, arms outstretched, whooping and squealing. They caught Katie around the waist, nearly knocking her sideways. "We're here!" they yelled over one another, not quite in unison. "We're here!"

"You're here," Katie agreed, laughing a little too loudly, hoping she sounded as over-the-top wired as they were. Which she was. But not the way she'd wanted to be.

She'd heard a story once about a favorite method actor defraying some personal bad news until after the day's movie shoot. *I can't know this right now*, he'd explained, though, of course, he'd just been told. It was his way of ducking the blow, apologizing that he couldn't react until the day's prescribed tasks were done.

That was how Katie felt waking up to this day, her mind snapping to her uninvited visitors from the night before. She couldn't know this right now.

Never mind that it might be dangerous not to.

Fortunately, she hadn't had time to think this morning. One minute, she was lying there, wondering how she'd fallen back to sleep, the next, Bess was calling from the porch that she'd brought muffins, not wanting to miss Gigi. Katie hurried to let her in, unease running laps through her veins, and found herself bursting out in a genuine laugh at Bess's sweatshirt, which said, *Sorry I'm late, I saw a dog*. Then Jude's truck pulled up, and it was just as well Katie hadn't had a chance to survey the pond to see if anything looked amiss in the light of day.

She never had to decide how to keep calm and carry on. It just . . . happened.

That's what she told herself, anyway, as she rushed to shower while Bess went with Jude to survey his boardwalk-in-progress. Katie watched through the bathroom window as they disappeared down the trail, and a sad, frightened numbness washed over her, aware she'd crossed a line from being unsure how much to tell Bess to being certain she absolutely should not speak of the Sequence ever again.

She kept coming back to the same two words: *plausible deniability.* Repeating them like a mantra, or a safety net. Or a terrible dream she couldn't wake from.

Gina had called them *words to live by*, without even knowing—or *had* she known?

Katie wasn't sure which was worse.

Technically, Katie hadn't seen a body. Technically, as far as Katie knew, she'd talked sense into Dottie and Sienna last night about *whatever* was attached to the shoe in their wheelbarrow. *They didn't grasp the terrible timing. I bet as soon as I went back inside, they talked it over, realized there had to be a better way, and wheeled that barrow right out of here.*

It didn't matter if this was likely. It mattered that it was *plausible.* The reality deniable.

Given no choice but to return to her old habit of lying to herself, maybe the new Katie could reframe this. Not lying, but manifesting. That's what Cora had called it, wasn't it?

A child's misunderstanding of what the mind was capable of.

Now here were her nieces, looking so much bigger than when she'd last seen them, bubbling that this place was *as great as they expected*, and it was *so cool* she'd had to buzz them through a *real* gate, and *that bridge was wild*, exuding innocence, youth, absolute trust—all things Grove sorely lacked. And here was Gigi, hugging Bess, showing no signs of sensing danger. Only admiring the raised garden beds, fragrant with basil and mint.

"I love this!" she said. "Remember how we'd swipe sugar snap peas from old Mrs. A's garden, only we didn't even like to eat them? We just liked the *idea* of them. Such a waste."

Katie swallowed the lump that kept rising in her throat. *Sugar snap out of it, Katie. Get your head together.* "I forgot about that. Mom found piles of them rotting in our clubhouse and made us go apologize. What were we even doing with them in there?"

Both sisters squinted at Bess, as if she could explain.

"Don't look at me," Bess said. "I had brothers."

"Did you ever," Gigi teased, and they all laughed again. Gigi and Bess got on fine every year during "Sibs Weekend" in college. On one of those visits, Gigi and one of Bess's brothers got on *extra* fine. At the time, Bess had gagged, and Katie had been just as glad it didn't go beyond that weekend. But here, together all these years later, she had a wistful vision of how nice it could have been, linking their families that way.

She never had been the best at thinking ahead.

"I know what you mean," Cora said, braided pigtails swinging, "There are *so many* things I like the idea of more than the reality." She glowered at her big sister, and Katie stifled a laugh.

"All gardening still falls into that category for me," Gigi mused, expertly ignoring Cora's jab at Nessa. "Also, indoor pools. Water parks. All theme parks, really. Baseball games."

"*Mom.*" Nessa rolled her eyes. "You're just listing things you're glad to be off the hook for this summer." Something about her had transitioned from big kid to preteen. Not so much the outfit—girlish pink shorts and a T-shirt—or her wrist full of scrunchies, but her expression. A look that said, *I'm figuring things out for myself now.* And maybe, *You can't get anything past me.* Oh, how Katie hoped she could. Nessa stood apart from Cora, arms crossed, but smiling.

"Am I?" Gigi took mock offense. "How about . . . movies based on books! Never as good, but we keep on liking the idea of them."

"Margaritas," Bess added. "They give me heartburn."

"Cute boys," Nessa piped up.

Everyone looked at Katie. But the most honest response she could think of was *caretaking*, which would not land well.

"Make that all boys," she said. No one argued with that.

Cora was bouncing around the porch, gushing about everything she was "obsessed with." The porch swing, the weather vane. "Miss Bess?" she asked. "Are our camp counselors with you?"

"I told them to let you get settled first. I'll bring them by tomorrow, okay?"

"Won't take long to get settled." Nessa scowled. "Mom didn't let us bring *anything*."

Gigi scowled back. "It's a guest room at your aunt's house, not a college dorm. Personalized is hardly required."

"I did bring copies of our activity schedules for the summer." Bess changed the subject smoothly. "Anything you girls want to join, say the word and I'll add you to the list." She handed glossy packets to Katie and Gigi too. "Ignore the fees, obviously."

Katie skimmed the first page. Things had picked up here after Memorial Day, but the place was far from bustling. Now, though, she could see the nature center followed a more pagan summer calendar, Grove included. Beginning with this week's solstice, the days were surprisingly full: Wildflower hikes. Edible plants workshops. "Creek Week" and other themed day camps. Scavenger hunts with prizes. Firefly talks after hours. Even guided full-moon walks.

She fought a wave of dizziness as the words swam before her eyes. *After hours. Full moon. Scavenger hunts.* The gates open on the brightest nights. The trails full of people searching, paying close attention to everything, hoping to find something truly unexpected. Children—Gigi's children—chasing fireflies down to the water's edge.

Surely it had been like this every year, she reasoned. Grace had managed it. The Sequence must know better than to venture back again. But what if the danger was in what was already left behind? Hidden, but how well? Hidden, but for how long?

Hidden, but for whom to find it?

"Who's that?" Cora asked, pointing, startling them all. They turned to see Jude loading wood planks onto his dolly by the shed—right where Dottie and Sienna had stopped to presumably raid his tools the night before. Tools they'd better have returned exactly as they'd found them. He waved but kept a respectful distance.

"Is that your boyfriend?" Cora stage whispered. "He's more muscly than Uncle Clark."

"Cora," Gigi said sharply, but Katie laughed.

"He's not my boyfriend. He works here. He's a handyman."

"I can see that," Gigi teased.

"If you think he's good looking, wait till you see the nature photographer," Bess sang.

Cora tugged Gigi's shirt. "Mom, you need tips from Aunt Katie. You're always telling us you can't find any boyfriends in the city, and in the middle of nowhere she found *two*."

"Thank you," Gigi purred, "for that astute observation." She turned to Katie. "You've been holding out on me. I need to call Bess from now on for the real story, huh?"

"Nope. There's no story." *Not a romance anyway. Can I interest you in a murder mystery? A missing person thriller? A cozy about an incompetent amateur sleuth?*

"No story *yet*," Bess corrected her, winking at Gigi. "It's fair to say Katie has yet to take full advantage of her newfound freedom. But she has options when she's ready."

Katie wanted to cry. Leading up to today, she *had* felt more ready to embrace whatever came next. Yet overnight, *newfound freedom* had ceased to apply to her life. Who could feel free when any moment could bring police roaring up, sirens blazing, search warrant waving?

She finally understood exactly why everyone had warned her, over and over, the less she knew, the better. Somehow she still didn't know anything, yet she'd seen too much.

Chevy took this moment to make her grand entrance, emerging from the barn for a showy stretch in the sun, and the girls skipped off to meet her.

"Since when do you consider Jude an *option*, anyway?" Katie asked Bess, deflecting. "This is the second time you've brought it up."

"You said he was growing on you. Can't he grow on me too? It's nice to see you bring out the best in a man for a change. As opposed to the previous arrangement."

"*Ooh,*" Gigi purred. "Are we hating on our exes? I'm in."

"I'm out," Katie said.

"You're too nice," Bess said. "And no fun."

Katie entertained a brief fantasy of cheerily announcing, *As a matter of fact, for your information, someone's ex is rotting in the pond right now! How's that for nice? Is that fun enough for you?* She had a flash of Dottie singing along to "Goodbye Earl."

She clapped her hands. "Gigi, want to stay for a bite?"

Gigi glanced at her watch. "Maybe. Girls," she called, "should we unload? Find your room?"

They really hadn't brought much. Katie hung back while Gigi directed her daughters. Cora carried in two armfuls of stuffed animals, and after debating whose bed was whose, set to work arranging them around her pillows to stand sentry over the room. Nessa, in the quintessential role of big sister, had exactly one plush, a cocker spaniel worn thin with love that she stuffed under her pillow, out of sight. She'd brought a glittery pouch of gel pens, notebooks, a tangle of earbuds, and one of Gigi's old phones, which she explained with another eye roll had no calling or texting enabled, only music and games.

"Basically," she summarized, "not a phone. A device denied its purpose in the world."

"If you find it so useless," Gigi said, unbothered, "I'd be happy to take it home with me."

"I'll take it," Cora chirped. Gigi went on folding clothes into drawers with the bored patience of a mom who's had this conversation a hundred times and will have it a hundred more. You'd never guess last night she'd been crying to Katie, questioning herself, and Katie was glad.

Worried, but glad.

"You can call me," Katie said, handing over a pair of walkie-talkies to the girls. She and Gigi had agreed on this in advance, deciding to present it as a fun surprise instead of what it really was: a safeguard. "These are the long-range ones our staff uses over at the main campus. I got one too. This way, when I'm working or you're playing, we can stay connected."

Nessa tried to remain aloof, but it wasn't long before Cora had her sister testing out the channels from across the room, giggling and speaking in spy code. Success.

Except that Bess kept sneaking sidelong glances at Katie, even pulling her aside in the upstairs hallway to ask if she was okay.

Fine. Just wrapping my brain around the plausibility of what's deniable.

"I just hope I can handle this," Katie whispered. She gestured through the doorway where, despite her assertion this was not a dorm, Gigi was hanging a corkboard for the girls' mementos from home. Soon she'd drive off, leaving Katie fully responsible for these children she saw maybe twice a year. Not strangers, but not much more than acquaintances either.

"You've *already* been handling this," Bess said, squeezing Katie's shoulder. "Every decision you've made lately has been with them top of mind."

Katie blinked back tears. It wasn't her decisions she was worried about.

It was everything beyond her control.

Gigi found her in the kitchen later, with the kids on her heels looking more subdued than they had upstairs. Katie could tell she wasn't the only one who'd had a rush of *Holy whoa, this is really happening.*

"They've talked me into staying for lunch," Gigi said, "if you're sure that's okay?"

"Better than okay." Katie gave Gigi a peek under the foil of the platter she'd made—triangles of grilled cheese on sourdough, kettle-cooked chips, salad greens, watermelon.

"I'll give you all some time," Bess said. "Gigi, great to see you. Girls, I'll bring the counselors by in the morning, if you're up for a creek walk first thing?"

"We'll wear our shirts," Cora promised.

Bess showed herself out, and Katie carried lunch to the picnic table alongside the porch. Jude had helped her cut a center hole so she could add an umbrella for shade, but she hadn't bothered with it yet this overcast week. Now, the clouds were thinning, the sun gleaming off the vinyl tablecloth and raising sweat beads on the pitcher of lemonade.

"I'll grab the umbrella," Katie fussed. "Go ahead and start."

She jogged to the open garage where she'd unloaded her stash of summer fun, still in the bags from the big box store, away from the dusty clutter of the barn. Yesterday, as she'd backed in with all her purchases, she'd found herself looking up at the ceiling and reciting yet another *Bess was right.* Thank goodness Katie had listened. Thank goodness she wouldn't have to fret that her nieces might detect some presence in the loft overhead. Thank goodness she wouldn't have to nervously hover as they perused this buffet of surprises from their super prepared, super together aunt—bubbles, hula hoops, glow sticks, sparklers, hammocks to string between trees.

How quickly that sense of assurance had evaporated. She wanted it back.

She wheeled around the corner and crashed smack into something tall and soft. Or rather, *someone*. He jumped back, startled, the leather camera bag bouncing at his hip.

"Ryan!" she gasped. "You scared me."

"You scared me back." His hand went to his chest. "I'm so sorry."

This was her fault, leaving the garage door wide open. Just because the loft wasn't in use didn't make it okay to let her guard down. She couldn't have people wandering in off the trails, thinking this was a public building. Yikes.

Then again, Ryan wasn't some clueless random hiker. He knew his way around by now.

"What are you doing in here?"

"I was looking for you. But I saw you had company and . . ." His face reddened. "You want the truth?"

The way those translucent eyes were looking at her—something bubbled in her core. A chemical reaction transforming her unease into a different kind of nerves. She could only nod.

"I worked out what I planned to say. I was going to just come out with it. But then you all filed outside and my mind went blank. Clearly, the smooth thing to do was panic and duck out of sight. And get caught, of course."

"Clearly." This was so not the time for any of this. Yet Katie couldn't help fighting a smile, the bubbling intensifying. "What was it you planned to say?"

He stepped closer, looking down at her so earnestly she understood how it felt to have all your thoughts erased.

"That I haven't run into you for a few days. And I've missed it. That maybe we shouldn't leave seeing each other to chance anymore." He blushed again, grinning in a way that seemed to ask permission. To assure her he could take it back if she wanted him to.

And she didn't. Even though maybe she should.

"Do you need help with the umb—" Gigi came around the corner and stopped short. "Oh! Hello." Katie watched as her sister eyed the camera bag, her gaze sliding up Ryan's tight-fitting T-shirt to his windswept hair, correctly surmising this was *the* nature photographer Bess had alleged had one up on Jude. Gigi agreed, judging from the look she shot Katie.

An amused, affectionate look that said, *You really do find them in the middle of nowhere, you magnificent bitch.*

"Ryan," Katie said, "this is my sister, Gigi. She's here dropping off my own personal summer campers."

"Nice to meet you, Ryan." Gigi glowed. "Katie was about to lug over this big heavy umbrella for our lunch . . ."

"Let me get it." He hoisted the umbrella with one arm, the stand with the other, and set off in long strides, biceps tightening.

"*Big, heavy umbrella?*" Katie hissed under her breath.

Gigi flashed the universal grin used by sisters everywhere to signify, *I can be a magnificent bitch too.*

Ryan was making quick work of the setup by the time they caught up, while the kids watched with interest. "These are my nieces, Nessa and Cora," Katie said, resting her hands on their shoulders. "They're staying with me while Gigi finishes her MBA."

She figured he'd wrap up and make himself scarce—their conversation to be continued. But instead, as she slid onto the bench next to Gigi, he turned his attention to the kids. "What a hardworking mom you have. I've looked into an MBA if my grants applications don't pan out, and it takes a *lot*. You're lucky to have such a cool aunt too."

"I bet they will pan out," Nessa said, though he hadn't even said what the grants were for. She looked dangerously close to flashing Katie an indiscreet thumbs-up, or maybe taking a cue from her mom and asking him to pour a lemonade from that "big, heavy" pitcher.

The feminist in Katie had her work cut out for her.

"Aunt Katie *is* cool," Cora agreed. "The other summer campers only get to come for a few hours a day, but we get to stay. Plus, it's better than Girl Scouts, because her shower isn't open to the outside and full of daddy longlegs."

Ryan and Katie exchanged amused looks. Gigi shrugged. "What can I say, their open house left quite an impression."

"What's in that fancy bag?" Nessa asked.

Ryan obliged, unzipping the flap to reveal his neatly packed gear. She whistled.

"I'd love to learn to use a camera like that," she said. "That's like, professional."

"The equipment is professional, but not me. Not yet anyway. I thought I knew what I wanted to be when I grew up, but here I am, trying to learn something new in my thirties."

Cora nodded knowingly. "I'm learning a lot in my nines." Everyone laughed.

"Why don't I come out one day," Ryan suggested, "and let you try it? As a part of your camp. I'll help you take all the photos you want, and you can each pick a few favorites to print."

"You don't have to do that," Katie began, but was drowned out by the girls' cheers.

"Girls," Gigi said, leaning over the table. "You can see his camera is not a toy. It's expensive." But Ryan waved her away.

"It'll be good practice for when my daughter is old enough to learn," he said. "I'm happy to do it." He beamed—not at Gigi, but at Katie. "Why don't I put my number in your phone?"

Gigi's knee bumped Katie's beneath the table, and Katie handed her phone over. Not that she'd needed the nudge.

"When?" Cora persisted. "How soon can we do it?"

"You girls just got here," Gigi reminded her. "You have plenty of time."

"It'll fly by," Nessa said, looking right at Ryan. "Then Aunt Katie will be all alone again." Katie wanted to crawl under the table.

"Why wait? How about tomorrow?" Ryan asked. He keyed in his number and handed Katie's phone back. "The sun creates harsh shadows this time of year, though. It would be easier for your first time out if we could do it closer to, say, dinnertime. If that's okay with your aunt?"

"Maybe you could stay for dinner after," Cora suggested. "Aunt Katie can cook it up while we're having our lesson. She even has a garden. And none of those sugar snap peas. Only things that taste as good as they look."

Beside Katie, Gigi choked on her water.

Ryan's eyes twinkled. "No culinary compensation required."

Katie looked down at her plate, feeling the heat of all eyes on her. This whole day had taken on a momentum of its own, and it was only lunchtime. Would every day with the girls here be this way? Not that there weren't worse things, considering.

"It's the least we can do," she said. "You're welcome to stay if you'd like."

Ryan was not even back to the tree line yet before everyone at the table was giggling, Katie included. She had to admit, she was grateful for the distraction.

"Well," Gigi said later, leaning on the hood of her car. Katie had waved off her offer to help clear the table, busying herself to give Gigi and her daughters space to fiercely hug and exchange last-minute promises (Cora), reminders (Gigi), and *I knows* (Nessa). Now, Katie stood holding a dish towel while Gigi jangled her keys, stalling. Across the lawn, the girls were practicing cartwheels, waiting to wave when their mom drove away. "I can see you'll be in great hands with my girls," Gigi teased. "Or is it the other way around? I'm not sure anymore."

"Neither am I."

Gigi stepped closer, lowering her voice. "Everything all right with Bess, by the way? She seemed kind of . . . I don't know. Distracted."

"Did she?" Katie had been so preoccupied just trying to hold it together, she supposed she wouldn't have noticed. Then again, how perceptive could Gigi be if she hadn't sensed anything off about *Katie*?

"She's got a lot going on," Katie said. "You saw that activity calendar."

"True. Speaking of. A word of advice?" She was being so careful with Katie's feelings—not dispensing advice, only asking if she wanted it. Katie wanted to cry, to tell her *Wait, before you leave them with me, there's something you should know.* She settled for a nod.

"I always think of the first time I took them to the zoo. They were babies, but I was determined to have this perfect day. And we did. But halfway through, I realized it wasn't the animals they were entertained by. We'd be feet away from a massive elephant, and they weren't even watching it."

Katie laughed. "What were they watching?"

"The other kids. Every time a kid yelled, 'Look!' or 'Wow!' or roared like a lion, that's what drew their attention. We might as well have been at the park, for free. Or in line for ice cream somewhere."

"So you're saying . . . Don't try too hard?"

Gigi nodded. "Don't overthink it. All these preplanned activities, special photography outings, that's all great—but it's extra. Don't feel like you have to turn this place inside out for them to have a good summer. All they care about is spending time with you."

Don't overthink it. The advice was well intended; the point was wise. Except if Gigi only knew how much there was to overthink, she'd pack her daughters back in the car, withdraw from her intensive, and possibly never speak to Katie again.

This was what Katie had hoped for with her sister: This teary, heartfelt moment of understanding, of repairing their bond, taking their trust to a new level, being something they hadn't been to each other before. A different kind of sister. A better kind of aunt. All the things she'd wanted in the first place. All the things it was too late to back away from now.

Because now, this moment was upon her. A moment she didn't want to squander. A moment she didn't want to live to regret.

"Thanks," she said. "It's all I care about too."

32

As far as the girls were concerned, Camp Aunt Katie was off to a good start. Katie took Gigi's parting advice to heart: instead of running them down every trail for a tour, they spent the afternoon hanging around the house, getting reacquainted. They ate popsicles under the new umbrella while the girls taught Katie a card game called Trash. They pulled books about butterflies off the living room shelves, gushing over every glossy picture. Jude came bearing gifts on his way out for the day, presenting to each girl a perfect four-leaf clover for luck, drawing them a treasure map to a whole patch by the pond where the genetic mutation for the fourth leaf was prevalent. The irony did not escape Katie—luck was relative, she supposed. Chevy kept a wary distance from the energetic new guests, sunbathing nearby with one eye open.

As the evening turned golden, Katie packed up lunch leftovers and drinks and led the girls to the overlook where she'd perched on her own first hike, thanks to a tip from the hiker who turned out to be Gina. Strangeness of that memory aside, it remained Katie's favorite view on the entire property. Now that the woods were at their lushest, the ridge seemed even higher above the river shimmering in the distance, and the creek beckoned invitingly as it snaked through the ravine far below. They draped a blanket over the massive, benchlike branch and swung their legs while they ate, chatting about their friends back home. Later, backtracking through the parking lot that had emptied for the day, Nessa sang Katie her song from the choir concert. Cora put a lot of effort into arranging her face to convey that Nessa wasn't *that* good.

Nessa was excellent.

"I could listen to you sing all day," Katie said, meaning it.

"Don't worry," Cora quipped. "You will."

By the time they reached home, Katie was dragging, her sleepless night and the day's emotion catching up to her. She was prepared to rally if the girls asked about the fire ring and s'mores, but they seemed just as wiped, having hit the road before sunrise.

They got quiet as they settled for bed and didn't squabble over who got which bathroom shelf or whether to use the night-light, though Gigi had predicted they would. Katie wondered if they were missing home, but they both hugged her tight when she said good night, each curled under the covers with a chapter book.

She took a last look as she left their door ajar and slipped across the hall. The sky wasn't quite dark, but Katie had no plans to do anything but collapse into bed.

They could check "Camp Orientation" off the list. Everyone was okay. No one had cried. No one had pulled the *Black-Eyed Susans* book from where Katie had stuffed it between the two least interesting, most oversize field guides she could find. No one had regretted they'd come. At least, no one had voiced it.

A new countdown had begun. One day down, five weeks and six days to go.

Every day that didn't meet with disaster would inch them closer to accomplishing what they'd set out to, pulling this off with everyone safe, happy, and blissfully unaware. Everyone but Katie, of course. In the meantime, Katie would take her wins this way, in a baby-step Sequence of her own—a sequence of survival.

As she climbed under the covers at last, she told herself she was just going to have to get used to leaving unfinished business unfinished. She still had one job, and it hadn't changed. Even this terrible incident with the pond, once she got past the initial shock, was really more of an extension of what she'd known about the Sequence, a stretched measure of how far they'd go. Dottie had always been up-front that she was the one calling the shots, and Sienna had always been on the *act first, think later* side.

In fact, the only truly out-of-character thing that stood out in the past twenty-four hours was Gigi asking about Bess. *Had* Bess been distracted? Had Katie been preoccupied to the point of not noticing something was up with her friend? Her heart sank at the thought of it: things were on their way to being so much better between them. She rewound the day, but through it all, Bess was more of a vague peripheral presence. The specifics she did recall were unremarkable: Bess arriving in her Sorry I'm Late shirt, walking with Jude to see the boardwalk, pulling Katie aside to ask if *she* were okay.

Katie wanted nothing more than to drift off to sleep, but her overtired brain couldn't seem to stop playing it all back. She kept rewinding, to Bess the day before that, and the day before that, looking for any other sign that all was not well, any other out-of-character thing.

She'd almost drifted off when her eyes shot open in the darkness, remembering.

No: picturing.

Flicking on the light, she fumbled on her nightstand for the brochure Bess had left, the summer activity calendar. She flipped it open and sure enough, next to the description for "Buddy Up With Bugs!" camp, was a close-up photo of a woman's hand holding a squirming mound of wood roaches. The woman's out-of-focus face was in the background, smiling a genuine smile.

It was blurry, but unmistakably Bess. Looking not at all squeamish.

Katie was wide awake now. She knew handling bugs was not the same thing as being trapped in a tiny building infested with them. *That was a lot, even for me,* Bess had said.

Still. She thought of the *un-Bess* way she'd swiped at her hair as she'd exited the summer kitchen. The way she'd ordered Katie to stay at a distance. The way she'd boarded over the window the second she dropped out.

The way her hands had been shaking with what Katie took for fury.

Katie threw off the covers. There was only so much she could do during the day without drawing the girls' attention to places she didn't want them playing. But now, she could hear Cora's soft snoring from here. If she hurried, she could be out to the summer kitchen and back in half an hour. They'd be locked up safe and fast asleep, never knowing she was gone. And if by any chance they did wake up, their walkie-talkies were right there on their nightstand, giving them a line out and her ears on the ground. She grabbed her own handset and rushed to get dressed.

This was one piece of unfinished business she could finish up right now.

For nearly a mile, the beam of Katie's flashlight was all she could see as she followed it down the path, darkness encroaching from all sides, mosquitos dancing ahead of her. Her long sleeves and pants warded off the swarms but left her sticky with June humidity by the time the summer kitchen came into view, so far off the path she might have missed it entirely.

Except for the faint light illuminating the cracks in the windows, the shape of the door.

That, she hadn't expected, and she briefly wished she hadn't given her mace to Sienna. The weight of the phone in her pocket was a cold comfort. Yet her fear barely even registered as surprise. True surprise would require faith that the Sequence had already shattered.

She was, however, horrified. Angry. And resolute.

She didn't know what Bess had seen in the summer kitchen. She didn't understand why she hadn't told Katie the truth. Whatever was going on here, it was wrong.

What kind of women's group didn't understand no means no?

But then, she heard the most nonthreatening sound there was, beckoning her from inside the walls: a faint, female humming. Katie couldn't pick out a melody, but the tone was unmistakably soothing, like you'd use to comfort a child.

She began picking her way toward it through the thick weeds off the trail. Was it possible that when she'd closed her loft for the summer, the Sequence had simply moved their safe house to the summer kitchen instead? No caretaker, stay at your own risk? After last night, she couldn't put anything past anybody. If this so-called summer break wasn't a sham, it was at minimum a pact they were willing to void.

The padlock dangled loose from the slightly ajar door. Katie didn't knock. She didn't hesitate. She was done asking permission.

She steeled herself and pushed it open.

A woman knelt in a circle of lantern light holding a baby, swaying with a practiced bounce. The summer kitchen interior was not dirty or infested, but swept clean as a dirt floor can be, and empty save for the makeshift changing pad and open diaper bag at the woman's side. When she looked up at Katie, her eyes weren't even startled. Only tired, apologetic. She carried no safe haven card that Katie could see.

A baby? Katie's brain swam against the currents of exhaustion and deepening confusion. The Sequence might break their own rules under the right circumstances—even unspoken rules pertaining to, say, disposing of inadvertently dead attackers' bodies—but a baby would *never* be one of them. Not if they hadn't even bent for a pregnant woman like Sky.

But Sky had heard a baby weeks ago.

"We were on our way to see you," the woman said, as if she didn't have to guess who Katie was. As if she already knew. "Pit stop for a diaper change."

Katie shook her head. It didn't matter that she couldn't allow this even if she wanted to, even if Dottie had made some exception without consulting her. She'd never in a million years be able to hide a baby *anywhere* on the property without someone hearing—Nessa or Cora or Jude or Bess or anyone. Babies cried. A lot. Babies were unpredictable, oblivious to what delicate balance they were disturbing.

This one, bundled loosely in a muslin blanket, was squirming even now. Looking flushed. Uncomfortable. Sweaty.

"I don't know who sent you here, but there's some mistake. I can't help you."

"I need you to call Dr. Clooney."

Katie recoiled, still gripping the door. If this woman hadn't been—couldn't have been—sent by the Sequence, how could she know they had a doctor, much less his alias?

"I wouldn't be here if I had another choice." The woman's voice shook. "The baby, she's really sick. I'm scared."

Only now, as the shock at seeing the baby subsided, could Katie process the woman holding her. She did indeed look desperate and frightened and still, genuinely, sorry.

Also, familiar.

"I'm Grace."

33

Katie and Grace faced off across the loft. Katie sat stiffly at the table, fiddling with the laminated welcome sheet laying out all the rules. Rules that had so impressed her with their ingenuity the night she'd found them. Rules that, apparently, no one but their tenants had the sense to follow.

Katie waited for relief to set in. Grace was accounted for, in the flesh. This was what she'd wanted, wasn't it? Proof that Grace was not rotting somewhere on the property, her abrupt absence a cautionary tale that Katie had not heeded. Grace was okay.

Yet that was obviously not entirely true.

Grace perched on the edge of the mattress, where the baby was coiled in the restless sleep of the unwell. She kept a hand on the curve of the baby's back, eyes darting around the room.

There's no one else who can help, she'd begged. *Please.*

Not here, Katie had said, eager to get back, to not let the girls out of her sight again. Drawn as she was—irresistibly—to the prospect of finally learning why Grace had left, Katie was caretaker now. The one with the keys and codes, title and responsibilities. The one who said who could stay and who had to go. Grace had walked away from the whole full-course meal, sticking Katie with the bill. She wasn't entitled to dessert.

Now, the stillness of the stuffy loft was a facade. They might appear to be sitting in opposite corners, but they were barreling toward each other, playing chicken on a one-lane road.

"There are kids asleep in my house," Katie said. She'd checked to make sure they were still locked up tight and undisturbed, but still. "They can't wake up and find me gone."

Clearly, this wasn't news to Grace. She didn't look at Katie the way anyone would in meeting their replacement for the first time. More like some aloof coworker who'd finally gotten around to saying hi.

"I'll talk fast," Grace promised.

Her story started by getting one thing straight: she'd never intended to quit.

The way Grace told it, she knew of at least one woman she'd sheltered in the loft who never reached safety. At least, not for long. She'd made a fatal slip, calling her cousin, who'd jotted down pertinent information her ex had been watching for. Within days he'd tracked her down, and that was that.

Weirdly, it wasn't those stories that haunted Grace. She'd done what she could. It was the stories of the women she couldn't help that haunted her. The ones who didn't qualify or had someone they were unwilling to leave, even to save themselves—and could you blame them? On paper, those women, conversely, often had more to live for: children, parents, siblings, friends. People who'd not only notice but care if they vanished. People who'd do anything to find them, unwittingly making things worse—or more horrifically still, putting themselves in danger.

People like Grace's own mom.

She didn't get into those details, and Katie didn't pry. The point was that at first, this whole system had seemed like a beautiful way to honor her spirit, but eventually, Grace couldn't escape the idea that the very woman who'd inspired her role in the Sequence would never have benefited from it. Grace's only sibling, a half sister her mom gave birth to in high school, was eighteen by the time things got really bad, but Grace had still been a dependent in every sense of the word. Even if her mom had ventured to a shelter, she'd never have been pulled aside for a late-night heart-to-heart with Dottie. And the biggest reason why? Grace herself.

No matter how many women Grace went on to help, what kind of tribute was that?

Yes, Grace had made peace with every story she'd inked into the *Black-Eyed Susans* journal. It was the blank pages that started keeping her up at night. What began as an itch became a drive, then an insatiable greed to fill *all* the pages, fuller, faster, better, smarter. Sequence policies that had once seemed sensible started feeling cowardly. It wasn't enough.

Grace had ideas for fixing that.

Dottie didn't want to hear them.

Grace told her anyway. Or, at least, she tried. Yes, more ambitious saves would require more ambitious risks—but surely that didn't mean they weren't worth considering? All Grace wanted was to put some ideas up for discussion by the group, but Dottie wouldn't allow it. She told Grace that attempting anything beyond what they were already doing was reckless, that *Grace* was getting reckless, that she was going to get them caught, charged with identity fraud or worse. She reminded Grace—as if she needed reminding!—there was not always room for nuance in the law. With the tougher cases, they had to keep faith that the traditional systems in place would eventually help, imperfect though they may be.

Grace had called Dottie "unimaginative." Just because they'd hit on a Sequence that worked didn't mean they couldn't try to innovate a better one. But *any* kind of ongoing conversation made Dottie squirm— she saw no room in their quick, choreographed exchanges for sarcastic swipes or passive-aggressive emails. She said if Grace didn't "snap out of it," soon they wouldn't be helping anyone at all. She even implied she'd find a workaround to Grove entirely.

Grace found it all the more infuriating because deep down, she was bluffing. If Dottie wouldn't help expand their offerings, Grace was unlikely to make good on her own threat to find someone who would. But if she kept at it, maybe Dottie would meet in the middle.

"I don't get why no one else is frustrated by this," she'd vented to Gina. They were up late one freezing February Saturday, playing rummy at the bar table inside the balcony of Gina's apartment. Gina got lonely when her "other half" was out driving, and as for Grace, well, she was getting sloppier about Sequence social constraints as her resentment grew.

"Everyone's frustrated by it," Gina insisted. "It's not great to feel like you're doing the best you can, yet every damn time you turn on the news you see it's only a drop in the bucket. But I don't think you're mad at Dottie, CT. I think you're mad at the world." Grace didn't want to hear it. She distracted herself by wondering where Gina had managed to find a pink leather couch.

When Grace's doorbell rang unexpectedly a couple of weeks later, like Katie, she knew as soon as she laid eyes on the young woman—or, more specifically, on the baby she was holding—she couldn't have come through the Sequence.

"Who sent you here? Why?" she asked the mother, who shivered in her puffy coat and peered at her blankly through eyes swollen from crying. Grace couldn't ask for the safe haven card without giving herself away, but glanced over the woman's hands and pockets, seeing none.

"I just . . . heard you could help."

This was concerning, on a multitude of levels. Either someone inside the Sequence was challenging Grace to find a better way on her own, if she was so sure there was one, or someone on the outside had gotten wind of the safe house.

Heard from whom? Grace needed to know. The woman refused to say. *How did you get here? Who dropped you off? I need names.* That's when the icy rain started. Grace crossed her arms, unmoved. *Let me drive you someplace safe. You heard wrong—there's nothing I can do for you.* That's when the mother's sobbing began, one word, over and over. *Please. Please.*

"I don't know her name," she said finally, desperately. "She was just . . . someone who changed her mind about doing this herself. She offered for me to take her place."

Grace's mind raced. "Someone where? In the shelter?"

The woman paused, as if deciding whether it would be okay to answer. Then she nodded.

Grace wavered. There remained a slim chance her phone would ring any minute and Dottie or someone would explain. But she doubted it. The truth was, wishing they could help mothers like this one—without broaching shaky legal or ethical ground—did not mean she had the first clue how it might be done. Later, she'd have to get to the bottom of who had sent this woman and how they'd known to do so and where the hell she was supposed to go from here.

In the meantime, having a policy against these guests was one thing, but closing the door in their faces on a miserable March night was another. Even Dottie would have to acknowledge that they were here, like it or not, and carrying an infant around in the dark woods was not the safest of choices for myriad reasons. What harm was there in waiting a few hours? Emotions were running high, but after some rest and a hot breakfast, clearer heads would prevail. As the saying went, things would look brighter in the morning.

Grace should have known better.

Maybe part of her did. Because it took only an instant to process what was happening when she opened the loft door after sunrise and found it empty except for the baby, ensconced in a makeshift bassinette made from couch cushions. And, of course, the note.

Forgive me. I can't. But she can.

The woman had said so little in her brief stay. *Please. Thank you.* And now, *Forgive me.* Were there any other words that said so much and yet never enough? Grace had run outside, yelling pleas of her own. *Wait! Come back! This is a mistake. It doesn't work like this.* But she was sure the woman didn't hear—long gone by then.

The gravity of her mistake sank in as she rushed back inside and took stock of the essentials the mother had left: formula, bottles, pacifiers, diapers, clothes. A week's supply, maybe, though Grace didn't know enough about babies to estimate, or even how old this one might be. Three months, six? There was a carrier you could wear like a reverse backpack, around the front. The baby was making little grunts of displeasure, setting up for a proper cry, and Grace quickly strapped it on and threaded the baby's tiny limbs inside. She grabbed a handful of Grace's hair and pulled, settling down.

There was no point in beating herself up over making the wrong call. Suppose she'd told the mother no and sent her away. Driven her somewhere, even. Now that she knew where to find Grace, what was stopping her from leaving her baby here anyway? If not today, tomorrow?

Nothing, that's what.

Whoever had sent this woman here for help—allegedly letting her take her place—had made the gravest error of all. Because from that moment on, Grace's fate had been sealed.

She snapped into action, firing off an email to Dottie.

> Random question: Has anyone ever changed their mind about going through the Sequence once you get them started? If so, curious about their reasons why.

She added the last bit to make it seem less out of the blue—she'd been pushing to review their best practices after all. If Dottie acknowledged someone had reversed course, at least they'd have a starting point—a source who might lead them to this mystery mother. But Dottie wrote back within moments.

> CT, you know I don't even think the word Sequence
> in the presence of a woman who's going to change
> her mind.

She thought back on the way the mystery mother had paused before nodding when Katie asked whose place she was allegedly taking in the loft. *Someone where? In the shelter?* What a foolish, leading question that had been. Then again, Dottie had gotten overconfident too. How could she possibly know whether their operation had become an open secret among some subset of the women in the shelter? Grace wanted to believe some version of the mystery mother's story was true, even if she was only "taking the place" of a woman who merely *wished* she could pull a Sequence escape hatch. It was as plausible as any other explanation she could think of. But it wasn't much of a lead.

Her mind skipped ahead the way her years in the Sequence had taught her to, as if on stones across the creek, looking for the solid ground of the next possible solution. And she landed on an educated guess, a gamble she was prepared to double down on: the mother would return.

Wherever she was right now, she'd already be feeling the twinges of regret. She might feel prepared to go home and face an angry husband, but nothing could prepare you for an empty crib. For abandoned onesies that say "I Love Mommy" and the sweet scent of baby lotion.

The only thing babies needed as much as nourishment and safety was a mother.

And a mother needed her baby every bit as much. She might tell herself she could loosen that knot tied around her heart, but it would only pull tighter with each day they were apart. Eventually, she'd realize that while this had seemed the best solution in principle, it would never feel that way in practice. The only way either of them could truly escape whatever danger they were in was to find a way to do it together.

Besides, what about the logistics? Sooner or later, she'd have to account for her baby's whereabouts. Sooner or later, coming back would start to seem easier than staying away.

When that happened, she'd return.

The logical thing to do was to wait her out.

One big problem: Grace couldn't account for the presence of a baby any more than the mystery mother could for the absence of one. Babies needed constant attention, as did Grove. Grace could not sit inside, hoping no one would notice, even if she wanted to. Which she did not.

She thought of her own mother and all she'd sacrificed to keep Grace safe. Her sanity, her very self. Grace couldn't let another mother make the same mistake. If she could talk to the woman again, she could make her see. Grace may have done the exact wrong thing last night, but she was the exact right person to change this mother's mind. All she had to do was find her.

Assuming, of course, that the woman was the baby's mother and this situation wasn't even worse than it appeared. Grace pushed the thought away and went on talking herself through it. Two ways out of this: either find the mother or wait for the mother to find her. Luckily for Grace, her closest Sequence friend was a private investigator. Unluckily for Grace, she couldn't employ her services.

She'd messed up, spectacularly, proving Dottie had been right all along: any cases with kids involved, no matter how heartbreaking, were too risky to take underground. It was going to cost Grace more than she'd ever imagined one misstep could.

But Dottie wouldn't get the chance to say, "Told you so."

As of now, if Grace were caught with a baby that had been, say, reported kidnapped, she had no idea how she'd explain—but that was her problem and hers alone. If, however, she reached out to anyone in the Sequence for help, she'd implicate them. It was one thing to have to step away from the organization she'd help build. But to see it torn down with her, everything they'd built reduced to nothing . . . She couldn't let that happen.

Any lingering doubt faded: *The Sequence hadn't claimed responsibility for this mother and baby because they had no responsibility for them. Which meant they'd come some other way. Which meant someone else knew what went on here. Even if that "someone else" was just some scared woman keeping her ear to the ground in Dottie's shelter, that was one person too many. It meant, theoretically, the mystery mother wasn't the only one who could find her here, be followed here. Come looking for the baby too. Which meant they weren't safe waiting here while figuring things out.*

Which meant she had to drop everything and leave.

All she could do was search, wait, and pray.

Somehow, she had to leave and stay at the same time.

She couldn't seek help from the Sequence, but she'd never manage it alone either.

That's where Bess came in.

34

"Hold it right there," Katie said. "Bess *knew*? All of this?"

Grace shook her head, adamant. "She was perfect because she *didn't* know. I told her only the bare minimum—that I had a personal situation requiring discretion and needed help getting out in a hurry. I thought if I had one sympathetic contact on the inside, I had a better chance of ducking out gracefully without drawing too much scrutiny. The idea was to use her to stay in the loop about what was going on here and call in favors if I needed them."

"Like, if someone showed up crying about missing her baby?"

"Exactly."

A noise escaped Katie, somewhere between a whimper and a sigh. To think Bess had made her feel guilty for not sharing everything about the Sequence, when the whole time, Bess had known more about Grace than she'd let on. The "bare minimum" seemed relative. Bess had watched Katie go from uneasy—at arriving to a half-inhabited house—to downright frantic after Lindsay's arrival that first night, and Bess had volunteered nothing.

Katie didn't know what to believe anymore.

"At no point did you tip Bess off about *anything* to do with the Sequence?" Her voice rose, and the baby stirred. "Even knowing she was bringing me to take your place?"

"I saw no reason to tell her. I'd pulled the plug instead—the Sequence was supposed to be done with Grove. Plus, obviously I hoped they'd find a way to continue without it. Why blow their cover? And why blow mine? I think I was in denial about never coming back."

Katie looked around at the loft, thinking back to her first time here. How even in the heat of the moment she'd marveled at all the special touches, the cozy hiddenness of it all. Had Grace really thought no one would ever find a key to that door, or even wonder what was behind it?

Maybe—the room had remained secret for this long. More likely, it was one of too many things she simply hadn't had a chance to think through.

"And what about all those times Bess told me she couldn't reach you?" Even as she grew more incredulous at the idea of Bess lying, things were making more sense. The way Bess hadn't seemed surprised not to find Grace at her forwarding address out of state. The way Bess had remained so sure Grace was okay, even when she couldn't articulate why, then got extra frazzled every time they found out more about what had really been going on here.

"I was obsessed with trying to reach you," Katie went on. "I was worried something had *happened* to you. Do you have any clue what I've been through? You were the only person who could've helped, and not only did you stay away, you got my own best friend to leave me hanging."

"That is *not* what happened. None of it worked out like I planned. Starting with Bess."

"What do you mean, *starting with Bess?*"

As she'd recounted her harrowing ordeal, Grace had seemed indignant, even defensive. Only now did she look ashamed. "I got cold feet—shot myself in the foot, is more like it. I got paranoid I couldn't trust Bess to know how to reach me after all."

"Why?"

"I got paranoid about everyone. Can you blame me? I had a contraband baby, for crying out loud. I kept replaying all Dottie's warnings that I wasn't careful enough even before all this. There was only one person on the nature center staff I'd ever thought might be suspicious of me, and suffice to say, he did not seem sympathetic. I started second-guessing everything. If he raised concerns, who's to say Bess wouldn't put two and two together and turn me in? When I woke up the day I was supposed to pack, he was here, unannounced, and I just . . . couldn't risk another second on-site. I panicked that I still wasn't being careful enough, that the risks of trusting Bess outweighed the benefits. I never planned to leave things that way."

"Who?" Katie asked, heart sinking that she already had a pretty good guess. Where she'd expected relief at hearing Grace's story at last, she was finding resentment instead. There were so many things she'd deserved to know all along. "Who made you so nervous?"

"Jude. Are you aware he comes from a long line of cops? Went all the way through training, and yet he's here? I'm not so sure he isn't on their payroll too."

It was funny. This whole time, she'd assumed Grace was so much smarter than her, about everything. Now here Grace was, admitting to bigger mistakes than Katie had made, allowing the possibility that— even at her most compassionate and vigilant—Grace could also be wrong.

Sure, Jude made Katie plenty nervous, too, with his uncanny knack for showing up at inopportune times. She hated the thought of him toiling all day next to the pond where a body may or may not have been dumped, and where who-knew-what had gone on before she got here.

But Jude hadn't hidden his background from Katie, the way Grace obviously assumed from her smug, *Are you aware?* He'd explained it. Made himself vulnerable, even. Somewhere along the line, Katie had inched closer and closer to accepting that Jude was . . . well, Jude.

"I heard you butted heads," Katie said, "but he's not as 'unsympathetic' as he seems."

Grace looked at her with something like pity. "No offense, but you've been here less than three months. Try years. I know I'm making a bang-up first impression, but I didn't last this long by being clueless. Careful with your assumptions."

Katie didn't know what to think anymore. Things might be coming together, but they still didn't fit, like puzzle pieces that look correct but won't quite click into place.

"Back to Bess," Katie said. "What do you mean, you got paranoid?"

Grace's guilty look returned. "I'm not proud of it, but I ended up ghosting her. Which was a crummy way to repay her for helping me out. And, by extension, you. You have to understand, I had no way of knowing that woman with the safe haven card would show up and kickstart things again. As soon as Bess was on to the Sequence, I couldn't be in touch with her anymore. It would've put everyone at risk. I'd done everything I could to disassociate the Sequence from my mistake. I even deleted their contacts from my phone, then got a burner—so nothing I did from that point on could be traced to them." She picked at the baby's blanket. "And if I'm honest, so I'd never be tempted to reach out if things got desperate."

She didn't need to spell out that they had. After all, she was here.

"But how did you even know?" Katie asked. "About the woman showing up and me and Bess figuring things out?"

"Like I said, I had to leave and stay at the same time."

Katie let this sink in, sorting piece by piece of her evidence log over to the Grace column. The smell of a campfire. The footprints in the snow. The sounds that had made poor Sky—and the rest of them—question her own sanity. The sign to keep out of the summer kitchen, presumably to ward off anyone who'd happen upon her pit stop. "All those times I was looking over my shoulder, feeling like someone was watching me . . . ?"

Grace nodded.

"You dragged a baby around the property all this time? How did you even come and go?"

She looked sheepish. "A back way, on foot. Not *all this time*. She's happiest when she's being held, which made it easier to keep her with me at first, except she'd nap in the carrier all day and be up all night. I ended up having to hire this retired lady in the complex where I'm renting to babysit, which stretched my funds—and my comfort zone. I need to lay low, obviously. Plus, now that it's hot, we're miserably sweaty. I've been relying more on the trail cams."

"Trail cams?" Katie didn't bother to hide her alarm, and Grace looked confused.

"I assumed you knew. I mean, last week Bess came and took the boxes from the summer kitchen, the user manuals and everything but the actual cams, which she hasn't found . . ." Her voice trailed off as it became obvious Katie did *not* know. "Well," Grace muttered. "She could have left my stash of diapers. It's not like I didn't get the message to get the hell out."

"You didn't get the message," Katie pointed out. "You're still here. Keeping tabs on me with trail cams, like I'm some endangered species. Which, thanks to you, maybe I am."

"It was never about watching you! Other than to make sure you were safe. It's about looking for the mom to come back. Or for the dad to come looking—assuming there is one. Not that I'd know what he looks like."

Katie wanted to laugh. *Crummy* didn't scratch the surface of what Grace had done. This woman had used her best friend for favors she had no intention of repaying, entrapped Katie here without any clue what she was getting into, and basically stalked her. Now she wanted Katie to put herself on the line to help her. She had nerve. And to top it off, she'd waited until Katie's nieces arrived to confess it all.

"Grace," Katie said evenly, "I'm sure I don't have to point this out, but there might be stuff on those trail cams the Sequence doesn't want anyone to see."

"No kidding. I'm a little more worried about that now that I know Bess didn't tell you."

Katie would have to sort out Bess's role later. Grace was the one here now, and the clock was ticking. "This has gone on too long. Please, tell me this ends with some kind of update."

Grace's voice went flat as she filled Katie in: She'd searched night and day for any hint of a matching missing person's report—combing news articles, lurking in neighborhood forums, looking for any local social media referencing an MIA mom, baby, or both. Crickets. At the beginning, she was sure every new day would be *the* day she identified the mystery mom, but in time, hope began to fade, and catastrophizing set in. The mom's note had said she couldn't leave, so maybe she'd come up with some cover story as to where the baby had gone. But how long could she keep that up before someone, especially the father, caught on that something was amiss?

And when the father did catch on, what would he do to his wife? What stories might he spin to prevent anyone else from reporting *her* missing? Grace shifted to obituaries, like a search and rescue downgraded to a recovery, but came up empty there too.

As for figuring out who'd sent the woman, that was another dead end. If Grace took her at her word, infiltrating the shelter was out of the question. And even if that story had been a lie, well, it was all Grace had. Meanwhile, she struggled with her crash course in child-rearing, knowing the baby deserved better. Grace didn't even know her name. Every night at bedtime, she'd pile on tenderness, read aloud picture books procured from little free libraries, sing her to sleep in a room that could never feel like home, and lay awake worrying she'd stretched the limits of a short-term solution without long-term consequences. Time was running out.

When the baby got sick, it felt inevitable, a miracle they'd made it this far before something went this wrong.

"So you didn't want to involve the Sequence, or even Bess, but you're involving me?"

"No. But I need you to call Dr. Clooney. Not that I want to involve him either." Grace's eyes filled with tears. "I keep asking myself what he'd want me to do. Her fever topped a hundred and four. In the worst-case scenario, he'd never forgive me for not calling him. I'd never forgive myself." She shook her head. "I've made such a mess of things. Even if I get through this crisis . . . Honestly, I have no idea what I'm going to do."

By rights, Katie should have been furious. Should have pulled her nieces out of bed and hauled Grace and the baby to a hospital right then. But she couldn't deny feeling one connection with Grace that Katie had never had, could never have, with anyone else.

They were the only two people who knew firsthand what it was like to be caretaker.

What it meant. How it felt. Every second of every day.

Maybe when it got down to it, that's why Katie could never let all these questions about Grace go unresolved. Why she'd been so intent on finding her. And now she had. Even if it was only making everything worse.

"You know," Katie said quietly. "I never could figure out what to make of the Sequence, coming in blind the way I did. Whether I could trust them."

Grace's face softened. They might have shared the same role, but they'd come to it with different baselines of what they'd accept as truth. She simply hadn't been here to catch Katie up. "I regret that," she said. "It wasn't fair. To any of you."

Katie tried to think of a tactful way to phrase what she needed to ask. But maybe they were beyond tact. "I understand you had differences of opinion on things they didn't do," she said carefully. "But what about things they did? Did anything ever make you question that they're, you know . . . the good guys?"

Grace didn't hesitate. "Never. I'm not sure of much, but I'm sure of that. If they ever did anything I wasn't crazy about, and sometimes they did"—Was it Katie's imagination, or did Grace's eyes slide in the direction of the pond?—"I trusted they had good reasons. And they always did. Things come to light eventually. You'll see."

Would she see? Did she want to? Or had she already?

Katie may have been at this for only a few months, but those months had pushed her beyond what she'd thought herself capable of. Months of faces she wished she could check up on over coffee, of stories she wished she could tell. Months of embracing things she'd never set out to do.

Of course that would pale in comparison to Grace's years. How many more things had she witnessed in that time, how many more women had she met who'd challenged her view of the world, of her place in it all, of what it really meant to do the right thing? No wonder she'd stitched and hung that maxim from Mark Twain where she'd have to walk past it many times a day. No wonder she'd left it there for Katie, her lone bit of unsolicited advice: "It is never wrong to do the right thing."

Between the two of them, was it any wonder they'd ended up here, sizing each other up across the loft, together yet alone, tangled in catastrophe?

Katie took a deep breath and dialed Dr. Clooney.

Grace might be out of ideas, but the new hire had a few of her own.

35

"A raging ear infection," Dr. Clooney told Katie. "And I do mean raging. We're lucky the eardrum hasn't ruptured. Since I'm here, I'll go ahead and write the prescription. But I think we both know this is not the kind of emergency I had in mind when I gave you my number."

He said this gently, but Katie had known she'd be taking this hit when she'd devised the plan. The Sequence had been aware, of course, that her nieces were coming, but not how many or how old they were. Thus, Aunt Katie had acquired a third camper. An infant fresh "from Tennessee" with a scary high fever. Concocting the story was easy. Looking Dr. Clooney in the eye, while Grace witnessed it all from her hiding place behind the shower curtain, was something else.

"I do know that," she told Dr. Clooney now. "I can't thank you enough for being so nice about this. When I realized how sick she was, I wasn't thinking straight—I just didn't want my sister to think I couldn't handle this. Or to wake the other girls and frighten them on their first night here."

"Your sister just brought her today? And not a word about her being fussy or unwell?"

He was right to be suspicious. Grace said the baby had been inconsolable for days.

"Gigi's plate has been so full," Katie demurred. "Please don't judge her."

"Nobody's judging anybody. But it's better for the baby to be seen somewhere she can get follow-up care if she needs it. During daylight hours."

"You're right. I won't put you in an awkward position like this again. I promise."

"Any known antibiotic allergies?"

Katie felt her cheeks color. "No. Actually . . . will I need any documentation to fill this? As her guardian for the summer, or . . ."

His frown deepened. "If you haven't already gotten their insurance info from your sister, obviously you should. But all the pharmacy needs is a name and date of birth for the baby, if you don't mind paying out of pocket."

"Great." Her whole face was blazing with embarrassment now, but at least she'd had the foresight to invent those details in advance, so she didn't stammer. She listened, trying to be patient, as the doctor directed her to the nearest twenty-four-hour pharmacy and instructed her to alternate infant ibuprofen and acetaminophen every three hours until the fever came down. Grace had insisted on hearing all this firsthand rather than hiding at a safer distance, but Katie's fear that she'd sneeze or otherwise give herself away made it all drag on interminably.

At last, finally, he packed his bag and went to the door.

But he didn't open it. He just stared at the knob for a long, conspicuous moment while Katie held her breath, heart hammering so fiercely it seemed impossible he couldn't hear.

Finally, he cleared his throat. "Now that we've established this as a judgment-free zone," he said, "want to tell me what's really going on?"

The room tilted. Of course Dr. Clooney was too smart to fall for this. The Sequence had partnered with the best, after all. He deserved the courtesy of the truth.

But he'd be better off without it.

Katie gave a self-deprecating laugh. "I already told you. I just have no idea what I'm doing. I hope I'm not in over my head."

"Mmm," was all he said, but there was so much trust in it, she wanted to cry. "I hope so too."

※

By the time Katie got back from the pharmacy, it was almost morning. The baby was awake and crying again, refusing to latch onto a bottle, and Grace was past ready to go. The diaper bag was loaded, her hoodie zipped to protect against the relentless mosquitos, and Katie felt bad she couldn't at least offer her a ride to her car. But the girls would be up soon.

When Grace held out her hand for the white paper pharmacy bag, Katie hesitated. The whole drive back, she'd been mulling this over, but she still didn't know what to do. With any luck the medicine would work quickly, this immediate crisis averted. But then what? After all this, Grace would just . . . disappear back into the night?

In a way, that would be best. Who in their right mind would want anything more to do with this mess? But if they said goodbye now—goodbye and nothing more—Katie didn't know how she'd ever stop looking over her shoulder, wondering if and when Grace might reappear. Worrying what would become of this sweet little baby and the family who must be missing her. Ruminating on questions she hadn't thought to ask or should have demanded better answers to.

"I owe you," Grace said, seeing her hesitation. "Starting with an apology. I underestimated you. Worse, I envied you. This has been so much harder on you than it had to be, and that's my fault too. But even on your hardest days here, I would have given anything to switch back. Now that I've met you, though . . . all I feel is grateful."

The idea of anyone envying all the stress and uncertainty she'd been through would have been laughable coming from anyone else. But Katie knew what she meant.

They had too much in common not to.

Even if you removed all the legal and ethical complications from this mix—which, of course, you couldn't—what was left was almost worse: the sheer terror that could drive a mother to hand her child over to a stranger. That kind of terror didn't abate or discriminate. It would attach itself to everything this tragedy touched. It would linger indefinitely, lying in wait. Ignoring it would do nothing. If you truly wanted it gone, like the other invasive species at Grove, you had to yank it out by the roots.

Katie wasn't about to get her hands dirty. But she could at least look over Grace's garden with a fresh eye. See if anything stood out.

"If you really mean that," Katie heard herself say, "then promise to come back. I don't think we're done here. Rest up, take care of the babe, and we'll pick up where we left off. I'm supposed to be on a summer break from the Sequence anyway. We can put our heads together without involving them. You're not getting anywhere on your own."

"Well, you're right about the last bit," Grace said. Katie handed over the medicine.

"Also," Katie said, "I have a letter for you. From your mom's . . . Betty. Plus artwork."

Grace winced. "I don't want it," she said quickly. "This might sound cold, but I left the artwork on purpose. It makes her happy to send it, but believe me, I'd rather she didn't. I can only come face-to-face with what my dad did to her once a month. That's my limit."

Katie took a step back, struck by her weary tone. The one you use when someone brings up something you've been over a million times before. Though, of course, they never had.

"Please don't ask me to recount the whole sordid story. I'll do the abridged version, okay? I'm the one he was mad at that day. She literally took the fall. Head trauma. My sister still hates me for it. He pled no contest to a minor charge. I was the only witness—at least, the only one capable of speech—so my word against his. They said we were lucky he'd pled to anything at all. And that she was lucky to be alive. I wasn't so sure about that. I'm even less sure now."

There was that word again, *lucky*. Katie's heart twisted for her.

"I'm so sorry," Katie said. "I can't imagine. Betty's letter is personal, though. You should have it. I don't want to risk waking the girls to get it now, but I'll bring it when you come back. Okay?"

She could practically see Grace recalibrating. Asking herself: Was she really going to do this? She probably hadn't intended to tell Katie more than the "bare minimum" she'd tried with Bess. But look where that had gotten her. She might have been losing faith in her own judgment, but Katie could see that she was gaining faith in hers.

"Do you know that saying," Grace said, "'No good deed goes unpunished'?" Katie nodded. It had certainly crossed her mind. "Well, I own my stupidly good deed. But the Sequence guards against that. They're better connected than you'll ever know. If they accidentally get one of their own into trouble, they'll get you out. Same can't be said for this. Understand the difference?"

It was a safety net and a warning, tangled into one. "I'll keep it in mind," Katie said. "Where's this apartment you're renting?"

Grace shrugged in a way that had nothing to do with the apartment. But she was smiling.

"Quick drive from Grove's back border. It's a short-term . . . well, shithole." She gave a self-effacing little laugh. "I never exactly stockpiled massive caretaker savings, and I couldn't pay on credit without being traceable. But at least the building is safe. Cleanish."

Katie nodded. "I don't like sneaking out like this with the girls asleep. But they'll be busy with a photography lesson tonight. Meet me here at seven?"

"I'll be here." Grace was halfway out the door when Katie called after her.

"For the record? I would've done the same thing you did. I'd be in the same mess."

She smiled ruefully. "Hate to tell you, but I think you already are."

36

It was setting up to be one of those unpredictable days. Katie and the girls woke to a shining sun, but by the time they'd finished breakfast, rain was pouring down in sheets, just in time for Bess's minivan to pull up, delivering their camp counselors. Emory and Ethan were undeterred: they somersaulted out the back hatch, laughing into the downpour, exuding their usual brand of manic happiness and unapologetic chaos. Nessa and Cora ran out to join their dancing across the grass, and Katie followed as far as the cover of the porch, huddling with her coffee cup.

She kept her eyes trained on the kids as Bess opened her umbrella and ran up the walk. It was funny, seeing the "counselors" looking so much younger and smaller next to Nessa and Cora, but the girls showed no sign of minding as they squealed at the soaking rain. You'd never know they were meeting for the first time.

And you'd never know Bess was the last person Katie wanted to see right now. At least, she hoped not. Because they desperately needed to talk.

"How worried should we be about these weather alerts?" Katie asked, not ready to meet her eyes quite yet. "Some counties say severe thunderstorm watch, some say flash floods."

"Some say sunshine," Bess chirped, leaping onto the porch, umbrella and all, looking deceptively like Mary Poppins. *Deceptively* being the key word. "It's anyone's guess around here. They cover their bases anytime something is remotely possible, so you can't say they didn't warn you."

"It is courteous to warn people," Katie agreed. It was petty, but she couldn't help herself. Though she'd only had a couple of hours of sleep—again—she'd thought she might wake feeling at least some sense of resolution, but far from it. Even the weather felt like a bad omen.

Bess narrowed her eyes, turning to see if she'd overlooked something amiss. The outbuildings were dark, the forest bleary through the rain, but already the sky was lightening, almost enough to start looking for a rainbow. "Well." Bess tried to laugh. "You good with the kids rain or shine? I can't stay—my boss is noticing how much I've *not* been at the center. But I'll have them out of your hair before the photography lesson starts."

She clearly expected Katie to brighten at the mention of Ryan. But Katie wouldn't give her the satisfaction.

"Mom?" Emory called across the lawn, already linking hands with her new friends as her brother zigged and zagged around them. "Can we go along to the fancy camera lesson?"

"Please, Aunt Katie," Nessa and Cora chimed in. "Please, please can they come?"

"I don't know if anyone's going," Katie said, "if this rain doesn't stop."

Right then, it did. A cheer went up from the kids, though she hadn't said yes.

"Better not," Bess said under her breath. "Four of them is a lot to ask."

"We are not a lot to ask!" Ethan insisted, though Katie had no idea how he'd heard. She'd have to be careful of this childhood superpower, overhearing things they weren't supposed to.

"We'll be wonderfully behaved," Cora sing-songed. "We won't ruin your *daaaaate*."

"It's not a . . ." Katie sighed, giving up. "*Maybe* I'll ask him, if you do your best to run around and air-dry. I need a minute to talk to Ethan and Emory's mom."

"C'mon, guys," Nessa called out. "Race you down the driveway and back!"

Bess jangled her keys as they took off running. If she'd been distracted yesterday, it hadn't taken much to make her downright nervous today.

Best to get on with it then.

"I'm only going to ask this once," Katie said. "Think hard before you answer."

"Okay?" Bess frowned.

"Is there something else you want to tell me about what was in the summer kitchen? Or what really happened with Grace?"

Bess took a lot of interest in toeing at the porch with her Birkenstock.

"Or maybe," Katie went on, though she was less sure about this part, "why this new boardwalk project is suddenly so high priority? Putting Jude here all day every day, right where he asked to be weeks ago?"

Bess cleared her throat. "What do you mean," she ventured, "*what really happened with Grace?*" The way her voice shook—Katie couldn't take it anymore. All the hurt she'd been doing her best to swallow came bursting out of her.

"Here's what I'm not clear on: What the hell did she say or do to convince you to cover for her all this time? Even at the cost of my sanity? Meanwhile, you're laying on guilt trips, making *me* feel bad for not telling *you* every little thing I know about the Sequence!"

Bess's face flushed. "I don't know where you're getting this, but—"

"From Grace! I'm getting it from Grace! She was here. Last night. Would have been nice to know *that* was a thing that might happen, what with the kids and all."

The words hung between them, in the open at last. But Bess didn't move to explain herself. Instead, she clasped her heart, like all she could do was contain her relief.

The kind that bowls you over so completely that for an instant, nothing else matters.

"She's okay?" She grabbed Katie by the shoulder. "Grace is okay?"

Katie nodded stiffly, every inch of her tense body signaling that Bess should back off, but apparently Bess didn't care. She threw her arms around Katie, and a sound that was half giggle, half sob escaped her. "She had me so worried. You have no idea."

"You're right about that," Katie said icily, teetering in the embrace. "I don't."

Bess pulled back, chagrined. Finally realizing.

This *was* a lot. Enough that you had to process it in layers.

"Listen, Katie, I—"

"Since when do you lie to me? Right to my face? I don't even know where to start. *The roaches, Katie, are they on me?*" She flopped her arms, mimicking Bess's performance outside the summer kitchen. "Thinking back, you even used the word *surveillance*, but when I asked why, you still didn't tell me you'd found trail-cam packaging in there. And if that's not insulting enough, you go behind my back to reassign Jude to babysit me?"

Just like that, Bess went from yielding to defensive. "First of all, who cares about Jude? You keep saying all you do out here is look the other way—it's nothing you're doing I'm worried about. It's the rest of the world. So yeah, I'm okay with having someone here who's trained to notice anything amiss. Who's protective of nature center property *and* the people on it. It's reassuring. And I had to do it behind your back because you'd stopped listening to reason. Every time I implored you to put your own safety first, inform some authority of what's going on, you wouldn't let up until you'd talked me out of it."

Katie crossed her arms and glared at her.

"What's the big deal?" Bess huffed. "You said yourself he was growing on you. You're on break from the Sequence anyway."

"What's the big deal?" Katie repeated, even as a self-conscious flush spread across her cheeks, remembering how hard Bess had pushed for the break.

Bess cocked her head. "You are on break, right?"

"*I* am, yes." Bess's eyes widened at her unintended emphasis on the word "I," so she rushed on. "The big deal is, I was dealing with this on my own terms, Jude included. The big deal is, you went behind my back. Both of you. You seem to have decided 'Bess Knows Best.'"

"What would you rather I do? Call the actual police? If I'd told you what was really in the summer kitchen, it was way too easy to picture you refusing to let me report this and then taking it upon yourself to track down the trail cams and whoever's behind them, alone out here at all hours. I was reasonably sure they were Grace's, but then again, where the hell *was* she? Standing in that creepy little building, it hit me how far out of our depth you and I both were."

"That wasn't for you to decide unilaterally."

"Calling in Jude seemed like a compromise. I didn't want you storming in there and messing up evidence. Not until someone who knew what they were doing could take a look. And yeah, while he's working on that—discreetly—he helped get the boardwalk fast-tracked so we'd both feel better about you and the girls out here. Now, tell me again what a terrible friend I am."

Bess had . . . some points. But Katie wasn't ready to back down yet. Jude was far from the worst of it.

"Did you tell him about the Sequence?"

"No." Bess averted her eyes, and Katie realized: it would have implicated her too. "I glossed it over, okay? Told him I was pretty sure they'd been Grace's and with her gone, we needed to figure out where they were mounted, *if* they were out there, and get them down. Though, of course, we'd want to look at the footage, just to be safe. I even floated a theory that one of our members undertook an innocent project without permission. In short, I played dumb."

"And you think Jude bought that?"

"Not all of it. He's the only one other than you who seems to give me too much credit to buy the dumb part." Bess tried to smile, but it was more of a grimace. "Anyway, he called in a favor through a friend on the force who knew a guy who can hack the trail-cam app. Problem is, we have to wait our turn behind authorized requests. Any day now."

"Grace thinks he's lying, you know, about not finishing the police academy. She thinks he might be undercover."

Bess sighed heavily. "I always thought it would be boring to be one of those people who are constantly trying to do the right thing. Now I know the truth: it's exhausting."

That was it. Exactly. Katie softened, in spite of herself. "It is," she agreed. "No wonder so few people do it." Then she closed her eyes, took a deep breath, and asked Bess if they could start again. From the beginning.

They sat down right there on the steps, and Bess told her. How she'd come by to discuss their member survey and found Grace right here, pacing the porch, admitting she didn't need to know the results—because she'd made up her mind to resign. Problem was, she explained, she couldn't give two weeks' notice. It would be a stretch to wait two *days*.

"What's the rush?" Bess had asked. "Is there some emergency?" And that's when a baby had started to cry somewhere inside.

"Sorry," Grace had said, flushing red. "I'm babysitting. Hang on. Let me get her."

She'd been so awkward, returning with the baby hanging half off her shoulder, swiveling her little head in search of steadier ground, that Bess had jumped in.

"I haven't held a baby in years," she'd cooed. "May I?"

Grace handed her over readily. "You can probably tell I don't know what I'm doing."

Bess had shown Grace how to support the baby's back, how to bounce in a way that was more soothing than jolting. That was all the prompting Grace needed to pepper her with questions—how warm to make the bottle, and what exactly babies *did* all day. The baby seemed hungry, so Bess demonstrated how to regulate the formula temperature and avoid air bubbles. She barely knew Grace, but she did know it wasn't like her to be rattled. She settled with the baby at the kitchen table while Grace made them tea.

"Is it a family emergency?" Bess asked. "Maybe a leave of absence in lieu of resigning."

"No." Grace's eyes darted around the room, as if she'd been accused of something. "I don't want my family brought into this. I just . . . need to sort some things out."

"Maybe if you tell me what's going on, we can sort it out together."

Grace said it was too complicated to explain. "Long story short . . . I need to take someone's place for a while. To pull it off, it's important no one comes looking for me."

Katie interrupted Bess's replay with a bark of incredulous laughter. The sun was out now, dry spots dotting the pavement. Across the driveway, the kids had taken to spinning themselves dizzy and seeing who could run the farthest without falling.

"She borrowed her excuse," Katie marveled, shaking her head. "I guess she figured if it worked on her . . ."

Bess looked confused. "Whose excuse?"

"Never mind. I'll explain later. What then?"

"Honestly, I thought she was kidding about the whole switching-places thing. I said, 'Like *The Parent Trap*? Do you have an evil twin?' But she made me feel bad for joking. She said this had more at stake and she wouldn't ask me to cover her unless she truly needed help."

"That's a pretty big favor to do for someone."

"Right? She was going on about how her family wouldn't understand. Her sister's house was the only forwarding address she could give, but she didn't want them getting questions about how to reach her. I said, 'This seems like a lot. Sure it's worth it?' She claimed she'd been antsy to move on anyway, so this seemed a good excuse. That's when I realized, I'm holding this baby"—Katie's eyes went wide—"and I said, oh God, is this her baby? Whoever you're switching with, is she going to rehab? And Grace was adamant that it was unrelated, she just happened to be babysitting. But I've played it back a million times, and I think that's when she started to shut down. When she started thinking she'd said too much."

A weighty pause fell between them. "I meant you," Katie said at last. "It was a pretty big favor for *you* to do for her."

"Yeah, well." Bess gave a little laugh. "You know me."

"Yeah," Katie said. "I do." She leaned back and crossed her arms. Waiting.

"Fine." Bess sighed. "Her need to get away from everything and everyone, start over without sticking around for the third degree? I didn't need to know her reasons for it to remind me of someone I love who was going through something similar at the time. And once she'd reminded me of her . . . I couldn't say no."

Katie's eyes filled with tears. She gazed up at the sky, patches of blue in layers of gray. She no longer knew what to say, how to feel. All this time, Grace had been this idea she had to live up to, this gold standard precedent. But Bess had never seen it like that. She'd looked at Grace and been reminded of Katie. How could Katie not be moved? How could she not feel, however tangentially, responsible too?

When she looked back at Bess, something in her had shifted. Something that said, *I would do the same for you, but damn it, do you have any idea what you've done?*

"None of this worried you," she asked, "when you thought about bringing me here?"

"It did. And then it didn't. Then it did again. But I'd asked Grace a thousand ways if there was *anything* I should know as far as the new caretaker was concerned. Whatever she was dealing with seemed personal, nothing to do with the nature center. I had no reason not to believe her. Grace was always like that student who never raises her hand but gets straight A's. The quiet kid in the back row you never have to worry about. Until apparently it turns out you do."

"But then she ghosted you," Katie finished.

"To put it mildly. I touched base with her after we saw how she'd left the house. She remained insistent I not share anything about the details of her quitting, even with you. Once all this Sequence stuff started, I stopped hearing back from her altogether, and it scared me. It seemed like it must be connected, like maybe she was helping one of these women on her own or changing roles on the back end—that's why I got frustrated you wouldn't tell me more. I thought if you did, I could put two and two together. I didn't know if I should be scared for *you*." She shuddered. "Grace did say the cams are hers, right? Nothing to worry about there?"

Katie nodded, but Bess didn't look less worried. "But what was she looking for?"

"That's a long story," Katie said. "How much time do you have?"

Bess glanced at her watch. "Not enough. There's too much here to unpack right now. Can we reconvene tonight? I'm no good to anyone if I get fired. I have to get going."

Katie tapped her foot. "Grace is coming back later, too, when the kids will be busy shooting photos with Ryan. Never mind that I'm supposed to be cooking dinner for us all."

"That sounds . . . overscheduled. Why on earth did you suggest that?"

"It was the next opportunity that came to mind." Katie pulled a face. "Believe me—all I can think of is reasons I wish I hadn't. What if the kids get shy and want me to come with them? Or what if one of them runs back here for something? They'll have the walkie-talkies, but . . . I don't know. Anyway, I have no way to change it even if I want to. Grace didn't give me a number to reach her."

"Wouldn't matter if she did," Bess said. "She hasn't answered the burner number she gave me for like two months. Listen, I'm going to come too. If you don't want to ask Ryan to include my kids, I'll have

Vince pick them up. But Nessa and Cora are already begging to bring them, right? And it's not like they'll be far—this place is your backyard. This ends tonight. No more sneaking around, no more secrets. Everyone spills the tea. Then we'll clean it up together."

Katie bit her lip. "I don't know . . ."

"I'll get to the loft first, so by the time she sees me it's too late to change her mind."

What choice did they have? "Okay," she relented. "I'll text Ryan, see how much of a saint he is."

"Tell him I owe him another latte run. And fingers crossed for no more rain."

This—all of them in a room together, at last—was all she'd wanted since the day she arrived. Yet now that it was finally about to happen, she couldn't shake this sense of dread. Katie and Bess and even Grace were coming clean at last, but Grove still harbored secrets of its own.

37

Katie sent a tentative text to Ryan to let him know she had a couple of extra campers today, and seconds later her phone rang.

"This is actually perfect," he said. After all the tension with Grace last night and Bess this morning, she could just about collapse into the warm, uncomplicated friendliness of his tone. "Change of plans here, too—my daughter is with me today. So it's a whole kid crew, I guess. We can reschedule, or . . . we can run with it?"

This was even better, honestly. With a whole gaggle of kids, no way would they finish early. "Considering they're the ones asking to bring their friends along, the more the merrier."

"Sounds like a plan," he said. "But also . . . less like a proper first date. Should we rain check on dinner afterward?"

This should have been a relief, on many levels. So why did Katie feel disappointed?

Maybe because he hadn't said the words "first date" before. They sounded so real.

"I have to admit," he said, his voice turned deeper, softer, "I've pictured it many times. But never with an audience. Or a children's menu."

Katie found herself smiling. In her life before Grove, she'd have gotten worked into a fit of anxiety at the thought of putting her heart out there again. Now, it seemed comparatively simple. Not an awkward first to get out of the way, but something to look forward to. Something to save, even, for when she was free at last from looking over her shoulder.

"I think a rain check will be worth waiting for," she agreed. "That way, I can give you the whole Grove After-Hours Tour. But how about a preview tonight? There's this great overlook where the kids picnicked last night, and it'd be special for them to get some photos up there."

Please say yes, she thought. It was just far enough that the kids wouldn't wander back for any little thing.

"Consider it done. Hey, if you're not going to cook, want to come along?"

"I wish. But some work stuff came up. Would I be the worst if I take advantage of the chance to get it done while they're gone?"

"You'd be the smartest. Happy to help. And hey, I'm glad I called."

"Me too. So much easier than figuring this out over a long text thread."

"I'll pretend that's why. And not because it's making my day to hear your voice."

The heat of his words radiated down her neck as she ended the call. A gust of wind blew mist through the screens of the porch where she stood, bringing cool relief. It had been raining again for an hour, and the kids were inside finishing lunch while laughing uproariously at "epic fails" videos on YouTube. But the forecast for this evening was mercifully clear.

She'd been thinking a lot about what Grace said, about how everything the Sequence did turned out to have a good reason. Now, as she faced this day and the closure she hoped it would bring, it felt like more than an insight. It felt like smart advice.

Did Katie have a good reason to tell anyone about Dottie and the baker appearing the other night? About what may be in the pond? About the existence of the Sequence at all? Did wanting to cover her own ass—for things she hadn't been behind—really qualify as a reason?

Plausible deniability had gotten her this far. Losing sight of those "words to live by" had been the game changer for Grace, the point of no return, unleashing torrents of trouble that could never be reversed. If Katie wasn't careful, that would be the biggest danger to her too.

The thing she could not plausibly deny was not a body in the pond, or the activity in the loft, or any of the unauthorized comings and goings in between.

It was Grace. The things she'd done. The secrets she'd shared. Grace had warned of this, too, in her own way. *Understand the difference?* Katie hadn't been ready to heed the warning right then and say goodbye for good, just like that. But she'd have to heed it eventually.

Katie didn't know that there was any real hope of determining where the baby had come from, or where the mystery mother had gone—but at the very least, Katie and Bess could listen. Grace had been alone for so long, and now, she had two intelligent, compassionate sounding boards. Tonight, they'd do what they could to help her find clarity.

But that would be the extent of it. Like it or not, Grace was a liability. This was Katie's post now, and she would *not* look the other way while Grace stayed around. Not with her nieces here. Katie had spent many sleepless nights and anxious days attempting to honor Grace's legacy, take up the torch, even take to heart the motherly chiding of a caregiver named Betty. She'd already taken too many risks, culminating with Dr. Clooney last night. He'd looked at her like he hoped she knew what she was doing. Like he knew there were limits to the help anyone could give in good faith, and they were all counting on her to understand what those limits were.

Meeting Grace had reassured Katie in ways she'd needed all along. Even in showing her how awry the best intentions could go, Grace had inadvertently made her feel more capable.

Katie had done enough.

She'd put this behind her after tonight. One way or another.

38

"Where *is* she?" Katie paced the loft. "She promised she'd be here. Something isn't right."

"Mmm," Bess mumbled. "Grace ghosting—how unlike her."

Katie didn't blame her for the sarcasm, considering. Still. A half hour had passed since she and the kids met Ryan in the parking lot. Their little legs had marched in front of her, walkie-talkies bouncing at their hips, rain boots squishing in the mud, not a care in the world now that yet another deluge had stopped. Ryan's daughter had fallen asleep on the way, and all the chaos Katie had pictured leaving him with was decidedly . . . unchaotic.

The kids instinctively dropped their voices, and Ethan peered through the tinted window into the car seat and groaned. "Another girl? No offense, but I'm already outnumbered."

"I know the feeling, kid," Ryan told him, shooting a sideways look at Katie that said Ethan would grow to like being outnumbered by women just fine.

The thought warmed her on the short walk home, and Bess pulled in right on cue. They had plenty of time—Ryan promised to bring the kids back by eight, when storms reappeared on the radar—everything going to plan. Until they'd entered the loft only to wait, and wait, and wait. Eyes on the door. Hearts in their throat.

"You don't understand," Katie told Bess now. "She's exhausted all her options—she wanted this meeting as much as we did."

"Then make me understand," Bess said, putting up her feet on the coffee table. "We're here, wasting time otherwise. Might as well start unpacking all this without her."

Katie put the question to her new test. Did she have a truly good reason to tell Bess? Other than to ease her own conscience?

She decided she did. Grace might have doubted whether she could trust Bess, and the Sequence had tried to make Katie doubt it too. But Katie's only regret was that they'd succeeded.

Grace had helped build the very network that taught Katie the power of women helping women. A power that Katie had already experienced herself solely because of Bess—who'd taken a risk of her own in bringing Katie here. Who'd made Katie feel, for the first time in a long time, she was worth it. Bess might have misstepped since then, but Katie had too.

She settled in next to her oldest, best friend on the couch, tuning her ears for the sound of the door opening downstairs. When she heard nothing, she started to fill the silence, starting with finding Grace in the summer kitchen last night.

But even when the light in the loft turned softer, when Bess's eyes widened and the air thickened as the evening heat blazed through the sloped roof overhead, Grace still didn't come.

"I've had a bad feeling all day," Bess said when she had finished. "Now I know why."

"No offense," Katie said, "but if you're so sensitive to energy, how come all your alarm bells didn't go off when Grace resigned in the first place?"

"Because she didn't have bad intentions," Bess said, like it was obvious. "The opposite. She was trying *so hard* to do the right thing she let herself get trapped in one wrong move. And now what?" She looked longingly at the door. "I take back what I said about her being a no-show. It is weird. She has to stop running, one way or another. The longer she keeps the baby, the worse it looks."

"Well, trust me, it's obviously not a case of getting too attached, wanting to keep playing house. Besides, otherwise she wouldn't still be here."

"She isn't here, though," Bess pointed out. "Did she say where her apartment is?"

But Katie wasn't thinking of what Grace had said. It was Bess's words echoing in her mind: *She let herself get trapped in one wrong move.*

Katie sat up straighter. "Maybe it's nothing, but . . . I had this random conversation with Jude last month. I said I resented people thinking I'd been trapped in a loveless marriage, and do you know what he said?"

"He said . . . Clark is a coward who blamed you for feelings he never owned up to and tragically let your marriage be consumed by his shame?"

Katie did have to love Bess's assessments. Even if it was best to ignore them. "He took issue with the word *trapped*. He said he'll never understand how so many people claim they're trapped when nothing is stopping them from walking away. Whereas the people who actually are trapped are often in denial."

"Deep."

"Yeah. At the time, I thought he was being a little too insightful for comfort. But . . . You don't think he meant me, do you? That I'm more trapped now than I was then?"

Bess pulled a face. "Knowing Jude, I think he meant exactly what he said. I don't suppose you've seen him today? He never showed at work."

Katie shook her head. "I figured with the rain he was working at the visitor's center?"

"Nope. Didn't call me back either." She smiled sheepishly. "I was going to warn him you were onto us and he'd have to face your fury."

Katie couldn't smile back, couldn't shake this nagging feeling. She and Bess had both made excuses for Jude—how he wasn't so tough. How it was easy to be too hard on him.

But maybe they'd also been too quick to let him off the hook entirely.

If hearing Grace out had taught Katie anything, it was that you can't always think things all the way through, no matter how hard you try—because no one person has all the information to foresee every possible outcome.

The fact was, Jude had been acting in such a way that made Grace nervous. He'd also poked around Katie's barn without real explanation, not to mention her bookshelves and who knew where else. He'd gone out of his way to spend time here, and after spooking Grace, had given lip service to respecting Katie's boundaries, even as he pushed them. He had challenged her, doubted her, then done an about-face and praised her ingenuity. He'd felt compelled to look out for Katie in a way Bess had chalked up to a crush . . . but as worried as he allegedly was, had never insisted they escalate any suspicions to any supervisor but Bess. Even the first advice he'd ever given Katie carried uncanny synchronicity: to take things *one step at a time*.

Now, the day after Grace had finally resurfaced, Jude was nowhere to be found. And so was she.

Katie's body tingled, and she wondered if this was how she was going to be from now on. If she'd no longer be able to tell the difference between excitement and fear.

She forced herself to speak at a normal pace, though her heart was racing.

"Before Grace ghosted you entirely," she asked Bess, "what *exactly* did she say, about why she left in such a hurry, leaving the house the way she did?"

Bess pulled up the text thread. "*Sorry. He was looking for me, I had to bounce. I asked who; she didn't answer.*" Bess blinked at her. "I forgot about that, honestly. We had bigger fires to put out, and—"

The door flung open, and they whipped around, expecting to see Grace.

But it wasn't her in the doorway.

It was Jude. He stood panting, disheveled in a way Katie had never seen him. The bottom third of his jeans were muddy and wet, to say nothing of his shoes. His eyes lit up when they met hers, as if he'd run a great distance through all manner of terrain to find her.

Here.

In the *loft*.

Katie's mouth dropped open. But he did not look around the room like he was seeing it for the first time. He showed none of the shock Bess or Katie had felt in marveling that this safe haven had been hidden above the garage all along. He only looked at her with manic urgency.

"The flash flood watch," he gasped. "It's been upgraded to a warning."

Bess leaped to her feet. "It's not even raining. You're sure?"

"The downpours hit upstream and stayed there. The water will overtake the bridge. Leave now or be stuck at Grove."

"How long do we have?"

"Not long. I left my truck at the gate and ran the four-wheeler up to warn you. I have to get to the parking lot next, evacuate anyone else here."

Bess pulled an elastic from her wrist and twisted her hair into a ponytail, as if getting it off her neck would solve something. "Thanks. I've got to get Emory and Ethan—they're out on a photography lesson with the girls and . . ."

But Katie couldn't hear her anymore. She was still staring at Jude. Watching him realize that he'd stormed into the loft as if it were the most natural thing in the world. Watching him realize that *she'd* realized it.

"Hey," Bess said, suddenly. "How'd you know where to find us? And where've you been all day?"

"Jude," Katie asked, narrowing her eyes. "What did you do?"

He looked past Bess, back at Katie, and his face held no denial. Only resignation, and something else—a helpless kind of fear. He took a long breath, and the air in the room stood still.

"I was only trying to help," he said.

39

"You sent a woman here, didn't you?" Katie asked. "Right before Grace resigned."

He nodded. She wasn't sure whether to lash out at him or fall to his feet in relief. This was the break Grace had been waiting for, the key to identifying the mystery mom, putting it all back together, and getting the hell out of Dodge. Where *was* she?

"You knew what Grace had been doing? All along?" Bess did not manage to ask this without the obvious undertone that she would've liked to know too.

"It was only a hunch at first. Then I encountered one of the women by accident, stepping outside for some air. She was so scared I was going to ruin the whole thing for her, she begged me not to say anything, even to Grace. So I didn't."

Katie closed her eyes. It wasn't hard to imagine the panic her guests might feel, like they'd done something wrong by not being sneaky enough. So many of them were used to being blamed for things that weren't their fault. "Grace never knew you were onto her?"

"I wondered if she suspected. But I never told her, no."

Fair enough. But Katie had had enough of the men in her life thinking they knew best. Even when they were clearly out of their purview.

"How did you think it worked?" she demanded. "Were you not aware that those people had to come through a system to vet them? A system with criteria and rules?"

"Not exactly," he said, looking sheepish. "Though in retrospect, that seems obvious."

"Retrospect is a bitch," Bess said. "The woman you sent here—who was she?"

"A neighbor. But . . ." He glanced at his watch. "Listen, they don't call it a flash flood for nothing."

Bess crossed her arms. "Then you'd better talk fast."

Jude began to pace from the kitchenette to the door and back. "I didn't even know this couple. I only talked to the guy once, later. But I'd noticed the young mother because she was in such a bad way. She had this infant and was always coming and going loaded with bags from a breast cancer center. She had the pink ribbon on her car, started wearing one of those chemo turbans, looked more and more tired and thin and just . . . unwell. And covered in these little bruises, I figured side effects of her treatments. Until late one night when I heard what they were from. And it wasn't any treatment, I'll tell you that."

Katie looked at Bess and saw all her own swirling emotions reflected back at her, both of them helpless to stop what they knew must be coming.

"I went to confront the guy." Jude kept pacing. "I knew it wasn't the smartest, but if I'd called the cops, they have limits, and he needed his ass kicked first. He was drunk, throwing things across the kitchen—plates, silverware, pans—and in the process he broke the window, so I could hear everything. I stood outside it shouting, 'Ma'am, you okay in there? Do you need help?' I made sure to address her, but of course it was him that darted out the back door, fists flying."

Bess cringed. "Jude! The kitchen? He could have had a knife."

"I did think of that later. Luckily he wasn't thinking, either, only reacting, yelling that I should mind my own business. I yelled back that it was everyone's business when a man was so low he'd shove around a woman who was battling cancer and raising a baby at the same time."

Jude was picking up steam now, fired up by the replay. "You won't believe what he said. I'll never forget. He said, 'Oh, you've got that wrong. She only *wishes* she had cancer. That way someone would wait on her hand and foot.'" Bess gasped aloud. "He said playing 'angel of the cancer battlefield' was her favorite excuse to ignore her husband. And I looked up at her through the window and wouldn't you know, she had a full head of hair under that turban. She'd been wearing it in solidarity."

"Wow," Katie said, for lack of more adequate words.

"Anyway. He stormed back to the bar down the street, ranting that if she tried to leave again she'd be sorry. The *again* was what got me—clearly she'd tried before, and here she was. She came outside, and we just stood in the freezing cold dark. She looked so embarrassed. All I could think was that she wasn't the one who had anything to be ashamed of. And yet he wasn't ashamed, not even when I called him out. It was chilling. He was too brazen for her to be safe there even one more night, one more *minute*. I wanted to involve the cops then, but she got hysterical, said it would make things worse for her in the long run. Same when I suggested the abuse hotline—she said the shelter was no place for her baby."

"So you told her she'd be safe here." Katie tried not to sound judgmental.

"I overstepped. I should have gone to Grace the next day and explained what was up. But there didn't seem time for that. I made assumptions that it would be okay. Assumptions I'm now pretty sure were untrue."

"Why didn't you come with her? Why didn't you bring her yourself?"

"I wanted to. She wouldn't let me. She swore if he saw us together, if he ever found out I was the one who'd helped her, he'd kill me. She said he'd once sent a man to the ER for *looking* at her. I wasn't scared of that coward, but she insisted she'd only go if I didn't come. 'You have no idea,' she said, 'what he's capable of. And neither does anyone else. Except me.'"

"You didn't say something to Grace the next day? Tell her you'd sent someone?"

"I tried. Retrospect really *is* a bitch. Grace and I didn't have the greatest relationship. When I came by in the morning, she either wasn't home or was pretending not to be. I decided I'd keep trying nicely for a day or two, and if that didn't work I'd plant myself here until she talked to me. I wanted to help however I could. But by then, she was gone."

Bess sat forward, elbows on her knees. "What, exactly, did you think happened next?"

"I don't know. She just quit, just left, and I had the immediate feeling I'd done something very wrong. I've been trying to figure it out. So I can fix it."

Katie sighed. "Why didn't you just have your neighbor tell Grace, 'Hey, I know you're not expecting me, but Jude sent me'?"

He shrugged. "Grace didn't trust me. She'd make these little comments, calling me a narc. For all I knew, she'd think I sent some poor soul to her doorstep as a trap. Plus, I admit, I'm not the best at thinking things through on my feet. That's why I'm *not* a cop. I fed my neighbor a cover story, told her to tell Grace she was taking someone else's place in the safe house. I figured that would get her in the door until Grace could see for herself how much this woman needed her."

Katie had heard enough. She knew Jude had only meant to help. But the idea that history could have repeated itself, that Jude could have inadvertently done this to her, putting her in the position that he'd put Grace in—it was too much. Too heartbreaking, for all of them.

If he thought Grace wasn't his biggest fan before, wait until she got hold of him now.

Was it really Jude's fault, though? Jude said it himself: the one person who deserved to feel shame never did. The abusers were the ones who should have to slink out of town, disguising themselves, fearing for their lives. The abusers were the ones who should have to pay the steepest price, losing everything they cared about. But did they? No. They almost never paid. And even when they did, it was rarely enough.

"You didn't think it odd," Bess asked, "when the mom resurfaced without the baby?"

He looked at her in confusion. "Without the . . . What? She didn't resurface. I haven't seen her since. I mean, I knew something wasn't right when Grace left the way she did, but I figured they'd skipped town together."

Katie squinted, grasping his meaning. "She didn't resurface," she repeated, "and no one reported them missing?"

"People leave their husbands all the time. What's he going to do, call the cops and say, 'I beat my wife and now I can't find her?' Plus, he was rarely home. I figured he'd taken over caring for their sick family member or whoever it was. But today . . ." He squinted at them. "Why do I get the feeling you know something I don't? Do you know where Grace is, what happened?"

He was asking them both, but his eyes were pleading with Katie, asking forgiveness—and something more. "I'm sorry," he said, more quietly. "For my part in the mess you stepped into. All I've wanted is to make it right somehow. Once I saw how this thing could go sideways, I knew someone had to look out for you. And . . ." He stood straighter. "I wanted it to be me."

Katie bit her lip. Oh, Jude. She just hoped by the time they pieced this all together, there wouldn't be any reason he couldn't forgive himself.

"Well," she said, "your plan got her in the door, all right. Just long enough to leave her baby. Grace wakes up and mom's gone, with a note to take good care of baby, please, and thanks."

Jude went as white as the walls. "Oh, God. I never dreamed . . ." He stopped cold. "Wait. How do you know this? Has she been back?"

"Last night," Bess answered for her. "As a matter of fact, she was supposed to meet us here now, and who should show up instead but you? After ditching work today and dodging my calls? Quite the coincidence."

He braced himself on the counter, like he might keel over without the support.

"That's not the only coincidence," he said. "The scumbag was finally home today. Home and in a wildly good mood. He had the baby; first time I'd seen her since that night. I thought something must have made his poor wife change her mind and come back. That's why I didn't come to work—I spent all day trying to get a glimpse, see that she was okay. But I never did."

His explanation pulled at Katie like a persistent kid on her shirt-tail. She wanted to yank free, and yet she knew it was trying to tell her something important. But Bess looked skeptical.

"You sure it was the same baby? From a distance, babies look alike."

He ran a hand through his hair. "I'm not sure. But he was *acting* like it was his baby. Seems odd to be doting so enthusiastically over someone else's."

"Maybe he really misses his own," Bess suggested, but there wasn't much feeling in it.

"If he has the baby," Katie asked, trying to keep the panic from her voice, "and Grace isn't here, then where is she?"

The same baby. Doting so enthusiastically. The exchange continued to nag at Katie. *Tug, tug, tug.*

"Where has Grace been staying?" Jude asked.

"Nearby," Bess answered for her, infusing the word with meaning. "Coming and going on foot." Katie watched as the two exchanged a look of understanding—confirmation of what they'd found in the summer kitchen. But she no longer felt excluded at the idea of them whispering behind her back. She was glad not to be the only one working to connect the dots.

Jude's phone dinged. He fished it from his pocket, then looked at them eagerly. "Maybe we can get a hint from the trail cam footage.

We're finally in. What time did Grace leave last night? I'll see if anything set off the cameras in that window."

"It was more like this morning," Katie said. "A little before five."

"I'm gonna go grab the kids, alert anyone else who's here," Bess said. "We don't need to be in the same room for this, right? Clock's ticking on that high water."

Jude was nodding, not looking up from his phone as he fiddled with the trail-cam app, but Katie's mind snagged on the words. *Alert anyone else who's here.*

"Your neighbor," Katie asked Jude. "What's his name? Do you have a picture?"

"I've looked him up. Let me pull up one of his profile pages—hang on." He glanced up at her, frowning. "You don't think he could've been here looking for her? I haven't seen him."

She tried to act casual, as if her blood wasn't chilling with fear. As if her pulse wasn't surging with hope that the lines she'd drawn to these particular dots were wrong.

"Grace kept an eye out but didn't know what she was looking for," she said. "If he knows you work here, maybe he was smart enough to avoid you."

"I do drive the truck home sometimes. But I don't think he pays attention to me. We talked only that once, and he was so far gone, I'm not sure he even remembers."

Jude flipped his phone around to reveal a profile image of a beaming, tanned man with a baby strapped in a hiking pack. A man whose eyes seemed so open and friendly no one would ever imagine his face could be paired with the story of Jude's cruel, violent neighbor.

A man who was pointing his own high-end camera right back at whoever had taken this photo.

And next to it was his name. Same as on his membership card.

Ryan Kenzie.

40

Katie, Bess, and Jude were a pack of restrained panic aboard the four-wheeler as it beelined for the parking lot. The first thing they needed to check was that Ryan's SUV was still here. As long as it was, there was no reason to think he and the kids weren't doing exactly the tame, ordinary photography lesson they'd set out to do.

The tame, ordinary photography lesson with the baby along. All these months, Grace had carried her around without knowing her name or who she belonged to. Well, now they knew. Her name was Mabel.

She belonged to Ryan. And his wife.

Who'd been unaccounted for, for *months*.

They'd raided the barn for a few tools that looked innocuous enough. A shovel. A crowbar. Zip ties. Clanging around in the back of their bumpy ride, the combination turned equal parts ominous and pathetic, and again, Katie cursed herself for giving the bear mace away. She'd ordered more, paying extra for expedited delivery, but it hadn't arrived yet.

Her memory rifled through its files, running a new search for moments she hadn't realized at the time were relevant. It flashed her an image of Ryan inside the garage yesterday. Beneath the loft. She'd so easily bought his story of feeling shy about approaching her. A story he'd probably had ready the entire time he'd been skulking around *Katie's* property, using Katie herself as his cover as he tried in vain to retrace his wife's escape route.

What a fool she'd been.

Jude drove, Katie riding shotgun, scanning both sides of the path for any sign of the kids. Her conscience was screaming at her to call them back on the walkie-talkies immediately, but they'd all hastily agreed it seemed riskier to tip Ryan off before they were better positioned to head him off or confront him. Bess was busy on Jude's phone in the back seat, searching the trail-cam footage for some sign of Grace. "It's all animals and wind," Bess muttered, continuing her rundown of things that had triggered the trail cams to start recording. In other words, things that moved. "Deer, deer, birds, more birds, squirrels, wind, indeterminable . . . *ooh*, owl."

"Keep looking," Katie urged. She bit her tongue not to nag Jude to drive faster, though the trees were whipping by with terrifying speed as it was. Overhead, the sky was turning an ominous gray, but Katie didn't spot a thunderhead.

Jude had said those were upstream.

"There!" Katie pointed to Ryan's SUV as they crested the top of the hill, exhaling relief at the sight of it. The only vehicle left in the lot on this day of iffy weather.

"That's not his truck," Jude said, heading straight for it. "This is what he's been driving?" Katie nodded. "No wonder I didn't notice him. Wonder whose it is."

He slowed to a stop beside it and cut the engine as Katie hopped out to peer through the tinted side window. The same one Ethan had stood outside just an hour ago, peering in at Ryan's sleeping daughter. Why hadn't Katie looked too? If anything happened to these kids . . .

"The car seat base is there," she reported. "They're still here."

Bess kept scrolling through the trail-cam app. "These are so dark I can't see anything. Cheap piece of crap."

Katie's mind kept racing. "I know where they planned to set up their shoot. Do we go get them? Or . . . Do I call his phone about the flood warning, or radio the kids and ask them all to head back? He has no reason to think we suspect anything, right?"

"People doing suspicious things always have reasons to think you suspect something," Jude pointed out.

"*Shhhh.*" Bess put her finger to her lips. "Did you hear that?"

They fell silent again, and sure enough, there came a faint, muffled tapping. "Is that . . ." Katie paused. There it was again. "Is that coming from *in there*?"

"You don't think . . ." Jude's eyes met hers. "Grace?" He called tentatively. All three of them sprang into action at once, surrounding the vehicle, faces to the dark glass. Every other time Katie had seen this SUV, it was tidy except for the camera equipment and maybe some spare hiking gear, muddy floor mats. Now, it was a mess. Scattered Cheerios and fast-food wrappers, a diaper bag with half the contents spilled.

"The blankets!" Bess cupped her hands, peering in the rear hatch. "I swear they moved."

Jude and Katie rushed to join her, eyeing the mound of blankets heaped in the trunk, but the sun chose that moment to glare through the clouds, obstructing their view. "What is it with you and me and hatchbacks?" Jude murmured, nudging Katie's arm. Just as quickly, the sun disappeared behind the clouds. And there was no mistaking it: the fabric was *moving*.

"Holy mother," Bess breathed.

Jude ran to the four-wheeler and produced a tool from the glove box. "Stand back," he called, jogging over with it. He must have fiddled with the latch for only a minute, but it felt like an eternity. Every nanosecond they spent here was one more heartbeat the kids were in the care of an adult who was not safe. Every breath marked the instant the water could rush over the bridge, trapping them all inside. Trapping help from *getting* inside.

The point of no return.

"Maybe it's a puppy?" Katie reasoned. As if leaving a dog in a hot car would be okay. Dizziness swarmed her. She'd gotten them into this. She saw now the dangerous overfamiliarity of having someone around so often without stopping to realize she didn't truly know him.

But was that bias unique to her? Gigi had sat right there when Ryan offered the photography lesson, batting her eyes, and her only concern had been the kids breaking the camera. How many times had Bess boasted they didn't need to police Grove for the simple fact that their members were inherently good? Even Jude had poked fun at how forest bathing passed for excitement around here.

No one here was communing with the woods today. Instead, the woods were closing in.

"Got it!" Jude pulled the hatch free and ducked underneath. He yanked at one blanket, then another, and to Katie's horror, they were staring down at the curled form of a woman, bound and gagged and, judging from her sluggish attempts to wriggle free, waking from heavy sedation. Then Jude was cradling her, easing her toward the ledge. Bess was cursing in disbelief, Katie repeating Grace's name.

The woman's head rolled toward them, and Katie's heart skipped like that old record player in her parlor. Even with the sweat slicking hair to her forehead, even with the thick tape over the bottom half of her face, even with the ties around her wrists, elbows, knees, and ankles, the woman's eyes looked more alert already, buoyed at the sight of them. But she wasn't Grace.

"My God," Jude breathed, hurrying to undo the ties. "It's his wife."

41

"Are you all right?" Jude crouched below the woman's eye level to speak to her in the most nonthreatening posture possible. She was sitting on her own now, legs dangling over the tailgate, rubbing the abrasions on her wrists. She gave a shaky nod. "I'm sorry," he said, "I don't know your name. I tried to look it up, after—after. The auditor lists only his name on your house."

"Michelle Kenzie," she slurred. She opened her jaw wide, stretching the muscle, and blinked hard a few times, though her pupils were dilated, struggling to focus as she panned their faces, clearly trying to shake the effect of whatever drug she'd been given—and the stifling heat of the closed car. "Thank you. I don't know how you . . ." Her eyes widened in panic. "My baby! We have to . . ."

"Michelle," he repeated, with measured calm. "We've got you. Take a breath. There are four of us, only one of him." She closed her eyes and inhaled, nodding. "Good. Now, can you walk us through what's happening? We'll call the police—"

"No police!" The words came out with more force than she looked capable of. "He'll turn it all on me. He's already planned it: he'll say how unstable I am, how I tried to give our baby away and he had to rescue her. Like it hasn't been killing me . . . Like he didn't force me to . . ."

"They won't believe him," Jude insisted. "Look how we've found you."

"He'll find a way to make sure they will. He always does." Her eyes shifted to the parking lot. "Where's the caretaker?"

Katie and Bess exchanged an uneasy look. "She doesn't mean me," Katie whispered.

"The last caretaker?" Jude asked calmly, his eyes never leaving Michelle's. "Her name is Grace. We want to find her too. Have you seen her? Has he mentioned her?"

"He said he was taking me to her. He said if we both thought we were so much smarter than him, we deserved to find out how wrong we'd been together."

Her speech was still sloppy, but not unintelligible. With every revelation, her sentences grew a little sharper, her body language a little stronger.

"What did you think he meant by that?"

"I didn't think, I knew. He was going to kill us both. He went on and on about how he'd already found a replacement for me, how she was prettier and kinder, how he'd make sure our daughter had a mother who was worthy of her *and* him."

Katie's face burned as both Jude and Bess looked to her, the obvious "replacement." For a heady moment, she thought she might vomit. She forced herself to focus on what Michelle was saying.

"He said I'd actually done him a favor. Things turned out better than he could've planned—but I still had to pay. Same goes for—you said her name is Grace?" Jude nodded, and she began to cry. "I shouldn't have dragged her into this."

Katie knew there was nothing they could say to console her. But she and Jude had both acted out of desperation. Only one person could fairly be held responsible. Was he watching them now, with the kids at his side? Plotting his next move? Katie turned in a terrified circle, but the woods all around them were still.

"Any idea if Ryan is really off doing the photography lesson right now?" Bess asked, sheer terror behind her words.

Gigi would never forgive Katie if anything happened to the girls. Neither would Bess—nor should she. Katie had had ample opportunities to leave well enough alone. Plenty of people, Bess included, had practically begged her: *Let it be.* But she hadn't listened. And here they were.

"I think so," Michelle said. "He said he had something more important to do before he got around to me. Then he'd pick up Grace and deal with us after. He was in no hurry to be done—he loves having the upper hand." She sniffed. "That's what's driven him so crazy these past months: no matter what he did to me, he couldn't take my leverage away as long as I refused to tell him where Mabel was. Now that he has her back . . ." She shook her head.

Katie kept trying to make sense of it. The words swirled into the nausea threatening to overcome her. *Past few months. No matter what he did to me.* And back to her own role: *replacement.* Jude looked as dumbstruck as Katie felt. It was Bess who finally spoke.

"Where on Earth have you been all this time?"

"At my mom's house," she said simply. "She is—was—sick. The reason I couldn't leave. She didn't have anyone else. It forced me to make an impossible choice, like he knew it would. He knew I'd stay for my mother, but he didn't count on me finding a way for our daughter to go. Even if it meant she had to go alone. It was the biggest gamble of my life, but I took a chance. Please . . . I'm not a negligent mother. He's proved my point: anything is better for her than this."

Katie reached out to steady herself, and Jude caught her arm. She couldn't even look at him, at anyone. Had the signs been there all along? They must have been. And she, of all people, on constant high alert for this very thing, had missed it. Not just missed it, fallen for it.

Ryan had told her himself, the day he'd spent hours waiting for the luna moth to move: *I've been told I never know when to quit.*

He'd come right out and said it, and how had she reacted? She'd thought it was a good thing. The way he could admire a beautiful creature from afar.

"I'm lost," Bess said. "This whole time, you've just been staying with your mom?"

Michelle made a strange noise. "The first few weeks, I was. I held him off as long as I could, asking for space after our last big blowup, until he finally lost patience and realized the baby wasn't with me. My mom's house is in the country . . . Scary how easy it was for him to hold us captive there. He canceled her appointments, told her doctors she was exploring options 'outside of Western medicine.' I begged him not to, and he promised she could resume treatment the instant I told him where Mabel was. Which, of course, I couldn't. Much as I love my mom . . ."

Katie pictured an old farmhouse not unlike hers, with no neighbors as far as she could see—also not unlike hers. A dank basement. No one around to hear her scream.

"What do you mean *captive*?" Bess asked for her.

"He kept us apart. He'd come out to untie me and walk me in to see her, ask me every day if I'd changed my mind yet. I knew he was drugging our food, but I couldn't not eat. I did whatever exercises I could, so my muscles wouldn't atrophy, so my brain wouldn't turn to mush. He'd taunt me, asking if I was really going to let her die. I almost got help once, there was this delivery . . ." She shook her head. "He has an explanation for everything, everyone. I knew he wouldn't ever let me go, and—well, I was right."

"Sick bastard." Jude's voice broke. "I should have realized something wasn't—"

"Don't do that. You tried. You couldn't have known."

"Michelle." Katie stepped toward her, urgently. "We *have* to call the police. Ryan is dangerous. He has Mabel and my nieces and Bess's kids with him as we speak."

"Then there's no time to call them," she said, getting shakily to her feet.

Katie was about to launch a protest, but Jude snapped into action. "You said he was taking you to Grace—any idea where?"

"In the summer kitchen!" Bess blurted out, startling them all. She looked up from Jude's phone, face white, and turned the screen so they could see. The freeze-framed image had that eerie high-contrast look of low-budget night vision. It clearly showed the figure of a man dragging a woman toward the propped-open door. Her right foot was twisted at a grotesque angle, her pants soaked through with a dark substance that could only be blood, her face slack. His face wasn't visible, but there was no mistaking Grace, in the clothes she'd been wearing when she left. The baby was nowhere to be seen, but the pharmacy bag protruded from the back pocket of his jeans.

At least he'd realized the baby needed medicine. It was no consolation.

"My God," Katie cried. "You think she's still in there? You think she's . . . alive?"

"There's no audio, and no time to go through the rest. But let's hope, from what Michelle said—plus he canceled your dinner, right? Quite the multitasker, this one."

"What's the alternative to calling 9-1-1?" Jude asked, thinking out loud. "He gets back here and then what? He realizes you're out and we're witnesses. For all we know, the bridge is already impassable. He'd be trapped with us."

"Like you told me that night," Michelle replied, "there's always an alternative." She took a few tentative steps, testing her legs. "That advice kept me going. I repeated it every day to my mom. *Keep faith. There's always an alternative.* I don't even know if she could hear me." Her eyes filled with tears. "Do you have any idea what he's done to her? She's gone. Right before my eyes. She had so much life left. He talks like she was some old hag, but she was barely sixty."

Her tears were falling freely now, but she stood straighter. "I've tried everything. I can be sure there's only one way this nightmare ends for me. Only one way, you understand." The slur had grown less noticeable, her eyes clear, determined. Katie was afraid she understood perfectly. She was no stranger to guests with one-way tickets—just not this kind.

"Now," Michelle said. "Where did you say he is? You can help me or stay here. But I'm going to get my daughter back."

42

Katie and Bess forced smiles as they approached the group huddled around the tripod. Katie should have been relieved to find them so easily, but all she could think was that she wished they'd detoured somewhere else. This spot had always felt like hers to share, and now it would be marred forever.

Ryan had set up the tripod a safe distance from the edge, behind the branch they'd used as a picnic bench, and angled his lens toward the rushing river in the distance. The kids were previewing their shots on the little screen, and a roar of laughter went up as Katie and Bess approached. "Aunt Katie!" Cora called, catching sight of them. "You've got to see this. We got photobombed by a beetle!"

Ryan was grinning broadly, looking as charmed by the children as they did by him—and by Mabel, who was strapped inside a carrier on his back, cheeks slightly less flushed than they'd been last night, fussily gumming her fist, which was slick with drool. Katie's heart sank at the confirmation: this was indeed the same baby left in Grace's care. Katie must have been clinging to a last strand of hope this was all some terrible mistake, because now she had a momentary sense of losing hold, flailing at the mercy of gravity.

She fought through it. "Ryan," she said brightly, "you remember Bess? These little camp counselors belong to her. Plus, as program director here, the photography contest is her brainchild."

"Some brain you've got there," he said warmly. "I've already spent all my would-be prize money on trying to win." Bess wore a deer-in-the-headlights expression Katie had never seen before. Even now, it seemed impossible this man had driven here with his *wife* bound in his trunk, and yet here he was, bantering like always. The whole time he'd been coming and going, flirting with Katie, not only had he been someone else's husband, he'd also been the same someone else's captor.

No wonder Michelle was so sure he could get away with anything. He already had.

Katie's mouth went dry as he turned to her. "You two decide to join the lesson?"

"Actually, we have to cut it short." She tried to sound apologetic, but it was all she could do not to yank the kids out of his reach. "There's a flash flood warning impacting our entrance bridge. We need to evacuate."

He frowned. "Seriously? The river does look high, but we haven't felt a drop of rain."

"Nature has a mind of its own," Bess trilled. "Kids, grab your things—you're coming with me back to the house, not a moment to spare, okay? Katie will hang back and help Ryan pack up his gear. But he was so nice to give you this lesson: What do we say?"

"Thank *yoooooou*!" they chorused.

Bess turned back to him, all business. "We'll have a staff escort waiting in the parking lot to see that you make it out safely."

"That's not necessary . . ." he began, but she'd already turned tail, hurrying after the kids.

Ryan shot Katie one of his trademark smiles—a smile she'd woken up every day for weeks hoping to catch a glimpse of out on these trails. Never again. Never again would she ever feel this humiliated and used by anyone. Man, woman, child.

"Was it something I said?" he joked, but there was an edge to the words. Either he was the sort who really disliked having plans ruined or he sensed something amiss.

"I hope the kids behaved well for you?" She bent to pick up a teething ring Mabel had dropped to the forest floor. She would *not* let him rattle her.

"They were great. Makes me wonder what Mabel will be like at that age, you know?"

"I bet. Is she okay, by the way? She looks a bit flushed."

"Babies are resilient," he said, "thank goodness." Goose bumps rose on her arms. Under other circumstances she might not have even noticed the odd nonanswer.

She handed him the teething ring. "Well. Want me to hold her while you pack up? We really should get her out of here. That bridge is no joke."

Come on, she thought. *Hand me the baby, and the rest goes easy.*

"Nah, she's happiest with me." He made no move toward the tripod, but instead leaned an elbow against the tree roguishly. "Are you my staff escort?"

"No," came a voice behind them. "I am."

Ryan's smile fell.

"What's the matter?" Jude asked, stepping out onto the trail from the cover of the trees. "Did you hope to keep avoiding my notice here? Or was there just something else you planned to do before you go?"

"Sorry," Ryan said, "do I know you? I think you're confusing me with someone else."

"Someone who drives a banged-up blue Silverado? But who is here right now in a vehicle registered to his mother-in-law? At 207 North Riverbend Road?"

Katie was impressed. Jude didn't give himself enough credit. He claimed he didn't fit in with the other police, but he'd fit enough to make friends among them. Real enough friends to call in favors. And to think Grace had taken Jude for too much of a stickler for rules. A tattletale.

Ryan narrowed his eyes. "You sure you want to do this, mate? Until now I've let you off easy. You don't think I could have busted up your little citizen's patrol? Unlike you, I don't stick my nose where it doesn't belong. I only care about keeping my own house in order. Provoke me again, and you'll leave me no choice but to mess with yours."

"Like you haven't already. You're the one who jammed the entry gate," Jude said.

Ryan threw up his hands. "You're upset about *that*? I only wanted to meet the caretaker and keep her occupied away from the house, so I could look around. That was the nicest possible way. No damage, no one got hurt."

Katie's mouth fell open. But he wasn't even looking at her. He was way too focused on one-upping Jude. Just as Michelle had said he'd be.

Ryan had to be talking a good game. A better game than he had. Sky had been in the loft that day of the gate jam. If he'd found the loft—at least, right then—Katie would know.

She wondered how much time had passed since Bess and the kids had left. Not in minutes, but in distance. Would the kids drag their feet and complain after a long day of running wild, or would they keep up, make good time? Was it too much to hope they were almost to the house by now? Would they listen and do as Bess asked when she settled them in front of a movie as planned? Would they buy it when she said she didn't mind being trapped here, that they'd turn camp into a sleepover, moms included? Most important, would they stay put, locked up safe, their attention on the screen while Bess rode the four-wheeler to the summer kitchen to retrieve Grace, praying she wasn't too late?

"I wouldn't say I'm *upset*," Jude said. "I am curious: What made you think to look here?"

"Oh. Are you concerned it's your fault? Worried I followed you?" He sneered. "Look, it's not like you're not turning heads with your fancy uniform and company car. But rest easy: I was smart enough to know I couldn't trust her in the first place. I didn't rely on phone or GPS to track her—I had backups. Last place they showed her, before Mabel disappeared, was here. At a strange late hour. Not that there was much mystery as to whose dumb idea it was to send her."

Ryan moved so quickly, Katie didn't even see him reach into his pocket or bag. Only that when he extended his hand toward Jude, it was holding a gun. She traced the straight line it was aiming directly at Jude's chest and found Jude pointing one right back. She couldn't even say who'd drawn first.

Katie wished, incongruously, that Bess were still here. Bess hated guns so vehemently Katie could imagine her marching up and kicking them out of both men's hands without a second thought, launching into a lecture about *this* being what was wrong with America. But Bess wasn't here.

No one was.

"Let's do it," Ryan said. "Have a little shoot-out. Draw the authorities up here to see what's going on. Bet they'll have a lot of questions. They might even want to dredge that pond."

Katie was surprised at the wave of emotion that hit her. Not fear, not guilt or remorse.

Only anger.

"Is that where you're planning to put your wife?" Jude asked. His voice never wavered from that steady calm. "Or is she already there?"

"She's none of your concern. And none of mine anymore either, now that I have Mabel back." He laughed, tossing his head in the direction of his daughter, who was still gumming her fist feverishly, none the wiser. "Speaking of which. Come on, put that thing away. Do you expect me to believe you'd shoot me with a baby strapped to my back?"

Katie cleared her throat. Both men had been handily ignoring her, but this was it. She was up. She had to get that gun away from Ryan. And get the baby to safety.

"You're still married?" she asked, hating how her voice shook. She had to keep him talking, and it seemed the best way to do that was to stoke his ego. Even if she had to make herself look weak. "The whole time we were getting to know each other, that was all fake? I thought we had a connection. But you were using me? The whole time, you were thinking of your wife?"

His eyes turned to her greedily, drinking in the emotion. The attention. The idea that she'd felt anything for him was repugnant, but she couldn't let that show. She had to channel her real hurt, her disappointment, her pathetic shattered hopes. That things with Ryan could be different. That a man could still find reason to adore her. That he represented one of the more mindless, frivolous pleasures here at Grove. Something to look forward to when the chaos cleared at the end of the day, rather than something to be feared.

The source of all the madness in the first place.

His face softened. She *hated* how it softened.

"Our connection was real," he promised. He was dripping with sincerity, because she was speaking his language. Jealousy and betrayal— things he understood. "And I wasn't thinking of her. Only of my daughter. You wouldn't want a lesser man, a man who wouldn't go to the ends of the earth for his family? That's what I did. I even quit my job so I could search for my daughter and look after my wife full time."

Look after his wife? His *prisoner* was more like it. Katie's skin crawled.

"Maybe you care for me now, but at the beginning, you only wanted to get closer to me under false pretenses. So you could hang around up here."

"No, I swear. The first thing I did was rule out anything to do with you. That first morning when you were manning the gate, I could tell from the house and the empty boxes in the barn that you were telling the truth about being brand new. Honestly, I was about to give up on finding any leads here until the day I found that moth. You remember, how you asked if I'd heard a baby crying? That was how I knew I was on the right track. But by then, I was doubly glad. Because not only did it give me hope of finding Mabel but it also gave me an excuse to keep seeing you."

Her heart sank at the realization that she'd tipped Ryan off. Although what if he had given up? What would have become of Michelle then? Katie sneaked a look at Jude. His face was hard to read. There was enough truth in this act she was putting on that she was embarrassed to do it in front of him. But she had to keep Ryan talking—to see what they were up against. How much further he could possibly justify his truly unjustifiable actions.

"Sounds like if your wife hadn't been the one to leave, you'd still be with her." Katie sounded like an indignant teenager, but Ryan seemed to be considering her words seriously.

"You're right about one thing. I was the one who tried. Right to the end. That last night, when your esteemed colleague here decided to butt in, I tried once and for all to make her see. I told her if she wanted to leave me, she'd have done it already. We were meant to stay together, work this out." He shook his head, incredulous. "She called me delusional. She had this crazy idea I'd been holding her in our marriage, in our family, against her will. She talked about me like I was a fool. Like our marriage was a joke. Then, like laughing at me and my unconditional love wasn't cruel enough, she said the only reason she hadn't taken our daughter somewhere I'd never find them was because of her *mother*. That *her mother* was the one she loved too much to leave, not me."

It was the strangest thing: even though he was still pointing the gun at Jude, eyes wearing a path back and forth to Katie, he still had that overly friendly manner he'd always used speaking to her. But there was a mania to it now, almost like Ryan was hovering above himself just enough to expose a shadow underneath she hadn't seen before.

A very dark shadow.

Behind him, Katie caught sight of Michelle slipping between the trees, making her slow, unsteady way toward her husband. Or, rather,

her daughter on his back. Katie knew how to keep him distracted, for now. But how to get the baby free—that much she was still working out.

She gathered all her courage. "So you were never . . . physical toward her?"

His eyes darkened. "I never meant to be. That's one of the worst things about her: she'd drive me to be this version of myself I didn't want to be. Especially since the baby was born—she had no time for me. And even then, did I turn my back on our vows? No. I figured it's a stressful phase, things will turn around. I offered her nothing but second chances. In sickness and health, and she wasn't even the one who was sick. How does she repay me? By acting like I'm an existential threat, that our daughter is better off with a stranger. What kind of mother is that?"

Katie willed herself not to risk another glance in Michelle's direction. As Ryan became more impassioned, his stance on the gun was going slack, his attention lingering longer on Katie and flicking less often toward Jude. Jude took advantage and sneaked a few steps forward.

"After she brought the baby here, though," Katie asked, "she went home to you?"

"She did not." At the clipped response, Katie's body clenched in fear. But he didn't seem to notice.

"So what then?" Her voice was barely a whisper. "What did you do to her?"

"I didn't do anything to her. I figured if she wanted to be with her mother so bad, I'd give her exactly what she wanted. Set them up real nice together. Figured they can enjoy each other's company all they want while I'm being the real parent and bringing my daughter home." He said this so naturally she was transfixed. Was he so far gone he'd look her in the eye and admit to what he'd done? She had to know.

"You kept them . . . locked up?"

"Of course not. They were free to come and go as soon as she told me where Mabel was. It's not my fault she refused. Her choice."

"But you have Mabel now. So you can let them go."

He looked at her sadly. "No," he said, "I can't." He renewed his stance on the gun, as if he'd just remembered Jude. "And not you either, Mr. Neighborhood Patrol."

Jude froze, looking afraid for the first time that Ryan might shoot. Because of course Ryan was right: Jude couldn't act first with a baby in the strike zone.

"What about me?" Katie blurted out. Her blood was pounding in her ears, but she forced her voice to soften. "Do I still fit into your plan? If I really was more to you than a front while you looked for Mabel?"

Ryan shot her a sideways smile, like he'd known she'd come around. "I hoped we'd start with a rain check on that dinner date."

"Make it official," she agreed. "No need to rush in."

"Exactly. But eventually, the three of us—you, me, and Mabel—I could see it. Someplace far away from here. A new start. Does that sound crazy?"

Tears stung Katie's eyes. Somehow, even with the gun, he managed to look vulnerable. It was so far beyond crazy, so far beneath it, she could almost relate.

That was the key: to relate.

"I don't talk about this," she said softly, "but my ex and I nearly had children. I got pregnant but it didn't work out. I always wanted to be a mom. I thought I'd make a good one."

"You would. I've seen you with your nieces."

She started to move toward him, crossing the distance one slow, small step at a time. One foot in front of the other, in sequence, like she'd learned. "Let me hold Mabel," she said, tossing her head toward Jude. "While you two . . . work this out. You don't want to risk exposing her, damaging her hearing. What she might see . . ."

He was wavering. "Babies are resilient," he said again.

"Yes, but *your* baby has already been through so much. She deserves better. Think what her mother already put her through, leaving her with a stranger like that." Michelle was back in her line of sight now, nodding encouragingly. *Yes, that's it. Keep stepping.* "With you should be the warm, safe place where Mabel knows she's home, where she belongs."

He never said she could take Mabel. But almost imperceptibly, he bent at the knees so she could reach. Katie forced herself to kiss him on the cheek as she undid the buckle and pulled Mabel free. To keep him off balance. He smelled as good as he always had, of musk and leather. She cradled the baby in her arms and turned away, still moving slowly and carefully, soothingly, humming the first song that came to mind—the song Nessa had been singing on their way home last night, not stepping tentatively but running out ahead of the pack, confident and carefree, the way any girl had a right to be.

There was no gunshot. Only a grunt of surprise, as Michelle hurled herself out from the massive tree in his blind spot, hoisting a broken branch like a gladiator pole, and shoved her tormentor, hard, off the rocky edge of the ravine.

But Katie didn't see.

She was looking the other way.

43

It took thirty-six hours until the floodwaters and debris receded enough for the rescue crews to investigate what Katie and Bess reported finding at Grove. One of those senseless, avoidable tragedies, this one involving a nature photographer who'd had the ill-conceived idea to photograph a flash flood in action. Who'd set up his tripod too close to the edge, intent on getting the perfect shot. It remained teetering precariously at his last perch, hundreds of feet above where his lifeless body lay in the ravine, but the camera itself had been smashed in the fall, the final images he took irretrievable, his gear scattered down the rocky outcrops of the ridge. His wife could not say for certain how long he'd been missing, as she and her infant daughter had been staying with her ailing mother, who—in a double tragedy for the family—succumbed to cancer after a long battle the very same day.

The caretaker had noticed the man's truck in the parking lot but was delayed in discovering his remains by a separate medical emergency, when a hiker was badly injured after muddy conditions prompted her to venture off the trail. Fortunately, a courageous employee was able to transport her to safety on an all-terrain vehicle after recognizing the dangers of her compound fracture, blood loss, and dehydration.

Thirty-six hours proved more than enough time to stage certain details. The best trained among them volunteered for the grimmer tasks: scaling the ledge to retrieve the baby carrier and gun. The rest was straightforward: moving the tripod to the danger zone, cleaning out the car.

Getting their stories straight didn't take long—there wasn't much to debate. Or to say. Not that they didn't have mixed feelings about never holding Ryan accountable, moving on as if he'd never held Michelle and her mother captive, never abandoned Grace in the summer kitchen, never intended to do away with them both. It didn't seem right how easy it was to go along with the story that Michelle and the baby had been MIA the past months because they'd been staying with her mom. It didn't seem fair to pretend her ultimate death was a natural end. It didn't seem just to dismiss Grace's horrific ankle break from the trap he'd laid as an accident.

But Michelle was adamant: it was easier this way. This was the silver lining in all the groundwork he'd done for them, becoming more and more possessive over the years until she'd quit her job, until her friends got used to her never returning their calls, until the only one left to notice was her mom. Now, letting the world know who he really was and what he'd done would only invite scrutiny into his death and where their baby had been all that time, and so much else. They were seeing right now for themselves how easily he would have gotten away with it.

So in that way, he did. He was allowed to remain that nice, good-looking guy behind the camera. The tributes poured in about what a shame it was, and Michelle was reeling in enough shock to fit the part of grieving widow, no questions asked.

But they knew the truth. And that was enough. Besides. He'd paid the ultimate price.

"There is still plenty of good, safe summer fun to be had at both nature center properties," Bess assured the people of Cincinnati in the news coverage. "Just use good judgment, favor the buddy system, and when in doubt, err on the side of caution."

Not that the kids saw her interview, or the emergency crews making quick work of the recovery. Bess got them into a structured day camp at main campus—gushing that there were a few last-minute openings, and with special presenters coming from the zoo, they *had* to take advantage—and with all week spent off-site, the kids never noticed anything amiss. They asked a few times when they were going to get their photo prints, and why Ryan didn't come around anymore, but after Katie said their first date was off, they felt sorry enough for her not to ask again. Same went for Gigi.

Finally, Katie's track record of heartbreak worked in her favor.

But this time there was no need to run off and be rescued by her best friend. She'd rescued herself. And her best friend was already here, closer than ever. Even if they had agreed certain subjects would stay off-limits from now on. No hard feelings.

Katie visited Grace in the hospital once, between surgeries, the letter from her mom's caregiver in hand. Grace got teary when she read it. She didn't promise to call her sister, but she did promise to "start thinking about it." Apparently, she'd done a lot of thinking already, drifting in and out of consciousness on the dank summer kitchen floor.

"You know the craziest thing?" she asked Katie. "I can't even be mad about this stupid ankle. I'd be lying if I said I didn't have regrets. But I'm not sorry about how things turned out."

Jude had something to do with that. And not just because if she'd been more open with him, she'd have found out Jude could relate to what made her impatient with the Sequence. He'd seen his share of gray area from the outside—as a trainee cop, a son, neighbor, coworker, friend, and a bystander who didn't know what to do but did try, to his credit, to do something.

Needless to say, he also had regrets, but he was trying to atone for them. He'd visited, too, turning her on to a new nonprofit designed to work within the system. One of his dad's retired colleagues helped found it after decades of being one of the only women policing their district. Jude made introductions, vouched that Grace would be perfect for the new liaison job if they'd give her a chance.

"It's early stages, and funding could be better," she told Katie. "But the benefit of being out in the open is that we don't put limits on who we can help. The idea is to improve intervention between law enforcement and domestic violence victims, provide both sides with better training and better options. I might even bring in Gina for a consult after her honeymoon—if anyone can work this aboveboard and below it, it's her." Grace would be discharged just in time to officiate the wedding. Katie couldn't go, of course, but she was glad Grace could.

"I think your mom would approve," Katie told her, and Grace nodded, looking quickly away when she saw Katie getting emotional.

"We'll see. No system is perfect, but I like being part of conversations about how we can do better. I mean, wouldn't it be great if eventually the Sequence wasn't needed anymore? If you were the last caretaker anyone would ever need, other than a bunch of naturalists?"

"It would be great," Katie said, and meant it.

Grace fidgeted with the stiff sheets of her hospital bed. "I must admit, after so many years, I'm glad I'm not under the radar anymore." She raised her eyes to Katie's. "But I feel better knowing someone still is."

Afterward, Grace sent a gift to the caretaker's house: a large pot of "Prairie Sun" black-eyed Susans. Katie hadn't known such a varietal existed: distinguished by their unusual centers, which were not black at all but a light, lemony green. She planted them by the porch, where they would bloom every summer, through the fall. When you approached the house from a distance, they looked gold the whole way through—distinctive and bold, like they stood for something.

She was looking forward to seeing how much taller they'd grow.

44

"You'll never guess who I ran into." Gigi started in as soon as Katie answered the phone. "He was today's guest speaker for the whole program and—well, you'll never guess. But seriously. Guess."

"Um . . ." Katie said. Normally, she hated this sort of thing, but she was way too glad to hear Gigi sounding so normal. Unsuspicious. And not just that—happy. Grateful.

Every time Katie thought of how she'd put Gigi's entire world in harm's way, no matter how unknowingly, no matter how they'd escaped miraculously unscathed, she felt as if she'd run into oncoming traffic and somehow come out the other side. This was what people meant when they said *too close for comfort*. There was no comfort afterward. Only sweaty palms and a terrible sense of something akin to déjà vu. *What if.*

Bess kept telling her, *no harm no foul.* And here was Gigi, sounding not just happy and grateful but happy and grateful because of Katie. When was the last time that had happened?

"Steve!" Gigi announced, unable to wait. "And you'll never guess what he's doing now."

It took a beat to realize who she meant: *Katie's* Steve. *Clark's* Steve. Who they'd hurt so irreparably. Who their whole college circle said they'd all "lost track of" because it was nicer than the truth: that he'd lost track of them. Intentionally.

"Seriously," Gigi went on. "*Guess* what he's ended up doing."

"Um," Katie said.

"Because you know how we always said he was like a human Labrador? Of course he founded one of these companies where you can subscribe for quality pet products delivered at a discount."

"You're kidding."

"Apparently after college he canceled all those plans he'd been making and moved back home. He ended up volunteering at an animal rescue, and he's married to their, like, community outreach coordinator now, because obviously."

Katie found herself smiling. "Obviously." She'd always thought it unfair that most people had to choose between an exceptionally goodhearted career and a high-earning one. Leave it to Steve to end up with both, and not even by design.

"Anyway. He was there to talk about 'innovating business models to meet evolving market needs.' We grabbed coffee afterward, and . . . he was sorry to hear about you and Clark."

Katie's smile morphed into a cringe. "I bet." She didn't know what was harder to picture, Steve having a friendly coffee with her sister, or Steve being sorry about her divorce. She wondered if he'd presumed she and Clark never looked back. If he had the slightest inkling he'd been the third person in their marriage the entire time.

"No," Gigi insisted. "He was sorry. He said he'd thought of reaching out to Clark over the years, just to tell him that it was okay. That he'd ended up where he belonged, in an odd way *because* of you two. But he never did, and . . . I think he feels bad. Maybe things would have been different if he had."

Katie waited for the old longing to reach around her and latch on to these words. To turn that *maybe* into a *probably* and why, why, why couldn't things have been different? It wasn't hard to imagine that if Steve had ever made that call, she'd be home with Clark right now.

But she didn't want to imagine it. She only wanted to be glad for Steve. And she was.

"It's just as well he didn't," she told Gigi. "But it means a lot to know. So thanks."

"Isn't life strange?" Gigi marveled. "If I hadn't done this intensive, I never would have run into him. And I never would have done the intensive if not for you."

Katie wasn't one of those people who believed things always worked out for the best. Frankly, after some of the women she'd met in her loft, she never would. But a funny thing happened as she thought of all the things that *had* worked out for her after all: a loyal best friend, nieces who kept proclaiming this their "best summer ever," a sister who felt like a friend again, and a new start that she wasn't afraid of anymore.

She felt something she never expected to: lucky.

Katie thought Jude might retreat to the main campus once the board-walk was done, but he found reasons to stop by nearly every day. He was a surprise hit with the girls, who'd line up for four-wheeler rides, lectures on such marvels as caterpillars and river otters, and his hilarious specialty: forest-bathing demonstrations.

The next time Katie invited him to stay for a beer, he took human-size sips. In fact, if she didn't know better, she'd think he was nursing the bottle. They sat on the porch and watched the girls by the barn, trying to untangle a kite they'd found. Chevy kept pouncing on the matted string, sending them into fits of giggles.

"You doing okay?" Jude asked, his voice low.

Katie nodded. She honestly was. But she was glad he'd asked. She'd been wondering the same about him. "And you?" She cleared her throat. "You're not feeling a deep-down obligation to come clean about any of it? To your friends on the force or the nature center board?"

Jude shrugged. "Like I told you before, I see everything as compli-cated." He turned and met her eyes. She wasn't used to seeing him so close, really looking at him. She'd been realizing how much the caretaker gig had in common with any other job. Ask anyone what made them like their work—or not—and they'd give the same answer: the people.

Without so many questions hanging over her, she liked this job better every day.

"What about you?" he asked, and Katie grinned, bumping his shoulder with her own.

"You see shades of gray. Whereas I . . . didn't see anything at all."

Bess came around the side of the house then, with a handful of wildflowers.

"Talk about shades," she said, waving the colorful blooms. "I keep telling Katie how much she's going to love this place in the fall."

Katie knew every season at Grove would bring its own challenges. But Bess—who'd never been a fan of heat waves or humidity—had been on and on about autumn lately. Specifically, she thought Katie might be interested to know more about how leaves change colors to such a brilliant new array. Because the thing is, they don't.

They merely lose chlorophyll. Revealing what their colors were all along.

Jude gave Katie a gentle shoulder-bump back. "Think you'll stick around then?"

She didn't hesitate. "As long as it feels like the right thing to do."

Finally, she understood what the caretaker gig required.

It wouldn't always be easy to keep simple.

In fact, it could get quite messy.

But she no longer doubted she was strong enough to handle any knock at her door. To take her guests by the hand, look them in the eye, and assure them they'd come to the right place.

Katie wasn't doing this because anyone thought she should, or to prove anyone wrong for thinking she shouldn't. There was only one explanation for how this place, this life, this role could fill her up the way nothing else had.

She was a natural.

And her true colors were just starting to show.

ACKNOWLEDGMENTS / AUTHOR'S NOTE

The initial inspiration for this story, perhaps unsurprisingly, did indeed come during a walk through the woods at a members-only property maintained by the Cincinnati Nature Center: the real-life best-kept-secret Long Branch Farm & Trails, where there is in fact a residential caretaker—who, it's worth noting, I have never met. While the existence of this beautiful place prompted me to dream up Grove Reserve and all that might happen there, my reimagined version has been wholly fictionalized, from the geography of the property (which begins with some basic similarities, as a respectful homage, but quickly diverges) to the operational details to the staff and other people who set foot through the gate. While none of the events or characters in these pages have any intentional basis in real life, I'm grateful to everyone behind the scenes at Cincinnati Nature Center for maintaining the kinds of spaces that invite nature lovers of all kinds to come stretch their legs and let their creativity roam free. Novelists included.

I have written about themes surrounding domestic violence before, in my 2018 novel *Not That I Could Tell* (which had the honor of being a Book of the Month selection during Women's History Month, in part because of these themes) as well as my 2014 *New York Times* Modern Love essay about my personal experience losing a close friend in a related tragedy. In the years since, I've spoken with countless book clubs, women's groups, and readers and writers across the US and beyond about the heartbreaking nuances surrounding this issue (which, while most prevalently impacting women, occurs across gender, race, class, sexuality, etc., and ultimately impacts us all, however indirectly). I've been invited into homes where book club members have confided about hiding friends who were in danger; I've been pulled aside by teary-eyed librarians who were themselves survivors; I've met selfless volunteers through organizations such as the Assistance League of Greater Cincinnati, who have "personal reasons" of their own for dedicating time, energy, and other valuable resources to helping victims. I am grateful to them all for sharing their stories, for opening their hearts until we're crying and laughing together like old friends. I have never professed myself to be an authority on this subject (not by a long shot), nor do I have firsthand knowledge of how much truth there is to the whisper networks we may have heard, well, whispers of. But I've come to believe that having these conversations, even and perhaps especially at our own kitchen tables with friends and neighbors, is key to combating damaging misconceptions and stigmas, because statistically, domestic violence is happening to people you know and love. Fictional stories can be conversations, too, and I try to have my end of them responsibly, even while taking artistic license for the sake of the story. While the Sequence portrayed in this novel is imagined, the solidarity that connects so many of us in spirit is real, and I believe it will lift us all at one time or another, perhaps in ways we will never know.

Years ago, I had the good fortune of volunteering with the YWCA of Greater Cincinnati's public awareness campaign for Domestic Violence Awareness month, which was instrumental in shaping my thinking around this complex issue. In more recent years I've been heartened by the emergence of initiatives such as Women Helping Women's Domestic Violence Enhanced Response Team (DVERT), which aims to improve crisis responses across Cincinnati-area jurisdictions—an example, it's worth noting, of real work underway to improve upon areas where this novel's characters lament that the system can do better. Education is crucial, so I was particularly appreciative of the 2021 webinar hosted with the University of Cincinnati,

"Coming Together in the Fight Against Domestic Violence: Building Multi-Agency Partnerships to Implement and Evaluate a Domestic Violence Enhanced Response Team (DVERT)." I also admire the quiet power of small but mighty organizations like Thrive Empowerment Center in Covington. Every voice can make a difference—and thank goodness for that.

If you or someone you know is involved in an abusive situation, help is available. If you're not sure where to start, the National Domestic Violence Hotline offers free, confidential support around the clock: (800) 799-SAFE (7233).

In many ways, the publication of my sixth novel feels as surreal as the first. I owe no small part of them all to my agent and friend, Barbara Poelle, who is steady and patient when I waver, brilliant and fierce when I'm indecisive, and hilarious and kind when I need it most. BP, you might not remember our first conversation about this book, but I do. *This is it,* you said. *Can't you feel it?* I would never have dared say so, but you did, and that pretty much sums it up.

Enter senior editor Alicia Clancy, who shared our enthusiasm for this project from the jump. It's a full-circle moment and a privilege to be working together after years of cheering each other on from afar. Thank you for providing just the right editorial guidance to coax this book into a stronger version of its best self. Kyra Wojdyla: thank you for keeping production running so smoothly, and for your clear communication at every step. Molly von Borstel, your cover design is a dream. Molly von Borstel, your cover design is a dream. Katie Kurtzman, I appreciate your enthusiastic approach to PR. The entire team at Lake Union has been so welcoming: heartfelt gratitude to all of you for your hard work and your vision. I couldn't ask for better publishing partners and am thrilled to be along for the ride.

Special thanks to my dear friend Sharon Short, a.k.a. Jess Montgomery, for a thoughtful beta read on short notice, for being the captain of Team Jude, and for all the fellowship in these overlapping phases of our writing lives. So grateful to have formed our lovely, lopsided writers circle along with kindred spirits Katrina Kittle and

Kristina Purnhagen: may we all be folding in the cheese together for many years—and stories—to come.

When it comes to the nitty-gritty, I owe quite a few favors to Jamie Mitchell, my favorite pharmacist, for always being game for a quick consultation, this time about filling prescriptions for minors. Thanks also to J. M. Petit, MD, PSC (and his good-natured middleman, Zac Petit), for fielding questions about RX writing on the fly. Abbey Bayer: your gift of the "Prairie Sun" black-eyed Susans could not have come at a more perfect time.

To the Career Authors team of Hank Phillippi Ryan, Paula Munier, Dana Isaacson, and Brian Andrews, you have become much more than colleagues: every time our group text pings, I truly can't believe my luck to be on the receiving end of your generosity, good humor, insight, and friendship. Jane Friedman, your referrals have meant the world to me in my editorial life, and I'm so grateful for the mutual respect that has kept us linked through two decades of our careers. Further thanks, yet again, to the team at *Writer's Digest* for keeping me in the family. And to the Tall Poppy Writers and the Fiction Writers Co-op for community and camaraderie.

No writer can succeed without the word-of-mouth excitement of readers, reviewers, booksellers, and librarians, and I appreciate every one of you. Much gratitude to all the venues who've been kind enough to host and recommend me, with winks to the wonderful people at Joseph-Beth Booksellers, Books by the Banks, Penguin Bookshop, the Public Library of Cincinnati and Hamilton County, the Clermont County Public Library, and Thurber House.

There are pros and cons to living with a writer, and I'm beyond lucky that my amazing family has embraced them all without complaint—and with a great deal of love and support. My dad, Michael Yerega, is without a doubt the most underpaid champion of my work. My husband, Scott, did not know he was marrying an eventual novelist (What do you know? Neither did I!), but, Babe, you sure are amazing at it. Kids, I love you more than words can say, and I'll keep on saying it anyway. Thanks for filling every day with adventure and joy just by being you.

READING GROUP
DISCUSSION GUIDE

1. On paper, would a resident caretaker job description read as your dream come true or your worst nightmare (or something in between)? In what ways do you imagine the reality of that lifestyle might differ from the idea of it? Do you think anyone can ever really know whether they're suited to that kind of solitude and independence until they experience it firsthand?

2. How might another character have reacted in Katie's position when she opened the door to her first frantic, wounded middle-of-the-night visitor? What factors contributed to Katie being reluctantly willing to do anything other than call the police? What might you have done?

3. What are some of the unexpected ways Katie finds herself relating to the women in her loft? Do you think relating to them ultimately made her decisions regarding the Sequence simpler or more complicated?

4. How is shame a common thread among many of the characters and their motivations, beyond the women who are assisted by the Sequence? Consider how Katie confronts (or buries) feelings of shame versus how those

feelings have manifested in Bess, Sienna, Gina, and even Jude. Why is shame so powerful, and how does it feed the cycle of domestic violence? Is there a way to take that power back?

5. Both Katie and Dottie struggle with the idea that she doesn't have a "personal reason" to remain involved with their network, though Katie eventually comes to realize she does have reasons she hasn't been able to articulate. Do you think most people could find a "personal reason" to help if we look hard enough?

6. Katie and her sister both want to repair their relationship but aren't quite sure how. Did seeing them together reveal anything new about what "the old Katie" might have been like? Did it give you a hopeful picture of what the future might hold for them both?

7. Would Katie have been as interested in Ryan if Bess hadn't been so cavalier about pushing her toward anyone whose "name isn't Clark"? Have we all been guilty of egging on friends without thinking it through? Or of the kind of overfamiliarity the comes with having a coworker or neighbor around so much that we overlook how little we know about them?

8. What frustrated you about Jude? What did you like about him?

9. Was it inevitable for something to go wrong for Grace sooner or later? If it hadn't, do you think she would have remained caretaker indefinitely—and would that have been the right call?

10. People talk a lot about getting "closure" after a big life change like a divorce. Do you think it's possible Katie found closure at Grove Reserve in ways that had nothing

to do with Clark? Or was she looking for something else all along?

11. Bess says, "I always thought it would be boring to be one of those people who are constantly trying to do the right thing. Now I know the truth: it's exhausting." What aspects of this story changed or challenged the way you look at the gray area between right and wrong?

ABOUT THE AUTHOR

Photo © Corrie Schaffeld

Jessica Strawser is the author of five previous book club favorites: *Almost Missed You*, *Not That I Could Tell* (a Book of the Month selection), *Forget You Know Me*, *A Million Reasons Why*, and *The Next Thing You Know*, a *People* magazine Pick. She is editor-at-large at *Writer's Digest*, where she curates the Learn by Example column; a popular speaker at writing conferences; and a freelance editor and writer whose work has appeared in the *New York Times*, *Publishers Weekly*, and others. A Pittsburgh native and graduate of Ohio University's prestigious E.W. Scripps School of Journalism, she lives with her husband and two children in Cincinnati, Ohio, where she served as 2019 writer-in-residence for the Cincinnati & Hamilton County Public Library. For more information, visit www.jessicastrawser.com.